PENGUIN BOOKS

BOOKENDS

Praise for Jane Green's earlier novels:

'Any woman who's suffered a relationship trauma will die for this book ... wickedly funny ... it may not improve your life but it will make you squeal with laughter' *Cosmopolitan*

'You'll want to gulp it down' *Essentials*

'Green writes with acerbic wit about the law of the dating jungle, and its obsession with image ... as comforting as a bacon sandwich' *Sunday Express*

'A great read: sharp, funny and packed with familiar situations for all those who've ever embarked on the dating game ... cancel all engagements and read it' *Tatler*

'A brilliantly funny novel' *Woman's Own*

'An immensely enjoyable read which more than lives up to expectations' *Prima*

'The literary equivalent of an evening gossiping with your mates ... funny and honest, it's superb stuff' *Company*

'Compusively readable ... the ultimate makeover novel made over with irony ... one for the beach' *Sunday Times*

'*Cinderella* with calorie-counted knobs on and first class feel-good factor' *Ms London*

'Irritatingly accurate, this is a hilarious and poignant look at love and sex in the 90s' *Elle*

ABOUT THE AUTHOR

Jane Green is the author of five bestselling novels: *Straight Talking*, her first novel, was published in 1997 and was followed in Penguin by *Jemima J.* (1998), *Mr Maybe* (1999), *Bookends* (2000) and *Babyville* (2001). Jane, who is expecting her second child, divides her time between London and Connecticut with her husband and son.

Bookends

JANE GREEN

PENGUIN BOOKS

PENGUIN BOOKS

Published by the Penguin Group
Penguin Books Ltd, 80 Strand, London WC2R 0RL, England
Penguin Putnam Inc., 375 Hudson Street, New York, New York 10014, USA
Penguin Books Australia Ltd, 250 Camberwell Road, Camberwell, Victoria 3124, Australia
Penguin Books Canada Ltd, 10 Alcorn Avenue, Toronto, Ontario, Canada M4V 3B2
Penguin Books India (P) Ltd, 11 Community Centre, Panchsheel Park, New Delhi – 110 017, India
Penguin Books (NZ) Ltd, Cnr Rosedale and Airborne Roads, Albany, Auckland, New Zealand
Penguin Books (South Africa) (Pty) Ltd, 24 Sturdee Avenue, Rosebank 2196, South Africa

Penguin Books Ltd, Registered Offices: 80 Strand, London WC2R 0RL, England

www.penguin.com

First published 2000
17

Set in 10.5/13pt Monotype Century Schoolbook
Typeset by Intype London Ltd
Printed in England by Clays Ltd, St Ives plc

Acknowledgements

I would like to thank the following people for their support, kindness and help: Dr Patrick French at the Mortimer Market Centre; Adam Wilkinson at Body Positive; Marek, Jessica and all at the Primrose Hill Bookshop; James Phillips and Andrew Benbow at Books Etc. in Whiteleys; Laurent Burel; Yasmin Rahaman; Tricia Anker.

My 'inner circle': Annie, Giselle, Caroline and Julian, and finally David, for everything.

Chapter one

The first time I met Josh, I thought he was a nice guy but a transient friend. The first time I met Si I fell hopelessly in love and prayed I'd somehow be able to convert him.

But the first time I met Portia I thought I'd found my soulmate.

She was the sister I'd always longed for, the best friend I'd always wished I had, and I truly and honestly thought that, no matter what happened with our lives, we would stay friends for ever.

For ever feels a long time when you're eighteen. When you're away from home for the first time in your life, when you forge instant friendships that are so strong they are destined, surely, to be with you until the bitter end.

I met Josh right at the beginning, just a few weeks after the Freshers' Ball. I'd seen him in the Students' Union, propping up the bar after a rugby game, looking for all the world like the archetypal upper-class rugger bugger twit, away from home with too much money and too much arrogance.

He – naturally – started chatting up Portia, alcohol giving him a confidence he lacked when sober (although I didn't know that at the time), and despite the rebuffs he kept going until his friends dragged him away to find easier prey.

I'm sure we would all have left it at that, but I bumped into him the next day, in the library, and he recognized me instantly and apologized for embarrassing us; and gradually we started to see him more and more, until he'd firmly established himself as one of the gang.

I'd already met Si by then, had already fallen in love with his cheeky smile and extravagant gestures. I was helping out one of the girls on my course who was auditioning for a production of *Cabaret*. It was my job to collect names and send them into the rehearsal hall for the audition.

Si was the only person who turned up in full costume. As Sally Bowles. In fishnet stockings, bowler hat and full make-up, he didn't bat an eyelid as the others slouched down in their hard, wooden chairs, staring, jealous as hell of his initiative. And his legs.

He went in, bold as brass, and proceeded to give the worst possible rendition of *Cabaret* that I've ever heard, but with such brazen confidence you could almost forgive him for being entirely tone-deaf.

Everybody went crazy when he'd finished. They went crazy because he so obviously loved, *loved*, being centre stage. None of us had ever seen such enthusiasm, but even though Si knew every song, word for word, he had to be content with camping it up as the narrator, as Helen, the director, said she never wanted to hear him sing again.

Eddie was a friend of Josh. A sweet gentle boy from Leeds who should probably have been overwhelmed by our combined personalities, but somehow wasn't. He was easy company, and always willing to do anything for anybody he cared about, which was mostly us, at the time.

And then of course there was Portia. So close that our names became intertwined: CatherineandPortia. Two for the price of one.

I met Portia on my very first day at university. We were

sitting in the halls of residence common room, waiting for a talk to begin, all sizing each other up, all wondering whom to befriend, who seemed like our *type*, when this stunningly elegant girl strode in on long, long, legs, crunching an apple and looking like she didn't have a care in the world.

Portia, with her mane of dark auburn hair that reached down between her shoulderblades. Portia, with her cool green eyes and dirty laugh. Portia, who looked like she should have been a class-A bitch, but was, then, the greatest friend I'd ever had.

Her confidence took my breath away, and, when she flung her bag down on the floor and sank into the empty chair next to mine, I prayed she'd be my friend. She stretched out, showing off buttersoft suede thigh-high boots, exactly the boots I'd dreamt of wearing if I ever got thin enough, and, taking a last bite of the apple, tossed it with an expert flick of the wrist into the dustbin on the other side of the room.

'Yesss!' she hissed triumphantly, her cut-glass accent slicing through the room. 'I *knew* all those years as goal shooter would pay off sometime,' and then she turned to me. 'I'm Portia. When does this bloody thing start?'

Portia had more than enough confidence for both of us. We found, within minutes, that despite our different backgrounds we had the same vicious sense of humour, the same slightly ironic take on life, although it took a few years for the cynicism to set in.

We made each other laugh from the outset, and there never seemed to be a shortage of conversation with Portia. She had a prime room – one of the most coveted in the building. A large bay window overlooked the main residential street, and Portia repositioned the armchairs so that they were in the bay, draping them with

3

jewel-coloured crushed velvet throws. She sat there for hours at a time, watching people go by.

Most of the time I'd be there too. The net curtains would be rolled around the string of elastic from which they hung, and in summer the window would be open and we'd sit drinking bottles of Beck's, Marlboro Lights dripping coolly from our fingers, waiting for the men of our dreams to walk past and fall head over heels in love with us.

They frequently did. With Portia, at any rate.

Even then she had more style than anyone I'd ever met. She would go to the hippy shops in town and pick up brightly coloured beaded dresses for a fiver, tiny mirrors sprinkled all over them, and the next day I'd find her finishing off two stunning new cushions, the mirrors glinting with ethnic charm.

She did have money, that much was obvious, but there was never anything snobbish or snooty about Portia. She'd been brought up in the country, in Gloucestershire, in a Jacobean manor house that could probably have provided accommodation for most of our campus.

Her mother was terribly beautiful, she said, and an alcoholic, but, Portia sighed, who could blame her when her father was sleeping with half of London. They had a pied-à-terre in Belgravia, to which Portia eventually decamped when she refused to go back to boarding school, opting to do her A-levels in a trendy tutorial college in London instead.

It was a world away from my own background. I was intimidated, impressed, and in awe of her life, her lifestyle. My life had started in deepest, darkest suburbia, in an ordinary pre-war semi on a main road in North London. My father, unlike Portia's landowning, gambling, semi-aristocratic parents, is an accountant in a local firm. My mother is a housewife who works occasionally as a dinner lady in the local primary school.

As far back as I can remember I would escape from my humdrum world by burying myself in books – the one true love of my life when growing up.

I love Mum and Dad. Of course. They are my parents. But the day I went to university I realized that they had nothing to do with me any more, nothing to do with my life, with who I wanted to be, and never was I more aware of cutting the umbilical cord than when I met Portia.

I used to wonder whether style was something you were born with, or whether it was something you could buy. I'm sure that it's something you're born with, and Portia was just fortunate in being able to afford the very best as well. I still have no doubt, however, that she could have made a bin bag look sophisticated. The rest of us would shop at Next, but she always looked like she was wearing Yves Saint Laurent. She'd joke about it, about our sweaters covered in holes, and our faded old Levis, the more rips and holes in them the better. She'd laugh about how she found it physically impossible to walk in anything with less than three-inch heels due to a birth defect. She'd sink to her knees and grab the bottom of my favourite sweater – a sludge-green crocheted number that, with hindsight, was pretty damn revolting – begging, pleading, offering me bribes to burn the sweater and have her N. Peal cashmere sweater instead.

There were a few people who were jealous of her. There always are. I remember one night when Portia was cornered by some big rugby bloke in a pub. She politely declined his offer of a shag, to which responded by screaming obscenities at her and telling her she was a rich bitch and the most hated girl at university. He made some references to her being a

Daddy's girl, and then said she was the university joke. Eventually, when she recovered from the shock, she slapped him as hard as she could and ran out to the garden of the pub.

I found her there. I hadn't known what was going on. I'd been in the other room, chatting to people, and it was only when I noticed Portia hadn't come back that I went looking for her.

She was curled up in a heap at the bottom of the garden. It was raining and she was soaking wet, her hand covered in blood, her skin torn through to the bone. She was sobbing quietly, and I took her in my arms. After a while I insisted she go to hospital for stitches. Even there she refused to say what had happened, and the next day the rumours flew that he, the rugby oik, had hit her, had pushed her down the stairs. She never said anything about the incident, neither confirmed nor denied, thereby making the rugby bloke into something of a pariah with women.

Months later we were sitting in a café on the high street, when Portia suddenly said, 'Do you remember that night? The night of the bloody hand?'

I nodded, curious as to what she was going to say, because she'd never spoken about it before.

'Did *you* think he'd hit me? Pushed me down the stairs?'

I shrugged. I didn't know.

'I did it myself,' she said, lighting up a cigarette and examining the tiny scar on the knuckle of her right hand. 'It's this thing I do,' she said nonchalantly, dragging on the cigarette and looking around the room as if to say that what she was telling me wasn't important. 'I have a tendency to hurt myself. Physically.' She paused. 'When I'm hurting inside.' And then she called the waitress over and ordered another coffee. By the time the waitress had gone, Portia was on to something else and I couldn't get back to the subject again.

It was the first indication I'd had that Portia wasn't perfect. That there might be things in her past that weren't perfect. It was only as I got to know her better that I realized the effect her parents had had on her.

It wasn't that they *didn't* care, she said. It was quite simply that they hadn't been around enough *to* care. Her mother lay in bed all day, in an alcoholic haze, and her father disappeared to London, leaving Portia to fend for herself.

This cutting, this occasional self-mutilation when life became too hard, was clearly an act of desperation, of Portia screaming to be noticed, to be heard. But if you didn't know, you wouldn't know, if you know what I mean. She was funny, generous and kind. When she got fed up with my persistent moaning about my mop of dull mousy hair, she whisked me to the hairdressers and instructed them to do lowlights.

The girl at the hairdressers didn't like Portia, didn't like her imperious manner, but Portia's mother went to Daniel Galvin, so Portia knew what she was talking about. When Portia said not the cap, the foil, they listened, and when she chose the colours of my lowlights, they listened. And when they finished, Portia showed them a photograph of a model in a magazine, and they cut my hair so that it fell softly around my face, feathery bits brushing my cheek. I had never felt beautiful before, only ever mildly attractive on a very good day, but for a few minutes, in that crappy local hairdressers surrounded by old dears with blue rinses, with Portia smiling just behind me, I felt beautiful.

Portia was the most sought-after girl at university. As

the builders at the end of our road one summer used to say, 'She's got class.' When I walked past they'd scream, 'Cor, fancy a night out, love?' To which I'd smile coyly and continue walking, faintly irritated by the interruption, but nevertheless flattered that they had even bothered to notice me.

When Portia walked past they'd fall silent. Downing their tools one by one, they'd step to the edge of the scaffold to watch her glide by, her face impassive, her eyes fixed on the middle distance. And once she'd passed they'd look at one another with regret, regret that she wouldn't talk to them, regret that twelve feet up a collection of steel poles was the closest they'd ever get to a woman like Portia.

But the thing was that underneath, beneath the designer trappings and *soigné* exterior, Portia was just like me. We were both eternal romantics, although we hid it well, and both desperately needed to be loved.

Portia had been practically abandoned by her parents since birth, and, though my background wasn't quite so dramatic, I was the product of people who should never have got married, of people who spent their lives arguing, shouting, who led me to believe, as a young child, that it was all my fault.

My parents were still together, very much so, but I suppose every family has its problems, and mine no less than anyone else. We just don't talk about it. Everything is swept under the carpet and forgotten.

Perhaps that's why I loved Portia so much. She was the first person I'd met with whom I felt able to be completely honest. Not immediately, but she was so warm and so open herself (years of therapy, she said) that it was impossible not to fill the silences after her stories with memories of my own.

We gradually allowed more people to enter into our world. Only a select few, only the people who shared our humour, but eventually, by the end of the year, we were a small group of misfits, all from completely different walks of life, but all somehow feeling as if we had found another family.

So there was Eddie, Joshua, Portia and Si. It never occurred to me that we didn't have any close female friends, but with each other we never needed them. Sarah entered halfway through the second year, by virtue of going out with Eddie, but, although we made her feel welcome, she never really belonged.

I longed to bring someone into the group in the way that Eddie had brought Sarah. And I had my fair share of flings. Of going on drunken pub crawls and ending the evening in a strange bed with a stranger, waking up knowing that you weren't going to see one another again, but praying that, nevertheless, you would. But they were only flings. The grand passion of which Portia and I talked, relentlessly, eluded me during those years, and one-night stands were the best I could get.

I remember how philosophical Portia was after her first one-night stand. She had lost her virginity the summer before starting university, on holiday, with a strapping Swede on the Greek island of Mykonos, and had said that one-nighters weren't for her.

I dragged her along to a pub crawl one evening, and tried not to look too horrified when she staggered up the road with a boy who had already worked his way through our entire hall of residence.

And possibly more horrifying was seeing Portia drunk. She simply wasn't the type. It didn't suit her.

'Don't worry,' she slurred, throwing her arms around me just before she left, 'I'vegoddacondom . . . hic' and with that she was gone. I sort of knew what she was doing. When we talked about our own one-night stands, Portia always seemed to feel slightly left out, and I suspected she was trying it, just to see what it was like.

I'm ashamed to say that I slept with pretty much anyone who wanted me at university – my self-esteem so low, that show some interest, the faintest bit of interest in me, and I was yours.

I still vividly remember the craving for affection. It wasn't the sex I wanted, it was the cuddling afterwards. It was the lying in bed, arms around one another, softly murmuring as they stroked your hair. I would sleep with them, then wake up, eyes pleading for one more taste of the affection I had had the night before. But invariably the orgasm of the previous night had taken the intimacy with it, and I would either be ignored, or have to indulge in polite conversation before getting out of there as quickly as possible.

I was sitting in Portia's room when I saw her walk up the road, still in her little black dress, high strappy heels swinging back and forth from her left hand. As she got closer I could see she had washed her face free of all make-up – something few of us did at home, never mind when away – and she grinned as she saw me, and waved.

I switched on the kettle in her room and was scooping Gold Blend into a mug as she came in.

'Well, I've done it,' she announced, 'and I don't know what the big deal is. I walked home and on the way I decided that I could do one of two things. I could either feel dirty and ashamed, because, let's face it, Cath, I've been well and truly used. Or,' and she paused. 'I can write it down to experience, learn from it, and move on.'

'Need I ask which one you've chosen?' I asked, impressed by her confidence, because, frightened though

I was to admit it, after each one-night stand, each rejection, I felt more and more unworthy.

'I'll tell you one thing,' she said, sinking into the chair and lighting up a cigarette, 'the sex was terrible. I can't imagine why *anyone* would want to sleep with a stranger. *And* he's supposed to be one of the best lays in this whole bloody town.'

There wasn't anyone good enough for Portia, I decided. Not here at the university. But then, towards the end of the second year, when we were sharing a little house just off the high street with Josh, Si and Eddie, Sarah not yet having made her mark in the way she was evidently hoping to, Portia came home smiling. She said she'd met someone lovely at the library, and would we mind if he came over that night for supper?

I did mind a bit, actually. It was the first time Portia had ever seemed interested in anyone, and I suppose I must have been jealous, but as soon as Matt walked in, we all fell in love with him.

Matt really was the perfect man. He was funny, charming, kind, bright, and he adored Portia. *Adored* her. You know how some couples just look perfect together? That was Matt and Portia. And I didn't lose her. Rather like fathers of the bride who say they're not losing a daughter, they're gaining a son, I gained another best friend.

But it didn't last. It never did, in those days, with Portia. For a year they were inseparable, and then, out of the blue, she split up with him. No reason, no explanation, nothing. She just decided it was time to move on, but what was an easy decision for her, left the rest of our tiny group devastated. And that was when it all started to go horribly wrong.

Chapter two

There was a girl called Elizabeth. A friend of Eddie. Someone with whom he had been to school, his best friend, who had opted for a job rather than university, and who had secured for herself the rather grand-sounding title of Marketing Assistant.

Eddie adored her. Throughout the first term we kept hearing about Elizabeth: Elizabeth this, Elizabeth that. How Elizabeth taught Eddie to smoke, and borrowed her parents' car while they were away, and how at sixteen Elizabeth and Eddie were driving, drunk, all over town, piles of their schoolfriends hanging out of the sunroof.

Eddie admitted that when he first met her he had a huge crush on her, but then everybody did, he said. She was gorgeous. Far and away the most beautiful girl in school, and even at fourteen she was the talk of the sixth form.

Elizabeth began to take on mythical qualities. She was the elusive beauty that we had heard so much about, but none of us was entirely sure that she really existed, at least not in the way that Eddie had described.

We assumed that Eddie's crush had blinded him to her actual attributes. We assumed she'd be pretty. Striking, even. But unassuming.

And then Eddie announced she was coming to stay for the weekend. He was giving up his bed, he said, and would be staying the night at Sarah's so that Elizabeth would be comfortable.

'Yeah, yeah,' Josh ribbed him. 'Bet you'll be sneaking

back into your bed in the middle of the night, Sarah won't be too happy about that.' Sarah was not, at that stage, a permanent fixture, but we could see that Eddie had, up until this visit from the infamous Elizabeth, fallen for her.

Eddie looked shocked. 'Absolutely not. I'd never dream of doing anything. You know how I feel about Sarah, and anyway Elizabeth is my friend. That's all.'

We all caught Eddie's excitement in the days before Elizabeth was due to arrive. All of us except Portia.

'Don't you want to meet this paragon of female loveliness?' I asked her, and Jesus, how clear this memory is. I remember asking that question. I remember exactly where we were, and the memory is so strong I can suddenly smell it.

I can smell the old seaside café, perched on the side of one of the narrow cobbled streets running up from the beach. During term time it was filled with students, noisily chattering, shouting at one another, sitting for hours over one cup of coffee, but then during the holidays it was full of old ladies, scarves wrapped around their hair, gnarled fingers clutching iced buns.

I loved it best during the holidays. I loved staying there, seeing the town in a completely new light, feeling like a local rather than an unwanted student. I loved sitting in the café by myself, often with a book, but usually the book was only for show, enabling me to listen in on their conversations.

I remember that day with Portia. I was supposed to be at a lecture, but I skipped it, vowing to make up for it later. I remember queuing for two steaming mugs of sweet, milky tea, and debating whether to treat myself to a bun, but deciding against it because those were the days when I actually cared what I looked like.

Portia and I were sitting at a tiny table with our lighters precariously balanced on our packets of Marlboros, the air smelling of smoke, and freshly baked cakes, and salt from the sea. I remember being full of the joys of a flirtation with a boy called Sam, and telling Portia everything about the night before, in minute detail.

And, being Portia, she listened and laughed in all the right places, and encouraged me every step of the way, and when I had finished I said I couldn't wait to meet Elizabeth. And Portia didn't say anything.

'You're coming with, aren't you?' I asked, having told her that all of us were going with Eddie to the train station to pick her up. Portia shrugged.

'Why wouldn't you come?'

She shrugged again, then smiled suddenly. 'I'm sure I will,' she said brightly. 'I've just got to go to the library, so I might have to miss the grand arrival.'

And it didn't occur to me at the time that there might have been more to it.

'What do you think she's like?' I giggled. 'Do you think she's as perfect as Eddie makes out?'

'She's probably a total bitch,' Portia said, which seemed out of character and took me by surprise, but then I entered into the spirit of things.

'Or hugely fat,' I chuckled, mentally applauding myself for resisting the bun.

'Yup. She's probably put on ten stone since Eddie last saw her, eating for comfort now that he's gone. Either that or she's balding.'

I looked at Portia as if she were mad, and we both cracked up laughing.

Portia didn't come with to pick up Elizabeth, and in the end neither did I. Josh took Eddie and Sarah, as he was the only one of us with a car, and I sat in the kitchen at home, waiting for them, and waiting for Portia to come back from the library.

I'd just made tea – which is all we ever seemed to do that year – when the front door opened and I heard a babble of voices. As soon as Josh and Eddie walked into the kitchen, I could see they were both in love. Their eyes were alight and they were laughing, excitement making their cheeks flushed. Right behind them in walked Elizabeth, and I understood what had caused their reaction.

She was, simply, gorgeous. Not in the way that Portia was, in a slightly imperious, untouchable way. Elizabeth was the classic girl next door, and as soon as she saw me she came over with a huge smile – whaddya know, perfect teeth – and I could see how the others had fallen under the spell she had cast.

Sarah had gone off to the library, but Josh whispered that even she seemed to think Elizabeth was lovely, and I remember being hugely impressed that she wasn't racked with jealousy in the way that I'm sure I would have been had I been in her shoes.

Si came back from a drama rehearsal soon after, and it didn't take long for her to work her magic on him, but the person who was quite clearly the most affected was Josh.

I hadn't seen Josh like that before. He couldn't take his eyes off her, and as the afternoon progressed I began to notice that she started paying him more and more attention. It started with a few looks – her eyes would come to rest on him slightly more frequently than on the rest of us, and soon she was laying a hand on his arm, begging him to stop teasing her. Because this was the only way that Josh, at nineteen, knew how to flirt.

'Isn't she amazing?' Si said, when we left to go to the corner shop and buy some more cigarettes.

'I didn't think I'd say this, but she is. I totally understand what Eddie was talking about. She's just so nice, and natural, and funny! I've been in stitches all day.'

'And gorgeous,' Si said as we stamped down the street, our breath clearly visible in the crisp, cold air. 'If I were straight she'd be my perfect woman.'

'What about Portia?'

'Nope.' Si shook his head. 'Portia's beautiful, but there's something impenetrable about her, something slightly cold. Elizabeth's just so natural. Jesus, what's Portia going to think of her?'

'What do you mean?' We went into the shop and picked up the cigarettes, milk, and a Pot Noodle for Si.

'She's going to hate her,' he said smoothly. 'She'll be eaten up with jealousy.'

I stood stock-still and stared at him. 'Portia? Jealous? Don't be ridiculous.'

'Cath, she won't be able to stand not being the centre of attention, and have you seen Josh? He's practically salivating over her. I adore Portia, but I wouldn't want to be the one pushing her off centre stage.'

'But what do you think she'll do?'

'Dunno,' Si said with a wicked smile, 'but, whatever it is, I'm sure it'll make bloody good material for my improv.'

When we got home Portia was there. She was sitting at the kitchen table, talking to Elizabeth, and, although I refused to admit that Si had been right, the atmosphere had definitely changed, and was I going crazy or did Portia suddenly seem to have a cold, flinty look in her eyes?

'So what's on the agenda for tonight, then?' Si put his shoes on the table as he slurped his Pot Noodle.

'We thought we'd do a pub crawl,' Eddie said, looking at Elizabeth for her approval.

'Sounds fantastic,' she laughed. 'Haven't done a good pub crawl for ages.'

'Elizabeth pissed is not a pretty sight,' Eddie said as she hit him, but neither Portia nor I missed the fact that Josh had not joined in with the laughter, too busy gazing at Elizabeth's lovely face.

Portia came downstairs at seven o'clock, and Si nudged me to turn and look at her as she stood in the hallway, shaking out her hair in the hall mirror.

'See?' he mouthed silently. 'She's dressed for battle.'

And she was. She was wearing a tight red dress that Josh once claimed gave him an instant orgasm just by looking at it, and what Si always referred to as her Fuck-me Shoes.

Si raised an eyebrow at me and I shook my head, because I really didn't want to believe Si, but all the evidence was pointing to Portia being very definitely up to something. I just didn't know what it was.

But it didn't take me long to find out. Eddie had established that Elizabeth thought Josh was 'cute', and Josh didn't need to say anything to anyone for his feelings to be established.

Eddie told us this with a mixture of pride and jealousy. Pride because Elizabeth was everything he had described, and so much more, and jealousy because it was absolutely clear that a part of him would always have a crush on her.

We started out at the King's Head. Portia, as always, turned heads wherever we went, but Elizabeth was also generating a fair bit of attention, not just because of her undeniable looks, but because there was a sweetness about her, and of course it may simply have been that she was fresh blood.

Nothing happened until we hit the club. At every pub we'd been to Josh had sat next to Elizabeth, and by the fifth pub they only seemed to have eyes for each other. Eddie shrugged resignedly, and Si and I just sat quietly, watching the blank look on Portia's face, wondering whether she would dare to say anything to Elizabeth.

Because of course Josh had always had a thing for Portia. From the moment we had all met, right through the first year, and on through the second. It had become a standing joke in our group, and even Josh was quite happy to be teased about it. Portia knew, and he knew that Portia knew, and he'd accepted that it was never going to happen. He used to joke with Portia, saying, 'A guy can dream, can't he?'

But the strange thing was that out of all of us, Josh and Portia seemed to make the best match. Josh might have come across as a bit of an upper-class twit at times, but underneath he had a heart of gold, and he was the only one who came from a background that was similar to Portia's.

Up until that night, Portia had always laughed when Si and I teased her about Josh's unrequited crush, saying that Josh was far too nice for her, but tonight I could see that she couldn't deal with another woman in the picture.

And sure enough, in the last pub we went to, the last one before hitting the local nightclub, Portia literally shoved Elizabeth out of the way, sidled up next to Josh and started whispering things in his ear, her coat flung casually on the seat to prevent Elizabeth from coming close.

Poor Josh looked as if he'd been hit by a truck. Stunned. Here was the woman he'd lusted after coming on to him for the first time in his life, and yet here was this other woman, who was also gorgeous, who simply didn't know how to deal with Portia.

Elizabeth sat quietly next to Sarah, and Si tried to act as if everything were normal, even while Portia did her Mata Hari impersonation. In other words, as Si put it later, acting like a complete bitch.

As soon as we walked into the club, Elizabeth went to the toilet and I joined her to tame my hair and put on some more lipstick just in case Sam should walk in the door.

'Are you coming?' I asked Portia, but she shook her head with a smile and followed the others to the bar.

'Josh is lovely, isn't he?' Elizabeth said, as she washed her hands. 'Eddie thought that I'd love you all, but he never mentioned how gorgeous Josh was.'

'He obviously likes you too,' I said, smiling, as she turned to look at me.

'Is there something going on with him and Portia, though? Eddie said absolutely not, but I feel like she's defending her territory or something.'

'Don't worry about it. Portia's fine, she's just not used to you, that's all, and no, there's nothing going on between her and Josh,' and we left to go back into the club.

Elizabeth saw it first. I heard this little gasp, and I turned to look at what she was looking at, and there was Portia. Well, Portia and Josh. Locked together in a passionate embrace in the middle of the dance floor, Portia entwined around him like a snake.

I couldn't tear my eyes off them, not least because I had never seen Portia do this, she wasn't a believer in public displays of affection, and it was an extraordinary sight, to see such blatant passion in public.

I knew Elizabeth was walking away, and I know I should have gone after her, but then Eddie and Sarah were tearing past me to reach her, and I found myself walking over to Si, never taking my eyes off Josh and Portia.

'See?' he said gravely, having to shout into my ear above the loud din of the Housemartins. He tried to look shocked, but the Gossip inside him was completely loving this drama. 'Told you so.'

I watched as Portia and Josh finally broke apart, and I could see that Josh, while thrilled to have finally got together with Portia, was also completely bemused. He looked like a little boy lost, whereas Portia was positively triumphant.

She led him to our table by the hand and picked up a triple vodka, downing it in one before reaching up and whispering something into Josh's ear, sucking Josh's earlobe as Si kicked me hard under the table.

'Where are the others?' she shouted above the din.

'Where do you think, Portia?' Si said, and Portia smiled, as a flash of what I swear must have been guilt passed over Josh's face.

'Oh well. May the best woman win,' she said, picking up another vodka before dragging Josh over to the dance floor and wrapping herself up in his arms.

That night we all got drunk, but what I do remember quite clearly, even to this day, was lying in bed and hearing Elizabeth's quiet sobbing coming from Eddie's room next door, and the rhythmic creaking of Josh's bed upstairs.

That old Victorian terraced house wasn't built to hide

feelings of betrayal, of jealousy, of misplaced passion, but I hadn't known that until that night.

I remember hearing Portia's soft moans, and feeling like a voyeur, even though I couldn't see anything. I remember pulling the duvet over my head to block out the noise, and eventually falling into a dreamless sleep.

Elizabeth had gone by the time I woke up. Eddie had left to take her to the station, and Si was already up, watching children's television with a plate of greasy fried eggs and toast balanced on his knees.

'What a night,' he said, in between mouthfuls. 'I could hardly sleep with all that noise.'

'Is she okay do you know? Elizabeth?'

Si shrugged. 'Not particularly, but I'm sure she'll get over it. Eddie's taken her to the station. She couldn't face spending the weekend here, apparently, so she's gone.'

'How's Eddie about all of this?'

'Upset because Elizabeth's upset, and because he doesn't understand what was going on last night. He knew that Josh liked Elizabeth and that Elizabeth liked Josh, and he said he knew they were going to get it together and he didn't mind at all. Actually, he said he was bloody pleased it was Josh.

'But most of all he doesn't understand what happened with Josh and Portia. One minute they were just walking in the club, and the next Portia and Josh were all over each other, and Eddie says he doesn't understand it.'

'God, poor Elizabeth. I have to say I don't really understand it either.'

'You're not serious?' Si looks at me in amazement as I shrug. 'Cath, don't be thick. Portia's chosen us as her friends because we're all a bit in love with her. She has to be the centre of attention, and she couldn't stand the threat that Elizabeth posed.

'It was bad enough that we all thought Elizabeth was fantastic, but the one thing she absolutely couldn't cope with would have been if Josh and Elizabeth had ended up together.'

'For one night? What's the big deal about them spending one night together?'

'Because,' Si said slowly, 'it might not have been one night. One night would have been fine, but what if Elizabeth and Josh had turned out to be an item? What if Elizabeth started coming up here every weekend to see Josh? What then? She *had* to sabotage it. She didn't have a choice.'

'Of course she had a choice,' I said defensively, 'and anyway, Portia's not a bitch. I can't believe she'd do that.'

'So you think that Portia coming on to Josh last night was just a coincidence, and that she's secretly been harbouring a massive crush on him for years, but now that she's finally found the courage to do something about it, they're going to live happily ever after?'

'They might.'

'Cath, I promise you that this is not a situation that will be repeated. Portia slept with Josh to make sure he stays in love with her, and, providing he does, she'll never sleep with him again. It's definitely a one-night stand between them. Trust me,' he sighed. 'I'm the expert.'

And, sure enough, it was a one-night stand. Of course Portia didn't say that. She said that she adored Josh, had always fancied him too, but that they were better off as friends. She wouldn't be able to bear it if they got involved and then it ended, and she lost him as a friend.

I think Josh was bewildered by the whole thing: he just nodded mutely and seemed to agree with everything she was saying. And after that everything changed. Josh was bewildered, hurt and confused, and the worst thing was that she didn't just destroy him, she destroyed all of us.

She destroyed our friendships, and, although we tried to forgive her, she'd somehow driven a wedge into the heart of our group, and things really were never quite the same after that.

For a while we still tried, even though we didn't trust her any more. We were still sharing a house, and Portia would make coffee in the mornings and bring it into my bedroom, curl up at the end of my bed like the old days, but *then* we never ran out of things to talk about.

A stiffness hung in the air, imbued our conversation with a peculiar formality, and after a while it became more and more difficult to look one another in the eye.

'Where will you be living?' she asked, as we were packing up the house, graduating, getting ready to start our real lives in London.

'With some old school friends,' I lied, knowing that Portia would realize I was lying but not really caring. I pretended to be busy folding knickers so I didn't have to look at her. 'Natasha and Emily. You don't know them.'

I never asked her where she was going to be living. As it turned out, she ended up renting a tiny flat by herself, which I suppose is exactly what she would have done, given that I had, quite clearly, made other plans.

Eddie moved to Manchester, still unable to forgive Portia for hurting Elizabeth as much as she did, and Josh and Si moved to London with me.

All of us had huge plans, but, as we tried to forge ahead with our careers, we drifted further and further apart from Portia. Suddenly I realized that I hadn't spoken to her in over three years. None of us had.

I had heard she was living in Clapham. I was in West Hampstead by that time, as were Josh and his wife, Lucy, and Si was in Kilburn, so I knew that with the North/South divide it was unlikely we'd see each other by chance.

She'd gone into journalism, and after a while I gathered she'd joined the *Standard*. I'd see her by-line first in tiny letters, and then gradually bigger and bigger, eventually accompanied by a picture in which she looked absolutely stunning.

I was working in advertising. I started as an account executive for a big, buzzy trendy ad agency that had recently scooped armfuls of awards, and I loved it. And every night I'd get on the tube with my copy of the *Standard* and look out for Portia's pieces, savouring every word of my former friend, who was now almost famous.

But then, about two years ago, her by-line disappeared. I went through a stage of buying every single paper for a couple of weeks, just in case her name should pop up somewhere else, but it never did, and after a while I gave up.

Josh and Lucy, and Si, were, are, my closest friends. Eddie is married to Sarah, and has become a hot-shot director for a television company, so we don't see him very often, but he comes down to stay from time to time. Apparently he remains in touch with Elizabeth. She was at their wedding four years ago, as lovely as she had been back then, but even after all these years she avoided us.

Si is still on the hunt for the perfect man, as indeed was I up until a few years ago, but I've given up now, particularly given that Si is the perfect date for those social and work occasions I can't face on my own.

The funny thing is, if you had asked me whether we would all be friends ten years after graduating from university, I would have said yes, but only if Portia were included, because she was the star around which we all revolved. Yet even without her, it works.

We do talk about her, though. Do still miss her. They say time heals all wounds, but I find myself missing her more as the years go by. Not less.

Josh has a friend who was a journalist on the *Standard*, and it seems she'd left to write a book. Josh said she was still single and was now living in Maida Vale. I remember feeling a pang when I heard that. Maida Vale. Up the road. I could bump into her at Waitrose. Or drive past her in Swiss Cottage. Or maybe I'd see her having a coffee in West End Lane.

It wasn't that I didn't want to see her. I did, it's just that the more time passed, the harder it was to pick up the phone and call her. Then a few more years went by, and my career took off. I had relationships, and flings, and my wonderful friends, particularly Si, and they all conspired to fill the void that Portia had left all those years before. Gradually I stopped thinking about Portia as much, although if I'm honest she was always there, in the back of my mind.

Once I thought I saw her. I was grabbing a coffee in the West End, and, as I turned to leave, out of the corner of my eye I could have sworn I saw Portia walking past, rounding the corner. She had such a distinctive stride, and all that mahogany hair. If it was her, she looked amazing, far more stylish than before, but I wasn't sure, and I was in too much of a hurry to follow. And even if I had gone after her, what would I have said?

Chapter three

'What shall I wear?' Si is, as usual, moaning at me down the phone.

'Oh, for God's sake, Si. I'm busy. How come you don't understand the concept of work? Why do you never seem to *do* anything except phone me a million times a day?'

I can almost see Si stick out his lower lip in a pretend sulk. 'Fine,' he says, in exactly the tone I would have expected. 'I'll leave you to your work, then, shall I?'

Before I can say anything I hear a click, then the dialling tone. I sigh wearily and punch out his number, knowing that the phone won't even ring before he picks it up.

'Have I ever told you how much I hate you?' he says, picking up the phone.

'No you don't. You love me. That's why I'm allowed to say these things to you.'

'Oh, okay, then,' he grumbles. 'But what are *you* wearing? No, no! Let me guess. Black trousers perhaps? A large black tent-like jumper to cover your bum? Black boots?'

'Well, if you know so much, how come you're asking?'

'Cath, you're not a student any more. *Why* do you dress like one? I keep offering to give you clothing lessons, but you're still as sartorially challenged as you ever were. What *are* we going to do with you?'

'Darling Si. I'm just not interested in clothes, like you. I'm sorry. I wish it were different.' I throw in a few sobs for good measure and Si laughs. 'I'm a hopeless case,' I continue, throwing caution to the winds and crying hysterically. 'A lost cause.'

'There, there,' he soothes. 'No such thing as a lost cause. We'll get you to Armani if it kills me.'

'Can I go now?' I say, in my usual exasperated tone, wondering whether I should signal my secretary to come in and tell me in a loud voice that my three o'clock appointment is here. 'Have you finished with me? I *am* busy, Si. Seriously.'

'You're no fun,' he says. 'I'll come over to yours at seven thirty.'

'Fine, see you la – ' and I stop with a sigh because he's already gone.

I smile to myself for a few minutes after I put the phone down, because it is extraordinary that Si manages to do this. He's supposed to be a film editor, although God knows exactly what that means. All I do know is that he works in Soho, which is, as he readily admits, completely perfect for him, because he can go out cruising every night, if he wants to.

He did throughout his twenties, and when Soho became the new gay village and all the seedy hostess bars were replaced with minimalist gay bars, Si thought he'd died and gone to Heaven (which he did fairly often in those days), but he seems to have settled down now. He used to talk about beautiful boys, and six-pack stomachs, and buns of steel, whereas now he talks about finding someone to cook for, to make a home with, to share everything with. But he's so desperate for commitment, a relationship, anyone who comes even vaguely close is frightened off within days.

'It's my chocolate mousse, isn't it?' he says to me,

humour doing a pretty bad job of hiding the pain. 'I *knew* I'd over-whisked those egg whites.'

'Either that or the fact that you slid the onion ring on to the third finger of his left hand after half an hour,' I say, and we both sigh with disappointment, because neither of us can understand why he can't find someone.

He's not drop-dead gorgeous, but he's certainly cute in a Matthew Broderick sort of way. He's funny, sensitive, kind, thoughtful, has a vicious sense of humour when he feels really comfortable with you, but would never use it against his friends. Or so he tells me.

And his body is – and I'm trying to be as objective as possible – really rather gorgeous. As he says, despite hating 'the scene', he appreciates that he's unlikely to meet Mr Right at the local McDonald's, and if you have to do the bars and, even more occasionally, the clubs, you have to look the part, and white T-shirts, apparently, require toned, tanned flesh underneath.

Every New Year's Eve Si and I make a deal. If neither of us is married by the age of thirty-five, we'll marry each other. Actually, it used to be by the age of twenty-five. Then thirty. And doubtless by the time we hit thirty-five it will move to forty.

I suppose I am slightly in love with him, if only in a platonic way, although there are plenty of times when I wish it could be different. Put it like this. I'm fairly genuine about our New Year's Eve promises. Si is everything I've ever looked for in a man. Apart from the being gay bit, of course. And he'd make a wonderful husband and father. I'd never have to lift a finger at home – he'd do all the cleaning and cook me wonderful gourmet meals every night.

We'd have a hell of a lot of fun, Si and I, if we were married. But I know Si would never marry me. I know he loves me more than anyone else in the world, but I also know that when Si goes to bed at night he closes his eyes and dreams of Brad Pitt, and he could never sacrifice that. Not even for me.

The phone rings again. My private line. Which means it's one of three people. My mother. Si. Or Josh. I'm always amazed that Josh manages to call me quite so regularly, but then again I'm not entirely sure I know exactly what he does, money and finance having always been something of an anathema to me.

I do know that he works for one of the big banks in the City. That he is in charge of a team of ten people, and that the only reason he manages to get home every night by seven o'clock is because he's in the office by six a.m. every day.

Other than that, I think he has something to do with Mergers and Acquisitions, or M & A, as I believe you're meant to call it in the trade. I know he's doing well enough not to have to worry about money, and I know that his public school background, minor though it was, has almost certainly helped him reach the position he now occupies.

'You must work to live, not live to work,' Josh always laughs, when Si and I tease him about having such an easy life at the age of thirty-two when he should, by rights, be working like a madman. But, although I am constantly surprised by his lack of ties to the office, I am also impressed, and I know that his family is so important to him that he would never sacrifice his life purely for money.

My line is still ringing, and it could very well be Josh on the phone now, so I pick up, taking my chances.

'*Now* what do you want, Si?'

'Just to tell you that' – he pauses dramatically – 'Mr Gorgeous has phoned!'

'Fantastic! So when's he coming over to break your heart? Oops, I mean, coming over for dinner?'

'And how do you know this one isn't The One?'

'I'm sorry, my darling. You're quite right. He might be. So you haven't invited him over, then? Let me guess, *he's* taking *you* to some fantabulously swanky restaurant for dinner tomorrow night.'

'Nearly,' he says brightly. '*I'm* cooking *him* a fantabulously swanky meal at my place tomorrow night.'

'You're hopeless,' I say.

'I know,' he replies, but his voice is bubbling over with excitement.

'No chocolate mousse, now,' I warn sternly.

'I know, I know. And I've buried the onion rings in the back garden.'

I get home at seven, cursing the fact that I haven't got a parking space at work, and fantasizing about going freelance and never having to take the damn tube again. There are times when I really don't mind it, when I actually quite enjoy it, but then there are times, like tonight, when there are no seats, and you're all crushed together, and everyone is wet from the pouring rain so the carriage is filled with that awful damp smell.

I grab a towel from the bathroom and pull the elastic band out of my hair, rubbing the towel vigorously over my head, rolling my eyes as I catch sight of myself in the mirror. I should not have been born with this hair. It is just not fair, because my hair is barely human. It is a frizzy mess that used to circle my head rather like a fuzzy halo, and, now that I have tried to grow it, looks increasingly like Marsha Hunt's on a very bad day. It would have looked fantastic in the early seventies, but it looks ridiculous now.

I have a bathroom cabinet stacked with various defrizzing, smoothing products that Si keeps accidentally-on-purpose leaving at my house, saying that he didn't really need them and I should keep them, but I just can't be bothered. Occasionally I read the labels, but invariably I forget to use them, and run out of the house with wet hair scraped back into a ponytail, which is the only way I can look halfway decent for work.

I used to make an effort. I used to wear make-up and have highlights and flirt with strange men in bars, but the older I get the less interested I am. I used to believe in love, in passion, but now I believe that the two cannot go hand in hand, because passion is not love, can never be love, and the one great passion of my life was someone I didn't even like, although naturally I didn't realize it at the time.

I was twenty-four when I met Martin. He really wasn't anything special, not that first time I met him, at a marketing course in Luton. We were there for four days, executives from all over the country, and Martin was leading the course.

I remember he took the stage, bounding up to one of those flip charts, holding an electric-blue marker pen in his hand, and I mentally wrote him off as a boring marketing man. He was ordinary looking. Medium height. Nondescript clothes. Nothing, in short, to write home about.

But by the end of the day I thought he was, quite simply, the most incredible man I had ever met. We all did. Even though none of us *had* actually met him at that stage. That came later. Afterwards. At the drinks party where he singled me out, came over to talk to me. Looked deep into my eyes and told me I had interesting ideas. And all of a sudden the colours in the room became far brighter, the lines sharper, and I remember thinking that perhaps this was what it was like to fall in love.

Eventually we sat at a table in the corner, with other people who had paid fortunes to come on this course, and Martin fascinated all of us with his stories, his confidence, his charm. But I knew I was special. I knew that there was some sort of link between the two of us, something magical, something that would lead to more.

Our table-fellows gradually started to leave. 'Got an early start tomorrow,' they'd say with a wink at Martin, who would laugh politely. Each time he heard it. And eventually it was just the two of us, and Martin turned to me and tugged the elastic band out of my hair, which actually hurt terribly, but I winced in silence because I was aware it was supposed to be a romantic gesture.

'You have beautiful hair,' he said to me, while I blushed furiously and tried to think of something to say.

'It's a frizzy mess,' I ended up muttering, instantly regretting spoiling the mood.

'No, no,' Martin murmured, 'it's quite lovely. Would you like to come up for a drink? It's rather noisy down here, don't you think? And I have a wonderful Scotch upstairs.'

Of course I knew that whisky meant sex, but I was somehow mesmerized by him, by the fact that the man to whom everyone in the room wanted to talk was giving me his undivided attention, and I meekly followed him upstairs.

We spent the next three nights together. I would sit in the front row during his lectures and feel a glow of warmth each time he looked at me, aware that the rumours had already started to circulate, but not caring. Only caring that Martin would look at me again by the time I counted to twelve, because that would mean he was going to fall in love with me. Even I wasn't naïve enough to believe he might love me already.

I like to think that if I had met Martin with the wisdom and cynicism of my current thirty-one years, instead of the romanticism and dreams of twenty-four, there are two things that would have been different.

The first is that I would never have slept with him in the first place, because now I know that these course lecturers regularly look for someone as I was then: a young shy girl, preferably rather plain, who would be flattered and impressed with their false charm and attention.

The second certainty is that when the relationship continued after the four-day course, I would have known that those times when he said he couldn't see me because he was working, those nights when he'd rush out of bed after sex and leave, the fact that he never gave me his telephone number, only a pager, meant only one thing.

Of *course* I should have known he was married. But you see what you want to see, and you hear what you want to hear. I didn't know better. I was so flattered, so swept up by someone, *anyone*, telling me I was beautiful, I didn't stop to think about anything else.

Si knew. Although he didn't say anything at the time. He once tentatively asked me if I thought he might be married, and I was so furious with him he never brought it up again. Until I knew for certain. At which point Si sniffed and said, 'I told you so.'

'I hate it when people say I told you so,' I said.

'I know. I'm sorry. But I told you so.'

And so it went on.

The whole *Martin Malarkey* (Si's expression, not mine) lasted two years. Two years that gradually wore me down until there was almost nothing left. Two years that shattered my dreams of romance and everlasting love. Two years that taught me never to open myself up again for fear of getting hurt.

In fact the only good thing to come out of it was the weight loss. Even after he confessed he was married, I continued to believe that he loved her but wasn't *in love* with her. I believed that she had happily consented to his wishes to sleep in the spare room and that they hadn't had sex for two years. I believed that the only reason he was staying was because of the children, but as soon as they started school he would leave.

I believed this until I found out she was pregnant again. Don't ask me how I found out – a long and complicated story – but I did, and Martin denied it until he could see I wasn't buying the lies any more, and then it was over.

So, as I was saying, the weight loss. I couldn't eat. Quite literally. Could. Not. Eat. For weeks.

'You know you're becoming a lollipop,' Si would say. 'You have this huge hair and a little sticky body. *Please* eat this,' he'd beg, proffering home-made coconut pie with chocolate sauce, or treacle tart, or salmon fishcakes. 'We're *worried* about you.'

Josh and Lucy would invite me over for dinner and exchange concerned glances when they thought I wasn't looking, too busy sighing and poking at pastry with my fork.

Finally Si dragged me up to Bond Street. 'We might as well take advantage of the fact that you now have hipbones,' he sighed, pulling me into Ralph Lauren.

'But I'll never wear this,' I kept hissing at him,

although I had to admit, if I were into clothes and had unlimited finances, I probably would have bought them.

Eventually we settled on Fenwick, much to Si's horror, and I bought a couple of size 10 trousers and a tight sweater, just to keep him happy, although I was slightly smug about not having to buy a size 14 for the first time in years.

'You're a woman,' Si said in disgust, shaking his head in amazement. 'You *must* understand the concept of retail therapy.'

I wore the trousers for a while, until I started becoming happy again, and soon I was back to my normal size and the trousers were given to my secretary. And since then I haven't really been involved with anyone.

There have been a few, but they've always been too short. Or too tall. Too handsome. Not handsome enough. Too young. Too old. Too rich. Too poor. Quite frankly these days I prefer a good book.

'What about Brad?' Si asked me one day.

'Brad who?' We were sitting at a café in West Hampstead, with Josh and Lucy, and a pile of the Sunday papers. It's become a bit of a tradition with us now. One o'clock at Dominique's, every Sunday, for coffee, croissants, scrambled eggs and papers.

We were all engrossed. I was stuck into the *Sunday Times* News Review, Josh had the Business section, and Lucy was reading Style. Si had the magazine.

'Brad who? Brad who?' he said indignantly. 'There *is* only one Brad,' he finally exclaimed, adding, 'Brad Pitt. That's who.' Si held up a picture of said man caught in a paparazzi snap coming out of a restaurant.

'What about him?' Lucy asked.

'What about him for Cath?'

'Yes,' I said slowly, as if talking to a child. 'Because

Brad Pitt would dump Jennifer Aniston for a short, plain, mousy . . .'

'You're almost blonde,' Si interrupted. 'And he loves blondes! Remember Gwynnie.'

Josh put down his paper and looked at Si, shaking his head. 'Si, what on earth are we talking about? What is this conversation? Have you gone mad?'

'No. I just meant that Cath finds fault with every man who even goes near her, and he's completely perfect, but she'd probably find something wrong with him too. Wouldn't you?' He looked at me.

''Course,' I said, examining the picture before exclaiming very seriously, 'His hair's too greasy.'

Josh and Lucy gave up introducing me to their friends a long time ago, but men never seemed to be much of a priority after Martin.

Not that I relished spending the rest of my life by myself, but I wasn't, not with Si, not with Josh and Lucy.

Damn. Si will be here in fifteen minutes and the place looks like a tip. As you would expect, Si's flat, despite being in the less than salubrious area of Kilburn, is immaculate. Not particularly smart, I grant you, but only because Si's work is so irregular he can't afford to re-create the room sets he drools over in *Wallpaper* magazine.

Mine, on the other hand, is a mess. The flat itself is in a mansion block, and therefore lovely and large, but interiors have never been quite my thing, and the fact that most of the furniture was passed on by elderly relatives or well-meaning friends has never particularly bothered me.

It bothers Si, though. Every time he comes over he sits on the sofa, growing more and more fidgety, before getting up and *re-arranging*. He pulls books off the book-shelf and arranges them in neat little piles on the coffee table, together with whatever bowls he can find.

He plumps up cushions and rummages around in my wardrobe for old scarves, which he drapes over furniture. Si's a big believer in draping, although he claims he hates it and is resorting to desperate measures to hide the 'hideous pieces of crap'. He collects mugs that are gathering mould, and, shooting me filthy looks, takes them into the kitchen, stands them in the sink and covers them in hot, soapy water.

He has been known to get the vacuum out of the cupboard and do the entire flat, but, as he says, hoovering has never been his favourite job. Give him a pair of rubber gloves and a can of Pledge, however, and he is as happy as anything.

I run around the living room, gathering papers, videos, books, and stack them in a precarious pile next to the sofa, well out of Si's view. The mugs are literally thrown into the sink, and then I remember the bed and rush in to shake out the duvet.

'Only *real* sluts don't make their bed,' Si said one day, after which point I have tried to remember to make it. At least when he's coming over.

At seven thirty on the dot the doorbell rings. I haven't had time for a bath, and I run to the door tugging a cream cardigan over my head because I can't be bothered to undo the buttons.

'Are my eyes deceiving me? Could that be . . . cream?' says Si. 'That's adventurous. What happened to basic black? I don't think I've seen you in a colour for years.'

'It's not a colour,' I say grumpily. 'It's *cream*. Anyway, would you like to come in for two seconds to see how tidy I am?'

Si pops his head round the living room door and marches straight over to the side of the sofa. The bit that's supposed to be hidden from view. One tap of his toe and the pile is once again all over the floor.

'Cath, my love, did you think my instincts would have failed me? Did you think, perhaps, that they had gone absent without leave? Or perhaps you think I'm rather stupid . . .'

'All right, all right. Sorry. But you have to admit it looks okay.'

'No,' Si says slowly. 'Although relatively speaking I suppose I'll have to concede it does.' He checks his watch. 'Josh said quarter to. Shall we wander over?'

I nod and grab my coat, turning to see Si watching me.

'Sweets,' he says. 'You really should make more of an effort. Put on just a tiny bit of make-up on this gorgeous spring evening. What if Mr Perfect turns up?'

'I don't need Mr Perfect,' I say, closing the door behind us and tucking my arm cosily into Si's. 'I already have you.'

Chapter four

Josh comes to the door with a tea-towel in one hand and Max in the other, looking, it has to be said, extremely cute in his little striped pyjamas. That is if you didn't know better.

Even Josh looks rather cute, come to that, with his dirty blond hair mussed up, his shirt sleeves rolled up to show off rather strong and sexy tanned forearms (well, they would be if they didn't belong to Josh).

It's funny how I've never thought of Josh in that way. Maybe it's just that he's too much of an older brother to me now, or maybe it's because I don't believe he's got any sex appeal, but I have never, could never, think of Josh as anything other than a friend.

And yet, looking at him now, purely objectively, he's a good-looking man. He is the sort of man who grows into his looks, who is just now, at thirty-two, starting to look seriously handsome in a boy-next-door kind of way. The deep laughter lines and creases at the corners of his eyes always seemed slightly incongruous in his twenties, but now they suit him, make him look worldly, as if he's been around the block a few times, which God knows he needed, because Josh was, still is, the straightest of all of us.

I remember Si and I going through our spliff phase just after university. Si would roll these tiny, tight little joints, and I would try to imitate them, ending up with Super Plus Tampons. We'd sit there, Si and I, rolling around on the floor and screaming with laughter, while

Josh puffed away awkwardly, looking slightly perturbed that it wasn't having the same effect.

'No, no, Josh!' Si would say, when the pair of us had recovered enough to actually breathe. 'You have to inhale,' and that would set us off again.

His only vice, if you can even dare to call it that, has been drink. First it was pints of Snakebite at university with the rugby team, then pints of lager with the City boys, and now it's good bottles of claret with dinner.

'Look!' Josh says to Max, after rolling his eyes at me briefly. 'Aunty Cath and Uncle Si! Do you want to give Aunty Cath a cuddle?' he says brightly, swiftly passing Max to me.

'No!' wails Max, turning back to Josh with a look of sheer panic on his face. 'I want Daddy!'

'Come to Uncle Si,' says Si soothingly, as he effortlessly lifts Max up and starts making him laugh immediately by pulling funny faces. 'Shall we go upstairs and find Tinky Winky?'

Max nods his head vigorously, as Si disappears up the stairs, concentrating hard on Max, who is now chatting away merrily. Josh sighs and closes the door, wiping his forehead with the tea-towel, leaving a big splodge of what could be cream, or could be something that's not worth thinking about, on the left side of his face.

'Face,' I say, gesturing to the cream, as Josh realizes and wipes it away.

'And it's lovely to see you too,' he says, leaning down and giving me a hug. 'Lucy's in the kitchen and I'm supposed to be helping her, but Max has been a bugger today.'

'Kids, eh?' I sigh. 'Who'd have 'em?'

'Tell me about it,' Josh says, but, tired as he looks tonight, I know that he adores Max, that although he might pretend to be unhappy about having to take Max out of Lucy's hair, he secretly loves it. Josh loves the fact that he can be a little boy again, can play Cowboys and Indians, teach Max the basic rules about being a man.

Josh and Lucy live in a terraced Victorian house in a narrow street. It looks like nothing from the outside, but is, basically, a Tardis house, i.e., it looks tiny, but once you're in, it's enormous.

It is always messy, always noisy, and most of the activity is focused around the large kitchen at the rear, which wasn't a large kitchen when they moved in two years ago, but, thanks to a smart conservatory extension, is now large enough for a huge dining table that usually has at least three people sitting round it, drinking coffee.

Tonight there is a man I don't recognize sitting there, strange only because I know most of Josh and Lucy's friends, and because I thought it was just going to be the four of us tonight.

Lucy has her back to us, chatting away, finishing an anecdote about work; she trained as an illustrator but seems to have done less and less since having Max. When she does have free time, she seems to spend it doing other things – displacement activity, Si always says. Her latest venture is a course in counselling, and I can hear, from the conversation, that the other person sitting at the table is from the course as well.

Lucy stops mid-sentence as she hears my footsteps. Her face lights up as she puts down the lethal-looking knife, and she gives me a huge hug, careful to keep her hands, currently covered with avocado, off my clothes.

Lucy is one of those people whose face always shines, despite not wearing any make-up. She is always radiant, sickeningly healthy-looking, always smiling, and is the best possible person to talk to if you ever have problems.

I love the fact that this is who Josh chose to marry. For a while Si and I were slightly terrified he was going to pop the question to one of an endless stream of identikit girls with streaky blonde hair, braying laughs and a lack of brain cells, but then he went and surprised us by falling madly in love with Lucy. Lucy, with her ruddy cheeks and raucous laugh, with her rounded figure in faded dungarees, with her winks as she ruffled Josh's hair and told him, repeatedly, that she was built for comfort and not for speed. Lucy, whose maternal instincts were such they were almost oozing out of every pore, who gave birth to Max five months after their wedding.

I love hearing the story of how they met. It gives me hope. Josh hadn't been working in the City long, when he met Lucy. He was, at the time, desperate to impress, and would spend his nights socializing with City boys who were very definitely not my type.

Josh tried to bring Si and I along a couple of times. I think he thought that if there were enough people going down to the pub, Si and I would just blend in. But of course we didn't. I had nothing in common with the gaggle of silly little girls that hung on to their every word, and Si had even less with the boozy, macho traders who'd relax in their spare time by having drinking competitions and seeing who could 'pull the best bird'.

A group of them decided to go off to France on a skiing trip one Christmas. They booked a chalet, and Josh came over one night and sat on my sofa, sighing over and over as he debated whether to bring his latest conquest.

'I do really like Venetia,' he sighed. 'I just know she's not The One, and I don't know what to do. She's already expecting to come, talking about going out to buy a new set of salopettes, but I'm worried she'll spoil the fun.'

It turned out he meant that Venetia would curl up on his lap every evening, gazing up at him with big blue eyes, taking him by the hand and leading him to bed at nine o'clock, thus preventing him from debauched nights with the boys. Venetia, he said, was gorgeous. She was the perfect trophy girlfriend, and all his mates were green with envy.

And everything would be fine, apart from the fact that Venetia's biggest problem was that she was far more mature than her twenty-three years. While Josh wanted to go out, have fun, play the field, and spend perhaps a few weeks with someone both adoring and adorable, Venetia wanted to get married.

And whom did she want to marry? A man exactly like Josh, and this was the problem.

In the end Josh had to take her. He was about to tell her he was going on his own, when she produced the aforementioned salopettes, together with a furry hat, gloves and moon boots, all of which had been bought that afternoon, paid for by Daddy's credit card. Daddy was delighted a chap as 'suitable' as Josh was showing the signs of making an honest woman of her.

A 'chalet girl', naturally, looked after the chalet they'd booked. Someone who had done a cordon bleu cookery course, who was adept at making the guests feel happy, and who would generally run around making beds and clearing up for a weekly pittance and the opportunity to grab a few hours' afternoon skiing on the pistes.

Josh and Venetia were the last to walk into the chalet, mostly due to Josh struggling with both his and Venetia's luggage, Venetia having packed for every eventuality, including, bizarrely, a bikini.

'Let me help you.' The chalet girl came bustling over and lifted up Venetia's suitcase with ease, striding in front of them, turning her head back and throwing a beaming smile over her shoulder as she walked. 'I'm Lucy.'

'God,' giggled Venetia in a stage whisper, as they followed her in. 'She's got bigger muscles than you.'

'Shut up,' hissed Josh, who was worried that the chalet girl would hear, and who didn't want to upset her this early on in the trip. Plus, she seemed pleasant, she had a lovely smile, and he wished Venetia wasn't quite so tactless.

For the week the group stayed at the chalet, the City boys treated Lucy like a serf. They would, by turns, ignore her, insult her and, when very drunk, manhandle her, guffawing about what they could do with a bottom that size. Lucy, to her credit, merely smiled and brushed their hands away, calmly placing steaming casseroles on the table and clearing the plates away as if she hadn't heard.

On the fourth day Josh fell and twisted his ankle. Not severely, but severely enough to miss a day's skiing. Venetia insisted on staying with him, but Josh wouldn't hear of it, and reluctantly she left with the others, ski pass swinging jauntily from her ice-blue jacket.

Josh settled himself in a large armchair with a good book, as Lucy built the fire and brought him endless mugs of hot chocolate. Within an hour the book was resting on his lap, and he was watching Lucy whirl in and out of rooms, a small smile playing on his lips.

And astonishingly, as he watched her ample behind disappear into a bedroom, he found himself wondering what someone like Lucy would be like in bed. And he closed his eyes and set off on what he claims was a really rather raunchy fantasy involving Lucy checking his pulse, then peeling off all her clothes and leaping on him. He opened his eyes with a shock to find Lucy standing over him, smiling.

When he tells this story now, they both roar with laughter. Lucy laughs about the guilty look in Josh's eyes, the fact that she knew he'd been thinking something dirty, not to mention the sizeable erection that she did her best to ignore. And Josh tells of his heart pounding while for a split second he thought his fantasies were about to come true, and then the combination of relief and disappointment as Lucy said, 'Penny for them.' His nervous laughter as he moved the book on his lap to hide the physical evidence of thoughts that were, as far as he was concerned, worth significantly more than a penny, and the realization that not only was this woman incredibly sexy, but that there was (and he only understood this as he looked at her) something very different about her, quite unlike anyone he'd ever met.

For one blissful half-hour in the afternoon Lucy came and sat with him, and they chatted. He found her funny, down-to-earth and refreshingly honest. She had an easy manner and an open smile, and, as she regaled him with horror stories from her cookery course, he found himself more and more attracted to her.

After a while Lucy bustled off to get ready for her daily treat of a couple of hours on the slopes, but not without asking Josh if he wanted her to stay and keep him company.

'Absolutely not,' said Josh. 'This is your free time, go and you can report back on the weather.'

'Are you sure?' Lucy hovered in the living room for a bit, and it was only years later that she admitted she was desperate for Josh to ask her to stay with him, that his appearance at the beginning of the week was like a shining light in a sea of dross, and that she had prayed for something like this to happen.

And Josh, being Josh, was waiting for Lucy to tell him that she simply refused to go out and leave him like that. So, because of their lack of communication, neither of them got what they wanted, and Josh was left on his own as Lucy reluctantly made him one final cup of tea before leaving to ski.

Venetia clambered noisily over the sofa when the others piled back in, showering Josh with kisses, her long blonde hair tickling his nostrils and making him sneeze, and it was all he could do not to push her away.

'Has old thunderthighs been looking after you?' she said, nuzzling his ear, as Josh did, finally, push her away, his throat constricted with anger.

'Don't call her that,' he said sharply, wishing fervently that the girl on his lap were Lucy.

But Lucy and Josh didn't get a chance to spend any more time together after that. Josh's ankle was fine by the next morning, and Venetia, sensing that Josh had distanced himself since the accident, now clung to him like a limpet, trailing after him in an extremely good impersonation of his shadow. Josh cleared the plates and took them into the kitchen, where Lucy was removing a pecan pie from the oven, and, just as Lucy's eyes lit up at the sight of Josh, Venetia tottered in on her spiked heels to see what Josh was up to.

Josh tried sloping off early, claiming the ankle was playing up, but this time Venetia refused to be left behind, and the two of them sat miserably, side by side, in the cable car going down, both of them depressed, both for entirely different reasons.

Finally, on the last day, everyone decided to go for one last ski. As they reached the cable car, Josh, furtively placing his ski pass in the pocket of his jacket, told the others that he had forgotten it and had to go back, and that they shouldn't wait, he would meet them on the slopes.

This time, when Venetia started to come with Josh, he told her she was being ridiculous, and it was bad enough that he should have to cut short his skiing time, but that there was no way she should as well. She couldn't say anything, she just miserably turned back to the rest of the crowd.

Josh went running into the chalet, nervous, exhilarated, unsure of what to say but determined to say *something*. He found Lucy in one of the bedrooms, cheeks flushed with the exertion of cleaning, shaking out one of the blankets, hair escaping from the elastic band holding it in a loose ponytail and falling in tendrils around her shining face.

'Lucy,' he said, standing in the doorway, his own cheeks flushed with the cold. 'I . . .'

And Lucy beamed at him, without saying anything, and just like in a Hollywood movie they moved towards one another as if in slow motion. Josh bent his head to kiss her just as the front door slammed and they jumped apart guiltily, before their lips had a chance to meet.

'Josh?' Venetia's voice rang through the house as Josh came to the door, the flush of cold rapidly becoming a flush of guilt. He turned round and looked at Lucy, who gave him a sad smile of regret and picked up the blankets again. Josh froze in the doorway, pulled between the two women, not knowing what to do.

But how was he to know Lucy was his future and

Venetia his past? All he knew was that he didn't really care if he never saw Venetia again, and he couldn't get Lucy out of his mind. And he'd come so close! To kissing those lips! Oh, Christ. How could he let her get away?

He did let her get away. Didn't have a choice because he didn't have a chance to find her on her own again, but before they left Josh scribbled Lucy a note, left his phone number in London, and shoved it under a pillow, knowing that Venetia wouldn't find it, but that Lucy, on making the bed, undoubtedly would.

Josh waited until they returned home before telling Venetia it was over. She seemed upset at the time, but a week later she was going out with a stockbroker called William, so evidently he hadn't broken her heart, and Josh then spent the next few weeks trying to get over Lucy.

She didn't phone. For the first couple of weeks every time the phone rang he'd leap on top of it, praying it was her, and then he tried to forget about her as he got on with his life and continued half-heartedly dating the identikit Venetias.

Eight weeks later Josh was at work when the receptionist buzzed him and told him to come down to collect a delivery that had to be signed for personally. He came down to be greeted by Lucy's sparkly eyes, and the rest, as they say, is history.

'Cath! So lovely to see you. Look at you, you look as fresh as a daisy in that sumptuous sweater. Sit! Sit! What are you having? Red? White? Or vodka? Gin?' Lucy bubbles away as she manoeuvres me into a chair, bustling away to open another bottle of red and pour me a glass.

'Where's that wicked Si? Not corrupting my Maxy I hope. Josh!' She screams, 'Come and be sociable! Oh

God. So rude. You haven't met,' and finally she stops to take a breath and grins at us.

'Cath. Dan. Dan. Cath.'

We smile warmly at one another, and I hope that this will not be one of those awkward evenings where strangers make small talk and ask questions like, 'How long have you known Josh and Lucy?'

'We're all on the course together,' Lucy explains, 'Dan lives in Camden and he gave me a lift, so it was the least I could do.

'Here,' says Lucy, thrusting a knife into my hand. 'You're on cucumber duty.' Dan is given red peppers, which might be an odd way of treating your dinner guests, but it breaks the ice and within minutes we are all laughing like old friends.

'I'm missing out on all the fun, aren't I?' says Si, rushing into the room behind Josh. 'Lucy, darling. You look gorgeous.' Si sweeps Lucy into a big hug, and Lucy blushes, gesturing at her faded apron, her hair tied back with a fraying old scrunchy. 'I look terrible,' she says, but she's delighted, as she always is, when Si compliments her.

'Hello. I'm Si.' He grins cheerfully at Dan, leaning over his shoulder to grab a piece of red pepper.

'Oi!' I dart over, covering Dan's pile of peppers protectively, hunger making me, as always, incredibly territorial about food. 'Hands off.'

'You can't speak to me like that,' Si says, in mock horror. 'You're not even in charge of peppers. If I'm not mistaken, you're doing the cucumbers, so M.Y.O.B.'

'I've got my hands full with one child, thankyouvery-much,' Lucy says, grimacing. 'I don't need another two this evening.'

'It wasn't me, it was her.' Si pours himself a glass

of red wine, grinning at Dan, who's laughing at this ridiculous exchange, before going to the stove and lifting lids off pots and sniffing.

I wish I could be more like Si at times. I know how insecure he is deep down, as insecure as the rest of us, and yet he has this ability to meet complete strangers and instantly put them at ease, make them feel as if they have known, and loved, Si for ever. Most of the time I think it's because he can be so childlike, so naughty, and it reminds us of when we were children, of what it was like to have no inhibitions.

He wanders over to the fridge and busies himself doing something, while the rest of us keep chopping.

'So how is the course?' I throw into the room.

Lucy and Dan groan at the same time.

'It was fine,' says Lucy.

'Until Jeremy,' says Dan.

'And now we can't wait until the bloody thing's over,' finishes Lucy.

'Jeremy?' I ask.

'Jeremy,' says Josh, in the tone of voice that says I ought to know who Jeremy is. 'Jeremy the class bore,' he continues, rolling his eyes, evidently having heard more than enough about him from Lucy. 'Who monopolizes every group session by talking about himself, having temper tantrums if he feels he's being ignored.'

'Oh, that sounds so mean,' says Lucy. 'I feel awful talking about him behind his back. It's not right. We actually shouldn't be doing this.'

'You're right.' Dan sounds contrite, for about two seconds. 'But fuck it. He is a major pain in the arse.'

Lucy remembers something, jumps up, checks her recipe book, and pushes Si out of the way to get to the fridge. She pulls the butter out, then stops as she closes the fridge door and squints at a point on the upper left side of the door.

'Si!' She shrieks with laughter as Si skulks over to the table, trying to look innocent. 'Luscious Sexy Smells Excite My Potent a r m p I t s'

'Armpits?' Josh looks bemused. 'That magnetic poetry kit doesn't have the word "armpits".'

'I spelt it out myself,' Si says proudly, and within seconds we are all clamouring round the fridge trying to out-do one another with ridiculously flowery poems, when the sound of concentration is broken by a wail.

'Daaaaaaaddy!' comes Max's shriek from upstairs, followed by a deafening silence. Then: 'Caaaaan youuuuu cooooome and wiiiiiiipe my bottttttttttttom?' Josh raises his eyebrows and leaves the room as the rest of us scream with laughter.

'God. So embarrassing. He's only just started using the loo on a regular basis, and Josh keeps showing him what to do, but he always wants one of us to do it,' Lucy explains, stifling a laugh.

'Quite right too. He doesn't want to get his hands dirty, and who can blame him,' grins Si. 'I hope those hands will be washed before they come anywhere near me.'

'Don't be so insensitive,' I chastise. 'You love Max, and if you love Max then you love *everything* about Max, and if you love *everything* about Max then you love his poo.'

'No.' Si shakes his head solemnly. 'My love does not stretch as far as to encompass poo.'

'Come on, then, guys, who's going to set the table?' Lucy hands me the cutlery, glasses to Dan, and napkins to Si, who instantly arranges them into little swans, prompting much oohing and aahing from Lucy, who has witnessed this many times before, but is just as amazed each time she sees it done.

'It's so pretty I don't want to undo it,' she says, placing it gently down on her plate.

The five of us sit down and help ourselves to Caesar salad.

'Bugger.' Lucy jumps up and runs to the oven, bringing out a familiar-looking silver loaf.

'Lucy, I love you!' Si blows her Parmesany kisses from the other side of the table. 'You never forget.'

'Si, I only do this for you, you know. I'd never *dream* of serving garlic bread to anyone else. It's just so seventies.'

'Seventies is in again now,' says Josh, shaking his head at Si, who's already eaten one piece and is now licking the dripping butter off his fingers. 'So as usual Si's one step ahead of us all.'

'God, do you remember that seventies party Portia had?' Josh laughs. 'When you and Cath set fire to my afro wig?'

'It practically stuck to your head.' I smile at the memory. 'I haven't thought about that in years.'

'Portia,' says Dan. 'I know a Portia. What's her surname?'

'Fairley,' say Si, Josh and I simultaneously.

Dan smiles as the rest of the table freezes. 'I knew that wasn't a common name. How do you all know Portia?'

How can a name, a name from the past that should have no power at all any more, still have such an impact on the three people in this room that knew her way back when? Time seems to stand still, and I'm too lost in memories to notice that Josh and Si are diving into those memories at the same time.

And the thing is, I can't help but wonder if she's forgiven us. I forgave her, forgave her for breaking Josh's heart, a long time ago. I figured that she must have had her reasons, that she wasn't doing it intentionally, but I've always wondered whether she has forgiven us for abandoning her friendship as a result.

And ten years on, none of us expected to hear her name in the comfort of this kitchen.

'We were at university together,' I eventually tell a bemused Dan, because he can see his words have had some effect, only he is not sure what it is. I smooth out my voice, careful of the tone, doing my best to keep the excitement contained. 'And you? How do you know Portia?'

'She bought my old flat,' he laughs, entirely unaware of the silent reaction her name has caused.

'Where?' I ask, suddenly desperate to know what's happened to her, if her life has fulfilled her expectations, if destiny has, as we all assumed, been kind to her.

'Sutherland Avenue,' says Dan. 'Nice flat. I miss it. Wish I didn't have to sell but there it is. Give up your job in the City for psychotherapy and bach pad goes with it, I'm afraid.' He shrugs and smiles at Si and Lucy, who offer him sympathetic smiles in return.

'She was always terribly beautiful at university,' Si says dreamily. 'One of those girls whose life was perfect. She had money, class, beauty, kindness. Born with a golden spoon in her mouth. We followed her career as a journalist for a while, but lost track. Do you know what she's up to now?'

'Sure,' says Dan. 'I'm surprised you didn't know. Haven't you seen that series on TV?' He mentions the name of a series we all love. A weekly drama that follows the lives of a group of thirty-somethings, and before Dan says anything I suddenly realize that she is the writer. She could not be anything other than the writer because, and I know it is ridiculous that this should not have occurred to me before, because all of the characters are based on us.

I look at the others and see Josh's mouth hanging open, Si's eyes wide with shock, both having had the same realization.

'Oh my God, she writes it!' Si finally snorts, half in wonderment, half aghast.

'She doesn't just write it,' Dan says. 'She apparently came up with the concept, sold it to the network, does all the writing and storylining, and to top it all has sold it on to seventeen countries worldwide. She's making a fortune.'

Si looks at Josh, his lower lip still somewhere near his knees, and coughs, attempting to regain some composure. 'Excuse me, can you pass the salt please, *Jacob*.'

'Don't be ridiculous,' says Lucy, 'they're not u – ' and she stops, because in the split second it took for her to verbalize that thought, she had another. A memory. She remembered the characters.

The central character in the series is Mercedes (good joke, I thought). Mercedes is the wealthy daughter of a millionaire who has spent her life struggling for independence. Mercedes looks like she ought to be a bitch. But of course she's not. She's adorable, although she can't seem to find a man who looks beyond the physical, who is really interested in getting to know her.

There's Jacob, world-weary, kind, but rather weak, who's married to Lisa, an overbearing Sloane who's too busy shopping and lunching to take much care of their toddler, Marty, who tends to turn up at Jacob's office on a daily basis.

Steen is the perfect gay best friend, who keeps the laughs coming in with his curt one-liners.

And Mark. Gorgeous, sensitive Mark, who loves Mercedes unrequitedly, for he is far too nice for Mercedes to love in return, and he, of course, could only be Matt, Portia's boyfriend from university.

And then, I realize with horror, there's Katy. Katy, who is plain, dowdy, but completely self-obsessed. Katy who only wears black. Or occasionally sludge-green. Katy, whose hair looks like it could house a few hundred sparrows in it if they were really stuck for accommodation.

Lucy suddenly chokes, and we all look at one another in panic, terrified she's choked with shock, but she has a sip of water and then starts laughing. And laughing. And laughing.

'It's hysterical,' she says, as we slowly see the funny side. 'You're Katy!' and she points at me and goes off into peals of laughter again, almost falling off her chair, arms weak with mirth.

'You can laugh,' I say in a nasty tone. 'She hasn't even met you. She's obviously just heard that Josh married someone who's name begins with an L, who has a son whose name begins with an M. I'm Katy, for God's sake. Katy, who's a selfish cow. I can't believe she'd do that to me.'

'Are you sure about this?' Dan says, looking more than a little worried about how this information has gone down. 'Are you sure the characters are you?'

'Look at us,' says Josh with a shrug.

'I'm happy,' Si says brightly. 'Steen's gorgeous.'

'Don't you mind?' says Dan suddenly. 'Don't you mind that someone whom you knew has written your life stories down and shown them to thousands of people?'

'Millions, according to the ratings,' adds Josh. Quietly.

'Not quite our life stories.' Lucy gets up to check the

pudding. 'Josh really isn't Jacob, or Jacob Josh. Josh is far stronger than that. And Katy isn't Cath. She's gorgeous, for starters.' She gives me a quick squeeze as she passes, which is supposed to make me feel better. And does, as it happens. 'As for Steen' – she eyes Si up and down – 'Si's far sweeter than Steen.'

'Not to mention far more handsome,' prompts Si.

'Of course,' she laughs. 'And far more handsome.'

'You know what it is,' muses Josh, staring into his glass of wine as if it holds all the answers. 'This is sort of her revenge, isn't it? She's taken the worst aspects of our characters and magnified them until that's all the character is. But the weird thing is, she's taken our characters as she knew them then, and I for one think I've changed immeasurably. We all have.'

'Go on,' I prompt, assured by Josh's interpretation.

'I *was* weak at university. I was insecure, had never been away from home, and so Portia's decided that at thirty-something I would have to be a wimp. You were selfish at university, at times.' He looks at me, and, although I don't want to agree with him, I know it's true.

'But not when it came to Portia,' he continues. 'She was the weak spot for all of us, but you were often thoughtless, so she's made you a self-obsessed adult.

'And Steen.' He looks at Si.

'I know,' says Si. 'You don't have to tell me I have a bitchy streak. I *have* calmed down, though, haven't I?' He looks at me, doubt written across his eyes. '*You* think I'm a nicer person now, don't you, Cath?'

I reach over and hug him. 'Of course,' I say, smiling. 'I think you're lovely.'

'Good,' he says. 'It's good of you to be so selfless for a change.'

I hit him, and he squeezes my leg and gives me a long, smoochy kiss on the cheek.

'Revenge for what?' asks Dan, intrigued, as a silence falls and we all start to look slightly shifty.

'It's a long story,' Lucy says matter-of-factly, able to do so because she wasn't involved, she simply heard about it many years later. Josh sat her down and told her, late one night, when they were having a conversation about first loves. Portia was his first love, he told her. She broke his heart and it took him a long time to recover, but it was all in the past now, and anyway, he hadn't seen her for years.

'A story for another time,' Lucy says brightly. The disappointment shows on Dan's face, but he's polite enough not to push the point.

'So what about Portia?' Si asks finally, when he's disengaged his lips from my face. 'Is she the breathtaking Mercedes? Perfect on the outside but unable to find lurrve?'

'Who knows,' shrugs Dan. 'She's very beautiful, but I only met her the few times she came to my flat with interior designers and stuff.'

'Interior designers,' I smile. '*So* Portia.'

'I can give you my old number if you like,' Dan says suddenly. 'I don't think she changed it, and it seems like you'd all like to get back in touch.' He smiles. 'If for nothing else but to shout at her.'

'No, no,' says Josh. 'It was all a long time ago.' I see him shoot a worried glance at Lucy, but she doesn't look bothered in the slightest.

'We were just curious.' Si's voice is nonchalant. 'That's all.'

'*I'd* like her number,' I find myself saying, even though I hadn't planned for those words to come out of my mouth. 'What?' I turn to Josh and Si, demanding to know why they are so shocked. 'What?'

'Bugger!' shouts Lucy, jumping up and knocking her chair halfway across the kitchen. 'Bloody bread and butter pudding.'

This evening brings up so many memories for all of us. Si and I walk back to my flat in silence, both immersed in thoughts of Portia, memories of our gang, the strength of our love for one another.

'I do still miss her, you know,' Si says softly into my ear, as he's hugging me goodbye.

I pull back and look at him. 'Maybe that's why we met Dan tonight. Everything happens for a reason, doesn't it, Si? Maybe I was supposed to get her number. Maybe none of us is supposed to miss her any more.'

Chapter five

I lose my nerve. It's not that I don't try, I do. For the last two weeks I've picked up the phone at least twice a day, Portia's scribbled number on a scrap of paper, mocking me from the table next to the telephone. I've even got as far as dialling all seven digits, but as soon as the phone starts to ring, I slam it down, not knowing what to say, heart pounding and breath coming in short, sharp spasms.

It's only *Portia*, I keep telling myself. It's not like I'm ringing someone up to have a confrontation, which seems to be the only other time my heart pounds and my breath is used up by fear. I'm only ringing her to catch up. There's nothing scary about Portia.

'Well?' Si asks, as he has now asked on a daily basis. 'Have you done it yet?'

'Yes,' I say earnestly, slowly. 'And I decided not to tell you that in fact I saw her last week, because I didn't think you'd be interested.'

'God, you're being such a wimp,' Si says. 'If it were me, I'd just pick up the phone and call her.'

'Go on, then,' I push the phone towards him. 'There's the number. Do it.'

It's a Thursday night, the night of Portia's series, and though Si has been coming over to my place to watch it for months, since our new-found discovery these evenings have taken on a greater significance.

We have still, these last couple of weeks, kicked off our shoes, curled up on the sofa, and pigged out on

59

takeaway Chinese for an hour before the show starts. But now, instead of laughing our way through, we are glued to the screen, desperately searching for clues to our own characters.

Earlier this evening we sat in silence, just the blue flickering screen lighting up the concentration on our faces.

'I'd *never* say that,' Si exclaimed indignantly, after Steen emerged with a particularly bitchy line.

'No one's saying you would.' I rubbed his back gently, eyes still fixed on the show, waiting for Katy to come back in.

'Jesus,' I whistled a few minutes later. 'I know it's meant to be funny, but she is so selfish. I'm not like that, am I?'

'Sssh,' urged Si. 'Here comes Steen again.'

And now it's over, and Si grabs the phone and dials the number, giving away nothing, looking as if he's just phoning Josh, just for a chat.

I watch his face intently, waiting for him to become animated, but he shakes his head after a few seconds and puts down the phone.

'Answer phone.'

'What? Didn't you listen? What does her voice sound like? What does it say?'

I grab the phone from him and press redial, and, although I know what will happen, why I'm phoning, it is nevertheless a shock to hear Portia's voice, and I would know that voice anywhere.

I'm so sorry neither of us can get to the phone. Leave a message and we'll get back to you. Thanks for calling.

'Neither of us?' I look at Si. 'Why didn't you say she said "neither of *us*"? That means she's married.'

'And what decade are *you* living in?' Si is horrified.
'The fifties?'

'Okay, not necessarily married, but living with
someone, then.'

'Could be her flatmate,' Si says.

'Right.' I raise an eyebrow. 'Because we *do* have flat-
mates when we're thirty-one and earning packets of
money.'

'We do if we're lonely,' Si says seriously, and it shocks
me that Portia might be lonely, and I want to step in and
stop her loneliness. 'Actually,' Si says, looking pensive,
'it could just be for security. There was an article in
Cosmo about looking after yourself, and it said that if
you lived on your own you should always refer to "we"
or "us" on an answer phone to deter potential burglars.'

'*Cosmo*!' I shriek with laughter. 'Jesus, Si, aren't you
a bit old for *Cosmo*?'

'I didn't buy it.' Si looks shifty. 'I just happened to
pick it up at a friend's house.'

'Yeah, yeah,' I grin. 'A likely story.'

'Look,' Si says, gesturing at the phone, 'this is the
perfect opportunity. You want to talk to her, but you
don't actually want to *talk* to her, and I know you're
terrified of how she'll react. I am too. This way you can
leave a message, and then it's up to her. She may not
call, but at least if she does you'll know it's because she
wants to.'

I grab the phone, hit the redial button and listen to her
message again, trying to smile so that I sound cheerful,
happy, successful, and keeping a hand on my heart to
try to calm down.

Beeeeeep.

'Portia, hi. Umm. This is, umm, quite strange, hearing

your voice on the machine.' Si rolls his eyes at me. 'I mean, it's not strange, because it's your machine, but we haven't spoken for ages. Years. Your name came up the other night at dinner – we met Dan, umm, the guy who sold you his flat, and it's just that we were wondering how you were, and it would be really nice to see you, to catch up. Anyway, umm, give me a call, if you want. Oh. It's Cath, by the way . . . *beeep*.'

'Shit!'

I redial, feeling like an idiot. 'Sorry. Your machine cut me off, but do call me, it would be lovely to hear from you . . .' I put the phone down, feeling incredibly pleased with myself.

'There,' says Si. 'That's done, then.'

'Do you think she'll call?'

'If she hasn't changed, she will.'

'You're right.' I nod thoughtfully. 'If she hasn't changed, she'll call.'

Ever since I can remember I have loved books. Not just loved, but been passionate about. I regularly spend hours at a time browsing in bookshops, losing track of time, losing myself in another world.

There's a bookshop near my office, and a couple of times a week I go there in my lunchbreak, and spend a good hour wandering around, smiling softly to myself, sometimes just brushing the covers on the hardbacks grouped on tables in the centre of the floor, other times spending the full hour engrossed between the covers of a new release.

My dream has always been to own a bookshop. Actually, my dream has always been to own a bookshop that also encompasses a café. I envision it as the sort of place that would attract regulars, lovable eccentrics who would step in to make the cappuccinos if I needed a hand.

It would be a laid-back kind of place. There would be beaten-up old leather sofas, squashy armchairs, possibly a fireplace in winter. Of course when it's summer, and I remember how much I love the sunshine, I envision it in a completely different light – my summer fantasies make it light, bright, breezy. It has stripped pine floors and slick chrome chairs, huge glass windows and Mediterranean-blue walls.

I indulge in this fantasy far more frequently as I get older. I used to think, in my early twenties, that I would work until I had enough money in the bank to open my bookshop, and that, as soon as I did, I would hand in my notice and get going.

But of course enough money is never quite enough, and now, although I seem to have amassed a fairly sizeable amount in the Abbey National (thanks largely to my lovely grandmother, who died and left me her flat in Wembley a couple of years ago), I know it will never be enough to allow me to jump ship, because actually it's not about the money at all.

Si says I'm scared, and of course he's right. Up until a year ago, I loved my job, I really did. I loved my clients, loved putting campaigns together, got a real buzz from it. But this last year it's felt more and more like hard work. I seem to be less and less motivated, but every time I think about leaving, fear clutches my heart and I know I haven't got the nerve.

What if the bookshop were a disaster? What if I lost all my money? What if I couldn't afford my mortgage? How could I give up my PPP? My pension plan?

One day, I tell myself, I will do it. I will fulfil that dream. It's just that I'm not sure when.

*

'Cath, darling! We need to meet. When are you free?' Lucy's voice is bubbling over with excitement, making me smile.

'Why? What's happened? You're not pregnant again, are you?'

Lucy shrieks. 'God, no. Not yet.' Then there's a silence. 'Bugger. I might be. When's my blasted period due?' she mutters. 'Oh, anyway.' Her voice is bright again. 'This is much more important. I have a proposal to put to you.'

'I can't marry you, Lucy,' I laugh. 'I'd love to, but you're already married.'

'If I were a big strapping chap, I would certainly marry you, but this, Cath, is something else entirely.'

'Go on, give me a clue.'

'Can't. Not on the phone. When can you meet me?'

'How about Saturday morning?'

'Saturday? I can't wait until Saturday. How about this afternoon? Or early evening? But afternoon would be better.'

I flick open my work diary on the desk and check the rest of the day. Thankfully there are no more meetings, and, although I don't do this often, I agree to scoot off early to go to meet Lucy. I shouldn't feel guilty about this, considering the hours I've been working recently, but I do, and if it weren't for her insistence, I wouldn't be doing this.

'Hoorah!' she says, when I agree. 'Come over to me, then, and we'll have a coffee. See you later. Bye bye. Oh, Cath, wait. Did you speak to Portia? Was she there?'

'I left a message, so now it's up to her.'

'Well done. Quite right. See you later.'

There's something luxurious about being at home, in my neighbourhood, at three o'clock in the afternoon. It's a completely different world at this time, the people so different from the ones I'm used to seeing at night or on the weekends, that I'm almost tempted to forgo Lucy and grab a window table in a coffee shop, just to people-watch for the rest of the day.

So many young mothers with their babies. Where do they all come from? Harassed-looking young men in dark suits, mobile phones glued to their ears, must be local estate agents, I decide.

But what astounds me most are the sheer numbers of people. Why are they not working? What are they all *doing* here, in West End Lane, in the middle of the afternoon?

My flat seems strangely quiet at this time of day. It's not like the weekend, when the phone never stops, or there's music playing, or Si's round, as usual, tidying up after my mess. It's absolutely still, so still I start to feel guilty, as if by being there I'm doing something I ought not to be doing, as if I have somehow disturbed the flat.

I dump my case, filled with research for me to look at over the weekend, pull off my right shoe by dragging the sole of my left down it, then use my bare right foot to do the same to the other side, thanking God that Si isn't here to witness this, as it drives him mad.

'*Don't* do that,' he'd say, wincing. 'You'll ruin your shoes, for God's sake. You can't just leave them there, haven't you got any shoetrees?'

The shoes rest on their side on the floor, daring me to look at the scuff marks I just made, so I kick them under the bed and pull on some flat boots, sighing with relief at being able to stomp around again, and run out the door.

I pause briefly at the entrance to the kitchen, tempted to grab something from the fridge, a quick snack, but of course I am going to Lucy's, and there is no better cook in London than Lucy, so why ruin a delicious pre-dinner snack with a piece of stale pitta from my own fridge?

'Hello, Max. It looks like you've been eating something yummy.' Max stands in the doorway, blocking my path, looking at me as if I'm about to start selling him dusters and dishcloths, a mixture of disdain and pity, which is quite extraordinary, bearing in mind he's three years old and half his face is covered in chocolate.

I'm not, as you may have gathered, a natural with children. In fact I'd go so far as to say that when God created me, he seemed to have forgotten all about my maternal instinct.

That first time Si and I pitched up to see Lucy in hospital, the day after Max was born, Lucy sat up in bed, looking tired but radiant as usual, and gestured to this tiny, tiny, little baby, eyes squeezed shut, fast asleep in her arms.

'He's divine,' whispered Si in awe. 'Look,' he said in amazement, 'look at those tiny hands, tiny feet. God, have you ever seen fingernails that small?' Si held his hands, his feet, while I lurked in the background, smiling awkwardly.

'Don't be frightened, Cath,' Lucy smiled, gesturing me forward with a nod of her head. 'Here,' and she offered the bundle in her arms to me, 'have a cuddle.'

Well, what could I say? I couldn't refuse, so I took Max in my arms, hoping that I'd suddenly feel all warm and gooey, but I didn't feel anything other than uncomfortable, and, just as I was about to start praying that the baby would keep quiet, Max opened his eyes.

He opened his eyes, looked at me and screamed. But screamed. His face was bright red, his eyes scrunched up, and he was screaming as if he'd seen the devil. I practically threw him back to Lucy, and of course the minute he was in her arms he shut up. I haven't picked up a baby since.

Si thought this was hysterical. For a good few weeks afterwards he was calling me *Scary Cathy*, and whenever I touched him – laid a hand on his arm, gave him a hug – he'd screw up his eyes and start wailing, collapsing in giggles every time.

It made me laugh at first, but after the forty-seventh time he did it, I started to get ever so slightly pissed off. Even Lucy told him off, which was most uncharacteristic of her, although she didn't actually mean it.

'Oh, Si,' she'd playfully berate him. 'Don't be so mean. Poor Cath. It wasn't her fault. Maxy's just nervous of strangers, aren't you, Maxy?'

Si would then have to prove her wrong by smugly taking Max from her arms and making faces at him or bouncing him up and down while he gurgled with delight.

And now, at three years old, Max still makes me feel as uncomfortable as he did when a newborn baby. But now, instead of screaming, he just has this habit of looking at me, and I find myself trying to befriend him, being extra-specially nice to make him change his opinion of me.

'If you're a good boy, Cath will give you a present. Would you like that?' I feel ridiculous, saying these things to him, but I don't know how else to talk to a three-year-old.

I've watched Si with envy, because Si doesn't treat Max like a child, he treats him like an adult. Si sits and has in-depth chats with Max about work. I know. Ridiculous. But it's true. I've actually seen Si walk in, sit down next to Max and say, 'God, what a terrible day. Do you want to hear about my day?' And Max will nod very seriously, as Si proceeds to talk at him about film rushes and editing, and things being left on the cutting-room floor.

But what's even more ridiculous, is that Max *loves* it. *Adores* it. He cannot take his eyes off Si during these conversations.

And then there was one time when Si sat down wearily next to Max, as Josh grabbed Lucy and enfolded her in his arms, covering her neck with kisses while she giggled and tried to push him away, and said, 'I wish I could find someone who loved me like that.'

Do you know what Max did? He put his hand in Si's and squeezed it, then very solemnly gave him a kiss on the cheek. Si said he nearly burst into tears.

But no matter what I say to Max, how large my bribes, he never seems to change with me.

I bring a lollipop out of my pocket and extend it to Max, who examines it for a few seconds without touching it, then takes it out of my hand, turns his back, and disappears down the hallway.

'Max!' Lucy shouts, running after him and sweeping him up. 'I saw that! Don't be so rude. You must say thank you when someone gives you something.' She rolls her eyes at me, mouthing 'sorry', as she drops Max at my feet.

'Fank you.' He looks at the floor, lollipop already in his mouth.

'You're welcome,' I say, as he trundles off again. I follow Lucy into the kitchen, the smell of freshly baked biscuits making me salivate. 'He does hate me, you know,' I say, pulling off my coat and throwing it on a chair.

'Well, he obviously has terrible taste in women,' she

says, 'and he doesn't really hate you, he's just at that difficult age.'

'He's been at that difficult age since he was born.'

'Bloody men,' she laughs. 'They're all the same. Now, how about some home-made, fresh-from-the-oven, apple-and-cinnamon biscuits?'

I rub my stomach in approval and take one from the plate Lucy sets on the table, not bothering to wait for the tea that ought to be the accompaniment.

'Lucy,' I mumble, mouth full, trying to catch the buttery crumbs that fall as I speak. 'Sorry for speaking with my mouth full, but these are amazing.'

'You're so sweet.' Lucy breaks into one of her dazzling smiles. 'That's why I adore having you over. So much nicer to enjoy what you're eating. I just can't bear all these sticklike girls who eat only lettuce, or have drinks filled with that ghastly sweetener stuff. Have some more.'

I happily comply, feeling only slightly guilty that I am not one of those sticklike girls who would wave the biscuits away, asking for a carrot instead, or perhaps a teaspoonful of cottage cheese. But even those girls would have trouble finding willpower if they had a friend who could cook like Lucy.

Lucy brings the teapot to the table and sits down. 'Cath, are you happy?'

'What? What do you mean?'

'I mean at work. Do you enjoy what you're doing?'

'I love my work,' I say, suddenly realizing that I am only saying this because, up until recently, it is what I have always said. Except there is no longer any conviction in my words, they sound hollow and empty, even to me.

I start again. 'Well, I *did* love my work. I suppose I

haven't really thought about it lately. Sometimes I quite enjoy it, but not like I used to. What a strange question, what are you up to?'

Lucy sighs. 'I've just been thinking an awful lot recently, about why we're here, and what we should be doing, and for years I always thought I wanted to help people, which is why I'm doing this bloody counselling course, although thank God it's practically over.' She pauses to drink some tea.

'But the thing is,' she continues, 'I haven't done any proper illustrating for three years, since Max was born, and to be totally honest I don't think I want to do it any more. This is going to sound awful.' She looks at me sheepishly.

'*But*,' I prompt.

'*But*,' she smiles, 'I feel like I've devoted these last few years to helping other people, looking after other people, being Josh's wife and Max's mother, and, although I adore looking after my boys, I think that now I need to do something for myself.' There's a long pause. 'What do you think?'

'I think that if that's what you want to do, then that's what you should do. Absolutely.' Even as I say it I know I should be applying those rules to myself, but then I haven't got a husband who would pick up the pieces if everything went horribly wrong. Who could afford to take on the entire mortgage if my money ran out. Who could, in short, be there for me.

'So what are you thinking of doing?' I ask, curiosity getting the better of me.

'Ah,' she says, breaking into a smile. 'Now that's where, hopefully, you come in.' She stands up. 'Grab your coat. We're going for a walk.'

As we reach the bottom of the stairs, Lucy yells out

to the au pair, 'Ingriiiiiiid? I'm going out. Won't be long.'

Ingrid appears at the top of the stairs. 'Okay, Lucy,' she says stonily, ignoring the fact that Max appears to be wrapping a lasso around her left leg. 'See you.'

'She is a godsend,' Lucy says, closing the front door, which slightly surprises me, as personally I think she's a cow. 'I honestly don't know where we'd be without her.'

'So where are we going?' I walk alongside Lucy, up her road, on to West End Lane, smiling because it's impossible not to feel good when the sun is shining and the pavements outside the cafés are crowded with tables and chairs, with people lingering over their coffees, just to enjoy the sunshine a bit longer.

'Surprise,' she says. 'But you'll see when we get there.'

Chapter six

'Here we are,' says Lucy, stopping in front of an empty shop and turning to look at me expectantly.

I look at what she's looking at. An empty shop in between the organic deli and the shop that sells strange wooden carvings. A shop that you can't see into because all the windows are obliterated by huge, multicoloured posters advertising bands, concerts, gigs.

Lucy's pressed up against the glass, trying to see in through the tiny gaps where the posters don't meet, and I join her, but the glass has been whitewashed underneath the posters and it's impossible to see anything.

I've passed this shop many, many times before. It's on the main drag, on West End Lane, opposite the bagel shop but before the Green. And I realize that although I've passed this spot many, many times, I have always seen the same emptiness, the same posters. I've just never registered it before now.

'And we are here why?' I ask.

'Look! It's empty!' Lucy's struggling to keep the excitement out of her voice.

'Yes?' I still haven't the foggiest what she's talking about.

'Oh, Cath, darling. You're being thick. This is the perfect place for my new business. Well, actually, hope-fully, our new business.'

'What business is this?'

'Your bookshop and my coffee shop.'

I look at Lucy, at her beaming eyes, expectant face, and I am amazed that she has remembered my dream, and more amazed that she wants to do it with me.

'I don't believe you.' I shake my head. 'How on earth did you remember that? I must have told you years ago.'

She links her arm through mine as we stand next to one another, trying to see into the shop.

'First of all, you go on about it far more than you think you do, and secondly that night, when we were talking about our dreams, I have never seen anyone as passionate as you, when you said this was the one thing you had always wanted to do.

'I suppose I never forgot that, and the one thing that I love, the one thing that I'd love to work with – '

'Food!' we both say at the same time, bursting into peals of laughter.

'I know it's funny,' she says, 'but it's actually true. I thought I'd stay in illustration for ever, but I just don't have the same commitment now that I've had Max. And even though it's your idea, to have the café/bookshop, I know, and darling Cath, do not be insulted by this, I know you couldn't cook a cake if your life depended on it.

'And the thing is,' she continues, barely pausing for breath, 'it actually wouldn't be that difficult, and Josh would help, and we'd only have to employ, say, two other people to make it work, and Cath, please say yes, because I think we could do it. I *know* we could do it.'

'You're serious, aren't you?' I stop and look at Lucy's shining face with amazement, feeling nervous and excited, and not sure whether we could actually pull this off.

Because isn't that the thing with fantasies? Fantasies are absolutely safe, as long as you never try to make them a reality. Whether you're fantasizing about wife-swapping, or café/bookshops, it's still a truism that they will always be safer when they are kept locked in your head.

But, as I look into Lucy's eyes, behind the sparkle I can see steely determination, and God knows Lucy could do it. Out of all the people I know Lucy is the only one who could not only bake cookies from heaven, but would also charm everyone who stepped over the threshold, and there really wouldn't be anything to be frightened of if Lucy were a partner.

'Have I convinced you yet?' Lucy grins.

'God, Lucy.' I shake my head. 'It's not as easy as that. There's so much to think about. My flat, the mortgage, my job. I mean, Christ, could I just walk out? My savings, because this would be it . . .' I'm so caught up in my world of problems I don't even realize that Lucy is steering me to the other side of the road.

I walk beside her in a daze, and I know that even though I have no idea what it will cost, how we'd get it going, or how we'd even think about running it as a day-to-day business, it's something I want to do.

I shake myself back into the present to find we're now further down the road. 'What are you doing now?'

'Come on,' she says, dragging me into an estate agent's. 'I found this site and I think it might be ideal, even though I haven't seen the inside, so I thought it might help to convince you.'

The door closes behind us as a young man in a navy suit looks up from where he's perched on the corner of a desk, sifting through a sheaf of papers.

'Hi.' He looks up, smiling broadly, putting the papers on to a desk and brushing a lock of mousy brown hair out of eyes that are surprisingly twinkly. 'Can I help at all?' His voice is deep, with just a hint of an accent that I can't quite place. Definitely south of England, possibly Dorset or Wiltshire, but whatever it is he looks far too *normal* to be an estate agent.

I always imagine estate agents to be smart and slick, dressed in sharp suits with mobile phones surgically attached to their ears, and though this man is wearing a navy suit, he looks slightly wrong in it somehow, as if he'd be far more comfortable in a chunky woollen sweater and a pair of faded jeans.

I realize I'm staring and look away quickly, pretending to be absorbed in the grains of wood on the floorboards.

'We're looking for James,' Lucy says, as the man stands up and holds out a hand.

'Let me guess. You're Lucy Portman.' His laughter lines grow deeper, and I comprehend with a shock that this is a seriously attractive man.

'James?'

'None other.' They shake hands, as I try to be as unobtrusive as possible. I glance up to see him looking at me with an eyebrow raised in a question.

'Hi, I'm Cath, er, Catherine Warner,' I mumble, reluctantly shaking his hand, because I'm really not very good at this business stuff, plus I'm suddenly feeling very awkward.

'Nice to meet you, Cath,' he says, looking directly into my eyes, as I look away and threaten to blush. He releases my hand and walks over to another desk, picking up a set of keys. 'Shall we go?'

We cross the road again to the empty shop, me still in a state of shock because it feels as if Lucy has completely turned my life around in the space of an hour, and, as James fiddles with the keys in an attempt to unlock the door, he turns to us.

'You know, the more I think about it the more I think

'it's a brilliant idea,' he says. 'A café/bookshop. Just what this area needs, and wait until you see inside. The space you're looking at is perfect.'

'You don't know of any others, do you?' says Lucy, vaguely anxiously. 'I've tried to find out, but I don't think there are any.'

'There is a bookshop, and there are plenty of cafés, but this area's so young and buzzy, the combination's bound to go down well. Plus,' and he lowers his voice as he says this, 'don't quote me on this, but a lot of the places here are a bit shabby, or quite dark and poky. A bright, sunny café with the advantage of the bookshop is bound to be a hit.'

Now I know he's only an estate agent, and I know he's got no experience of running a café/bookshop, but because he's a stranger, and because he has somehow validated this idea, I start to feel excited. In fact, by the time he's actually picked out the two keys, out of the forty or so, that fit, I'm almost ready to start dancing round the shop with joy. The door creaks open and Lucy takes my hand, giving it a quick, reassuring squeeze, as we both gingerly step in.

We don't say anything for a while, just wander around, trying to envisage whether it could be what we're looking for. What, in fact, I wasn't looking for up until an hour ago, but still. What the hell.

But as our eyes adjust to the gloom, lit by a solitary light bulb in each room, Lucy and I gasp, because the only thing this place is, it could ever have been, is a bookshop.

Surrounding the walls are beautifully made wooden shelves, stretching from floor to ceiling, the shelves acting as partitions, forming an open library. The craftsmanship is superb, and I realize how absolutely perfect this place is.

And the space is huge. The ceilings go up for ever, and, as my eyes adjust to the one swinging lamp bulb, I can see that there is a gallery in the larger room. I wouldn't trust the one rickety stepladder propped up in the corner, so I just have to assume you can stand up in the gallery.

'Can you believe it?' Lucy keeps whispering. 'Can you believe it?'

There's one large L-shaped room with a huge picture window at the back, another, smaller window in the gallery, and a slightly smaller room next door.

Lucy starts reading the details James has brought with him, and excitedly walks to the back of the shop, where she pushes open a door to reveal another room.

'Look! Cath! The kitchen!' And then she runs into the larger room and, sure enough, off the L-shape is another room.

'Let me guess.' I smile wryly. 'Stock room?'

'Isn't it perfect, Cath?' she says, whirling around. 'Can't you just imagine it? Close your eyes and can't you hear those pages rustling? Smell the coffee? The home-made cakes and biscuits?'

I smile at her, swaying gently in the middle of the floor, eyes squeezed tight, able to see exactly what it will be like.

And of course it is perfect. It would make the perfect café/bookshop. I'm just not sure that I have the nerve to get involved with something entirely different at this stage of my life.

'What was it before? It must have been a bookshop, but I don't remember.' My voice is clipped, businesslike, because I figure that at least one of us has to be if we're going to be taken the slightest bit seriously.

'Believe it or not it was empty,' James says. 'It's been empty for about twenty years.'

'Well, that explains the dust,' Lucy says, stifling a sneeze.

'It was owned by one of the local eccentrics,' continues James. 'Harry Roberts?' He looks at us, but we both shake our heads and shrug. 'Harry was always a bit of a local character. He died last year in his nineties, but up until the week he died he used to go to work every day, dressed in a three-piece suit, immaculately turned out.'

'And?' Lucy's eager to hear what happens, loving nothing more than a good story.

'We all thought Harry was a bit of a chancer.' James smiles fondly at the memory. 'He used to come into the office to talk about property, and we'd indulge him because we thought it made him feel good, but we didn't think he had anything. He was just an old man.'

'And?' Now it's my turn.

'The thing is he never actually seemed to do anything. He just had this office round the corner and he used to go every day, without fail, and then pop round to the local agents for chats because he was bored.

'And then he died, and you'd never believe it, but he turned out to be worth millions.'

'No!' Lucy breathes in awe. 'Really?'

'I'm not kidding,' James said. 'He lived in a hovel of a flat. Really disgusting. Threadbare carpets, chairs held together by string; most of the furniture hadn't been changed since the thirties, but he owned about half of the commercial property in the area.'

'But didn't you know?' I asked. 'You must have known?'

'That's the ridiculous thing,' James says. 'He just leased them all out, and most of the tenants were paying next to nothing to stay there. When they were going through his estate they realized that he had been sitting on a fortune that had hardly been making a profit.

'So they sold them off,' he continues. 'And this one had just been sitting here for years. We'd tried to find out who owned it. Everyone in the area had, but this was the one property he'd never leased out.'

'Oooh. How fascinating. Why do you think?' Lucy's eyes are wide and bright, hardly able to contain her fascination.

James shrugs. 'All sorts of rumours have flown about. Allegedly it was a bookshop, and the owner was a woman he'd had an affair with. She was supposed to be the one great love of his life, but she was already married and wouldn't leave her husband. He never got over it, or so they say.' He grins at us. 'But you never know with rumours.'

'That doesn't sound right,' I say. 'In his day women didn't really have careers, did they?'

'Who cares,' says Lucy, hugging herself with happiness. 'How romantic. How wonderful. This is it, you know,' and she looks at me, while I try to signal to say nothing further, because you should never let estate agents know what you're thinking.

'It's crying out for some TLC,' James says. 'But, as I explained to Lucy the other day, all the basics are here. Stick in a new kitchen, a bar in the middle here, and a coat of paint.' He scuffs the floorboards with his right foot. 'Even these are immaculate. They just need sanding down' – he looks up at us – 'and I really can't imagine a more perfect spot for your business.'

'Have you had much interest?' I ask casually.

'We've only just got it,' he says. 'So we haven't even started marketing it properly yet, but we're putting adverts in all the trade press next week. It will go like a shot.'

Lucy looks dispirited. 'That means we must act quickly, Cath,' she advises sternly. 'Come on now.' She grabs my arm and turns to James, flashing him a dazzling smile. 'James, you are an absolute angel for showing us at such short notice. We'll ring you in the morning.'

James, still stunned by the radiance of Lucy's smile, nods, and we leave him standing there, basking in the excitement and joy Lucy has left behind.

'Low-halogen spots, lots of pale wood, very sunny. What do you think?' Lucy's pacing round the kitchen, words tumbling out of her mouth.

'I think,' Josh says slowly, looking at me, 'you should (a) stop pacing round the floor, and (b) ask Cath what *she* thinks.'

Lucy stops in mid-step and looks at me, mortified. 'Cath! Darling! I'm so sorry.' She runs over and leans down, giving me a big hug. 'I just haven't stopped talking. God, I'm so selfish. Tell me. Tell me. What do you think?'

'It's all a bit much for me,' I say. 'I mean, it's not that I don't want to do it, it's my life's dream, but I just don't know if I could really leave my job and do this. What if it were a massive failure? What if we lost all our money? I'd have to put my life savings into this, and I could lose everything.'

'Not necessarily,' Josh says slowly.

'Come on, Joshy,' Lucy says. 'You're the clever banker. How could we minimize the risk?'

'You could go with a backer,' he says thoughtfully. 'But then again, maybe it's best to keep the investors to a minimum.' He sits in silence for a while as Lucy makes faces at me. 'You know,' he says eventually, 'it might actually be far less than you think.'

'Do you think it's worth it, then, Josh?' I trust his opinion.

'I do, as it happens,' he says, coming back to the present. 'Hang on,' and he leaps up, grabs something from his jacket pocket in the hallway, and comes back into the room. He opens a small black computer-type thing and starts typing on a tiny keyboard.

'What is he doing?' I raise an eyebrow at Lucy.

'Heaven forbid we should go anywhere without his beloved Palm Pilot,' she laughs.

'Just trying to work out some initial costs,' Josh says, snapping it shut. 'In fact one of the guys at work has parents who own a bookshop. It's in Derbyshire or somewhere, but I'm sure he'd be able to help, or at least give us an idea of the sort of money we're looking at, although at a guess I'd say around £100,000 once you've sorted out builders, alterations, stock cost, etc. Why don't I speak to him?'

'Sure.' I shrug, wondering why this fantasy appears to be suffering from a severe snowball effect.

'But as for the idea – ' he goes to the dresser and pulls out some plates, napkins, and lays them on the table – 'I do actually think it will work. You'll have to do your research, of course, but the cafés that are already there seem to be full all the time, so there's obviously room for one more, and we need a populist bookshop.'

'Populist?'

'Well, it has to be financially viable, so you have to provide something for everyone. In other words, a bookshop that stocks a good range of books across the board. You can't compete with Waterstone's or Books Etc., but you can offer a next-day delivery from the wholesalers.'

Lucy's looking at him with affection. 'Darling husband of mine, tell me how you know all this?'

Josh shrugs. 'And the other thing,' he continues, 'is that as far as I know most books are stocked in bookshops on a sale or return basis, so apart from the refurbishment of the shop, and the catering outlay, it wouldn't be as much risk as, say, a clothes shop.

'Plus, Lucy, we could always remortgage the house. God knows I'd rather use the money for a business venture than for a holiday or something.'

'What about your son's schooling?'

'We'll cross that bridge when we come to it. And Cath, what about that money from your grandma?'

I gasp. 'Josh, you're not supposed to know about that! How do you know about that?'

'Because you told me, Cath. You asked my advice on investing it, then promptly ignored it, and I bet it's been sitting in the bank all these years gaining nothing on interest.'

I choose to stay silent.

'Exactly. It's about time you made that money work for you. God, between the two of you, you can do this thing, no problem.'

'Have I ever told you how much I love you?' Lucy says suddenly, flinging her arms around Josh and planting a smacker on his cheek.

'Yes,' Josh smiles. 'Does that mean you love me enough to serve me dinner?'

Lucy flops into a chair with a grin. 'Nope,' she says happily. 'You cooked, you serve. That's the deal.'

'So let me get this straight. You're thinking of leaving your super-duper, high-powered fantastic job that pays you a fortune, to set up your own business with . . .' and at this Si pauses. 'Lucy?'

'What's wrong with Lucy?'

Si begged and pleaded for me to meet him for a drink after work in Soho, and, even though it's a pain, I succumbed, because, as Si often moans, I have become horrifyingly suburban in my old age. I remember thinking nothing of going straight out after work in my twenties. In fact, if I didn't hit the bars, pubs or clubs, you could be certain there was something wrong with me. Every afternoon, about half an hour before the end of the day, you'd find a pack of us in the loo, all hastily reapplying make-up, putting on spare clothes, hairspray, perfume, from the seemingly endless caverns of our handbags, ready to flirt with City boys until we were too drunk to stand up.

I used to think nothing of spending every night in 'town'. Of course, I tell myself now, those were the days when you could actually find a black cab when it was going home time. Unlike now, when friends of mine have been forced to walk home to West Hampstead from Piccadilly Circus, turning round every few feet, just in case they should experience a minor miracle and spot an orange light in the distance.

'So get the tube,' Si says. 'Mix with the common people for a change. See how the other half lives.'

But I spend enough of my working day crammed in with people on the tube. At least my salary should enable me to afford the luxury of a black cab when we go out. It's not my fault they all seem to desert the West End after seven p.m.

But tonight I thought, what the hell, I could do with a fun night out. Is this a sign of getting old? That going out for dinner now means popping up the road to a comfortable, cosy local restaurant? That I never have to even consider making an effort with my clothes? That not only am I always home by eleven o'clock, but that if I weren't I might possibly die of exhaustion?

I wasn't always like this. Honestly. In the early days, post-Martin, I threw myself into the club scene with wild abandon. Si would come and pick me up at midnight, and we'd hit the one-nighters all over town, ending up sipping coffee at Bar Italia in the early hours of the morning.

To be honest, I've been feeling for some time that I'm slightly stuck in a rut. I love my friends. Would die for them. But part of me would quite like to meet a man, and unless I manage either to convert Si or to steal Josh from Lucy, neither of which is a particularly appealing option, I think it's highly unlikely, unless I drastically change my life. Do something to meet more people.

And Lucy's plan seems to have come at exactly the right time. Think of all the new people I'd meet! Think about what it would be like to have my own business! To – oh joy of joys – go to work almost on the doorstep of my home!

Do you know what I thought today? I sat at my desk thinking what the hell am I doing still working here? Because although the events of yesterday feel like a bit of a whirlwind, I do think that if anyone could make it work, it would be Lucy and I.

Lucy of course doesn't have a clue about business, or bookshops, but – and I swear I'm not making this up – on the rare occasions I venture into coffee shops and order cakes, even if they're home-made they're not half as good as Lucy's.

And Lucy doesn't think it should be just cakes and home-made biscuits. She thinks easy sandwiches, beautifully presented on fresh ciabatta bread, slabs of basil and garlic focaccia with roasted aubergine and grilled mozzarella ... even hearing her descriptions made my mouth water.

It was all I could think about at work today. Work? I didn't do any. I sat in my office, closed the door and fantasized the day away. By mid-morning I'd planned the lighting. By lunchtime Lucy and I were playing the convivial hosts, loved and adored by the entire community, and by the end of the day we were being written up in the *Ham & High*.

'So what *is* wrong with Lucy?' I ask again, when Si refuses to answer.

'It's not for me to say.'

'Right,' I mock. 'If not you, then who?'

'Oh, okay,' he sighs. 'If you insist. It's just that Lucy's wonderful, and we all adore her, but she's not a businesswoman.'

'But that's the point, Si. That's why Josh is looking into it before we do anything, but anyway I'm the one with the common sense. Lucy's the creative person. She'll help with the design, the concept, and, let's face it, she is the best cook in London.'

'That's true,' he agrees. 'So explain to me exactly what you would be doing?'

'What do you mean?'

'Cath, sweets, I know you have good business acumen, but it's in advertising, not in bookshops. It's all very well Lucy being the creative person, but you know next to nothing about running a bookshop, and I'm not sure if this isn't too big a challenge for you.'

'Actually, I think you're wrong,' I say with certainty, slightly pissed off at Si for pointing out the obvious, but pleased that it is firing my determination. 'I mean, I'm sure Lucy wouldn't have asked me if she didn't think I could contribute something, and there's no way Josh would let either of us do it if he didn't think it was a viable proposition.

'Plus it's always been my dream, and I know the two of us could do it.'

'Cath,' Si says, suddenly serious. 'Do you want my honest opinion?'

I nod.

'My honest opinion, and remember I'm only giving you this because I love you and I want you to be careful, but my honest opinion is that you should definitely become involved on some level, but certainly not throw in your job or do anything drastic until it's established in the new site and it's successful.'

I know he's right. Of course he's right, but even as I hear his words I feel them float in one ear and out the other.

'Stop it, Cath,' Si says sternly, knowing exactly what I'm doing. 'You know that it makes sense. Lucy doesn't really have anything to lose, and if it went horribly wrong, then Josh could always pick up the pieces, but you would be the one with the most at stake here, and you stand to lose the most.

'I'm not saying don't do it, I'm saying think about it. Hell, get Lucy to do it by herself, work in the shop on weekends, organize reading groups, events, anything you want. Just don't give everything up yet, that's all.'

I know what he's saying makes sense. But I also know that there's no way on earth I will let Lucy fulfil my lifelong dream without me in it. I just won't tell Si. That's all.

'And by the way,' he adds with a twinkle, secure in the knowledge that I've listened to him and taken his advice, 'if I gave Lucy my application form for a Saturday job, would you make sure I got it?'

'Only if you pay me enough.' I squeeze a smile, and we sit in silence for a few moments, then Si looks at me and lets out a big sigh.

'I know you too bloody well.' He shakes his head.

'What?'

'You're sitting there thinking: screw Si, I'm going to do it anyway.'

I know I'm not supposed to be smiling at this, but I can't help it: a grin flashes up.

'Cath, I'm just saying that I don't want you to lose everything.'

I reach out and cover Si's hand with my own. 'Listen, my darling,' I say. 'I know you've got my best interests at heart, but I really do think I need to take a risk and I need to do this. At the very least I need to explore every option.

'And as for the money,' I continue, 'Josh was absolutely right. It has been sitting in the bank doing nothing, so even if it all went horribly wrong and I lost everything, I wouldn't actually be losing anything, if you see what I mean. And Si, I *hate* my job. I can't carry on doing it for much longer.' I pause for breath but before I have a chance to continue Si pulls the twizzler out of his rather revolting-looking daiquiri and sucks it slowly.

'So let me ask you this,' he says finally.

'Yes?'

'You basically want to be Ellen, don't you?'

'What?'

'That's what you've been describing all night. Ellen's bookshop. *Buy the Book*.'

'Oh my God!' My mouth drops open. 'Si, you're

87

brilliant! That's exactly what I want it to be like. If I did it,' I add quickly, in a mumble. 'Which I probably won't.'

'I know, I know.' Si waves me quiet impatiently. 'So you're Ellen. Lucy is Audrey, except she's not dippy, she doesn't have red hair, and she dresses better. Portia, if she were here, would be Paige. Josh, I suppose, being handsome and decidedly heterosexual, despite being taken, would be Adam. Or Spence. Depending on whether you're a fan of the early years or not.'

'Uh oh.'

I start to laugh, knowing Si so well, knowing what's coming.

'So that means that I'm the bloody fat bloke with the coffee, aren't I?'

'Absolutely not,' I wipe the smile off my face in a flash. 'So shall we make a move, *Joe*?'

Chapter seven

I cannot believe how quickly this all seems to be happening. Six weeks ago there I was, stuck in my job, dreading the tube, wondering if there would ever be an end to all of this, and praying for summer to arrive early just to make me feel better.

The next minute I'm caught up in Lucy's whirlwind of interior design, recipe ideas, hurried phone calls to the estate agent to make sure it's still ours. And God, am I glad I didn't take Si's advice. I cannot think of anything worse than watching Lucy do this without me, because I have loved, am loving, every minute of it.

The scariest bit was actually handing in my notice at the agency. They offered me more money to stay, but my mind was well and truly made up. Then, at my leaving do, my boss made a speech where he confessed that he'd always had a dream of moving to the country and buying a farm, and said he was deeply jealous that I was pursuing my own dream, when he didn't have the nerve.

But once I'd actually left, panic set in. That first Monday morning, when I didn't have to get up at the crack of dawn and catch the tube to work, I suddenly realized what I'd done: what a big step it was. What on earth would I do if it all went horribly wrong?

But then, later that day, Lucy dragged me to a meeting with the carpenter in the shop, and once we'd spent half an hour talking about bars and counters and display shelves, it started to feel real again and, more importantly, started to feel right.

And then the meetings started. We were hoping we wouldn't have to do a business plan, Lucy and I managing to raise £120,000 between us, but we hadn't banked on working capital: paying employees; paying the bills; managing the inventory; petty cash and all the other minor day-to-day expenses that you never think about when it's still just a fantasy.

So Josh said we had to go to the bank. We set aside the best part of a week and sat at Lucy's kitchen table, heads together, drawing up a business plan, and every night, when Josh got home, we'd run it by him, moaning and groaning because he kept telling us we had to make it more businesslike.

But eventually we got it right. We took it to the bank, and they agreed to lend us a further £100,000, which was far more than we'd even dreamt. And Josh and Lucy remortgaged their house, which meant we could buy the shop in the first place.

We then had to deal with the Health and Safety inspectors. We didn't need planning permission, as we weren't actually going to be cooking on the premises, and preparing food falls into something called an A1 Use Class, which was a good thing for us, because it didn't constitute a change of use.

Lucy and I travelled up to Derbyshire and spent the day with Ted and Linda, the people Josh had told us about who own a bookshop, and their advice was invaluable.

And eventually contracts were exchanged, with the completion date amazingly set for the same day, and we could actually start work. It was touch and go for a while, us getting the shop, but James managed to swing it our way, despite the competition that suddenly appeared at the eleventh hour.

James has actually been fantastic, and the more I know him, the more I like him. I know I shouldn't be that surprised, but he really does seem to be honest, straight, to have integrity. Lucy's also pointed out that he's rather dishy, but to be perfectly honest he's not my type. If I have a type any more, that is.

Plus, he's a child. Well, not literally, but he's got to be younger than us. I'd hazard a guess at around twenty-six, but Lucy thinks he's more like twenty-eight, an age, she says, at which they are unstoppable. Whatever that means.

She even managed to draw out of him the fact that once upon a time he was an artist, but lack of funds meant he had to find something else, and property seemed the most lucrative option at the time.

The snowball appears to be gathering momentum with every passing minute, and last week, when the builders had finally moved out, Lucy and I were able to do the one job we'd been looking forward to since the beginning – painting the shop.

We had talked, initially, of finding architects, employing teams of builders, paying for the most professional of jobs it is possible to pay for in England, in the nineties. But, as Lucy pointed out, all builders are a nightmare, so, rather than paying someone a fortune to have a hassle-filled life, why not pay someone *peanuts* for a hassle-filled life, and do a bit more yourself?

And, despite not being particularly house-proud, I will admit that I'm genuinely excited about painting *Bookends* ourselves. Corny name, I know, but it seemed to fit, and even Si had to admit it was probably right.

Lucy and I have been to Homebase. Have selected the perfect shade of sunshine yellow for the walls. Have contacted local hire companies for huge, professional sanding machines to sand down the floor ourselves. Have found a 'carpenter from heaven' – Lucy's words, naturally – who's building the bar in the middle of the room for a knockdown price.

Lucy's been developing new recipes, although no one's allowed to taste until she's absolutely ready, and I've run up huge phone bills calling Edward – a distant cousin who works in sales at one of the major publishers – and picking his brains about the how, what, when and where of stocking a bookshop.

Even Si, loath though he is to admit it, is impressed, although I know he won't actually come out and say so until we're up and running.

'Have you seen their house? Have you seen what's happened to their house?' Si's borrowed a huge, shaggy mutt called Mouse to walk in the park. Except we're not walking in the park simply to enjoy the pleasures that nature can offer. I know what it means when Si borrows Mouse for the park, or the hill, or the heath. It means that Si's on the hunt for Mr Right. Si has this theory that every woman, and/or gay man, should have a dog. This is because, he says, most men go weak at the knees over dogs. Not small dogs, though. Big, strapping dogs. Alsatians, Labradors, Retrievers. Real dogs.

Mouse belongs to Steve and Joe, and Si discovered the joys of Mouse when Steve and Joe bought a holiday home in Tenerife. Northern Tenerife, they said, and therefore far, far away from all the lager louts. Simply divine, they said, the only catch being that they couldn't take Mouse.

So Si, naturally, was enlisted to dog sit. We went together to pick up Mouse. Si drove his sparkling classic Beetle up to Steve and Joe's flat – both of whom I'd met several times, although I wouldn't classify them as friends of mine – and before we'd even made it halfway up the path we heard Mouse.

'Are you quite sure about this?' I said, looking at Si's face as we stood on the doorstep listening to what sounded like a Rottweiler hurling himself at the door.

'Quite sure,' Si said, but I could see he was having serious second thoughts, and then the door was open and this great big teddy bear of a dog launched himself upon us, covering Si's face with huge wet kisses, whirling round in ecstasy, crying and barking with joy.

Si phoned me the next morning, breathless with excitement. 'This is it,' he said. 'I have to get a dog of my own.'

'Because?'

'Because I've never met so many gorgeous men in my life!'

Apparently Si and Mouse had been minding their own business, walking up Frith Street, when three – three! – gorgeous men stopped to pat Mouse and say what a handsome dog he was. Never mind the fact that none of them had gone on to invite Si out on a date. It was enough, and Si decided that the only thing standing between him and Mr Right was the lack of a canine friend.

Of course a week later it all changed.

'Oh my God,' Si hissed down the phone. 'The bloody hair gets *everywhere*.'

'He's a shaggy dog,' I laugh. 'What did you expect?'

'I did not expect a carpet of hair over all my furniture. Christ. I've spent the last week hoovering and it still hasn't helped. *Mouse! Get Down!*'

'So you're not going out to buy Mouse Junior, then?'

'I don't think so. Except Mouse did find me a rather nice young man in Hampstead yesterday.'

Si no longer dog sits for Mouse, but he does take him out regularly for walks, trying to guess where the gay population of North London might be. And yes, I know you're thinking behind Spaniards Inn at the top of the heath, but, as Si says, he's not looking for a quick fuck. Plus, he wouldn't want to corrupt Mouse.

'What's happened to their house?' I ask Si, as I pull off my cardigan and tie it round my waist, thanking God I had the foresight to wear a T-shirt underneath, as the sun has finally managed to break through the clouds and it's turning into a beautiful day.

Confused, I look at Si, wondering exactly what he's talking about, although harbouring a strong suspicion he's talking about Josh and Lucy.

'The place looks like a bomb's hit it. Those book catalogues! Piles and piles of the bloody things all over the sofas. You can hardly move in there for catalogues.'

I shrug. 'That's the new business, I'm afraid.'

We slow down a bit to catch our breath, because beautiful as Primrose Hill is it's not called Primrose Hill for nothing, and when we reach the top we collapse on a bench to admire the view.

'So.' Si reaches into his pocket for a treat for Mouse, who gobbles it up, then bounds over to a mad Old English Sheepdog called Dylan for a spot of harassment. 'Aren't you going to ask me about my date?'

'Oh my God!' I'm absolutely mortified that I've forgotten – that last night Si saw Will again, and that, despite Si having cooked him dinner, Will does seem to be rather interested after all.

'I am that evil witch friend of yours, and I'm sorry. I want to know everything.'

'Everything?'

I roll my eyes. 'You can leave out the gory details. Start with your menu.'

'Fresh asparagus to start with. Garlic bread, naturally . . .'

'God, Si, you really must learn to outgrow that, it seriously is becoming increasingly naff. Wait! Let me guess. You consulted Queen Delia for the main course.'

'But of course,' he sniffs. 'Since when have I consulted anyone other than Queen Delia for my seduction dinners?'

'Hmm. Let me think. I'm guessing . . . fish?'

A faint smile spreads over Si's face.

'Okay. So . . . it was either the coulibiac or the salmon with a cous cous crust.'

'Good,' he says, eyebrows raised. 'But which one?'

'Well, I know you would have wanted to impress him, and, although both are equally impressive, the coulibiac is one step ahead on the presentation front, so I'm guessing coulibiac.'

Si laughs. 'If you're so bloody clever, what did I make for pudding?'

'I know what you didn't make.' I nudge him, and we both laugh at the memory of the chocolate mousse.

'Okay,' I say, thinking hard. 'I'm doubting a proper pudding because the coulibiac's pretty heavy, with all that rice and pastry. Am I right?'

'If you mean, did I make treacle sponge, then yes, you're right.'

I suddenly remember Si's last Queen Delia success, and I smile to myself as I say breezily, 'It was hot last night, wasn't it? Hot enough for' – I pause dramatically – 'a *strawberry granita.*'

'God, you really are a witch, aren't you?' Si hits me.

'Anyway, he now thinks I should give up my job in films and open a restaurant.'

'Yeah. You could call it Delia's Den.'

'Or Delia's Dinners.'

'Because of course she wouldn't have a copyright problem with that, would she?' We both snort with laughter at the thought.

'So we didn't stop talking all night,' Si says, itching to keep on the subject of Will. 'He is fantastic, you know. He's handsome, and bright, and funny, and charming. You'd love him, I can't wait for you to meet him.'

I look at Si with eyebrow raised sardonically. 'Si, you know what that means. It means I'll hate him.'

'Well, of course you'll hate him if you think you're going to hate him,' he says disdainfully. 'But actually this time I think the two of you would get on. And he works in PR, so you'd have something in common.'

'Si, how many times do I have to tell you that PR and advertising have practically nothing in common.'

'He's creative. You're creative. He has black shoes. You have black everything. You're bound to get on.'

'And what's his relationship history?'

Si looks at me with horror. 'Like I *know*?'

'But didn't you ask? You must have asked. That's always your first question.'

'Darling, Cath. He's a gay man with twinkling blue eyes and a body to die for. I'll have to assume he's been shagging for Britain, and is now tired of it and looking for security.'

'So how come you didn't ask?'

'Because he would have lied. They always do.'

Si takes my arm, and we walk down the other side of the hill, our stride perfectly in tune, Mouse and Dylan happily tearing around the field, chasing one another.

We walk in silence for a while, then Si asks, 'If you could meet anyone walking round this field right now, who would it be?'

'Dead or alive?'

'Alive, sweets. This has to be a fantasy that has potential. Otherwise what's the point.'

'Okay. Someone we know, or someone we don't?'

Si lets out a long sigh. 'For God's sake, Cath. Just get on with the game.'

'Okay, okay, sorry.' We trudge along while I try to think of someone, but, as each name flicks into my head, I mentally cross them off, knowing that they're *not* the person I'd really like to meet, but not quite sure who is.

And eventually I'm left with only one name.

'Portia.'

Si looks at me with horror. 'God, Cath. You're so sad. I thought you'd say Brad Pitt. At the very least I would have accepted Tom Cruise, but Portia? You really are obsessed, aren't you?'

Actually I'm not obsessed. In fact, apart from our weekly addiction to her series, made all the stronger now we know the truth, I've hardly thought about her since I left that message on her machine.

I was pissed off that she didn't call back. Pissed off that she'd obviously rejected us, wanted nothing more to do with us, but other than that I really didn't mind, it was just that there were so many unanswered questions. I suppose what I'm trying to say is that there never seemed to be closure with Portia.

I remember Lucy once saying that the relationships she carried with her, the ones that hadn't seemed to die, no matter how far in the past they were, were always the ones that didn't actually have an end. They were the ones that were cut short before their life span was up. The relationships where one person decided they'd had enough – invariably the men – and the other person never had a chance to say their piece, to explain how they felt, to be acknowledged at all. Lucy was using this analogy to talk about relationships she'd had before Josh, men she'd been out with, lived with, loved; but I see no reason why you can't extend this analogy to friendship, because what is that type of close female friendship if not a relationship? Without the sex, of course.

And relationship does sum it up far better than friendship: I remember feeling, at times, that Portia and I were locked into such an incredibly intense relationship, that it wasn't unusual for us to joke that we felt like lovers, except we didn't want to sleep together.

'If I could find a man like you,' she'd say, 'I'd marry him tomorrow.' And I'd say the same thing back to her.

There were occasions when I felt quite simply overwhelmed with love for Portia. She was like the sister I never had. The best friend, mother, father, brother, the everything, and I do not believe that you can simply walk away from friendships like that. You cannot simply drift apart and get on with your lives, never giving one another a second thought.

Which was perhaps what upset me, pissed me off most, about Portia not returning the phone call. If I had come home to find a message on my machine from Portia, I would have called her back. Immediately. I might have felt sick with nerves while doing so, but I would have done it. But then who knows, she may have changed beyond recognition. I might be remembering someone who doesn't exist any more, or perhaps in name alone.

'I think you might have been slightly in love with Portia,' Lucy said once, while I jumped in shock and dismay. And guilt, because this was something I already knew.

'I don't mean you wanted to have sex with her,' Lucy continued, seeing my reaction. 'I just mean you felt an incredibly strong emotional attachment. It's nothing to be ashamed of, loving someone like that. And you mustn't deny it to yourself, negate the memories. The nature of your friendship with her was incredibly special and pure, and you must remember that.'

So when Si makes the comment about being obsessed with Portia, I shrug regretfully and explain lightly, 'Unfinished business, Si. I'd just like to see her again.'

'You know that if she does happen to call you'd be duty bound to tell her about the bookshop? In fact I think you should call and leave another message on her machine, just to make sure she includes it in the series. She'd have to rework her storylines to give you a dusty little bookshop called something like Fully Booked.'

'And Steen would presumably be called in to do the decorating. Chintz armchairs and gingham cushions.'

Si laughs. 'Anyway. My turn. Now who, other than Will, would I most want to bump into right here, right now. Hmm. Let me think. Rupert Everett or John Travolta? Eeny Meeny Miny Mo . . .'

'No, Max,' Lucy says. 'Go and wash your hands before touching anything.' She turns back to the fridge, and Max walks over to me with a grin, which I take to be a good sign.

'Hello, Max. Have you been at school today?'

Max doesn't say anything, revolting Damien devil-spawn that he is, but, still grinning, he reaches out two chocolatey hands and grabs my cream cardigan, before running out of the room chuckling to himself, leaving me open-mouthed with shock. Not because I care about the cream cardigan, but because that child is a monster.

'He is a monster,' I shriek, proffering my cardigan to Lucy, who groans and starts to clean it with an old dishcloth while screaming for Ingrid at the top of her voice.

A shadow falls in the hallway and I smile faintly, wondering how on earth an au pair girl can manage to look so immaculately groomed, my immediate second thought being how on earth Lucy can trust Josh with Ingrid in the house, because isn't that always the classic scenario? Wife comes back to find husband in bed with young, nubile Scandinavian tottie?

Ingrid runs her fingers lazily through her hair and steps gingerly into the kitchen, which is when I notice that in between her blood-red toes are wads of cotton wool protecting her newly applied nail polish. So that's what they do all day.

'Were you calling me?' Ingrid asks, which is quite an extraordinary question, given that Lucy has been shrieking her name for at least three minutes.

'Ingrid. Yes. Look, would you mind keeping Max with you? Playing a game with him? Staying in the playroom? Something? Anything?'

Ingrid looks perplexed. 'But I have just finished my nail polishing. I cannot play any games at the moment.'

Lucy stares, dumbstruck, at Ingrid's feet. 'Well, I'm not actually saying you have to play cops and robbers,' she says finally, patience wearing thin, which is amazing, really, because Lucy has more patience than anyone I know. 'What about a quiet game?'

Ingrid can see that she's not going to win this one, so she shrugs and walks off down the corridor.

'How do you put up with her?' I whisper, when I'm sure the coast is clear.

'Oh, she's all right. Rather sweet, actually. She just seems to be obsessed with clothes and make-up. Maxy adores her, and that's all I care about.'

'So the fact that she doesn't really like Max doesn't bother you.'

'She does like Max.' Lucy grins. 'She just has a funny way of showing it.'

'And don't you worry about having someone like that in the house?'

'Worry? Why on earth would I worry?'

'Well, how does Josh get on with her?' Lucy looks at me, confused, and then starts to roar with laughter.

'Oh, Cath. Darling, Cath. Now that is funny. Josh and Ingrid! Ingrid and Josh!'

'So glad I've amused you,' I say grumpily, wondering what the joke is.

'I'm sorry,' Lucy says finally, giving my hand a squeeze. 'It's just that it had never occurred to me. I didn't know what you were talking about. As far as Josh is concerned, Ingrid's a naïve young girl, far away from home, who's doing a fairly good job of looking after Maxy.

'And as for Ingrid, she probably thinks Josh is old enough to be her father. Oh dear, Cath. You have made me laugh. Anyway,' she says, slipping her glasses on and sitting opposite me at the table, pulling a large notebook towards her. 'I've been trying out recipes for weeks, so here's the final list.' She passes me a copy.

'These sound amazing, Lucy.'

'I've made each one personally, just to check, and I've done a bit of experimentation and come up with some new ones. I know the virtually fat-free, sugar-free, choc-olate-chip banana muffins are probably desperately unhealthy, but they taste delicious and I'm sure they'll be a winner.' Lucy looks at me closely, then takes off her glasses again.

'I thought you might give me a pre-session opinion. Well? Will you?'

'You'll finally allow me to have a taste?' My eyes light up.

Lucy laughs and goes to the fridge. 'Your mother must have adored you,' she says. 'Other than myself, I've never met anyone who loves their food as much as you do.'

'I know,' I say regretfully, mouth already full of delicious chocolate-chip banana muffin. 'I just wish it wasn't quite so obvious.'

'What are you talking about?'

I start to laugh. 'Having a face stuffed with chocolate muffin is not the time to start bemoaning a weight problem, is it.'

'Weight problem?' says Lucy, who's no stick insect herself. 'What weight problem? You're a woman, Cath, and that's what women are supposed to look like. You're gorgeous and I don't ever want to hear you say anything else. And anway, that muffin, remember, is virtually fat-free.'

Amid sounds of ecstasy I finish the muffin, only to see Lucy looking at me sadly.

'Oh, Christ,' I say. 'What's the matter? You look like you're about to cry.'

Lucy shakes the expression off her face. 'No, no. I was just thinking how wonderful it is that we're finally fulfilling this dream, and the only thing that would make this complete would be if you found yourself a wonderful man. I just don't understand why you haven't got anyone. Josh doesn't understand it either.'

'I'm really not that interested,' I say, slightly disturbed

that she and Josh have spoken about this, although I'm not surprised. 'I'm quite happy with you, Josh and Si.'

'I know,' she says with a smile. 'That's what worries me.'

Chapter eight

Sundays have always been my take it easy day. The one day when I'll allow myself a lie-in, scooping up the papers to take out to brunch with the rest of the gang.

But today Josh and Lucy are taking Max to friends in the country, and Si is all loved up with Will, so there won't be a brunch. Instead, Si has decided that Will is definitely more than a fling, and that therefore it is time to seek my approval, so Si has decided he will bring Will over for tea.

I did say that tea might be better at his house, particularly given that Si's flat is so much nicer than mine, but they are going *antiquing* – 'revoltingly coupley', said Si, with glee I might add – and Si has decided they will come over on their way home.

I do not understand how, in the space of two weeks, Si has found someone with whom he can go *antiquing*. Isn't that the prerogative of long-term couples? Of people who are used to one another, who know all of one another's foibles?

But perhaps I shouldn't be so surprised, because Si has always done this. He always decides, within minutes, that this time he has met the right one, and instantly attempts to create the intimacy, the level of comfort, that you don't usually have for at least six months. And of course this always frightens them away. I hope this time it's different. I hope that Will could turn out to be someone special, and I suspect that after this afternoon I'll have a pretty clear idea of his intentions.

*

I clamber out of bed, pull on a pair of tracksuit bottoms, a baggy sweater and trainers, and shake my hair out on the way to the bathroom to get washed.

I know what Si's expecting. He'll be expecting Mr Kipling's finest, but today I'm going to surprise him. I plan to put on a proper English tea. Not quite scones and cream, but certainly cucumber sandwiches.

And, oddly enough, I'm in the mood for baking. Not that I actually know how to, but, in his quest to turn me into something vaguely resembling a female, Si has bought me a few cookery books over the years, and before I leave I pull out a few and look at the recipes.

Chocolate sponge. Not too difficult. I list the ingredients, shove the piece of paper in my pocket, and walk up to Waitrose.

'Oh my God!' Si's mouth is hanging open with shock, as Will and I stand in the doorway, watching him with amusement.

'Catherine Warner, I do not believe this.' Si's frozen by the coffee table, on which are piled plates of dainty cucumber sandwiches, a teapot that rarely sees the light of day, and delicate bone china cups and saucers.

Si sniffs. 'Something smells good too. What have you made?'

'Shit!' I run back into the kitchen just in time to stop the chocolate sponge from burning. Si follows me in.

'Well?' he whispers. 'What d'you think? Do you like him?'

'Si!' I start laughing. 'Give me a chance. I've just said hello to him.'

'But what does your gut tell you?'

'That I'm hungry.'

'Oh, come on. Seriously.'

'Si, I honestly have no idea. I know you think I'm a witch, but my powers only start working after twenty minutes, okay? Ask me again in twenty minutes.' Si makes a face at me before dashing back into the living room to look after Will.

I bring the cake in, to find Si sitting on the sofa next to Will, holding hands and looking like a match made in heaven. They do look good together – Will has floppy blond hair and classic good looks, but, and I would never say this to Si at this stage because I'm not even sure why I think this, but I'm not sure Will is someone I would trust.

Not that there's any reason for it. He was perfectly charming when we shook hands, but there's something hard and cold behind his eyes, and I am pretty damn certain that Si's going to come out of this one very hurt.

'Tea?' I start to pour for Will, who says, 'Actually, do you have Earl Grey?'

'You're lucky she's got PG Tips, her kitchen's so badly stocked,' laughs Si, while I apologize frantically for not having Earl Grey, suddenly feeling very inadequate at only being able to offer boring old breakfast tea.

'Sandwich?' I pass the plate to Si, who greedily shoves one in his mouth while putting another three on his plate, and then watch as Will takes one sandwich and puts it on his plate, which he then places on the floor.

Does this man think I have fleas?

'So,' I say, rubbing my hands together because suddenly there seems to be an awkward atmosphere, which is ridiculous given that Si is one of my best friends. 'Did you find anything good today?'

'I found a wonderful Victorian washstand,' Will says.

'So beautiful *and* he took a good offer, so a bit of a win for me.'

'Si?'

'Nah.' Si shakes his head, as Will starts laughing.

'He was trying to buy a huge Victorian dresser, but it was obviously repro.'

Will looks smug, and I wonder what gives him the right to patronize Si in this way, because it certainly does appear to be patronizing, even though Si doesn't seem to notice. Or perhaps simply chooses to ignore it.

'Will knows far more than I do,' Si says finally, deferring to his new partner. 'About antiques, that is. Not much else.' Si gives Will an affectionate squeeze, but this last comment doesn't seem to go down all that well with Will.

'So, Will. What do you do, then?' Now I really hate asking that question. Not because I'm not interested in what people do, but because it really does epitomize small talk, which I loathe and detest because it is all so meaningless. Very occasionally you will ask that question to discover that the askee has a fascinating job, and you, the asker, can then fall into a deep discussion with them for hours. But more often than not they'll say something like, 'I work in computer programming' or 'I'm a lawyer', and you quickly have to think of more questions that you don't really want to know the answers to, except you don't want to appear rude. 'Oh?' you ask, feigning interest. 'What sort of law? What sort of computer programs?'

'He works in PR,' Si says impatiently. 'Remember? I told you.'

'Oh yes, of course.' I try to think of the next question. 'Who do you work for?'

'I'm the Head of Press at Select FM.'

'Really? How interesting!' I strive for enthusiasm, trying to catch Si's eye to make a slight face, but Si's too busy gazing at Will in rapt adoration.

'It's actually a huge responsibility, but I enjoy it.'

'How long have you been there?' Jesus, this is like pulling teeth.

'I joined two years ago as a Senior Press Officer, and when the Head of Press left I was the obvious choice.'

'Right. Select is incredibly popular,' I say, remembering all the features I've read recently about their new image. 'You do a wonderful PR job. How many people are on your team?'

'We've got four people working across the group, all of whom report directly to me.'

'He's very important,' Si says, pride shining out of every pore. 'Aren't you?'

Will shrugs, too full of his own self-importance to give an answer.

Si leans forward and helps himself to more sandwiches.

'Have some,' I encourage Will, because if they don't go I'll be eating cucumber bloody sandwiches for the next week.

'I'm fine,' Will says disdainfully, still not having touched the sandwich on his plate.

'Oh God,' Si groans. 'I'll have to make a confession now. I'm sorry, Cath, but we went out for a huge lunch. That's why Will can't eat anything.'

Right, I want to say, and why can't Will speak for himself, but I know Si's just trying to protect him.

'Don't worry,' I say, 'not a problem,' although if this lunch were so huge, how come Si can still manage to stuff himself?

'You know,' I look at Will, suddenly interested, 'I know someone who works for Select.' Si looks thrilled: if I have a friend there he can find out everything he wants to know in one easy phone call. 'Alison Bailey?'

'Of course I know Alison,' Will says. 'How do *you* know her?'

'God, I've known her for years. We used to work together at an ad agency before she switched sides and moved into sales. She's pretty senior now, isn't she?'

Will lets out a short barking laugh. 'She's the *Deputy* Sales Director. So not that senior.'

I wish I could tell you that it got better. It didn't. It got worse. Even Si started to look vaguely uncomfortable and took the first opportunity he could to whisk me into the kitchen.

'You just hate him, don't you?'

I sigh and look at my lovely friend, wishing I could like Will, wishing, at the very least, I could lie about it, but I just can't. But nor can I be entirely honest.

'He seems very nice.' I grit my teeth.

'Oh, come on, sweets. You can do better than that. Be honest. Tell me what you really, really think?'

'Really really?'

'Really really.'

'Even if you might not like what I have to say?'

'If I can't rely on my best friend to tell me the truth, who can I rely on?'

'Okay.' I take a deep breath. 'It's just that he seems a bit arrogant.' I pause, checking that Si's okay with this. 'And you know that arrogance doesn't go down particularly well with me.'

'He's not usually like that,' Si whispers quickly, watching the door to make sure Will doesn't surprise us both by coming in. 'I swear, Cath. I haven't seen him like this before.'

'So you mean even you think he's a bit of a wanker today, then?' I say, smiling.

'I didn't say that. I just meant that he's normally very laid-back.'

'And you know that because you know him so well.'

'Now who's being catty? Anyway, more to the point, how well do you know Alison Bailey?'

'Do you mean do I know her well enough to ring her up and get her to dish the dirt on your friend Will?'

Si idly traces a finger along the kitchen table and looks at the floor. 'Maybe,' he finally concedes.

'Okay,' I say, as his face lights up and he gives me a big kiss. 'I'll ring her when you've gone.'

'Find out everything,' Si says. 'And I mean *everything*.'

'Cath? Christ, I haven't spoken to you for *ages*. How are you?'

'I'm really well. How are you?'

'Oh, you know, same old Alison, same old life.'

There's an awkward silence, because, much as I like Alison, we both know that I wouldn't be phoning just for a chat, because we hardly ever see one another these days, and there has to be a point. I now have a choice: I can either beat around the bush and ask about her family, her job, whether she has a man in her life, or I can come straight to the point.

I come straight to the point.

'I'll tell you why I'm ringing,' I start. 'I've just had your Head of Press over for tea, and I wondered what you thought of him.'

There's a silence. Then: 'You've had Will Saunders to your flat for tea?'

'Umm. Yes. Why?'

Another silence. Then: 'He's a cunt.'

And I have to tell you, I nearly drop the phone. Not just because of the abruptness of her response, but the 'c' word is not one I employ in everyday conversations. In fact, I can't even remember the last time I heard it, let alone used it.

And Alison is possibly one of the straightest people I know. She's so bloody sensible she makes Mary White-house look rebellious.

'You are joking,' I venture, still shocked at her language.

'Nope,' she says. 'And I can't believe you entertained him in your house. God, you should have told me. I would have come round and put arsenic in the sandwiches.'

'Why do you hate him so much?'

'How long have you got? I'll tell you this, though. When Will Saunders chooses, he can be the most charming man you've ever met. I suppose he charmed you senseless?'

'Well, no, actually, I thought he was slightly arrogant, to put it mildly.'

'He's an egocentric, self-obsessed, nasty piece of work.'

I let out a long whistle. 'You really have a problem with him, don't you?'

'Every single person here has a problem with him. This place is run by a guy who adores him, which is the only reason he got the job. Two of the girls on his team are really good friends of mine, and he's a bullying bastard. One of them had to take three weeks off work due to nervous exhaustion.'

'Why don't they just tell him to piss off?'

'You can't. I've seen first-hand what he does. First of

all he pretends to be your best friend, and then boom. Suddenly he's phoning you at home, every night, screaming at you, telling you you've fucked up, patronizing you, saying that you're the worst publicist they've ever had.'

She's on a roll, so I let her speak.

'Then,' she continues, 'the phone calls start coming in every day. He repeatedly put Caroline down in front of her colleagues.'

'Caroline?'

'My friend who almost had a breakdown because of him. He made her life a misery, and she's an amazingly strong woman, but he gradually wore her down. That's what he does. He's a total misogynist, hates women and hates anyone who threatens him in any way. Caroline wouldn't take shit from anybody, but after that campaign she wouldn't say boo to a goose. She became terrified of her phone ringing at home, and actually became ill through stress. I hate the fucker. What on earth was he doing at your flat?'

'He seems to have got involved with a friend of mine,' I say, not wanting to name names.

'Well, whoever it is, tell him to watch out. He's a deeply unpleasant character. Two-faced, deceitful and horrifically insecure. Also a compulsive liar. And an enormous snob, which is surprising, really, given that his family haven't got a pot to piss in, but I suppose that explains it.'

'Er, you like him, then?'

She sighs. 'I would tell your friend that he's not a person to be friends with, let alone have a relationship with.'

'God, Alison. I'm glad I called you. Now I just have to figure out a way to tell him.'

'It's my pleasure. Forewarned is forearmed, I always say.'

But how do I tell him? I've barely put the phone down when Si calls.

'Well?' he says. 'Have you phoned her?'

'Where's Will?' I stall for enough time to think of an excuse.

'Gone home,' he says. 'I dropped him off on the way back from yours.'

'I phoned her,' I say. 'And she's not there. I left a message, but I'll call you as soon as I hear from her.'

'Okay.' His voice is filled with disappointment. 'I suppose I'll just have to wait.' We say goodbye, and I thank God that Si didn't ask me any more questions about what I thought, whether I might change my mind, whether I thought they would make a good couple.

I flick through the TV guide to check the evening's viewing, then put the kettle on before realizing I've run out of milk. I head towards the door but turn back, because, typical English summer, there's now a chill in the evening air, and a T-shirt isn't enough to keep me warm.

I walk out to the corner shop, and just as I've picked up the milk I hear my name.

'Cath? Hi!'

I turn around to see James the Estate Agent standing there, beaming at me, and I almost start to laugh. He is wearing exactly what I would have expected him to wear, exactly what I pictured him in the first time we met, except the sweater isn't chunky and cableknit, but a fine grey lambswool.

'Oh, hi, James. How are you?' I'm amazed that my

voice sounds so normal, because I had forgotten how attractive this man is, how unsettling I find it to be around someone who might make me feel things I didn't think I could feel any more.

'Fine,' he says, at which point I sneak a glance at his shopping basket and note that it contains a packet of fresh pasta, one lemon, a packet of Parmesan cheese, one can of Coke and some salad stuff. One can of Coke? Interesting. Not that I'm interested, it's just that James didn't strike me as the sort of bloke who would be single, and, unless my powers of deduction have deserted me, I'd say the Coke proves he's having dinner alone.

'Supper,' he says, gesturing to the basket with a smile and running his fingers through his hair in what can only be described as a distinctly endearing manner, because even though he doesn't appear to be shy, something about this gesture says he is, and I like him all the more for it.

'I can see,' I say, smiling back. 'I thought all you estate agents would have cupboards full of Marks & Sparks ready-made gourmet food.'

'You've forgotten I'm not really an estate agent,' he grins, resting the basket down on the floor in front of his mountain boots, which, I note, are covered with splashes of multicoloured paint. 'The struggling artist deep down still feels guilty about spending that much money on food,' he says with a shrug and an apologetic smile.

'I know Lucy lives locally, but I didn't know you did as well,' he continues. 'Whereabouts are you?'

'St James's Mansions?' It comes out with a question mark, but of course James knows exactly where it is.

'I sold a flat there last month, so I know it quite well. You know what's fantastic about those flats? Most of them still have the original mouldings, and the ceiling heights are fantastic.'

I start to laugh and James stops abruptly.

'What?'

'I'm sorry. It's just that you sound so like an estate agent.'

He groans. 'Oh God. Thank you for pointing it out. If I ever do it again, a swift sharp kick should shut me up.'

We stand chatting in the middle of the tiny corner shop, as people squeeze past us, murmuring *excuse me*, trying to sort out their Sunday night suppers, and I realize that, even though this isn't exactly a social situation, I'm enjoying myself.

There's something incredibly down-to-earth about James. Even if it weren't for the accent, you would know he wasn't from London. He doesn't have that edge, that streetsmart nous, that the other local agents have.

He looks like he'd be completely at home in a pair of old green wellies on a farm, so it's no surprise when he admits, during the conversation, that his real home is in fact a farm in Wiltshire.

After a while James looks at his watch, and I actually feel disappointed that he's going to leave, because although there are occasions when I love nothing more than curling up on a sofa and slobbing in front of the television, tonight isn't one of them.

Si's obviously not the best person to talk to right now, given that the only subject on which he's prepared to speak is Will, and Lucy and Josh still aren't back from their country excursion. I even sat at home earlier this evening, flicking through my phone book, over and over again, desperately trying to find someone I wanted to speak to, but there just wasn't anyone.

And yet I'm really quite enjoying this chat with James. He's interesting and, as I said before, a genuinely nice guy, not to mention frighteningly gorgeous. Did I say that? I can't have done. Ignore that.

'Do you want to go for a coffee or something?' James suddenly says, 'it's just that it seems crazy to stand here in everyone's way.'

'Sure,' I find myself saying. 'Great.'

James grins, and we both head to the checkout, where we're given the evil eye by the bloke behind the counter for blocking his precious aisle for the last fifteen minutes, and we escape outside, laughing.

'La Brioche?' we both say at exactly the same time, and we head off up West End Lane.

'You know,' James says, as we walk along, 'if we'd bumped into one another in six weeks' time, we'd be going to the bookshop for a coffee.'

'Not at this time,' I say, pointing at his watch. 'We'd be closed by seven.'

'But you'll have events, won't you? Book readings? Local authors coming in for drinks? Maybe even book clubs?'

'We haven't really thought in detail about things like that yet, but yes, you're absolutely right, that's exactly what we need to be doing.'

'Word's got round, you know,' James says, holding the door of the café open for me. 'A lot of the local shopkeepers know what the building's being used for, God knows how.'

'And what's the reaction?'

James shrugs. 'Most people think it's a brilliant idea, but there are always a few who put a dampener on things. Really they're the people who have been trying to get hold of that building for years, and I think they're just pissed off that they never got a shot at it.'

'I can kind of understand that,' I muse. 'It is a great building.'

'So how is Lucy? Oh.' The waitress is standing by the table, waiting to take our order. James looks at me. 'Cappuccino?'

I nod. 'Incredibly excited but also pretty apprehensive. Jesus, even I'm apprehensive. I don't seem to have slept for weeks. Look at these bags,' I laugh, lowering my head to show off the shadows, but James shakes his head as if he can't see anything.

'You look fine,' he says.

'I don't, but thanks. All I've been doing is lying in bed planning the colour of the walls, going through the sanding of the floorboards. All night every night I've basically redecorated the shop from top to bottom. I wake up every morning feeling like I've done a hard day's work!'

'Or had a hard day's night,' he smiles. 'No wonder you're exhausted.'

I laugh before continuing: 'Exhausted but happy. It was the best thing I've ever done, handing in my notice. Even if it doesn't work, although God knows I hope it does, I'll never be able to look back and regret not having done it.'

James's face lights up. 'I know exactly what you mean. I've always thought that the one thing I would hate most in life would be to reach the age of seventy, look back over my life, and think *if only*.

'We have to fulfil our dreams, and I think you're incredibly lucky having a dream in the first place, and then being able to fulfil it.'

'So if your dream is to be an artist,' I say, trying to steer the conversation away from me, 'how come you're still an estate agent at the ripe old age of . . . how old are you anyway?'

James laughs. 'Thirty-six.' I practically fall off the chair. 'I know, I know.' He rolls his eyes and tries not to look exasperated as he says what he must say to everyone who accuses him of the same thing: 'I look ten years younger,' and then he laughs. 'But I've got it all worked out. Why do you think I'm not spending fortunes at M & S? I'm stashing every penny away so that when I'm forty I can chuck it all in and spend the rest of my days painting.'

I'm impressed. Impressed by his passion and commitment. By his ability to set out a plan that will actually work for him. By his confidence in everything turning out fine.

'I'd love to see your work,' I say.

'Would you really?' Suddenly he seems shy.

'I really would. I'm assuming you still paint.'

'God, all the time. My only extravagance these last few years has been the studio, because I couldn't live without my painting.'

How extravagant can a studio be? I know what his studio must be like. A tiny room splattered in paint and covered with canvases, smelling of turpentine and linseed oil; an easel propped up in the middle of the room, old coffee cups gathering mould, planted around like traffic cones.

I can see it all now, but actually I *would* like to see it. I'm sort of fascinated by this estate agent with an artistic side. I know very little about art, but I'd like to know whether his dream is a viable one, whether he has the talent to make it, although it doesn't sound like he cares, he just wants to pursue his passion.

'Why don't you come over some time? Maybe you'll even persuade me to cook.' He smiles, then looks slightly worried. 'Only if you want to. You're probably very busy.'

You know, if those words came from anyone else, I'd think I was being asked out on a date, but I know, quite categorically, that this isn't the case. I am definitely not his type. Which is quite a relief, really, because at least it means I don't have to worry about anything. He's just an interesting man with an interesting hobby. And I did say I wanted to meet some new people . . .

Chapter nine

'I can't *wait* to start decorating,' Lucy groans eagerly, stepping into her professional painters' dungarees, while George the carpenter looks at her as if she's gone completely mad.

'*You're* not going to do it, are you, love?' he says. 'You'll have to get some men in to do that. This is a huge job. Too much for you ladies.'

This immediately gets my goat, even though I know it's only George being George, but nevertheless I speak up on Lucy's behalf, telling them that they're talking nonsense, and *ladies* such as ourselves would do a far better job than some big oafish blokes.

Sam the Spark – as we've come to know the electrician – smiles to himself without saying anything, as Lucy and I walk round inspecting their work.

'I can't believe it,' Lucy says, stroking a single kitchen unit that is currently sitting in the middle of the café area. 'Don't you think it's bizarre? How you left your job in the middle of June, when this place looked like nothing, and now, nearly two months later, it's almost finished and you can see exactly how wonderful it's going to be?'

We look around, at the low-halogen spotlights that instantly bring the appearance of bright daylight into the room, at the sleek modern counter in the centre, solid maple with glossy granite surfaces, from behind which Lucy will reign as queen of the cakes.

And now it's almost done. The kitchen's almost

installed, the wiring's done, the shelves have been sanded down and re-stained, and, as soon as the decorating's finished, the floor will go down. It's almost D-Day.

And it's only now that everyone can start to enjoy it. Because it's been hell. Everyone said it would be, but Lucy and I thought we knew better. The first set of builders we had turned up at seven o'clock every morning, on the dot, which we thought was pretty damn amazing. Until we realized that they were stopping for tea breaks every fifteen minutes, and that at lunchtime they were off for the rest of the day.

We tried to give them the benefit of the doubt. The pair of us started turning up every morning, always with a reason, but actually just to chivvy them along, to see if we could get them working. And that was the extraordinary thing, Lucy kept saying afterwards, amid much laughter and disbelief. There we were, their employers, and yet still, every fifteen minutes, the foreman would announce that they should down tools because it was time for tea. Did they think we were stupid, she asked in amazement, eyes wide. Well, yes, actually, they probably did, and quite frankly I'm not surprised. We were both so shocked that they had the audacity to do this when we were standing right there, that neither of us said anything.

But then Lucy found George. She'd asked his advice in Homebase, thinking that he looked like a man who knew what he was talking about. George not only turned out to be a fantastic chippy, he also had a team of people who worked with him, all of them reliable, hard-working and nice.

In short, George was a godsend – despite being the sort of man who believes that men are the hunters, and their primary job in life is to protect women, who should, incidentally, be feminine, giggly and completely hopeless at anything other than cooking, sewing and bringing up children.

George, naturally, adored Lucy, and, though he seemed to be slightly wary of me at first, he warmed up pretty quickly after I found myself succumbing to the helpless female act, because, stupid as this may sound, it was just easier and it meant he'd get the job done.

But Christ, did it get results. I have never met a harder worker than George. Lucy literally had to force him to stop for coffee by bringing in huge slabs of cake and delicious sandwiches every day, trying to tempt him to take a break.

'I'll just have a bite now,' he'd say, carefully unwrapping it so as not to tear the tinfoil, 'and I'll save the rest for later.'

'Lucy, you put my missus to shame, you do,' he'd say, when he finished the mouthful, while Lucy briskly said he was talking nonsense, and she was sure that Mrs George was a wonderful cook.

And how do I feel about all this? I feel as if I'm walking around with constant butterflies in my stomach. I still can't quite believe that it's actually happening, and if anything I'm even more nervous now than when I left my job, but Lucy's so reassuring, so calming, that I try to push the negative thoughts out of my head when they appear.

So today is the first D-Day, as Lucy put it. In other words, decorating day. Josh is turning up later, and even Si has invested in some decorators' overalls to help out, but for now it's just Lucy and I.

We wait until George and Sam have packed up and

headed off to the pub for a well-earned drink, before tugging off the lids of the paint pots and starting to paint.

We work in silence for a while. Select FM is keeping us company, even though I'm tempted not to listen any more due to the ghastly Will, who seems to have slightly come between Si and I, if only by virtue of the fact that Si seems to spend all his time with Will.

I do feel incredibly selfish, disliking Will as much as I do, because surely I should be thrilled that Si has finally found someone, but I can't shake the feeling that Will is going to hurt Si – particularly after that conversation with Alison – and he just deserves to find someone so much better. Luckily Si seems to have forgotten that I was going to get the dirt on Will from Alison, and I figure that as I've now got away with it for a month, the chances are I'll get away with it for good.

After an hour my arm starts killing me. Lucy on the other hand seems to be thriving, and one wall's almost done, so I keep my moans to myself, figuring that I'm not going to be the first to crack.

Two hours later I climb off the stepladder and stretch, grinning as Lucy does the same thing.

'Cath?' Lucy says, leaning her head on my shoulder. 'Whose blasted idea was this?'

I start laughing. 'Thank Christ,' I say. 'I thought I was the only one thinking this is a bloody nightmare.'

'It's not quite a nightmare,' she sighs, 'but it's not half as much fun as it looks on the box.'

'On the box?'

'You know, all those adverts where young couples smile adoringly at one another while they're decorating the nursery.' Then Lucy starts to laugh. 'Tell me I don't look as bad as you.'

'What? What's wrong with the way I look?'

'Go and look in the mirror.' Lucy sternly orders me to the tiny loo off the stock room. I look like a slightly less *soigné* version of Cruella de Vil. In other words, my brown hair now has a sunshine yellow streak running along one side, about four inches thick. My face is splattered with tiny blobs of yellow paint, and there are smears of yellow on my forehead where I've obviously got some on my fingers, and without realizing have pushed my hair back.

In other words, I look a mess.

'I see what you mean,' I shout out to Lucy, who still looks as clean and shining as when she arrived. 'I look like Big Bird gone wrong.'

'Actually you look rather sweet,' Lucy says. 'Why don't we have a break?'

'I'll tell you what.' I reach for my purse. 'I'll go up the road to the takeaway and get a couple of coffees, how does that sound?'

'You can't go out like that!' Cath says. 'Even if you do look sweet. You stay here and I'll go.'

'Fine,' I say, shrugging, and off she goes.

With nothing else to do, I pick up the paint roller and carry on, and don't even turn around when I hear the door open five minutes later.

'Just put mine on the table,' I shout. 'I'll be down in a sec.'

'No rush,' says a voice that is definitely not Lucy's. 'I can see you're busy.'

I turn round to see James standing there, although for a second I don't quite recognize him because in the intervening weeks I've grown used to seeing him in the neighbourhood in his navy suit. Not that we've had time to chat – we've been far too busy for that – but we manage a wave and a grin through a window.

But now, in his weekend gear again, he looks like the boy next door. These clothes suit him far more than the suits. In the suits he somehow appears slightly uncomfortable, almost like a little boy playing at being an adult, although I know I shouldn't be saying that, given that he's five years older than me.

'Is this a bad time?' He's already apologizing, backing out, thinking he's made a mistake, but I clamber down the ladder telling him not to be ridiculous, we're only painting.

'I can see,' he laughs, and I laugh with him, frankly not caring that I look like a dog's dinner, although obviously, if I were interested, it would be a completely different story.

'Anyway' – I point my roller at him sternly – 'you should be offering to help. You'd probably do a much better job than me.'

'I doubt that,' he says, 'but I'd certainly do a cleaner one.'

'Yes, well. I'm sure that wouldn't be difficult.' I peer at him closely because he seems to be carrying something in his right hand. 'What are you doing here anyway?'

'I walked past earlier and saw you both in here, and I remembered that I had something for the shop, so I thought I'd drop it in.'

'For the shop? What is it?'

James hands over the package just as Lucy walks through the door.

'James! How lovely to see you!' She puts down the polystyrene cups of coffee and gives him a hug, which would normally surprise me, given that she hardly knows him, but it's typical Lucy behaviour and only seems to faze James very slightly.

'Oh damn!' She looks at the two cups of coffee. 'Let me run out and get another one for you.'

'Don't be silly,' James says. 'I'll go.'

'Are you sure?'

James nods.

'Okay,' she says. 'But come straight back and we can all have some strudel together.'

'Strudel?' I look at her.

'My latest try-out.'

I roll my eyes to the ceiling, wondering how on earth I'm going to manage to retain my voluptuous, yet normal size 14, when Lucy's bringing in these delicious things all the time. And Christ, it's only going to get worse. How am I going to resist?

Perhaps it will be as my friend Katy said: she used to love chocolate, but then she started to live with a man who was a confirmed chocaholic and kept gallons of the stuff all over the house. She swore blind that after the initial temptation she got so sick of bloody chocolate she never touched it. But then again, Katy is, and always has been, a size 10.

This is the last strudel I will eat, I tell myself, saliva already beginning to build at the very thought of Lucy's delicate filo pastry and spiced apple filling. From tomorrow morning I'm turning over a new leaf.

'So why is the handsome young James visiting our humble abode?' Lucy says slyly, when he's safely out of view.

I shrug.

'Might it perhaps be that he has a little bit of a soft spot for the lovely Cath?'

'You know what?' I turn round and give Lucy my innocent wide-eyed look. 'I think you're absolutely right. Because what man wouldn't adore me with canary-yellow paint all over my face?' I give my head an expert Jerry Hall-style toss, thus causing the afro to vibrate very slightly. 'Not to mention my gorgeous flowing locks.'

Lucy starts to laugh, stopping only when she notices the package on the table.

'What's this?' she asks, picking it up to examine it more closely.

'James brought it. It's for the shop.'

'For the shop? But this looks like a present. What on earth can it be?' As she shakes the parcel James walks back in and Lucy drops it guiltily.

'Caught me red-handed,' she blushes. 'I'm so sorry, James.'

'Don't be,' he smiles. 'It's for you.' He looks at Lucy and then at me as he says this and Lucy gives me a surreptitious wink. 'Actually,' James continues, 'it's really for the shop. But if you don't like it then you must tell me.'

'Go on, Cath,' Lucy says, suddenly making herself very busy with a tin of paint. 'You open it.'

I wipe the residue of wet paint from my hands on to my overalls and gently open the package to reveal a tiny painting in a simple wooden frame. It's an incredibly delicate abstract watercolour, deep royal blues fading into turquoise, strips of colour criss-crossing one another, the layers built up until they shimmer richly from the paper.

'This is beautiful,' I say, because it truly is.

'Are you sure?' James cannot hide the look of relief on his face. 'I just wanted to bring you something for the shop, a sort of good luck token if you like, and I thought the colours were very sunny, it reminds me of summer, so I thought you might like to put it up somewhere.'

Lucy puts down the paint pot and comes over, gasping when she sees the picture.

'Goodness, how extraordinarily beautiful. What a stunning painting. But James, where on earth did you get it? You didn't . . . It's not *yours* . . .?'

But of course it is. And I have to say, I'm shocked. Shocked because I didn't expect he'd be quite this talented? Well, yes, possibly. And shocked because this is such an incredibly kind thing to do. To bring a painting to people he hardly knows. To treat us as something other than just another business deal.

'You really like it?' James is now beaming.

'We love it,' Lucy says, and gives him a kiss, which means that I have to give him a kiss too, which is fine, except I'm not all that big on touching people I barely know. I'm not all that big on touching people I know very well, except for Si, Josh and Lucy, and that's only because they're so tactile themselves you can't help it.

But I cast my inhibitions aside and give James a kiss on his left cheek, pulling away sharply afterwards because I do find these situations so awkward, but then Lucy thankfully breaks the ice by loudly ripping open the cover on the strudel and cutting each of us a huge slab.

'It looks fantastic in here,' James says, admiring our counter, our shelves, our etched glass windows. 'Seriously. Even old Harry Roberts would be impressed.'

'Now that *is* a compliment,' Lucy laughs. 'So James, given that you're not just any old artist, but in fact a deeply talented and wonderful one, how would you feel if we had some paintings for the shop? We could give you a sort of mini-exhibition. What do you think?'

James looks thrilled as Lucy continues. 'Look. We can't promise anything, because it may not even be a viable idea, we really have to look at it from every angle, but even if we don't display them in the shop I'd love to buy some for home.'

'I'm astounded,' James says. 'And embarrassed. You must think I came here to try and wangle an exhibition, or somehow to make you feel obliged to buy my work. I . . .'

Lucy cuts him off mid-sentence. 'James,' she says gently. 'I am not a people pleaser. I am not a person who says things because she thinks it will make the other person happy, nor am I a person who offers things she cannot deliver because I want the other person to like me.'

James nods. 'Okay.'

'What I think is this,' she says, while I'm slightly dumbfounded, because isn't this the sort of decision that should be taken with a partner? Even though James's work is, admittedly, beautiful, shouldn't Lucy have waited until she and I had discussed it in private?

And what on earth is she thinking of when she says, 'I think that Cath and I should come over this evening when we've finished and have a look at your work. How does that sound?'

James gulps. 'This evening? Okay. Why not? Fine.'

'Oh bugger!' Lucy says immediately. 'I can't make it this evening. I have to go for dinner with some boring colleague of Josh's. Oh damn. I completely forgot. Oh well, never mind, Cath, you don't mind going by yourself do you?'

'Mind? Why should I mind?' I say. 'I'll just cancel the dinner party I was having.'

James looks completely stricken while Lucy lets out a snort. 'She's joking,' she says. 'She'll see you at . . . seven?'

James nods, and I try to catch Lucy's eye to let her know she's about to get a severe bollocking, but she refuses to look at me, just chats animatedly to James about the plans for the shop until he gets up to leave.

'What on earth were you doing?' I'm completely bemused, and more than a little furious, because this is supposed to be a joint business venture, and what the hell is Lucy thinking of, offering him a show without discussing it with me first? Not to mention pressganging me into going over there later, which I'm not happy about in the slightest.

'What do you mean?' she feigns innocence.

'I mean, Lucy, and put that bloody roller down and look at me, I mean first of all you made a work decision without discussing it with me first, which I find hugely insulting, given that we're supposed to be partners, and secondly,' I stop to breathe, 'secondly you then dumped me in it by saying that I could go and check out his work when I don't want that responsibility all by myself, plus I felt that you were arranging my evening for me like I'm your errant daughter. You had absolutely no right to do that, plus, how do you know I don't have plans?'

'Do you?'

'No, but that's hardly the point.'

'Darling Cath.' Lucy comes over to me looking sad. 'I'm sorry that I upset you, and I'm sorry that I didn't discuss it with you but it was all spur of the moment.

'I did tell the lovely James that it wasn't written in

stone, and that we may not go through with it, so I *have* provided a get-out clause, but I'm so sorry that I hurt you. It really wasn't my intention to do so.' She pauses and looks at the floor, scuffing the boards with her trainers like a naughty little girl. 'But I can't apologize for making you go there this evening,' she says slowly, still looking at the floor.

I'm speechless. 'What?'

'Face it, Cath.' She looks at me again and this time she's grinning. 'Not only is he gorgeous, but I'm sure he's got a wee crush on you. I know you'd never give him the slightest hint of encouragement, and this was the only way I could think of to get the two of you together this evening. And I've heard he's definitely not with anyone at the moment – apparently he was in a nine-year relationship that ended about a year ago.'

'He doesn't fancy me, and anyway,' I mutter, although my anger suddenly seems to be disappearing, 'you really didn't need to go to all the trouble of plotting to get us together. He already invited me over for supper, and he meant it in a purely platonic way.'

'I know he already invited you for supper, but that was *weeks* ago, and neither of you has done anything about it. I apologize for my intervention, but sometimes that's the only way.'

'God, you're a nightmare,' I say, shaking my head slowly. 'What makes you suddenly think I need a man so badly? I've managed pretty well without one up until now.' I sigh and look at her. 'I must have been mad taking you on as a friend.'

'What *are* you talking about?' she grins. 'You didn't take *me* on. I chose *you*.'

Chapter ten

'It's not bloody funny,' I hiss down the phone at Si, who's laughing hysterically at Lucy's conniving. 'And I can't get this bloody paint out of my hair.'

'I thought you just said you didn't care what you looked like?'

'I don't, but I'd quite like to give the Big Bird impression a rest for a while.'

Si snorts again. 'God, I never would have guessed it of Lucy. Amazing what she hides behind that innocent face of hers. So, what are you going to wear?'

'The usual,' I say, smiling, waiting for Si's predictable reaction.

'Oh Christ. Not bloody black again. At least try. Please? For me?'

'All right, then,' I mutter. 'Brown. But for God's sake, Si, I don't know why you're getting so worked up. I told you before, this isn't a date.'

'Not yet,' he says, 'but give it time.'

'You and Lucy,' I sigh. 'You're both as bad as each other.'

I've never heard of his road before, which is odd because I thought I knew West Hampstead pretty well by now.

'It's off Sherriff Road,' he said earlier, writing down the address while Lucy practically exploded with pent-up excitement. 'It looks a bit dodgy from the front, but the house is back to front, so follow the path round to the back and you'll see the front door.'

I've come empty-handed, unsure about whether to bring wine, which of course is what I would always bring when visiting someone's home in the evening, but perhaps wine would give a mistaken impression, would make him think that I might have had an ulterior motive, and I have no wish to embarrass myself.

I realize while trudging up the path that I haven't eaten anything since the slab of strudel earlier, and although I very much doubt that food will play even the tiniest of roles this evening, I am praying that James will not keep me long, so I can grab something on the way back home.

He did once upon a time mention he would make me supper, but this is so impromptu that there's no way he will be thinking of food. This is a business arrangement, pure and simple.

The back of the house is almost pitch black, but I can just about make out that almost the entire back wall is a huge arched window, and next to that is a front door. I stumble over a stone and feel around the door frame for a doorbell, but before I can find one the door opens and James is standing there grinning.

'You found it.'

'I found it.' I find myself grinning back at him, noting that he is holding a corkscrew in one hand and immediately wishing that I had, in fact, brought a bottle of wine because suddenly it feels like the right thing to have done.

'Come in, come in.' James gestures inside, and I shuffle in, apologizing for coming empty-handed, explaining that I had meant to bring wine but . . .

'Don't be silly,' he says. 'I've got plenty of wine. What would you like? Red or white?'

I'm about to answer him, but, as I walk inside, I just

stand there, open-mouthed, too dumbstruck to say anything, because out of all the scenarios I had imagined, this was definitely not one of them. This house was not what I would have imagined at all.

The room is enormous. Vast. At least double height, the entire ceiling is glass, and, although all you can see now is velvety blackness, it must be like the playground of the sun during the day.

It seems to be divided into three sections. The section closest to the door is obviously James's studio. The white varnished floors are splattered with paint, and everywhere there are canvases propped up against the wall, some finished, some blank, waiting to be started. Pots of paint are dotted around, brushes, rags, the smell of turpentine.

'Have a wander,' James says gently, enjoying my amazement. 'I don't mind. Oh, and take your shoes off, it's probably safer.' I kick them off, noticing that James is wearing thick red socks.

I pick my way through the pots of paint, purposefully not looking at James's paintings, wanting to save the best until last. I walk through the large opening into the second section, the open-plan kitchen, and through again to what is evidently the living room.

Sea-grass rugs cover the scrubbed floorboards, while huge white squashy sofas dominate the room. An old wooden chair sits at an angle by an enormous stone fireplace. It is, in short, spectacular. It looks like something out of a magazine, and I tell him this.

James manages to look embarrassed. 'It has featured in a couple, actually,' he admits. 'But I wouldn't do it again. I had to spend about a week tidying up before they'd come near it. Never again. Much too stressful.'

I laugh, as it dawns on me why this looks like a home.

Why, despite the designer-type furnishings, it is a house in which I feel immediately comfortable. The mess. Piles of papers dotted around, just out of sight, but nevertheless there.

In the kitchen sink there is a pile of washing-up, waiting to be tackled, and on the kitchen table there are distinct rings left by coffee cups.

James notices me noticing. 'God, I'm sorry,' he sighs. 'I'm just so bloody messy. I keep meaning to get my act together, but I'm just not naturally a tidy person. You're horrified, aren't you?'

I laugh. 'You'll be happy to hear you're not half as disgusting as I am.'

'Really?' His face shows the beginnings of relief.

'Really.'

James breaks into a grin. 'Red okay?' I nod, and he pours me a glass of wine as I wander back into his studio.

'This place truly is incredible.' I turn to him. 'It's the sort of home we all dream of living in but none of us could ever afford.'

'The one perk of being an estate agent,' he says with a smile. 'Not only are the commissions extremely welcome, you also get to hear about things way before anyone else.' He pulls out a chair for me in the kitchen and I sit down, wanting to hear more.

'How did you find this, then?'

'It was about four years ago,' he says, taking a sip of the wine and murmuring with pleasure, his expression inviting me to do the same. 'It was one of those ridiculous situations where this had been on the market for ages and the owner was desperate.

'He didn't live here, he'd moved to the country years before, and this place was slowly falling down. Everyone knew about it, but nobody wanted to touch it. In fact, everyone knew about it by reputation. Somehow word got round that there were problems of some kind, and it just sat here slowly rotting.'

'Until you came in and saved the day?'

'Well, sort of,' he grins. 'I'd always been curious, but I'd heard all the negative stuff, and then one day I heard a couple of other agents talking about it and I decided to come along and have a look.'

'And was it love at first sight?'

'Yes and no. I couldn't believe the building. The potential. But it was disgusting. There were rats here, rubbish that had been left for years. It had been lived in by squatters for a while, and you could hardly walk around for the smell.' He gestures up at the gallery. 'That was completely rotten, you couldn't even walk up the stairs to see what was there.'

'But you took a chance.'

'I'd never seen somewhere with such enormous potential in my life.'

'And did you get it for a knock-down price?'

'Yup.' He grins. 'And a week after I exchanged I was offered double for it.'

'You're joking!'

'Nope. That's property for you. As soon as one person's interested, everyone wants it.'

'But double the price? Weren't you tempted?'

'Are you kidding? This was my dream home. And now I love it. I can't imagine living anywhere else. Do you want the guided tour?'

'You mean there's more?' And as I say this I suddenly blush slightly because I realize I haven't seen any bedrooms, and there is something uncomfortably intimate about going into a strange man's bedroom, and what else could there be left to show me?

James stands up and walks to the arched window, flicking a switch to the left. Suddenly the outside lights up, and he opens two double doors hidden in the window, and we walk outside.

And I realize that the pitch blackness outside through which I stumbled to get here is in fact a huge garden, not particularly well tended, but breathtaking by the sheer fact of its size.

'Bit of a mess, but at least I get to grow my own tomatoes.'

'You are joking?' I start to laugh.

'No, I'm serious.' He points to a patch at the back where I can just about make out large black shapes that are evidently tomato plants. 'What else would you expect from a farmer's son?'

We go back indoors, James pours me another glass of wine – I didn't realize I'd finished the last quite so quickly – and makes me laugh with stories of drunken rides on tractors and escaping the clutches of braying horsy women at Young Farmers events, saying how moving to London when he was twenty-one felt much like winning the lottery.

'So where's your yokel accent, then?' I ask, after a while.

'You mean my Worzel Gummidge accent?' he says, doing a perfect impression as I splutter out my wine with laughter. 'I haven't spoken like that since my first day in London,' he laughs. 'It took about five minutes to realize that I didn't have a hope in hell of surviving here unless I changed the accent.'

'Did you really speak like that?' I'm amazed.

He raises an eyebrow and grins, pushing his hair out of his eyes. 'You'll never know now, will you?'

'Come and see the rest of the house,' he says, and I

follow him upstairs, where he proudly shows me two bedrooms and a bathroom, and I manage to control any lascivious thoughts that may or may not have been lurking somewhere in the depths of my mind.

And then it's back downstairs to sit in the kitchen, still chattering away.

'Look, I don't know about you,' James says after a while, 'but I'm starving. Are you hungry?'

I nod, although to be honest by this time it's a reflex answer, because the hunger seems to have disappeared completely, and I really couldn't care whether we eat or not.

'You saw me in the corner shop, so you know that my fridge is not exactly the most well stocked in the world. Would you mind getting takeout?'

'Whatever you want,' I say. 'I really don't mind.'

'Curry?'

'Great.'

James picks up a sheaf of papers from the kitchen counter and starts leafing through them. I stand up to see what they are, and laugh out loud when I realize that all of them are leaflets for Indian, Chinese, Thai and Pizza.

'You ought to be ashamed of yourself,' I admonish playfully. 'Thirty-six years old and you can't cook?'

'It's not that I can't,' James says seriously. 'It's that I won't. Actually, to be completely honest, I absolutely adore cooking for other people.'

I raise an eyebrow in doubt.

'No, seriously. There's nothing I love more than having my closest friends round and cooking for them, it's just that when it's only for me I really can't be bothered.'

'Mmm. I know what you mean.' I think of my own empty fridge.

'Okay,' he says triumphantly. 'Found it. What do you fancy?' He brings the leaflet over and stands behind me, looking over my shoulder as I read.

'What are you having?'

'Maybe a vindaloo. You?'

'Chicken korma, I think.'

'Okay. Plain rice?'

I nod as he picks up the phone.

'Hello,' he says, 'It's Mr Painting here.' I stifle a laugh as he shrugs his shoulders in resignation at the name they've evidently given him. 'I'd like to order a delivery. No, no. Not the usual. We'll have a chicken korma . . .'

I watch him with a smile, because he's the most un-estate agency estate agent I've ever met. Not that I've met a lot, but James is so normal. So nice. And it's been so long since I've met someone new with whom I immediately bond. And although it might be a little early to jump to conclusions, I would say that James is exactly the sort of new friend I've been looking for.

It's not just that he seems to fit in with me, I think, as I watch him put the plates in the oven to warm them up. It's that I could also see him fitting in with my friends. I mean, I know that Lucy already adores him, and I could see Si adoring him too. All in all, I would say he'd make an extremely welcome new addition to our cosy little gang.

'Onion bhaji?' He looks at me for approval and I shrug my shoulders. 'A nan and a peshwari nan. Oh, and vegetables. Maybe a sag aloo?' I throw caution to the winds and just nod, slightly bewildered at the amount he's ordering, but he must be a man with a big appetite.

Oh, and by the way. Just in case you're wondering, I do mean all of the aforementioned – all of that stuff about James fitting in – platonically. Okay?

*

'I've got a stomach ache,' I groan, sliding down the sofa until my head is practically on the seat, undoing the button on my waistband and rubbing my stomach to try to ease the pain of over-stuffing.

'Oh God, me too,' says James, grinning at me.

'I know this is a bit weird,' I say, downing the last glass of our second bottle of wine, 'especially because I hardly know you, but it is a bit weird that I feel comfortable enough to make a complete pig of myself in front of you.'

'That is weird,' James says. 'Does that mean that if you didn't feel comfortable with me you would only have eaten six grains of rice and a thimbleful of chicken korma?'

'Quite probably,' I say sternly, realizing that I have had an awful lot to drink, and that unless I sit up straight I'm quite liable to fall asleep in this position. Then I remember with horror that this is supposed to be a business evening.

'Oh God.' I manage to force myself upright. 'We've been having far too much fun. I'm supposed to be here on business.'

'Are you?' James looks completely bemused, which isn't surprising, bearing in mind he's matched me mouthful for mouthful. 'What kind of business?'

'I'm supposed to be looking at your paintings.' I stand up, in my best impression of an imperious gallery owner. 'In fact, as you already know, Lucy and I are considering giving you the opportunity to exhibit your work in our super-duper fab and trendy new gallery café/bookshop type thing. And I' – I pause dramatically – 'am here to do the dirty deed and decide whether to give you a chance.'

'Right-oh,' James says, trooping into the studio bit, as

I stumble in after him. 'Let's see what you think, then.'

One by one he starts gently pulling canvases out, laying them against walls, standing back to look at them, and as he pulls them out my heart starts beating faster and faster.

'James,' I say finally, when there are nearly twenty paintings displayed in front of me. 'I'm not an expert, but what the fuck are you doing working as an estate agent?'

James turns to look at me in confusion. 'What are you talking about?'

'No. What are *you* talking about? These are incredible. They are the most beautiful, subtle, inspiring paintings I've seen for years. And I don't even know what I'm talking about.'

James looks embarrassed. 'Does that mean you like them?'

I start to laugh. 'Jesus Christ, James. I love them. In fact, to quote Woody Allen, I don't just love them, I lurrrve them. I loooove them. We'll take 'em.'

'Are you serious?'

I ignore the fact that I've just done exactly what Lucy did earlier and have taken a decision without consulting Lucy. But what the hell.

'More serious,' I say, 'than I've ever been in my life.' Unfortunately I ruin that last statement somewhat by hiccuping at the end of it, but nevertheless the sentiment remains the same.

'James,' I say, extending my right hand, 'it's been a pleasure doing business with you.'

'And where the hell have you been until this time on a Sunday night?'

'Having sex.' I keep a straight face for a while but the

silence becomes too much for me and I collapse with amusement at my little joke.

'That's not your line, that's my line. I hope you're joking.'

'Why? What would be so terrible if I wasn't?'

'It wouldn't be terrible, as it happens,' Si muses. 'It would be pretty bloody cataclysmic, that's all. Headline-making stuff, as it happens. Big Bird Bonks Again.'

'Si! That's not nice. Anyway. No bonking. I've been with James.' I slur ever so slightly, but enough for Si to pick up on.

'James? James who? Oh my God! I've been so wrapped up in myself I completely forgot.' Si plays the innocent as I laugh, knowing that he'll have been sitting by his phone for hours, waiting for me to call him back, to give him the full report on my evening.

'But more to the point,' he continues, 'you, Catherine Warner, are drunk as a skunk, aren't you? Aren't you?'

'Shut up, Mum,' I intone in my best truculent teenager impression. 'Leave me alone.'

'Good God. Wonders will never cease. You don't mean to tell me, Cath, that you've been out having a good time? With a man, no less? Until . . .' He pauses, presumably to look at his watch. 'Quarter to midnight?'

'Yup, yup and yup.'

'So tell me about James, then, sweets. Is he delicious?' He smacks his lips together wickedly. 'Did you eat him up.'

'Whatever that means, Si,' I laugh, 'no. He's just a nice guy. A new friend. A new addition to the family.'

'We can't have any new additions until I've vetted them,' Si grumbles. 'Which means that I'll have to meet him pretty soon. So how was the evening from heaven with James the hunky estate agent who's got a crush on you? Was it heavenly?'

'Someone's been talking to Lucy a bit too much these days. He's not hunky and neither does he have a crush on me. He's just nice. And a fantastic artist.'

'Methinks the lady doth protest too much . . .'

'Si!' I stop him.

'Anway, you can't blame me for talking to Lucy too much these days. You're never around.'

I can't tell him that I'm still trying to avoid the Will issue, but perhaps now that drink has loosened my tongue, perhaps I can be honest with Si, tell him what I've heard, warn him to be careful.

'Si, I did speak to Alison Bailey.'

'You cow! I knew you had. When? I bet you spoke to her weeks ago, didn't you?'

'No,' I lie expertly, knowing that the truth would send him into a fury. 'Actually she phoned me back this morning.'

'So what's the story with William the Conqueror?'

'Well, he doesn't seem to conquer people's hearts. Their hatred, more like.'

There's a shocked silence and I know I've pushed it too far.

'Joke, Si.'

'Was it?'

'Of course,' I sigh. 'But she did say he's . . .' I pause, trying to think of a way to put the message across, yet couch it in terms that aren't too bitchy, 'he's got a side.'

'What does that mean?'

'I think she meant he's a bit two-faced. She just said be careful, that's all.'

'Oh God,' Si mutters. 'First you hate him, now I'm told

to be careful. Why is it that Will's the first man I've met in ages whom I've really liked, and everyone hates him?'

'Sod's law, I suppose.'

'Ha! Got you. Everyone does hate him, don't they?'

'Oh, Si, I'm sorry. I just think you can do so much better.'

'Well, if I can do so much better, how come I'm *not* doing so much better?'

'I don't know, my darling. I do know that I'd go out with you in a flash. If I were a bloke, that is.'

'Why? Why would you go out with me in a flash?' I know instantly that Si's in one of his miserable moods, feeling sorry for himself, sitting, as it were, on the pity pot. And I also know that most of the time I pull him up sharply, but tonight he needs to have his ego stroked. Just for a short time.

'Because you're handsome. And funny. And you're the second-greatest cook I know.'

'Is Lucy the greatest?'

'Yup.'

'Well, that's okay, then.'

There's a silence.

'You haven't finished,' Si says.

'Oh?' I smile affectionately. 'Haven't I?'

'No. You've forgotten about me being kind, and sensitive, and individual, and hating Barbra Streisand.'

'You hate Barbra Streisand?' I'm shocked.

'Well, no. But I can't stand being such a cliché.'

'Oh, Si. I do love you. Even though you are a pain.'

'I love you too, Cath. So tell me more about James. Is he a boxer shorts or briefs kind of guy? Or,' and he pauses, 'heaven forbid, a Y-front man?'

'Not heaven forbid if they're Calvin Klein,' I state seriously. 'You have taught me well, Si.'

'True,' he muses. 'Calvins will always pass. So which is he?'

'I think probably a boxer shorts kind of guy.'

'You think? You think? You mean you didn't find out?'

'Forgive me. Next time I go to his house I promise I'll rifle through his underwear drawers.'

'Next time you go to his house I expect you to strip him personally. So what's his house like anyway?'

'Oh, Si.' I snuggle down under the duvet and get ready for a long gossip. 'I've never seen anything like it. You would have loved it.' And off I go.

Chapter eleven

'You're impossible,' I say, raising my eyes to the ceiling, as Si rolls down the window of his car and urges me to hurry up.

'Come on, come on,' he says, pressing the horn to irritate me further, but I speed up and open the door of the Beetle.

'God, I love this,' he says, leaning over to give me a kiss. 'I can't believe it's September, look at that sun. On days like this I wish I had a convertible. Anyway, sweets, I can't believe you actually agreed to let me take you shopping. We haven't done this since . . .'

'Since I was thin?' I finish off his sentence for him and we both laugh.

'*You* might say that,' he says, pulling away from the kerb, 'but I couldn't possibly comment.'

'So, where are we off to? Not Bond Street again?' I groan.

'Actually, we are going to Bond Street, but don't worry, I'm not going to drag you into the top shops. I know how uncomfortable they make you feel.'

'And no skirts, Si. Please, no skirts.'

'What about gorgeous floaty summer dresses?' He looks at me from the corner of his eye, trying to hide the smile that's fighting to escape, while I make excellent vomiting noises.

'Okay, okay,' he laughs. 'Trousers it is, but Cath, sweets, you have to trust my judgement on this one. It's the opening party for the shop and you, my darling, will go to the ball.'

And I have to say that although Emporio Armani is not a shop I would ever normally enter, the clothes are actually pretty nice if you're into that kind of thing, and Si has picked out a selection of trouser suits, and this one, the black velvet one with the long fitted jacket and the beautifully cut trousers, looks pretty damn impressive, even if I say so myself.

Si whistles as I step out of the changing room.

'Jesus, Cath.' He's practically rubbing his hands with glee. 'You look gorgeous. If I didn't know better, I'd say you were a size 10.'

The very thin, very chic, very French sales assistant was obviously just about to agree, but stops suddenly, not quite knowing what to say. 'Yes,' she says uncertainly, 'it is very flattering.'

'Oh, fuck off,' I say, turning to Si, as the sales assistant pretends to spot something very important on the other side of the shop, although I'm grinning at my reflection as I say it.

'It's pretty nice, isn't it?' I continue, twirling while I marvel at how cleverly the jacket manages to conceal my rather Rubenesque thighs.

'No question about it. It was positively made for you. Now, if only you'd let me do something with your hair.'

'My darling Si, even you know that's pushing it too far.'

'Okay, okay,' he grumbles. 'But you can't blame a guy for trying.'

We get to the cash desk and the assistant rings it up, then turns to me and says nonchalantly, 'That's four hundred and fifty-five pounds.'

I turn white as Si grabs my arm to steady me.

'How much?' It comes out in a whisper but, before the assistant has a chance to repeat herself, Si drags me to one side. 'Cath,' he says sternly. 'I'm sorry, but for a suit that divine, that's how much you have to pay.'

'No way, Si.' I shake my head. 'I'm not paying over four hundred quid for a bit of black velvet when I can get exactly the same in Top Shop for a hundred and fifty. Forget it.'

'Fine,' Si says, much to my surprise. 'Let's go to Top Shop and see how we do.'

'Fine,' I say, as Si goes back to the sales assistant, presumably to apologize as I head out the door and wait outside.

We do Top Shop. We do Miss Selfridge, now seemingly renamed the funkier *Spirit*. We do Hennes. We do French Connection. We push through the Saturday crowds to do Oasis.

Three hours later we're back in shop number one, grinning rather sheepishly at the same sales assistant, who smiles without saying a word, disappears behind the desk for a second, then draws out the velvet suit.

'As my grandmother always used to say, if you pay peanuts, you get monkeys.'

'The stuff we've been trying on wasn't bad,' I say, doing my best to stick up for the chain stores.

'I'm not saying it was,' Si says smoothly, watching me physically wince as I pull out my Visa card, 'I was just saying that once you'd tried this on, you'd never find anything as nice.'

'God, it kills me to tell you you're right,' I say, shaking my head.

'But?'

'But you're right. Okay?'

*

'*How* much?' Lucy's having much the same reaction on the end of Si's mobile phone, and even I can hear her shriek.

'Four. Hundred. And. Fifty. Five. Pounds.' Si says very slowly. 'Only.'

'Let me talk to her!' and Si passes the phone to me. 'I don't believe it,' Lucy giggles, 'I didn't even know you could spend that money on a suit! Cath, darling, is it wonderful?'

'Well, it is rather special.'

'You're going to look like a princess,' she says firmly. 'Everybody deserves to splash out on themselves from time to time.'

'What are you wearing Lucy?' I kick Si as he rolls his eyes.

'God knows,' Lucy laughs. 'I'm sure there's something perfect in my wardrobe, I just have to find the time to actually look.'

'Are you as nervous as I am or are you ready for the grand opening?'

'I don't know,' she says. 'I just know that it's been a complete whirlwind and I haven't had time to stop and think about whether we're ready or not. Anyway. Onwards and upwards. Make sure you and Si come to the house first because there's no way Josh and I can manage all this stuff by ourselves.

'We thought, as a treat, we'll do champagne and preliminary tastings just for us, but remember we've got to be at the shop about an hour before it starts. I'll see you later, okay?'

We say goodbye and I relay what she's said to Si, but midway into the conversation he pulls up sharply outside an Italian menswear shop.

'Why are we stopping here?'

'And who says Cinderella is the only one allowed to buy a new outfit for the ball?'

'Hi, I'm Laura. I'm the babysitter.' Si stands back and lets Laura in, as he mouths to me, 'Babysitter?' in a question, then rapidly smiles as she turns round and catches him.

'Lucy's in the kitchen,' he says, showing her through before turning to me and saying, 'What the hell have they got a babysitter for? What about Ingrid?'

I shrug. 'Maybe it's her night off.' Si wanders into the living room to find Josh adjusting his tie in the mirror above the fireplace.

'Where's Ingrid tonight, then?' he says, sinking into the sofa as he simultaneously reaches for a tiny home-made spring roll.

Distractedly Josh says, 'Coming to the party. Do you want some more champagne?' I shake my head and go to help Lucy in the kitchen.

'Cath, be an angel and put some clingfilm on this, would you?' She hands me a bowl of baby ricotta and spinach tarts. 'And then can you take those boxes into the car for me? Max!' she shrieks. 'Come and say hello to Laura.'

The next thing I hear is a clattering downstairs as Max runs in and bashes my knees with a wooden fork, before trundling over to Laura and whacking her on the thigh.

'Hello, Max,' she says, beaming through her gritted teeth. 'Do you remember me? I came to babysit and we watched *The Lion King* together.'

Max stares at her uncomprehendingly, then bashes her again and runs out of the room, while I smile widely, grateful that I'm not the only one.

Lucy sighs. 'He's just impossible at the moment. I'm so sorry.'

Laura smiles. 'Don't worry. I'll go after him, shall I?' Lucy nods gratefully, and Laura follows Max upstairs. We do our best to ignore the ensuing shrieks as Max realizes we're all leaving him.

I enlist Si's help and the four of us start to load up both cars with food and drink, and soon the cars are sinking under the weight. We go back inside and collapse around the kitchen table to toast ourselves with champagne.

'So where's the lovely Ingrid tonight?' Si ventures.

'Coming to the party, of course,' Lucy says. 'I couldn't not invite her, not when she's seen all the preparations for the bookshop these last few months.'

'That's very nice of you,' I say, as Ingrid herself waltzes into the kitchen, whereupon my mouth drops open a few notches in amazement. Ingrid, while being one of those incredibly striking naturally blonde Scandinavian stereotypes, is usually to be found in a pair of faded jeans, a T-shirt and trainers. But tonight even Lucy stops in amazement as we survey Ingrid's get-up of tiny black mini skirt, plunging jacket and super-high platform strappy sandals that, quite frankly, wouldn't look out of place in a brothel specializing in S & M.

Ingrid, on the other hand, looks completely relaxed as she totters across the kitchen to help herself to a glass of water. Lucy gulps and looks at me.

'Ingrid,' she says eventually, and rather cheerfully it has to be said. 'Looking ever so glamorous. How on earth do you manage to walk in those marvellous shoes?'

'I am used to them,' she says, as Max comes running in and falls at her feet, clutching her calves. She raises her leg and for one happy second I think she might aim a sharp kick at Max in her killer shoes, but no, she just gives him a disdainful look and shakes him off as if he were something nasty, which I suppose he is, depending on how you look at things.

'Ingriiiiiiiiid,' Max wails, going in for the cling again. 'Don't go. Stay here with me.'

'No, Max,' Ingrid says, walking across the kitchen and thereby dragging Max with her across the kitchen floor, as Lucy ignores them and Laura stands in the doorway looking as if she'd dearly like to be anywhere other than here, 'I am going out tonight to party.'

'She can say that again,' Si whispers, doing a double take at Ingrid disappearing up the stairs.

'Blimey,' Josh says, with a huge grin on his face. 'Old Ingrid, eh? Who would have thought she'd scrub up like a sex kitten?'

'Sex kitten?' splutters Si. 'More like cheap hooker.'

'WHAT'S A HOOKER?' Max's voice reverberates around the house, and we all turn to stare at him in horror, Ingrid evidently having managed to disengage him from her leg just outside the kitchen door.

'Oh God,' Lucy groans, hiding her face in her hands. 'I knew this day would come. Max. Sssshhh. Don't shout.'

'BUT WHAT'S A HOOKER?' Max now realizes he's not supposed to be shouting this and naturally starts shouting louder than ever, before marching up to Si and screaming, 'YOU'RE A HOOKER! YOU'RE A HOOKER!' at which point we all do the worst thing possible, given the situation, and collapse with laughter.

'Maximilian, I have been called many things in my time, but I have to say that's a first.' Si scoops Max up on to his lap and smiles indulgently, putting him down pretty quickly as Max opens his mouth for another bit of attention-seeking shouting.

'Oh God,' Josh says, finally managing to calm Max down by offering him a handful of chocolate, 'do you think she heard?'

'And what if she did?' Si sniffs. 'Face it, she does look as if she's on her way to a street corner in Westbourne Park Road.'

'Oh, she's only young,' Lucy says. 'That's obviously all the fashion.'

'In Scandinavian porn films,' Si says, 'perhaps.'

Josh quickly stuffs some more chocolate into Max's face, then whisks him into the other room to distract him with the video of *Mulan*. Thankfully he manages this before Max can utter those immortal shrieks: WHAT'S A PORN FILM?

'Thank God.' Lucy rolls her eyes. 'Peace and quiet. Now, Si.' She turns to face him. 'Why are you here by yourself, is your new man coming later, and if not, why not?'

Si looks at me and makes a face. 'Cath hates him, so I decided not to ask him.'

'Does she?' Lucy looks at me, horrified, and I shrug dejectedly. 'I don't exactly hate him,' I say, 'I just didn't really take to him, that's all.'

'Never judge a book by its cover,' Josh says, putting his arms around Lucy and giving her a kiss on the cheek.

'And what's that supposed to mean?' She hits him playfully with a tea-towel.

'Nothing,' he says, 'just that you should judge people by yourself, not judge them by what you hear.'

'Speak as you find,' echoes Si. 'Exactly,' and he looks at me with disappointment in his eyes.

'God, it's not my fault!' My voice is as indignant as I feel. 'I mean, Jesus, you didn't have to not invite him because of me. That's ridiculous, to give me a guilt trip about it. I wouldn't have minded if he'd come.'

'Uh oh, now I feel guilty,' Si says. 'Actually, I was winding you up. I did ask him, but he said he had other plans.'

'What other plans?'

Si shrugs. 'He didn't say.'

'And you didn't ask?'

'Nope. Anyway, much better that it's the old gang. To be honest I'm not sure how comfortable I'd be if he were here now. Not that I think you wouldn't like him – well,' and he shoots me a dirty look, 'other than Cath, of course . . .

'It's just,' he continues, 'I'd be worrying about what you all thought about him, and what he thought of you, and quite honestly I just want to have a good time tonight and let my hair down. And of course,' he goes over to Lucy and puts his arm around her, 'give both of you my undying love and support.'

'I can't believe it,' I say, still unable to believe that it's actually happening, that tonight's the night. 'I can't believe this is the opening party. God, Lucy. Do you think it's going to be fine?'

'You tell me, my love,' Lucy says with a grin. 'You're the one who keeps telling me we're going to be a huge success.'

'I know,' I groan. 'I was hoping the power of positive thinking would work, but now that it's actually here I'm *so* nervous.'

'Here.' Lucy pops a prawn satay stick into my mouth to shut me up. 'The food's great, the shop looks amazing, and the local support has been extraordinary. You just wait and see, Bookends is going to be a huge hit.' And with that she takes off her apron and walks upstairs to freshen up.

'Shit,' I mutter quietly when I'm sure she's gone, spitting the satay into the palm of my hand. 'I'm allergic to prawns.'

We get ready to leave, and, as I walk out the front door, I almost have to kick myself to remember that this isn't all a dream. I can't believe that back in April this was just a fantasy, and in August, only a month ago, we were still decorating, and now we're opening!

But the truth is, it's all been so easy. Hard work, but lovely work, because it's ours. We've employed two young, local people, Bill and Rachel, to work in the shop with us – Bill will be on the till, while Rachel will take control of the stock and help Lucy in the kitchen. I, naturally, am in charge of the accounts.

The four of us have slaved to get the shop ready in time. Bill and Rachel took over the responsibility of sectioning up the bookshop, as Lucy and I couldn't manage to get it quite right, and between the two of them they skilfully divided the shop into sections: fiction, biography, cookery, travel, health/family, history, children's, local interest, poetry, plays and Shakespeare, gardening, humour, and a touch of mind/body/spirit, just in case.

We spent all of last week unpacking the boxes, while Lucy and I kept on catching one another's eye and giggling because we couldn't believe that it was actually happening.

All the orders have come from wholesalers – thank God – so I haven't had to deal with a million invoices and deliveries from all the different publishers, which, quite frankly, would have done my head in.

There's still a lot to learn, but we're learning fast, and thankfully Bill had a summer job at Waterstone's when he was at university, so he's been unbelievable, to put it mildly.

Now I used to go to parties quite a lot for work, and most of the time they weren't much fun. Even the ones that are supposed to be 'trendy' and 'media' were usually trivial and boring, and a couple of years ago I decided that I had become immune to parties, and that they were no longer my thing.

But look at this place! Look at the people squeezed into every available bit of floorspace in the shop! Listen to the buzz of conversation that's growing steadily louder and louder as people's tongues are loosened with champagne.

And watch their faces as they groan in ecstasy at Lucy's canapés – her delicious bite-sized morsels of food that, quite literally, melt in the mouth; and watch Lucy, weaving through the hordes, beaming with heat, pride and happiness.

A handful of local authors are here, each in turn being interviewed by the *Ham & High*, and each saying how thrilled they are that Bookends has opened, and what a great idea, and why hadn't someone thought of it sooner.

Si seems to be taking his role as chief coffee maker from the TV series *Ellen* quite literally, and is walking around offering people mugs of French vanilla cappuccino. Lucy tries to stop him, but he shakes her off. 'How else do you think I'm going to meet gorgeous men?' he tuts, making a beeline for a very pretty blond man in the corner.

'Cath?'

I turn around and James is standing there, smiling uncertainly. He's wearing his navy suit and a tie that is covered with tiny jewel-coloured books.

'James!' I give him a big kiss, not feeling the slightest bit self-conscious, as the copious amount of champagne I've had has loosened my inhibitions considerably.

'I love your tie!' I shriek, over the din.

'Thanks.' His lips brush my ear as he leans forward to be heard, and I shiver. 'I painted it myself. Appropriate, I thought.'

I laugh as I link my arm through his and lead him slightly unsteadily towards Lucy.

'Lucy! Look! It's James!'

Lucy's face lights up and she too plants a large kiss on his cheek, as Si rises up behind her.

'Hel-Lo,' he says, in his best Leslie Phillips impression, eyeing James up and down, then raising his eyebrows practically to the ceiling as he notes my arm linked through James's. I hurriedly unlink it and introduce them.

'Oh,' Si says. 'Now I've heard *all* about you.'

James looks surprised as Lucy starts to drag Si away. 'What a load of rubbish,' she shouts over her shoulder to James. 'He knows nothing about you. Nothing. He's just drunk.'

'Sorry.' I now feel slightly awkward, unsure what there is to talk about, when I remember the paintings. 'Look!' I gesture around the room. 'Don't they look wonderful? I think they've even sold one or two.'

'Are you serious?' James's face lights up. 'That's amazing. Will you come with me to see which ones?'

I nod happily as James suddenly seems to look at me again. He stands back and shakes his head slightly. 'God,

Cath,' he says, the smile disappearing from his face. 'You look fantastic.'

'I do? I mean, no, I don't. But thanks.' It's been so long since I last had a compliment I haven't the faintest idea what to do with it.

'Come on.' I take his arm again, if only to stop myself from fainting with happiness – what a compliment! What a man! – and we push our way through the crowd to see his paintings.

I'm having such a good time. I don't remember the last time I had such a great time. I'm high on champagne and life. My dream of opening a bookshop has come true, and could I be . . . am I . . . oh my God! I'm actually flirting with James, and what's more, I'm enjoying it. Christ, this feels good.

'Cath, have you seen Josh?' I turn and look up at the familiar face of Ingrid, towering above me.

'Nope.' I wave an arm lazily around the room. 'But I'm sure he's around here somewhere.'

'Hello.' Ingrid suddenly extends an arm to James. 'I am Ingrid.'

'Hello,' he says, taking in her twelve feet legs, three-inch waist and pneumatic breasts. 'I'm James.'

'Nice to meet you, James,' she breathes, in what I'm convinced is a deliberate take-off of Marilyn Monroe.

'Umm, yes. Nice to meet you too.'

'So what are you doing here, James?' Ingrid says, and I give up. My bubble deflates in a split second, and as I back away from the pair of them neither notices, each completely wrapped up in the other.

How is it that you can go from feeling on top of the world to feeling like shit in less than a minute? If this weren't our party, weren't the opening of my dream, I'd leave right now and go to bed. But of course I can't do that, so I choose the only other option available. Booze.

I drink and I drink and I'm about to drink a bit more, when Lucy comes over and gives me a stern look, subtly removing my champagne glass as she introduces me to yet another potential customer to charm. I give her a grateful look, because tonight, the opening of our shop, is not the time to be disgracing myself, and, although I'm definitely tipsy, Lucy has managed to save me from thoroughly disgracing myself.

At some point I become aware that Si is trying very gently to steer me into the stock room, and then I look over his shoulder and do a double take. Or perhaps that should be a quadruple take, because walking this way is someone who looks very like Portia.

'Hello, Cath,' she says coolly, as I practically keel over with shock. 'Long time no see.'

Chapter twelve

It's very strange to see someone again after ten years. Strange to see how that person has changed, whether they have, in fact, changed.

I remember bumping into three girls I went to school with a couple of years ago. I hadn't seen them in twelve years, and they were all mortified because I said they hadn't changed at all, but it was true. Their faces were older, their hairstyles more sophisticated, but I would have known them anywhere.

Yet although Portia should not have changed, I can see that somehow she has. Her face seems harder, and, even though she is still tremendously beautiful, her look more polished than even I could have imagined, there seems to be something brittle about her. We stand there for a few seconds, both half smiling, both unsure of how to greet one another after all this time.

And though I know my face doesn't give it away, I'm nervous as hell and I can feel my heart beating wildly, and I just hope that when I speak I'm not completely breathless with nerves.

'Oh my God!' Si's shrieking breaks the reverie, and he flings his arms around her in a bear hug before she can say anything. She laughs and gently disengages herself, then leans forward and gives me a kiss on the cheek.

'But how did you . . .? What are you . . .?' Si is as surprised as I am, and I realize that this isn't his set-up, his surprise.

'Don't ask,' she smiles. 'I got your message, but you never left your phone number. I read about this in the local paper and it mentioned your name, so I thought I'd pop in to say hello.'

'You look amazing,' I find myself saying, unable to help myself, because she does, she looks as if she has just stepped from the pages of a glossy magazine. Make that an *expensive* glossy magazine. Her hair is a rich sweeping curtain of mahogany, her eyes bright and clear, and her voice rings with a confidence and authority that has evidently developed tenthousandfold over the years.

Put it like this: if you spotted Portia walking down the street, even if you had no idea who she was, you would assume she was a high-powered media star who always gets exactly what she wants.

'Thank you,' she smiles. 'And it's a relief to find you look exactly the same. The same old Cath. Still presumably as disinterested in fashion as ever, although,' and she fingers my jacket and takes a close look, 'do I detect a hint of Emporio in here?'

Si gasps with pleasure. 'I told you,' he nudges me. 'Told you it was worth the money. I've been trying, Portia' – he looks at her with a shrug – 'but you know Cath. This is the first decent thing she's worn in the last ten years.' It's odd to hear his tone of voice, friendly, light, familiar. Almost as if it has only been a week since we last saw her.

'You look good too,' she says to Si. 'This is so weird, coming here and finding that you're all here and still friends and still looking the same.'

'Because you've had to imagine us these last few years?'

Portia looks bemused but is poised enough not to look embarrassed; she simply raises an eyebrow as a question.

'I should say I'm angry, but actually I'm rather flattered, because Steen is gorgeous.'

'What are you talking about?'

'Well, it's us, isn't it?'

Portia laughs. 'God, you wouldn't believe the number of times I've heard people say they *know* it's about them. Si, I hate to disappoint, but they are fiction.'

'Portia, we're not stupid,' I interject gently at this point, not wanting to push the point, because what if we are all wrong? Although I know we're not.

'But it's fiction,' she repeats, refusing to admit anything, doubtless for fear of being sued.

'Anyway,' I say brightly, 'you've done so well. We had no idea the show was yours.'

'Thank you,' she smiles. 'I haven't done too badly.' She looks around the room and says, 'Josh must be here. I'd love to see him.'

'And Lucy, you haven't even met Lucy,' Si says protectively, shooting me a warning look. 'You'll love her. Let's go and find them.'

I've always been fascinated by memory. Fascinated by the fact that you can avoid thinking about the past for years and years, and then something will trigger a memory, and you find yourself swept back to times you are absolutely certain you have forgotten.

As I lead Portia through the room, towards Lucy, and Josh, I remember Elizabeth. I remember Portia entwining Josh like a snake, before cruelly dumping him, and I think of Lucy's shining face and bright eyes.

And as I walk I thank God that these ten years have passed, and that Portia is not, presumably, the insecure girl she was at eighteen, and that Josh and Lucy are the strongest couple you could ever hope to find.

I say I thank God, but lying in bed, later that night, I realized that I was actually praying.

Chapter thirteen

By the time the three of us manage to reach the other side of the room, the party has thinned considerably. People have come, as they said they would, to show their support and have now moved on to feed families, step into local restaurants, and even, in a few cases, grab a minicab and whizz up to the West End to continue drinking in one of the trendy bars in Soho.

And yet, despite the thinning numbers, it is clear that Portia is known. I see one of the journalists from the local press turn to a colleague and whisper, pointing Portia out, and I notice other people nudging each other as we pass.

How did we possibly manage to miss all this? Me, I could understand. Lucy and Josh I could certainly understand, but Si? How could Si not have known how famous Portia is?

Lucy is perched on one of the stools at the bar, talking animatedly to Keith, a reporter from the *Kilburn Herald*, and, as I walk past, Lucy grabs me and pulls me over.

'This is Cath,' she says, 'and this is Keith, who's promised to write lovely things about us, haven't you, Keith?'

Keith smiles, and disappears to find another drink.

'Lucy,' I say, as Si and Portia stand behind me, waiting to be introduced. 'There's someone here I'd like you to meet.'

'More people?' Lucy laughs, looking behind me at Si. 'I thought I'd met everyone in this room.'

'Not everyone,' Portia steps forward, her right hand extended, and Lucy beams at her and shakes her hand.

'I'm Portia. And you must be Lucy.'

'Now this,' Lucy says, her gentle face breaking into a broad smile, 'is truly a surprise.' Lucy pats the stool next to her and Portia obediently sits down, her posture, her poise, her elegantly crossed legs making Lucy appear rounder and plumper than ever, but Lucy wouldn't notice, wouldn't care: too intrigued by this apparition from a past she never knew.

'So do you like my bookshop, Portia? Do you think it will be a huge success?'

'Yes and yes. I think it's wonderful,' Portia says. 'Although I haven't been here long. Just long enough to see Cath, and Si, and now to meet you. You're not what I expected.'

Lucy, to her credit, doesn't ask what Portia might have expected. She just smiles and says, 'And you, Portia, are far more beautiful, now that you have actually appeared in the flesh. Has my Josh seen you yet? He'll be, well, I don't know. Thrilled? Certainly. Speechless? Far more likely. Shall we go and find him?' and Lucy stands up, links her arm through Portia's and leads her off, as Si and I stand there watching them, open-mouthed.

'What do you reckon?'

'What do you mean?' I look at Si in surprise.

'Is she or isn't she up to something?'

'Oh, for God's sake, Si. Why do you always have to be so bloody negative and pessimistic when it comes to Portia?' Which perhaps isn't entirely fair, given that it's been ten years since we've seen her, but it is true that after that night with Elizabeth, none of us managed to ever quite trust her again.

He looks at me as if he's about to say something, then

shakes his head, as if to dislodge the thought. 'Come on. Let's go and see the reunion.'

We cross the room to find Lucy beaming at Josh, who does, as she predicted, look shell-shocked. In fact it would be fair to say that he is completely lost for words, and Lucy appears to be making conversation for both of them.

'Do you know what would be lovely?' she says, surveying the room. 'A proper reunion. We're all dying to know everything you've been doing, and I'd love to get to know you properly. Would you come to our house for supper one night, Portia?'

Portia nods and I realize that she probably doesn't know quite what to make of Lucy, that Lucy is not someone she knows how to handle, because even in the short space of time since they have been introduced, it is clear that Lucy is not intimidated by anyone, and certainly not by Portia.

And that, as I remember, is, or certainly was, the one thing of which Portia could always be certain, and the one thing that gave her that slight aloofness. Portia could be as giggly and girly as the rest of us, but that wasn't her natural demeanour, and in an instant she could switch to the cool, calm sophisticate, a manner that seemed to suit her far better.

But how could she not respond to Lucy? Lucy is so warm, so welcoming, Portia cannot help but be swept away by her charm, and she tells Lucy that supper sounds wonderful and that she can't believe it's been ten years, and that there is so much to catch up on.

Josh doesn't really say anything, but then again he doesn't need to, and once Lucy has pressed their phone number into Portia's hand, and Portia has handed over a thick cream business card of her own, Josh shakes

Portia's hand awkwardly and says he'll look forward to seeing her during the week. And then he excuses himself to help clear up.

Portia turns to Si.

Si has been watching this from a distance, observing as if it were a play. 'Come on you,' she says, nudging him. 'What's been happening in your life? Tell me everything.'

The three of us go to one of the leather sofas, recently vacated, and collapse gratefully on it as Si starts talking to Portia about work. She is fascinated, and it doesn't take long before they find people in common, television and film being so closely linked, and Si apologizes repeatedly for not realizing what she was doing, quite how *known* she had become.

And, as cautious as Si has been, I can see him loosen up, warm to his theme, and the more he talks the more Portia concentrates, and you could honestly believe that she has never in her life met anyone more fascinating than Si.

'And what about your love life?' she asks finally, and Si gives her a blow by blow account of his relationship with Will, insisting that this time, despite what I have told him, it may well be The One.

'What about you?' he says. 'You don't look married, and' – he picks up her left hand before letting it drop gently down into her lap again – 'there's no ring. So are there any potential Mr Fairleys lurking on the scene?'

'God, no,' she groans. 'The only men I seem to meet these days are middle-aged television executives who are all married and desperate for a glamorous bit on the side. I've lost count of how many times I've been invited for a "quick drink after work".'

'Do you ever go?'

Portia laughs. 'I did in the beginning. Before the

series, back when I was naïve and desperate for my big break. Also before I understood that a quick drink after work meant a quick bonk in the shabby hotel around the corner.'

'Oh.' I don't say anything else, too busy trying to picture Portia in a shabby anything, anywhere, but it doesn't quite work.

'They could at least have booked Claridge's,' sniffs Si, and we all start laughing.

'I know,' Portia says. 'That's exactly what I said to him when I turned on my heel and left.'

'So you didn't . . .' Only Si could have asked that question.

'No! I most certainly did not.'

'So how does it feel to be this huge success?' I ask. 'Do you love it? Has it changed your life?'

'Absolutely.' She looks at me. 'And it's wonderful, but it's also very strange. I always used to think that the one thing I wanted more than anything in the world was to be famous. I used to have daydreams about being a film star, or anything really, just being recognized, being loved by everyone.'

I catch Si's eye, and I know immediately what he's thinking. That of course Portia would have wanted fame, that the only thing she thought would make her feel secure would be the adulation of strangers, and that if anything it was astounding that she wasn't now starring in Hollywood on the silver screen.

'Not that I'm famous now,' she says quickly, 'but I am *known*. I've gone from being the journalist, the one who does all the interviews and asks all the right questions and has the power to rip someone apart if she so chooses, to being the vulnerable one, and I'm not sure how much I like it.'

'But I would have thought you'd love it.' Si echoes my thoughts. 'You must have changed more than we thought.'

'I don't think so,' she smiles. 'I haven't really changed, but I never expected to feel so vulnerable. You never know what someone's agenda is. And when the series first took off every paper and magazine wanted to interview me, and I thought I needed to do everything, so I did.

'So I'd let people into my home, trust them in my personal space, open up to them and be as honest as I knew how, and then open the paper a week later to see that they'd torn me apart. And I know I used to do the same thing, but then I thought that this was the price people paid for being in the public eye, and that it wasn't personal. Except most of the time it is.'

'Jesus,' whistles Si. 'Sounds like a nightmare. I'd be slashing my wrists every day.'

'It's amazing how quickly you develop a shut-off mechanism,' she says. 'But it never really stops hurting. You just try to avoid the negative pieces because all it's going to do is upset you, and it's not as if anyone's giving you constructive criticism, they're just slagging you off because they don't like you and because they can.'

'But what about the good things? Aren't you going off to amazingly glamorous parties and hobnobbing with the stars at premières and things?'

'Sometimes,' she says, shrugging, 'but actually it's not very exciting at all. If you're willing to play the game, then it's great – you go to two or three things a night, air kiss the same people, do a few lines of coke to keep you going, and have the same vacuous conversations as the ones you had the night before.'

'God, if you ever need an escort, I'm usually free,' Si

grins, throwing up his hands and saying, 'I'm joking, I'm joking' when he sees the look on my face.

'I would have thought the trick is to surround yourself with people you trust. Just the really good friends,' I say. 'So you can go to all these things, but you know that it's not real, and that the real people, the true friends, are the ones you spend your real time with, rather than the fake people you see at these do's.'

Portia thinks for a while. 'In theory you're absolutely right, Cath. Of course that's what you should do. I suppose I've just been so busy with my career I haven't had a chance to find the sort of people I'd want to surround myself with.' There's a long pause. 'I haven't found those sorts of people since university,' and with that she looks first at me, and then at Si, and I pray that my blush doesn't become any more fierce, for we, after all, chose to lose contact with her when we had all graduated. We were the ones who hadn't returned her calls.

So is she saying that she's missed us, that she valued the friendship we once had, that it isn't too late for us to resurrect it, which would be the point of her turning up this evening?

'God, I'm boring you!' she says suddenly, turning to me and laying a hand on my arm. 'Cath, you will never know how good it is to see you after all this time. It's your turn. Tell me everything.' And I do.

Half an hour later, or possibly an hour, or might it even be three, Lucy comes over with a tray of steaming lattes for us, refusing to sit down because there are still a handful of people here who need looking after.

'Oh, damn,' she says, turning round just as she's started to walk off. 'Cath, I forgot. The gorgeous James was looking for you.'

'Was he?' I perk up for a second, as Portia raises an eyebrow.

'The gorgeous James? I thought you said there weren't any men in your life.'

'There aren't,' I say quickly, as Lucy laughs and shouts over her shoulder, 'Not yet, but he's definitely her not-so-secret admirer.'

'I don't think so.' I haven't forgotten what happened earlier, but nevertheless it is encouraging to hear he's been looking for me.

'What's he like?' Portia asks.

'Gorgeous,' Si says. 'Young sexy Farmer Giles type. All dimples, floppy hair and big white smile.'

'Rather like him?' she says, gesturing to the door, as I sink back into the sofa, feeling sick at having thought there might have been a different outcome.

'Yes.' I watch in a deep dark gloom as James guides Ingrid out the door, her face lighting up in a most uncharacteristic way as she turns her head to laugh at something he has said. 'Exactly like him.'

I didn't mean to get drunk last night. In fact I think I was doing incredibly well. Lucy stopped me going hell for leather, and then I'd been knocked sideways by Portia turning up, which definitely sobered me up, and then, after all that, I had to deal with my admirer not actually admiring me in the slightest.

But once the guests had gone, once Portia had left with strict instructions to be at Lucy and Josh's house on Saturday the eighteenth (instructions from Lucy, needless to say, Josh having gone back home to pay the babysitter), once it was just Lucy, Si and I, I really let my hair down.

Bill and Rachel attempted to clear up, but Lucy and I

shooed them home with a bottle of champagne each, only regretting it afterwards when we saw the state of the bookshop.

Our newly polished oak floors were covered in cigarette butts and pools of liquid, and our sparkling coffee tables, strategically dotted close to the old, beaten-up leather sofas, now looked distinctly second hand. Books had been taken off the shelves and randomly shoved back where they clearly didn't belong, and the air smelt of musty smoke and too many people crammed into too small a space. But I have to say, it was worth it.

We took one look and decided to leave the clearing up until tomorrow, thanking God that we had had the foresight to leave the actual opening of the shop until Monday.

I was ready to drop, but Si and Lucy were so high on the success of the party, turning the volume of the CD up loud, dancing on top of the bar, that it was impossible not to join in. And Lucy, wisely (or perhaps unwisely, depending on how you look at things), had stashed a few bottles of champagne in the office for exactly this reason.

So we cracked it open, we danced, and we started drinking again. Properly. Before the champagne appeared, I was desperate to do the Portia post-mortem with Si, but I could see that it would have to wait until the next day, so I pushed all my questions aside, and Lucy and I toasted one another. Over and over and over again.

My memories of Si trying to teach us to salsa are reasonably clear. Si and I got the giggles at Lucy's complete lack of coordination, and when she stepped on his feet for the fourth time we lost it completely in the way that you only lose it completely when you are well and truly pissed, or well and truly stoned, and we hung over the back of the sofa, crying with laughter.

Si then decided it was time for a change of pace, and Abba went on the stereo, and Si and I did very poor impersonations of the two girls from *Muriel's Wedding* impersonating Frida and Agnetha. And, just in case you're wondering, Si was the blonde. Like you had to ask.

Josh walked in at some point. I think he was fairly shocked to find Lucy and I lying head to head on the bar, while Si attempted to pour hazelnut syrup into our mouths. Si said it was supposed to be done with tequila, but, since we didn't have any, the syrups used to flavour the coffees would have to be the next best thing.

He didn't seem to be very happy to find Lucy with sugar syrup smeared all over her face and hair.

'Now that,' he said disapprovingly, 'is the most disgusting thing I've ever seen. Look at the pair of you. You're covered in a sticky mess.'

Lucy hoisted herself up, climbed down from the bar and staggered into the loo to clean up, while I joined Si on the sofa and shouted at Josh.

'You're an old killjoy,' I shouted.

'Yeah. An old fart,' Lucy shouted disloyally from the depths of the loo.

'Why don't you just let your hair down and have some fun?' Si said, swigging from the last bottle of champagne and handing it to Josh to finish. Josh took it and tipped the rest of the champagne down the sink.

'Not that I like being called a killjoy,' he said, 'but one of us has to act their age, and you're going to have a hell of a job clearing this up tomorrow. I would suggest that unless you plan to spend the whole day in bed with the largest hangovers you've ever had, it's time to go home.'

'I think, troops,' said Lucy, as we all struggled up to say goodbye, 'that much as I hate to admit my boring old husband is right, we should all call it a night.' And although we all moaned and groaned, today I could kiss Josh for being so stern. I feel bad enough as it is, particularly getting up at the crack of dawn to be in the shop by seven, but if Josh had let us carry on drinking all night, I think my liver might well have collapsed this morning.

As it was, Si chaperoned me home, which was slightly ridiculous, really, given that he could barely stand. He then came in so we could both drink three bottles of water each, as he had read that if you consume the same amount of water as alcohol drunk that evening, you will wake up hangover-free.

Unfortunately we could only manage a glass and a half each, and, after his minicab arrived, I stumbled out of my clothes, leaving them lying in heaps on the bedroom floor, and climbed into bed.

I wake up the next morning to the doorbell ringing, except initially I think it must be the doorbell in my dreams, then it becomes the phone, and finally I realize it's the door. What the hell do they want at this godforsaken hour on a Sunday, and why the hell don't they shut up?

I stumble out of bed, groan as my head pounds like a drum, and walk as quickly as I can to the hallway.

'Hang on,' I shriek, cringing at the loudness of my own voice. 'I'm coming.' And mercifully, the doorbell stops.

I make my way gingerly back to the bedroom and

grab the towelling robe from behind the door, making a mental note to wash it because in the absence of a clean towel I've been using it daily for God knows how long, and what was once white is now an interesting spectrum of greys.

'Who is it?' My voice is back to normal now, I just wish that I were back to normal. My eyes feel like pinheads, my throat is dry and scratchy, and, as if the headache weren't bad enough, waves of nausea are threatening every few seconds, and I'm not sure whether to answer the front door or head for the bathroom just in case.

'Flower delivery,' a voice says, and through the frosted glass I can just make out a huge bouquet of flowers. Strange. Who the hell's sending me flowers? It doesn't occur to me that no one sends flowers on a *Sunday*. Ever.

I open the door quickly, hoping that no one's around to see me because I don't even have to look in the mirror to know I look like shit, although frankly with the way that I'm feeling I don't very much care.

'Thanks,' I mumble, reaching out to take the flowers, and as I take them they reveal the face of the delivery man. I stand on the spot, paralysed with horror.

'Hi!' James's smile fades as he gets his first good look at me. 'Umm, I didn't wake you, did I?'

'What? What do you want?' I don't mean to be rude, but what the hell is his game? He left last night with Ingrid, doubtless took her back to his amazing studio, probably shagged her senseless, leaving me to spend the evening doing Abba impersonations. And I'm supposed to be pleased to see him?

'Just leave me alone.' I ignore the bewildered expression on his face, shove the flowers back into his hand and slam the door, groaning as the bang reverberates through my poor thumping head.

Oh shit. I make my way slowly to the bathroom, sink to my knees on the floor and – to hell with it – stick my fingers down my throat. As soon as I've thrown up I start to feel better, if only because the nausea's subsided, so I go to the medicine cabinet. To Nurofen Plus. To redemption. I take three pills just to be on the safe side, consider drinking a lot more water but can't quite manage it, drop the towelling robe on the floor and stumble back into the bedroom, turning down the volume on the phone on the way. I draw the duvet over my head.

What is going on? And more to the point, why is it bothering me so much? Why should I care if James and Ingrid got it together? Why do I actually feel upset about this? Enough. I'm not going to do this any more.

This time I refuse to wake up until my head, my heart and my life have all returned to normal.

Chapter fourteen

'I can't move,' I groan, eyes still closed, phone lying on the pillow beside my head. 'Leave me alone. I've already been disturbed by that bloody James coming over this morning, and now you. Can't you just go away?'

'Nope.' Si's voice is as dodgy as mine. 'I feel like hell too, but we've got to do the post-mortem, and we've got to do it before we clean the shop. I mean, what the hell's the point in bothering to even talk to someone like Portia after ten years if we can't then get together and talk about her once she's disappeared again?

'Plus,' he continues with relish, his voice becoming stronger by the second, 'I need to know what's going on with Farmer James the Estate Agent Artist. And, the best way of curing a hangover is a fry-up. We need fried eggs, chips, sausages swimming in grease and baked bea . . .' Before he finishes his sentence I've jumped out of bed, run to the bathroom and shoved my head back down the bowl of the loo.

I lean my hands on the sink and look at my reflection, marvelling at the face that stares back. I haven't had a hangover this bad for years, and I'm sure I never used to look this awful the morning after. I smudge my fingers under my eyes to try to remove the mascara that's halfway down my cheeks, then splash my face, groaning with relief at the cold water.

And as I walk back to the bedroom I hear muffled shouts coming from the telephone. I pick it up in amazement.

'You're still here?'

'I refuse to put the phone down until you agree to meet me for breakfast. And I got the message about the fry-up, so we can just go for a cup of coffee, but I've told Lucy you'll meet her at the shop this afternoon, so you haven't got an excuse. You have to come.'

What can I do? I give in and we arrange to meet in an hour's time.

An hour later I'm sitting by the window of a cosy café off the high street in Hampstead, nursing a large black coffee and a head that's not thumping quite as badly as it was, but is nevertheless still thumping.

I hear a commotion coming down the street, and I peer out of the window to see Si being dragged towards a Yorkshire terrier that's straining at the leash by none other than Mouse. 'No!' he shouts at Mouse, who has managed to get himself wound around a lamppost. 'Naughty boy!' He eventually manages to unravel him before looping his lead through a railing just outside the shop and instructing him to sit. Mouse obviously decides to curb his natural exuberance for once, and sinks slowly to the pavement, his eyes looking rather pathetically up at Si as he walks inside and comes to sit down at the table.

He scrapes the chair away from the table, as I grimace and lift my hands to my tender temples.

'Sorry,' he whispers, leaning over to give me a kiss.

'What's Mouse doing here?'

'I forgot I'd promised to babysit. You don't mind, do you? I'm meeting Will a bit later on and we're going to take him for a walk.'

'Is Will coming *here*?' I try to make the question as nonchalant as possible.

'Don't worry, you won't have to see him.' Si can see straight through me. 'I'm meeting him at the tube. Now, we both need to order Cokes.' He goes off into this long explanation of why Coke is the best cure for a hangover, and, even though Coke is the last thing I want right now, once it arrives and I start sipping it slowly, it's extraordinary how much better I feel.

In fact, within half an hour I'm feeling so good that suddenly the thought of a fry-up doesn't sound too bad after all, and we both order exactly the same thing: scrambled eggs, sausage, bacon and fried tomato with copious amounts of white toast. Si debates going for wholemeal, as it's 'so much healthier', but in the end we decide that there really isn't any point, and that if white bread and brown bread were exactly the same in terms of nutritional content, you'd choose white every time, so what the hell.

'It's like those times you go into restaurants and see these rather large women ordering garlic bread, spaghetti carbonara with extra Parmesan, and a Diet Coke,' he snorts, as a rather large woman on the table next to us puts down her almond croissant, picks up her Diet Coke and shoots Si an extremely dirty look.

'First, James,' Si says, and I tell him what happened last night, up to the point I saw him leave with Ingrid.

'But I thought you weren't interested,' Si smirks, as I jump on the defensive.

'I wasn't. I mean, I'm not. It's just that everyone was so convinced he was interested in me, and to be honest it was hugely flattering. And he is a nice guy. At least I thought so until last night, and I suppose I just feel let down.' Something in me stops me from telling Si that I actually feel more than let down.

'But you don't know that anything happened,' Si said.

'You saw Ingrid last night. Do you really think he was just walking her home?'

Si thinks for a minute, then shrugs apologetically. 'I'm probably not the best person to ask. I'm gay, for God's sake, I can't judge Ingrid's attraction.'

'Bollocks, Si. She looked up for anything last night, and no man can resist that.'

'True, but if he's as nice a guy as you think he is, then he's not the type to jump into bed with her on the first night.'

'Not "think he is". Thought he was. The only thing I think right now is that I was wrong.'

Si shakes his head and laughs. 'I can't even believe we're having this conversation. This *is* Cath-the-celibate-one I'm talking to, isn't it? The one who hasn't had the slightest bit of interest in men since Martin?'

'I'm still celibate,' I grunt. 'Just in case you hadn't noticed.'

'I had noticed actually, but I still think it's strange,' he says pensively. 'Portia only re-entered our lives last night, but already I feel unsettled, that the dynamic suddenly seems to be changing.'

'What do you mean?'

'Well, that we should be having this conversation, for starters. I don't remember talking to you like this about men since we were third years. I feel as if I've regressed ten years, as if we all have. And then did you see Josh's face last night? If I didn't know better I'd say he was a lovestruck undergraduate. I almost expected Portia to wind herself round him like a snake and put her tongue in his ear.'

'Jesus!' My mouth drops open. 'I can't believe you just said that. That's exactly what I was thinking about last night. I hadn't thought about that for years.'

'Me neither,' Si says sourly, 'but isn't it interesting that that's the first memory that should come flooding back once Portia turns up. And, pissed as I was last night, I noticed Josh was not a happy bunny by the time he came back. I can't help but wonder what else is going to change?'

'Si, you're being a touch overdramatic, don't you think? She turned up because we were the ones who got in touch with her. Talking to you anyone would think she's spent the last ten years plotting her revenge and she's come back to steal all our husbands.'

'Well, Lucy's husband, because obviously you and I are husbandless,' I continue. 'But still, Si, I do think that's slightly ridiculous.'

'So you're saying that you don't think she's come back to set her sights on Josh once again?'

'Don't be ridiculous. Whatever for? The only time she's ever been interested in Josh was one night, ten years ago. She could have had him permanently then, but if you remember correctly she didn't want him, and I don't for a second believe she wants him now.'

'Not even because he's the only one out of all of us who's actually happily married to a divine wife with a gorgeous child? You don't think she might be jealous?'

'Did I just hear you use the word "gorgeous" in relation to Max Damien Devilspawn?'

Si grins.

'Look, if we hadn't phoned her that day, we wouldn't have seen her last night. This is all our doing, and you're just reading far too much into it. Josh was pissed off last night because we were all completely whacked.'

'I don't know.' Si shakes his head. 'It's just a feeling, but I hope I'm wrong. Anyway, I suppose we'll have to watch this space when she comes to Josh and Lucy for dinner next week. So, back to Farmer James the gorgeous Estate Agent. What was he doing coming over this morning, or is there something you haven't been telling me?'

Half an hour later Si manages to persuade me to walk him up to the tube to meet Will.

'You don't have to stay,' he begs. 'Pleeeeaaaase,' he pleads. 'I'll be your best friend for ever and ever, and I'll invite you to my party.'

How can I resist? I do, however, clearly state that I will be staying just long enough to say hello, and then I will be off.

The gorgeous warm sunshine of yesterday has well and truly disappeared, leaving the weather cold and windy, and truly autumnal. I'm grateful I brought my scarf to keep the wind away from bones that are fragile enough already. We stride slowly up the hill, apologizing as Mouse becomes entangled with people or runs across them, tripping them up with his lead.

My breath is visible in the crisp air, and Si clamps his hands under his armpits to keep them warm, as I dig mine deep down into the pockets of my coat.

'I love this weather,' Si says, taking a deep breath and exhaling with a look of intense satisfaction on his face.

'Are you serious? Give me the summer anytime. People in short sleeves, carefree, everyone smiling and milling round outside.'

'Nope.' Si shakes his head. 'Give me cold, windy winters. Or, even better, this time of year. Autumn. Anything where it's cold and you have to wrap up warmly. Kicking through the leaves across the heath, then going home to snuggle up under thick blankets with a roaring fire to keep you warm.' He sighs with pleasure.

'Any second now you'll be talking about melting marshmallows in mugs of creamy hot chocolate,' I laugh sarcastically.

'Well, yes, actually.' Si affects a wounded look. 'What would winter fantasies be without the ubiquitous hot chocolate.'

'God.' I shake my head in wonder. 'You really are an old romantic, aren't you? No wonder you haven't managed to settle down with anyone. Who could live up to those expectations? Who could live as if their life were a constant movie?'

Si thinks for a second. 'Rupert Everett,' he offers finally, smacking his lips together before licking them lasciviously. 'That's who.'

We reach the station five minutes late, and there's no sign of Will. Si immediately begins to worry that we've missed him, that he's been and gone, that he thought Si wasn't turning up.

'Don't be ridiculous,' I say. 'He's probably late himself.'

And, although it's really far too cold to be standing around a chilly tube station, that's exactly what we do. For half a bloody hour.

'Hasn't he got a mobile?' I ask eventually, and Si nods, so we troop down to the payphone down the hill, Si having forgotten to re-charge his. I lean outside, attempting to control Mouse, while he phones Will.

I want to eavesdrop desperately, but I don't want to look as if I want to eavesdrop, so I pull Mouse over to a shoe shop and try to appear amazingly interested in shoes, which isn't exactly a realistic proposition, but it's the best I can do on such short notice.

Eventually I hear the door to the phone box open, and Si comes out looking completely dejected.

'How do you fancy coming with us for a walk?' he says finally, his voice flat.

'Us?'

'Mouse and me.'

I look at my watch and shrug apologetically, because I have to get to the shop, but Si and I walk up the hill together, back to the tube station, in silence, as I wait for him to explain. Eventually he lets out a long sigh and says, 'He forgot.'

'He what?' I'm flabbergasted. And horrified.

'He's with friends in some brasserie somewhere, and he said he completely forgot.'

'Bastard!' I spit.

Si doesn't say anything, he just shrugs, so I take the opportunity to unleash a tirade of vitriol that probably isn't that appropriate, given I hardly know the guy, but I just can't help it. How dare he treat Si like that. How dare *anyone*. I look at Si's sweet, loving face, and I just want to kill this man for treating Si as if he's disposable.

'Okay, okay,' Si says, stopping me. 'I get the picture.'

'Does this mean you've realized he's not for you?'

'I don't know. Let's just say I might have started to see things a bit more clearly.'

'Si.' I try a more gentle tack. 'Don't you remember what you always used to say to me? That I deserved the best and when was I going to get enough self-esteem to realize that if somebody didn't appreciate me, then it was time to simply walk away without giving them a second thought?'

Si nods.

'Well, don't you think you're old enough to start listening to your own advice? Because, as you always used to say to me, you don't have to wait for someone to treat you badly repeatedly. All it takes is once, and if they get away with it that once, if they know they can treat you like that, then it sets the pattern for the future.'

'You forgot to say ugly enough,' Si says, with the vestige of a small smile on his face.

'What?'

'You said didn't I think I was old enough. You forgot to say "and ugly enough" too.'

'I thought that went without saying,' I grin, and Si takes my hand and gives me a quick squeeze.

'Thanks,' he says, 'you're the best friend a girl could ever ask for.'

I arrive back home, change into my oldest, most disgusting clothes, grab a bucket of cleaning stuff and dash to the shop.

Lucy's already there, cleaning up the kitchen, and she makes us both strong cappuccinos before we start work. We sit at one of the cleaner tables to drink our coffee and gossip about the night before.

And then, Jesus, do we work. We scrub, sweep, mop and polish, until the shop is positively gleaming, until you wouldn't have a clue that last night there were well over a hundred people crammed in here.

And eventually, when we've finished, Lucy looks at me with a twinkle in her eye and says, 'So what's on your agenda for the evening?'

I shrug, planning nothing more exciting than a long hot bath and an early night in preparation for the big day tomorrow.

'Before you have your hot bath and early night,' Lucy smiles, reading my mind, 'can I tempt you with a delicious savoury cheesecake that I'm planning to have for supper with a large salad and an even larger glass of red wine. Care to join me?'

'I'd love to. But can I take a raincheck on the wine?'

Lucy's kitchen is even more disorganized than usual. The dustbin lid is wide open like a gaping mouth as rubbish threatens to spill out all over the kitchen floor, and a couple of supplementary bins, rather cleverly disguised as Sainsbury's bags, are dotted around at the base of the main bin.

The sink is overflowing with dishes, and the board with messages, scribbled on various bits of paper, envelopes, scraps torn out of magazines, each in Lucy's illegible handwriting. The fridge is now evidently doubling up as a noticeboard, and the magnetic poetry kit has been completely hidden by several scraps of paper clinging on to the fridge with the help of some rather dusty hamburger-shaped magnets.

One of Max's videos is playing at full volume in the living room, and even in the kitchen the noise is slightly deafening, which isn't helped by Max zooming around the kitchen with a plastic aeroplane making vroom vroom noises.

Christ. I know I've been neglecting my flat for the past few weeks, but this takes neglect on to a whole other level.

But Lucy is, as always, the port of calm in the storm, blissfully unaware of the chaos around her. I follow her into the kitchen, and she sits down at the kitchen table to slice tomatoes directly on the wood, creating yet more criss-crossed gouges in the old pine that has definitely seen better days.

Max climbs on to her lap and attempts to grab the knife, while Lucy smiles and gently brushes him aside.

'Don't be silly, darling,' she says, 'you know knives are bad for you,' and I wonder again how she manages to stay so serene in the face of all this noise and mayhem. 'Go and tell Ingrid to get you ready for bed, and Cath, why don't you open that bottle of red on the side,' she continues, as I bristle at the very mention of Ingrid's name.

Max runs upstairs shrieking for Ingrid, and minutes later there she is, Ingrid, coming down the stairs looking as sullen as ever. I examine her face closely, trying to see whether she had sex last night, even though I don't really know what I'm looking for. She certainly doesn't *seem* to have any sort of post-coital glow, which is what people always talk about, how they say you *know*. Not that I think I've ever actually *seen* a post-coital glow, but I'm sure I'd recognize one if I looked hard enough.

I remember talking about it with Portia all those years ago. We'd just run into someone we knew on the high street, and she seemed to be in a particularly good mood. Once we left, Si looked over his shoulder knowingly and said, 'Well *someone* had a good time last night,' and neither of us knew what he was talking about, or how he could tell.

Not long after that I had a wild night of passion with no one very interesting, and the next morning I ran out without washing and hurried back to the house, dashing into Portia's room and grabbing her mirror from the dressing table.

'Well?' I said, sitting on her bed and examining my face in the mirror. 'Do you see it?'

'Hmm.' She took my chin in her hand and turned my face this way and that, making me stand in different positions around the room for the light. 'Do you want me to be honest?' she said eventually.

'Yup,' I nodded. 'Because I can't see it, although Si says you can never see it on yourself.'

'You look completely exhausted.'

'Oh. Is that *it*?' I wasn't disappointed in the slightest, and Portia nodded. 'Oh well,' I started walking out to run a bath. 'Perhaps that's what everybody's talking about.'

And here I am, examining Ingrid's face as she strides into the kitchen and stops in front of Lucy, left hand planted aggressively on her hip. Lucy looks up and smiles benignly.

'I would like to know where you think Max's blue pyjamas are,' she says, as Lucy shrugs.

'The wash?' Lucy says hopefully, as Ingrid shakes her head. 'Ironing pile?' Ingrid shakes her head and pulls her right hand from behind her back. 'They are here,' she says. 'In the laundry basket. Where they have been now for more than one week.'

Lucy grimaces at me, then starts to apologize to Ingrid, who merely says, 'He is your son and tonight he will have to sleep in his day clothes,' before heading for the fridge and helping herself to a yoghurt, which probably explains how she manages to stay so thin.

I haven't taken my eyes off her, but I've stopped examining her for the post-coital glow and now I'm just looking at her in amazement, astounded by how she can talk to her employer like that. When she turns around again, she catches me looking at her, and she just stands there watching me.

She peels off the yoghurt top, slowly brings it up to her mouth, and licks it, all the while looking at me, obviously trying to embarrass me for staring at her. I look quickly away as she smirks and leaves the room.

'So.' I stand up and put the kettle on to hide the expression on my face. 'What do you think about James and Ingrid, then?'

Lucy looks utterly bewildered. 'What do I think about James and Ingrid what?'

'Well, they left together last night. I'm assuming she didn't come home?'

Lucy starts to laugh. 'Sweet Cath, do you really think that Josh would have come back to rescue us from a night of debauchery if Max had been sleeping here alone?'

Why didn't I think of that? Thank God.

'But they did leave together,' I continue. 'And James looked as if he were practically salivating.' This last bit isn't quite true, as I couldn't actually see his face when they left, but, if I had been able to, I'm pretty sure that's what he would have looked like. 'I'm certain they both fancied one another,' I say decisively.

'Really? I can't see them together at all. Not that I know either of their types, but I wouldn't have thought she was James's type, far too obvious for him.'

'That's what I'm worried about,' I find myself saying involuntarily, clapping my hand over my mouth as it comes out, because really, I'm not worried at all.

Lucy puts the knife down and smiles. 'Does this mean that you're finally admitting that you might have some feelings for the lovely James after all?'

'Absolutely not,' I say. 'We're just friends. Well, we were, anyway.' And with that the kettle boils, and I busy myself with the intricate task of making a cup of tea.

Chapter fifteen

Bill's behind the till, Lucy's busy arranging fresh pastries and croissants in baskets on the counter, and Rachel and I are racing round the shop checking that all the books are exactly where they should be, all the sofas at exactly the right angle.

'I don't believe it,' I say, turning to the door with a grin as it rattles, and already there are two people outside, ignoring the fact that the closed sign is up, peering through the window and attempting to open the locked door, despite the sign saying we don't open for another ten minutes.

'Must be a good omen,' Lucy laughs.

'What do you think?' I check my watch. 'Shall we do it? Shall we let them be our first customers?'

The two women don't show any sign of giving up, so I grab a key from the counter and go to the door to let them in, the smile on my face completely obliterating the fact that I'm as nervous as hell. Our first customers! What will they think? Will they buy anything? Will they stay and have coffee? Will they approve?

I catch Lucy's eye, and she gives me the thumbs up. I swing the door open, wishing the women good morning and welcoming them in.

'We just couldn't wait,' one of them says, bustling in with her shopping bags.

'Sorry we're so early,' the other says, 'it's just that we've been watching this for weeks, and we were dying to have a look round. Goodness, are we your first customers?'

I nod, noting that all four of us have identical grins on our faces.

'What do you think, Shirley?' The shorter one turns to her friend. 'Coffee first or browsing first?'

Shirley sniffs, then looks over at the counter, where Lucy is beaming.

'We've got delicious home-made Danish pastries,' Lucy says, tempting them over, and the pair of them succumb to Lucy's smile and sit down in the café area to have coffee.

'I must say,' Shirley says, as they deposit their shopping on the floor, 'you've done a beautiful job here. Look at how lovely and sunny it is. Just what this area needed.'

'That's exactly what we thought,' Lucy says. 'I hope everyone feels the same way.'

'Just as long as I don't walk out without *Angela's Ashes*,' Shirley says. 'Don't let me forget, Hilary. I've been meaning to read it for ages.' Lucy winks at me from behind the counter, and I scurry off to dig through the pile of biographies and memoirs on the table at the front until I find Frank McCourt, and take it over to Shirley and Hilary.

'Oh, what an angel you are,' Shirley says. 'I wish more shops would take a leaf out of your book,' and I walk away feeling a deep satisfaction.

An hour later and there have already been six more people in the shop. Four of them are still here, quietly turning pages, two on the sofas and two in the café, and the others just ran in to buy new titles.

But everyone does seem to agree with Shirley, or perhaps they're just saying it to be polite, but people seem genuinely impressed with us, with what we've done, and by the end of the day we realize we've sold twenty-one paperbacks and sixteen hardbacks, plus taken orders for four more books that we haven't got in stock, which, all in all, as Bill said, was 'pretty damn marvellous'.

Not to mention the fact that every single one of Lucy's home-made cakes and pastries has been eaten, and there hasn't been a single minute during the day when the shop has been completely empty.

'I've got to tell you,' I say, turning to Lucy as we're closing up the shop, having shared a bottle of wine with Bill and Rachel to celebrate. 'I think we're on to a winner here.'

'As if you could ever have thought anything different!' Lucy laughs. 'Oh, Cath, you're such a worrier. It's going to be fine,' and she gives me a big hug.

I walk around the shop, picking up books that have been left on tables and putting them back in their rightful positions, and marvelling at the fact that this is mine! Ours! Our very own business! But, more importantly, as Lucy pulls out the mop and starts cleaning the floor, I understand for the first time that she really is right after all.

But the fact that she is right does not mean that she is not completely mad. Two weeks later she is busy organizing this dinner party on Saturday, when any normal person (i.e., me) would be (is, in fact) completely shattered, but Lucy's so fired up and excited she can't seem to sit still for more than about five seconds.

She hasn't been sleeping either, and at the moment she's doing an incredibly good impersonation of Superwoman, having woken up yesterday at the crack of dawn and spent two hours cooking a variation of some well-known chicken dish for dinner tonight, and that was before the shop even opened.

And the shop? Well, as everyone predicted, so far it seems to be doing okay. Despite the initial flurry of interest on the first day we opened, things have settled down a bit, and there have been a couple of very quiet afternoons. It's not, as Josh put it, what you might call an immediate runaway success, but then we are talking about a bookshop here, and you can't expect people to come in and spend thousands.

But what has happened is the curiosity factor. People have been popping in to see what all the fuss has been about, and have ended up staying far longer than they'd originally planned. The old leather sofas seem to have gone down a storm, and last weekend a handful of people decamped permanently from La Brioche, spending almost all of Sunday sitting around the sofas at Bookends with their Skinny Lattes and copies of the *Guardian*.

As I said, in a rather embarrassing interview in the *Ham & High*, we can't compete with the huge Books Etc. up the road, but then we're not trying to. This was always going to be more of a community bookshop, somewhere for people to meet, chat, have a snack, and then stop on the way out as an interesting book catches their eye.

And the partnership between Lucy and I really seems to be working, despite the reservations Si had.

I love the feeling of waking up every morning and knowing that I'm off to work, and that it's the job I've always dreamt of, and it's my own business. There's a hell of a lot to learn, and I know it will take a while before I'm completely comfortable with it, but I'm sure I'm getting there. We both are.

Lucy's doing what she does best – cooking and playing the convivial host, and she's completely adoring it. She's on her feet all day, which always makes me feel slightly guilty, as I tend to be either sitting behind the till or sitting in the stock room. Either way, I'm sitting.

Josh went out and bought Lucy a foot spa as a congratulatory present, which Si and I thought a bit of a let-down – as Si said, wouldn't diamond earrings have been preferable? But Lucy was thrilled, as her feet, she said, were absolutely ready to drop off by the end of the day, although she didn't mind, she laughed. It was worth every second of sore feet.

And now it's time for Lucy's dinner party. I spoke to Portia once last week. She phoned me after Lucy had invited her, and she said I should go to her flat for a drink first, and that it would be lovely to see me on my own after all these years, and how excited she was about seeing me properly, talking to me properly.

You know how I felt after that phone call? I felt exactly the same as I used to feel when we were at university. I felt *honoured* by Portia's interest.

I felt as if a small piece of sunshine were shining on me when Portia treated me like this, as if I were special, and, although I've relished breaking free from Portia's shadow over the last ten years, there's something about stepping into this old role that feels very familiar, very comfortable, and I wonder whether I'm happiest in the shadows after all.

'What about that lovely James?' Lucy asked last Tuesday when we were closing up the shop, ringing up the wholesaler to put through some orders that customers had requested. 'I'd love to invite him over, and the two of you seemed to get on so well. Can't I ask him, Cath, my love?'

'No!' I practically barked at her, almost dropping the pile of books I was carrying up from the stock room.

'You know,' she said carefully, 'there is nothing going on between him and Ingrid.'

'Oh?' I have to admit, my interest was piqued, even though I'd tried to put him out of my mind, particularly because I hadn't actually been in touch with him since the day he brought the flowers round, which I still felt fairly guilty about, although with every passing day it was getting harder to call.

'Nope. I asked her.'

'You asked her? What did she say?'

'Well, it was most peculiar, actually. For a moment she looked completely stunned, and then I realized she hadn't got the foggiest what, or rather who, I was talking about.'

'Maybe it was so awful she wiped it from her memory.'

'Cath, darling, come on. Seriously, I realized she didn't have a clue, so I reminded her that she'd left with him, and then asked if something had happened, and if she were interested in him.'

'And?' I was trying to look as if I didn't really care.

'And she looked at me as if I'd gone completely mad and then laughed uproariously for about five minutes.'

'Are you serious?' I was horrified. 'That's appalling. Jesus, I mean James isn't exactly Mr Universe, but she'd be bloody lucky to get someone like James. Who does she think she is?'

'I know,' Lucy said. 'I mean, I couldn't really say anything, but James is divine. He may not be her type, but still, there was no need to laugh like that.'

'Lucy, when are you going to realize that the woman is completely vile?'

'Cath, as long as Max is happy I don't really care. And anyway, these au pairs apparently never last long anyway. I was talking to a woman in the shop yesterday who's been through five au pairs in three months.

'Apparently the first one brought her boyfriend to stay when they were away for the weekend, the second was lovely but didn't have a bath in three weeks, the third was wonderful but decided her room wasn't big enough, and the fourth walked out after three weeks for no reason whatsoever.'

'And the fifth?'

'The fifth is apparently perfect. Although how long it will last she said she didn't know.'

'When did she start? The fifth?'

'On Monday. Anyway, according to this woman, Ann, I'm incredibly lucky to have a godsend like Ingrid, and I should be doing everything I can to make her life more comfortable because good au pairs are about as rare as gold dust on the streets of London.'

It's a good job Lucy had turned her back to pick up a stray magazine, as she missed the sneer on my face. 'I suppose you'll be buying her little treats now?'

'As it happens I did buy her one of those little gift sets of bath oils and delicious-smelling soaps yesterday. It smelt so gorgeous and I couldn't just walk straight past the shop after what that woman had said.'

'You realize she'll probably walk out now,' I chuckled evilly. 'She'll probably think you're trying to tell her she stinks to high heaven, and she'll be so offended she'll be gone by the time you get home, doubtless taking half your clothes with her.'

'Oh God,' groaned Lucy. 'Do you really think so?'

'Only if you're really lucky.'

'Anyway, the point is, Cath, that obviously nothing

happened between them, and I would love to ask him round, and please, please, please say that you wouldn't mind.'

'Oh God, Lucy. How can you emotionally blackmail me like this?'

'Does that mean I can ask him?'

'Okay,' I grumbled. 'But don't think this means I've given you my blessing.'

'Fine,' she said, and the grin on her face was huge as she picked up the keys and I followed her out the door. 'I'm ringing him as soon as I get home.'

Now you know and I know that clothes have never exactly been a big thing for me, but I think I do kind of owe it to James to make something of an effort after the last time he laid eyes on me.

In fact, every time I think about opening the door and seeing him standing there, and more importantly him seeing me, with my wild woman of Borneo hair and my smudged mascara, bleary eyes and grey skin, I feel positively ashamed.

And perhaps this is yet another symptom of what Si has started calling The Portia Effect, because, let's face it, the last time I made an effort with my hair, with make-up, with clothes, was probably about ten years ago.

But tonight I want to show James that I can look nice, and maybe, if I try really hard, I'll manage to wipe the image of me from the other morning out of his mind and replace it with one infinitely better.

So I did something this morning that I haven't done for years. I took a day off from the shop – only possible because Si is now dying of jealousy and wants to get in on the act and couldn't wait to take my place, even for a day – walked out of my flat at ten o'clock in the morning, jumped on the bus to Oxford Circus, turned a blind eye to the Saturday crowds and hit the shops, even though I didn't have a clue what I was looking for.

But in the first shop I went into I found a pair of grey flannel trousers that would have made Si proud, and then a few doors up I had to stop and admire a sophisticated window display that was so alluring it made even me want to step inside.

I walked past, hesitated, then stepped back and caught the eye of one of the sales assistants, who smiled at me, encouraging me to go in.

'Can I help you?' he said, and I found myself gesturing to the window display.

'The sweaters,' I said. 'How much are they?'

Clever sales assistant that he was, he pretended to ignore the question, and instead strode to the back of the shop and brought over an array of gorgeous pastel sweaters that were so soft, so feminine, I was almost upset that he disturbed the pile of perfection by unfolding them and laying them out on the table for me to admire.

'Why don't you just try one on?' he said with a smile, picking up the one I'd been tentatively fingering – as soft as butter, a delicate baby pink, it was the most beautiful sweater I'd ever seen. And remember, I'm not a person who goes in for sweaters. Or any clothes, for that matter.

I walked into the changing room as if in a dream, and when I pulled the sweater over my head and came out, even I had to admit that it was probably the nicest thing I'd ever worn in my entire life. There was something about the colour, about the softness, that made me feel soft, made me feel feminine, and even with my old black leggings that had definitely seen better days it still looked lovely.

'Do you have trousers to go with?' the sales assistant

asked, not even bothering to ask whether I was going to take the sweater, probably presuming that it looked so good, how could I not.

I pointed to my bag and told him I'd just bought some, and he insisted on having a look.

'Let's see them together,' he insisted, and for a moment – being bossed around by a gorgeous sales assistant who had far, far better taste than I could ever hope to have – it was just like having Si with me, and how could I resist?

They looked amazing. And what's more, the sales assistant approved, which was about as much as I could ever have hoped for. I couldn't believe how much this simple sweater cost, but I figured that it would be worth it after all. Because, to be honest, what would be the point in revealing your new image in the same old over-stretched black sweater that you've worn almost daily for the last five years?

I went, I tried, I paid through the nose. And I was intending to go straight back home, really I was, but as I was walking down the street a young, trendy-looking girl stopped me and pressed a paper flyer into my hand.

'We're doing a special offer,' she said brightly. 'At Snippers. Everything's half price today and you get a free consultation.'

On any other day I would have smiled vaguely at her and walked straight past, crumpling the paper into a tiny ball as I walked, and tossing it into the nearest rubbish bin, but today I stopped in front of her, listened, and then looked at the flyer. 'Bored with the same haircut?' it proclaimed. 'Looking for a new image? At Snippers we have a team of top experienced hairstylists ready to show you the new YOU!'

What's a girl supposed to do when something like that

is thrust into her hand, and she's been thinking about taming the frizz for, ooh, at least a week now? Up the steps of Snippers I went, and into the hands of – hopefully – top experienced hairstylist, Pezz.

'Mmm,' he said, picking up handfuls of hair and looking distinctly unimpressed. 'Yays, I see. Eet is very deefeecult to handle, no?'

I nodded meekly.

'You would like to have seelky smooth hair, no?'

I shrugged, then realized from Pezz's impassive face that this was evidently the wrong answer and proceeded to nod vigorously instead.

'We will give you the hair of Jennifer Lopez,' he said triumphantly, looking pensive again. 'Maybe you don't like the colour of theese hairs, hmm?'

Actually I hadn't stopped to think. Other than to note that far more grey hairs seemed to be appearing by the day, I really wasn't that bothered. Pezz, on the other hand, evidently was.

'I am theenking vegetable rinse, yes? I theenk nice reech brown. Strong warm tones weeth leettle beet of red, hmm?' Is it just me, or is his accent becoming more and more unintelligible? It seems that as Pezz becomes excited, his accent deteriorates, but I've never been the type to sit and chat with hairdressers about holidays and DIY, so I refuse to worry about it.

I accept the offer of a cappuccino, eat the two tiny little biscuits in about two seconds flat, and then settle back in the chair with a sizeable stack of crappy magazines that I'd never be seen dead reading anywhere else.

Two hours later – Christ, this is seriously decadent of me – and I'm sitting in the chair at Snippers looking into the face of someone who does look like me, only a far better version.

Because I would never have believed that *my* hair could be silky, smooth and actually *shiny*! My hair is *shiny*! But Pezz has worked wonders, and good God, I seem to have got a chestnut mane falling to slightly below my shoulders.

It looks amazing. I can't stop smiling at myself. The only problem is, and I only realize this as I keep looking at myself in the mirror, it's exactly the same as Portia's. Shit. And how the hell am I supposed to pass this off as coincidence?

But by the time I get the tube home, I'm allowing myself a damn sight more than a little smile. I'm actually getting a few looks. From men. Oh my God! Oh not many, not enough to start making headline news, but – and at first I thought this was my imagination – there have definitely been two men who have walked past me and have held my eyes for far longer than was absolutely necessary.

Sitting on the tube, I lean my body slightly to the right, so that I've got an almost clear view in the reflection of the black glass, and, though I have never been a vain person, it's definitely not too late to change, and I can't believe how I look!

I love this new hair. No, I don't just love it, I think I may well be completely in love with it. I can't stop stroking it, marvelling at how soft it feels, how it feels, in fact, like *hair*, rather than like pubic hair that had accidentally been planted in the wrong spot.

And the only reason I'm late for Portia's now is that I spent so long marvelling at my reflection in the mirror, I didn't realize what time it was. That and the fact that once I'd dressed in my new clothes and shaken my hair around a bit, I realized that the finishing touch would have to be a bit of make-up, the only problem being that it's been so long since I wore any I didn't even know what I had.

Luckily, lurking in the back of the bathroom cabinet was an old brown eyeliner and an old lipgloss that I vaguely remember being stuck to the cover of one of the glossy magazines that I must have bought aeons ago.

I dragged the eyeliner across my upper lid, and then a bit underneath, but I completely overdid it and a rather messy Cleopatra stared uncertainly back at me, so I grabbed a cotton bud and smudged it, after which it actually looked pretty good. In fact, I was astonished at how my eyes suddenly seemed double the size.

Hmm. What else could I do with the eyeliner? I decided to use it as a lipliner, and very slowly outlined my lips, before doing the cotton bud trick again, then filling it in with the lip gloss.

I smiled at my reflection, and then, lacking mascara and blusher, I did what I remember the girls at school doing when we were eleven years old, too young for make-up, but desperate to look grown-up and impress. I pinched my cheeks until they were red, and then licked my fingers, carefully brushing them against my eyelashes and holding them to try to curl the lashes. Not a fantastic curl, but a discernible difference, certainly.

And by the time I grabbed my coat and ran out the door, I was already fifteen minutes late, but what did I care? I looked the best I'd looked in ten years, and that, quite frankly, was the only thing that suddenly seemed important.

Chapter sixteen

'Cath, you look wonderful.' Portia comes to the door of her apartment, air kisses me on each cheek and beckons me inside, through a wide, airy corridor to an enormous living room with huge windows overlooking communal gardens off Sutherland Avenue.

Several scented candles are dotted around, and the air is filled with the sweet scent of orange and cinnamon. On the glass coffee table, next to the enormous bowl of white lilies, is a bottle of champagne, already opened, and two glasses.

There isn't a colour to be seen, and everything looks terrifyingly expensive. The sofas are so white, I'm almost loath to sit down just in case I should have some sort of ghastly period leakage or something, which of course would only happen if you were to find yourself sitting on an immaculate white sofa.

It is exactly where I would have expected Portia to live, the sort of apartment that you only ever normally see in the pages of a glossy interior magazine, the sort of apartment that I've never set foot in, in my entire life.

Portia pours me a glass of champagne and collapses elegantly on the sofa next to me, her knee-length skinny skirt more than adequately showing off the length of her legs, helped somewhat by high strappy sandals.

Portia looks rich. She looks as if she doesn't have a care in the world. And, although I am in my new grey flannel trousers, my new pink cashmere-mix sweater, with my glossy locks sitting sleekly on my shoulders, next to Portia I feel even more frumpy than I did this morning.

There is something about her appearance that looks effortless. If you look closely you will see that she is wearing make-up, and quite a lot of it at that, but unless you are standing nose to nose, she looks naturally beautiful, as if she has just fallen out of bed, brushed her hair, slicked on some lip gloss and run out the door.

And her whole look, the pencil-slim skirt, the elaborate brocade skin-tight top, trimmed with lace and thin velvet ribbon, the high-heeled sandals that cling to her feet with wisps of leather, screams *Vogue*. It screams super-expensive understatement.

She raises her glass to mine and smiles. 'Cheers,' she says, and then sips some champagne, sighing and sitting back, looking for all the world as if she should be in a film or, at the very least, a television advert.

'Your flat's amazing,' I say. 'I can't believe how huge it is, how high these ceilings are.'

'I know. The first time I came to see it, it was in the morning and light seemed to stream through every window. The minute I came into this room I just fell in love with the proportions. Do you want the guided tour?'

I nod, and she leads me through into the kitchen, the dining room, points out the terrace at the back, and shows me the bedroom. All of it is beautiful, and at the last door Portia hesitates and grins before turning the knob.

'This,' she says, 'is the real me. It's the room I never show people because it's in such an appalling state, so here goes. Tah dah,' and she opens the door. 'My study.'

No wonder she manages to keep her flat immaculate. All the junk, all the papers, all the books, are in here.

The walls are lined with bookshelves, and every available inch is crammed full of something. An enormous desk takes up one side of the room, and again piles of papers, letters, scripts, are threatening to topple over on either side of a state-of-the-art computer.

'This is my real home,' she says with a smile, gesturing around. 'It's the one room in which I feel really comfortable.'

Which of course doesn't surprise me, because the rest of the flat is like a museum. In here there's a navy blue sofa, the cushions squashed flat, and Portia flops down on it with a grin.

'I do all my read-throughs on here,' she says. 'My favourite place in the world,' and for a second I catch a glimpse of Portia before she felt she had to play a role, before she became the sophisticated adult she is today. Portia was always sophisticated, of that I'm sure, but at university it was far less well honed. You knew she came from a wealthy family, but you didn't *know*.

Now she wears it like a coat of armour, and it occurs to me that if I were in Portia's shoes, if I had developed an armour of sophistication to present to the world, I too would probably get in touch with friends I hadn't seen for ten years because surely those would be the only people with whom I could drop my guard.

We go back to the living room and I ask her. I ask her whether she is comfortable playing this role, and for a second she looks hurt, but she swiftly regains her composure and lets out a small laugh.

'This was a role I was always destined to play,' she says. 'And Christ, it could be so much worse. Far rather the single girl-about-town than a country housewife stuck in some crumbling pile in the middle of nowhere, with just the children, the Labradors and the horses for company.

'Anyway,' she says, peering at me closely, 'what sort of role do *you* think I'm playing?'

'God, I'm sorry, Portia, I didn't mean to offend you. It's just that everything about you is so perfect, so polished, and nobody I know lives like this. I mean, if this were my flat these sofas would be grey by now, and nothing would match, and there'd be washing-up all over the kitchen, and it just looks like it must be such hard work, living like this.'

She shrugs. 'Not hard work. You get used to it, and this is, I suppose what's expected of me.'

'What do you mean?'

'Well, every time anyone writes about the new league of single superwomen, I'm usually in there at the top of the list, and they always want to photograph me at home and examine the contents of my fridge, and quite frankly I wouldn't want to disappoint.'

'So what does a single superwoman keep in the fridge?'

Portia laughs. 'Help yourself,' she says, and I get up and open the fridge.

'Portia,' I start to laugh. 'Lucy would have a fit if she saw this.' Because there is, quite simply, nothing remotely edible in the fridge. There are two shelves devoted to champagne and white wine, another devoted to bottles of mineral water, both still and sparkling, and a few tins at the back which on closer inspection reveal themselves to be – surprise, surprise – caviar.

'What do you live on?' I come back into the living room, shaking my head in amazement.

'I eat out mostly,' she says. 'And occasionally I'll pick something up on my way home from work.'

'What if you have dinner parties? And I'm assuming

you must have dinner parties, given the size of your dining room table.'

'Darling,' she says, fixing me with a mocking look, 'what do you think caterers were invented for?'

I laugh, and then a question occurs to me. 'Portia, I can see why you're portrayed as a single superwoman, but why are you?'

'Why am I what?'

'Why *are* you single? I just don't understand it.'

Is it my imagination or does Portia suddenly look slightly uncomfortable? 'I just haven't found the right person yet,' she says breezily, but somehow I don't believe her. Then again, this is typical of Portia. She probably has some terrible tale of loss and heartbreak which makes my dalliance with Martin look like child's play, but this is what Portia does when she doesn't want to talk about something: she switches off.

She pours some more champagne for us both, and then sits back, looking at me over the rim of her glass, and before I have a chance to ask more questions she deftly changes the subject.

'How have these last few years been for all of you?' she says, continuing without waiting for an answer. 'You and Si told me a bit about your lives at the bookshop the other week, but what about Josh? Is he happy? I must say that Lucy seems . . . she seems *charming*. Not perhaps what I expected, but obviously the relationship works . . . Does it?'

'Does it what?'

'Does it *work*?'

'Josh and Lucy? God, they're amazing. Well, you'll see for yourself later on, but they're the most perfect couple imaginable. I know what you mean about Lucy not being what you'd expect – you should have seen the horrors he kept picking up throughout his early twenties. All these identical Sloanes called Serena who were desperate to get Josh into Daddy's business.'

'Lucy definitely doesn't fit into that category,' Portia says. 'So how come he ended up falling for Lucy?'

I think back to the story of how Josh and Lucy met, how they fell in love, and even as I think about it I feel a slow smile spread upon my face, because after all these years, after all this time, the memory of it still warms the cockles of my heart.

Josh and Lucy, as I now tell Portia, are in no doubt that they were meant to be together, and Lucy has always been convinced that fate played a pretty strong hand, because had it not been for that skiing trip, they would never have met.

Of course I don't tell Portia all the details. I tell her they met on a skiing trip, that Lucy was the chalet girl, that Josh was with a ghastly woman called Venetia. And then I look at my watch and let out a yelp, and we order a minicab and dash over to Josh and Lucy's.

And throughout the entire cab journey, Portia asks me questions about Josh, about Lucy, about Max, and I'm not entirely sure why I don't give her the full story, why I don't tell her more, but I find myself clamming up slightly. Perhaps I'm not entirely comfortable with her interest. Perhaps I'm starting to think that Si might be right, that she might be up to something after all.

Chapter seventeen

As usual, Si opens the door to Josh and Lucy's house and welcomes us in, giving Portia a brief hug before turning to me and leaning forward to give me a kiss. And then he stops.

'Oh my God!'

I smile.

'Oh my God, oh my God, oh my God!'

Lucy comes running out of the kitchen, and Josh comes running out of the living room, and within seconds all three of them are staring at me open-mouthed.

'Can I touch it?' Si whispers reverently, as he reaches out his hand and softly strokes my head as if I were a cat, while Portia looks on with faint amusement.

'Look at our Cath!' Lucy beams proudly. 'Quite the supermodel! Cath, you look gorgeous, look at your fantastic hair, and your sweater! Good Lord, Cath, pink will have to be your colour from now on.'

'You look amazing,' Josh says, when he finally recovers, and he catches Portia's eye and immediately goes over to welcome her.

I watch, and I can see Si watching out of the corner of his eye as Josh leans down to give her a kiss, and Portia, instead of kissing the air as she has done with the rest of us, plants her lips softly, but very definitely, on Josh's cheek, and I look at Si in alarm as he raises an eyebrow.

'Oh look, you daft thing.' Lucy walks past Josh with

my coat and, seeing Josh, laughs, then reaches up to wipe the lipstick off his face, as a slow flush creeps up Josh's face.

We go into the living room, and because we're so late I'm certain that James will already be in there, so imagine my surprise when the vile Will turns round from examining the bookshelves and gives me his evil lizard smile.

'Hello, Catherine,' he says, extending a hand that I reluctantly take, wondering how a person's eyes can make them look so cold. 'Nice to see you again.'

'And you,' I say, nodding, extracting my hand and shooting a filthy look at Si for not telling me Will was coming. 'This is Portia.' I do my best to appear polite by introducing them, and I edge towards the door.

I can see that Will obviously approves of Portia, as he suddenly flashes a charming and disarming smile at her, and for the first time I see a hint of what Alison Bailey was referring to when she said he could be the most charming man on earth.

But I am not fooled.

'I am not fooled,' I hiss to Si, as I go into the kitchen to try to discover what has happened to James.

'Be nice,' Si warns. 'It's only one evening, and I knew if I'd told you he was coming you wouldn't have come, would you?'

'Yes.'

'Truth.'

'No.'

'Listen, sweets.' Si stops and looks at me very seriously. 'I know you don't like him, but please try and make an effort. You don't have to love him, but I think he might be around for a while, and it would make me so happy if you could just come to some sort of amicable arrangement. Not friends necessarily, just being on polite terms.'

'Okay,' I grumble, as Si puts his arms around me and gives me a hug. 'I'll try. Is James in the kitchen?'

Si disengages himself from my arms and says, 'No. Why?'

'Oh, nothing,' and I walk into the kitchen, ignoring the eyes boring into the back of my neck.

Lucy hands me a bowl of Indonesian crisps and instructs me to take them into the living room, and just as I head out of the room I turn my head and say in a nonchalant manner, 'Isn't James coming tonight?'

'Oh bugger!' Lucy slaps her forehead. 'Oh blast! Oh damn! I knew there was something I'd forgotten.' She puts her head in her hands, then looks up at me with guilty eyes.

'Oh, Cath, I'm sorry, can you forgive me?' She looks mortified, and I feel a flash of anger at her because this is just so typical. Typical of her to be so scatty and to forget. This is exactly what Si was talking about, why he warned me off going into business with her. I mean, Christ, how could you forget to invite someone to a dinner party?

'Bugger. And you look so gorgeous, I can't believe it.' She's genuinely devastated and I start to forgive her. It's not the end of the world. I'm just disappointed.

'What happened?'

'I phoned him and then the machine picked up just as my call waiting went and so I left it and I just completely forgot to call him back. I don't believe it,' and then her eyes light up. 'Let's call him now!'

'No.' I lay a firm hand on Lucy's arm, which is reaching for the phone. 'If it's okay with you, I'd be much happier if you didn't.'

'Oh, Cath. I am so, so sorry. Can you forgive me?'

'Don't worry,' I say, but I feel like laying my head on my arms and sinking into a deep sleep. It's not even as if I'm terribly upset, I'm just weary. Weary of this whole relationship game. Weary even though I've only taken one tiny tentative step back into the lion's den, and already I'm learning that I'm just not equipped to win this one.

I like being alone. I always have. But it's not the present that worries me. What worries me is that I'll have to spend the next fifty years on my own, and that's something that I really don't want to have to think about. But in the meantime I'm used to my own company, and I haven't had to think about anyone else for months. *Years.*

But the thing is that since I've met James, since everyone started banging on and on about my not-so-secret admirer, I'd started to find it quite exciting. I'd forgotten that I don't get involved because the pain just isn't worth it. All that flattery and attention distracted me from any pain that might have been lurking around the corner, but of course the pain got me in the end. It always does.

I take the bowl into the living room and sink miserably into the sofa, as Josh looks at me with a worried expression, then leaves the room, presumably to find out what's wrong.

Portia and Will are deep in discussion, and, bizarre as this may sound, it almost looks as if he's flirting with her. Bizarre only because I had him down as a complete misogynist, but then again maybe it's just me. Maybe he only gives time to women like Portia.

I watch Si trying to push his way into the conversation, only to be ignored, and eventually he comes over to me with a shrug and an apologetic smile.

'They seem to be getting on like a house on fire.'

'I know. Thank God someone seems to finally like him.'

'Why? Have Josh and Lucy already expressed disapproval, then?'

'Not yet,' he says, wincing, 'but I've got a horrible feeling this evening isn't going to run smoothly.'

'God, you and your bloody feelings,' I laugh, as Josh and Lucy walk in, having finally got the food in the oven, the glasses on the table, and the devilspawn in bed.

'Will.' Josh pours him some more wine. 'Si tells us you live in Clerkenwell. How do you find it.'

'I love it,' Will says. 'I've got the most incredible loft in probably the best building in Clerkenwell, and there's always something going on in the neighbourhood.'

'Will's been thinking about moving to Soho, though,' Si interjects in his best husbandly way.

'Really? Why?'

'I'm not seriously thinking, it's just that the only problem with Clerkenwell is it's pretty much in the back of beyond and I miss being in the centre of things. Don't you feel the same way living here?'

The hairs on my back bristle, but luckily he wasn't talking to me and I leave it to Lucy to deal with that last comment.

'Here? Why on earth should we feel that living *here*?'

'Well, the suburbs.'

'But this isn't the suburbs,' Lucy says pointedly. 'It's West Hampstead. We're practically in town.'

'Oh, come on,' Will sneers. 'This is the nineties version of suburbia. A high street lined with cafés and local ethnic restaurants, and the whole area filled to bursting with young marrieds like yourself with their 2.4 children and a four-wheel drive. It's the updated version of *Abigail's Party*. Mike Leigh would have a ball.'

I'm dying to open my mouth, but I'm frightened that if I do the damage will be irreparable, not only to any future relationship I may or may not have with Will, but more importantly to the relationship I have with Si.

'You are joking?' Lucy says very quietly, as Will shrugs and says he's not. 'First of all, *Will*,' and I can tell by the inflection on his name that Lucy is seriously pissed off, which is something that doesn't happen all that often, 'I can tell you that West Hampstead is a fifteen-minute drive to the West End, and a ten-minute ride on the Thameslink to the City, which I think you'll find would not merit a labelling of suburbia anywhere.

'Secondly, irrespective of that, what exactly is wrong with an area that caters to the needs of, as you put it, *young marrieds*?'

Will shrugs disdainfully. 'It's just, well. Look at you all. You think you're so cutting-edge and trendy, with your stainless-steel top-of-the-range kitchen equipment and your Alessi corkscrews, but this, all of you, are just the nineties version of suburbia,' this last said with an unmistakable sneer, and I almost gasp in shock.

'I'm not entirely sure of the point you're making,' Lucy says, her voice ice-cold, 'but I'm certain that whatever it is I don't agree with it. So what if we have Alessi corkscrews and four-wheel drives . . .' She takes a breath and is about to carry on, but Portia steps in and expertly changes the subject to calm everyone down.

'Speaking of four-wheel drives,' she says coolly, 'I've been thinking about trading in my car for one of those jeeps. I quite fancy the idea of being so high up on the road – it adds a whole new perspective to my superiority complex.'

Everyone laughs, and the tension is shattered, and I wonder how I had forgotten Portia's ability to do this –

to diffuse situations, to calm things down, to take control. For a few seconds I am immensely grateful to Portia for coming back, because I'm quite certain that given a few minutes longer I would have punched Will in the mouth.

We somehow manage to sit and make small talk, and Si goes to sit next to Will, obviously protective of him tonight, and I watch Si watching Will with big, adoring eyes, and I can't help but note that Will barely even turns to look at him.

If I were to give him the benefit of the doubt I'd say that Will was trying so hard to make a good impression on everyone else that he was temporarily abandoning Si, but somehow I don't think it is that. I just don't think he's all that interested, really, but God, how I hope I'm wrong.

Eventually we stand up and all file into the dining room, as I give Lucy's arm a squeeze, because none of us has even been into the dining room for about two years – we always eat in the kitchen – and I find myself seated next to Josh at the top and then, thank God, next to Si.

Will walks past my chair on his way to his place, and as he passes he leans down and touches my sleeve. 'Very nice,' he says, and I open my mouth to thank him for such an unexpected compliment. 'Shame it's not pure cashmere,' and with that he walks off round the table.

Portia is on the other side of Josh, opposite me, and thankfully next to Will, and in the commotion as people take their seats Si leans over and whispers, 'Bet you a fiver she flirts with Josh all night.' I raise my eyes to see Portia watching us, and a guilty flush threatens to rise, but I give her a strained smile and ignore Si.

But Si is wrong about Portia and Josh. Not, perhaps, through choice, but for lack of opportunity. Will has evidently decided that Portia is the only person at this table worthy of his attention and proceeds to monopolize her from the moment she sits down.

The rest of us fall into our easy conversations. We talk about the bookshop, and I make everyone laugh with tales of mad customers. Already three people have come in and asked for a book, and, on being told it isn't stocked but it could be here the next day, have gone on to ask if Waterstone's have the book.

Lucy chuckles, as I apparently kept smiling through gritted teeth, even as I politely told them to go and find out for themselves. And where, the customers wanted to know, would they find the book? Which section would it be in, and on which floor?

The conversation dies down as Lucy brings in the chicken dish, and we all make the appropriate noises of delight at the smell as Lucy lifts the lid to release the steam.

All, that is, except for Will. He says nothing until he is served, and when we all start eating, all groaning with pleasure, Will chews for a while, then puts his knife and fork together on his plate and pushes his plate aside. We all stop and stare.

'Is everything okay?' Lucy asks.

Will sneers at the food. 'Not really, no. This is *supposed* to be a River Café recipe, isn't it?' he says, as Lucy looks worried. 'I sort of recognize it.' Lucy nods, as Will continues. 'I can't put my finger on it, but there's something not right about it. You've changed the herbs, done something different, what is it?'

Lucy's face falls, and I look at Si in exasperation, as he simply looks crestfallen.

'Well,' Lucy says uncertainly, 'the thing is, I don't usually tend to stick to recipes all that precisely any more. I'm not sure what I did differently, but I just used that recipe as a guideline, a base. You don't like it?'

'Put it like this,' Will says, picking up the knife and pointing it dismissively at the food as I hold my breath. 'Inedible would be one of the nicer things I would say about it.'

Si and I catch each other's eyes nervously, and nobody says anything for what feels like an interminably long time, when Josh stands up and the silence that has already descended on the table grows even more fraught.

'Enough,' Josh says slowly, and we all turn to look at him. 'Will, I would like you to leave.'

I would love to say that I sat there and smirked, but in fact I was so shocked at Josh saying this, doing something about this ghastly awful man, that I just sat there open-mouthed, and it didn't take long to realize that everyone else was doing the same thing.

'You're not serious,' Will says, half smiling, picking up his fork and prodding the chicken on his plate.

'Put. That. Fork. Down.' Josh says, and my eyes widen because I don't think I have ever seen Josh that angry before. I didn't know Josh could even *get* that angry. Portia looks as stunned as me, and Lucy and Si are both looking at their plates.

'I welcomed you into my home as a guest, and you have spent the entire evening making me regret ever allowing you across the threshold. You have insulted my wife, my friends and me. You are not welcome here, and I want you to leave this instant.'

Finally Will seems to realize that he's not joking. Si's face is purple with embarrassment, and, as Will scrapes his chair back, Si stands up as well, but he can't look any of us in the eye.

'Fine,' Will says, as he walks out of the room, Si

217

scuttling behind him to get their coats. 'I was here on sufferance anyway.' I keep my eyes glued to the table-cloth, terrified that if he catches my eye he'll start on me, and I really don't think I could handle that, because this man, I swear, is vicious.

Will storms out, slamming the front door, as we all wince, fully aware that there is a child asleep upstairs, and Si hovers in the hallway apologizing to Josh. And from what I hear, Josh is telling Si that it's not his fault, and that Si is welcome to stay, of course he is, but if he wants to leave we'll all understand.

Of course Si, loving, lovely, needy, insecure Si, leaves. And as soon as the door quietly closes behind him and we are all just about to breathe a sigh of relief, a familiar clattering comes down the stairs.

'Lucy.' Ingrid towers in the doorway. 'Why are there doors being slammed when Max is asleep.'

'God, I'm sorry Ingrid,' Lucy apologizes. 'It was one of our guests, he left in a bit of a hurry.' She pauses. 'Ingrid,' and I can already hear the placatory tone in her voice. 'Would you like some supper? We've got masses of this chicken left over.'

'And it's delicious,' I add, just in case there's any doubt.

'No,' Ingrid says, scanning the room. 'I have eaten already.'

'You know Cath, of course,' Lucy says, as Ingrid barely nods in my direction. 'And this is an old friend of Josh, Portia.' Lucy presumably wants Ingrid to feel as if she is one of us, and I'm waiting for her to invite Ingrid to join us, but thank God one nightmare guest is enough for one evening. 'Portia, this is Ingrid, our wonderful au pair.'

Portia smiles at Ingrid, and, Christ, does this woman's charm never cease, Ingrid actually smiles back, and I realize that in all the time Ingrid's been here, I've never actually seen her smile, and if I didn't know better I'd think Ingrid was as sweet as sugar from the beatific smile she now bestows upon Portia.

'Is there anything we can do for you, Ingrid?' Josh asks, and I marvel at how they both seem to tiptoe around her, when it's their bloody house.

'I would like some peace and quiet so I can read and Max can sleep,' she says, turning on her heel, then turning back. 'It was nice to meet you, Portia. I hope you all have a nice evening,' and she goes upstairs.

'You're unbelievable,' I say to Portia once she's gone.

'Why?'

'You're like one of those Indian snake charmers. You just manage to charm everyone.'

Portia laughs. 'What do you mean?'

'Oh, come on.' Even Josh is laughing. 'She's right. First of all you were the only one who managed to charm that awful Will bloke, and then you manage to charm' – and at this point he lowers his voice to a whisper – 'the scary Ingrid.'

'Is she scary?' Portia laughs, also whispering.

'God, yes,' Josh whispers back. 'Ask anyone. Ask Cath.'

Lucy's watching us with a broad smile, and she nods at Portia, who looks at me.

'No,' I whisper. 'If I'm being completely honest, I'd have to say she's completely bloody terrifying.'

'Speaking of which,' Lucy says after we've giggled childishly at the fact that we're sitting around a table, all of us in our thirties, and all whispering because we're frightened of the au pair, 'how terrifying do you find the fact that Si seems to be completely enamoured with that . . . that *pig*?'

'I told you,' I moan. 'Nobody believed me when I said he was awful, but he is, isn't he, he's disgusting.'

Portia looks pained. 'I didn't think he was that bad, actually,' and my jaw hits the floor.

'Oh, come on,' Josh starts laughing. 'You've got to be joking.'

'No,' she says earnestly. 'I know too many people like that, and all that arrogance hides tremendous insecurity. He wasted no time in telling me he'd spent the afternoon looking at company cars and that he was thinking of getting a Porsche Boxster, which I don't believe for a second, but he thinks that makes him better than everyone else.'

'Prick,' Josh says, as we all nod in agreement.

'But you know,' Lucy says, doling out second helpings, which Josh and I eagerly accept, but Portia declines, whispering it was delicious, but she's just too full, 'I'm not sure that insecurity is a good-enough excuse for that sort of behaviour. We're all insecure, and I really think he's old enough to have discovered the reasons behind his insecurity, and do something about them.'

'Darling,' Josh says affectionately, 'not everyone is a budding psychotherapist. He probably doesn't even care what the reasons are.'

'I bet I can tell you what the reasons are,' Portia says suddenly. 'At least some of them.'

'Go on.' I'm fascinated.

'I watch people all the time, it's how I do my job, and there were some obvious clues. First, he speaks in very polished tones. Too polished. If you listened closely there were some definite northern inflections, and after I'd asked him he confessed – reluctantly – that he was from Yorkshire.'

We're all very impressed and stay silent for her to continue.

'Before that he said his father was a bigwig at one of the City banks, and changed the subject when I asked which one. And then a while later he said that since he's been living in London, for the last ten years, he's been going home to his parents for the odd weekend and helping his dad with his accounts.

'So his father clearly doesn't work in the City. He's probably a dentist or something, in a sleepy northern village outside Leeds, and Will thinks that in order to run with the fast crowd in London, which is what he so obviously wants to do, he has to make up a pack of lies that he thinks will impress people.'

'That's the problem with lying,' Lucy says. 'You can never remember what you've said.'

'You're amazing,' Josh says, as Portia gives a self-satisfied smile.

'No. It's amazing what you learn about people when you look for the right signs.'

'But at the end of the day, even if he's from a family who didn't have a bean, it doesn't give him the right to be arrogant, superior and, well, as Josh put it, a prick.' I think about using the noun that Alison Bailey had used, but even among such good friends I can't do it.

'True,' Portia says. 'But I think he's terrified of people discovering who he really is and where he's really from.'

'Okay, clever clogs.' I give Portia a challenging smile. 'You're proving to be the witch tonight. Is Si going to stay with him for ever?'

'I have a feeling,' she says with a sigh, 'that it won't be long before we all find out.'

Chapter eighteen

Despite such an inauspicious start, the party at Josh and Lucy's ends up being one of the better ones. Si and I are there for dinner all the time, but somehow having a new person completely changes the dynamic, and I truly find it one of the most refreshing and interesting evenings I've had in ages. In fact, probably the nicest evening I've had since, well, since that evening with James.

My only concern is Si, and the first thing I do when I step through my front door, even though it's almost one o'clock in the morning, is pick up the phone and call to see if he's okay.

And of course I'm not surprised that his phone is picked up by his answering machine, and I leave a brief message, asking if he's okay and telling him that he can call me anytime if he needs me, because I'm praying that Will hasn't taken it out on him.

I don't hear from him until the next day, and then at around eleven a.m. I get a sheepish phone call.

'It's me.'

'I know,' I say, surprised he's taken so long. 'How are you?'

'Embarrassed,' he admits. 'I know I've got to phone Josh and Lucy and apologize, but I don't know what to say to them.'

'Why are you apologizing? It's your arse of a boyfriend who should be saying sorry. And before you start justifying him, he behaved appallingly.'

'I know.' And he does know, because I have never heard Si sound this contrite before. 'But he won't apologize. He doesn't think he needs to, because he'll never be seeing any of you again.'

'Charming. I take it he liked us as much as we liked him, then?'

'More, possibly. Except for Portia, whom he raved about all night, but then again she is a semi-celebrity, which seems to turn him on somewhat.' His voice sounds slightly bitter.

'So I take it all is not rosy in the garden of Eden?'

'God, I don't know, Cath.' He lets out a deep sigh. 'I thought it was just you, being difficult, but last night I saw a completely different side to Will. I went back to his flat, and he basically ignored me the whole night, and I was appalled by his behaviour at Josh and Lucy's. I just don't understand it.'

'You mean you didn't try to talk about it once you'd left? That's not like you, Si.'

'I couldn't. He was in such a foul mood that I just sat there very quietly and then we went to bed.'

'Si, what *are* you doing with him?'

'He's not all bad, you know, Cath. He can be incredibly sweet and loving, but . . .' and he stops and sighs again.

'So it's not over yet?'

'Not until the fat lady sings.' And with a sad smile that I can picture as he speaks, we say goodbye.

And when I get home that evening there is a message from Lucy, a message from Portia, three messages from Si, and finally, as I'm expecting a fourth message from Si, I hear James's voice on the machine.

'Hi, umm, Cath. It's James. Look, I'm not sure what I've done to upset you, but whatever it is I'm really, really sorry. I'd really like it if you called me . . .' and he leaves the number. I replay the message a few times, trying to work out if there is a subliminal message lurking in between the lines, or if perhaps I can pick something up from the tone of his voice, but there's nothing.

I kick off my shoes and wander into the kitchen, flicking the kettle on and opening my fridge to see if there's anything vaguely edible. Luckily there is a tub of houmous, and an open pack of thin cheese slices with only the top one having gone hard and orange thanks to my inability to wrap food properly. I take them out and go to the cupboard, where I discover an open pack of rice crackers shoved right at the very back – God knows where they came from, as I'm sure I'd never buy anything that healthy for myself – and then I head back to the fridge just in case something delicious has materialized in the short time it's taken me to open the cupboard door.

Nope. I didn't miss anything, so I make myself a coffee and take it into the living room with the food to think about James and whether I should call him back. The problem is, I think, as I take a bite of rice cracker that's so old it's now soft and pliable, that I actually do quite like James.

The problem is that if I were to even contemplate getting involved with anyone at this time in my life, James is probably exactly the sort of man I'd choose.

But the bigger problem is that I can't get involved. I can't go through all the shit that Si's going through now with Will – the hassle of introducing someone to all my friends and praying that they'll like him and that he'll like them. Although I suppose that bit's already been taken care of with James.

Look at me. I'm sprawled on the sofa, one leg flung over the back, crap sit-coms that I'd never admit to watching blaring from the television screen, and I'm cramming soft rice cakes topped with plastic-effect cheese and a healthy dollop of houmous (scooped from the tub by my finger, I'll have you know) on the top. I'm slurping the coffee because it's too hot, and the only reason I can do any of this is because I'm on my own.

I remember being with Martin. I remember being with other men at university, and going out with men in my early twenties. The whole palaver of having to make an effort all the time. Making sure you look nice. Ensuring he doesn't know you spend evenings stuffing your face with tasteless crap because you can't be bothered to walk the three minutes to the corner shop to buy something decent.

I wouldn't be able to do this if I were with James, with *anyone*. And even if I could, the risk of hurt, or loss, is always there, and right now I'm happy. I don't want anyone to come and spoil that.

'Not even if you could, potentially, be a thousand times happier?' Lucy once asked.

'Not possible.' I shook my head with a grin. 'Not when I've got all of you.'

'You can't grow as a person,' she said sadly, ignoring my joke, 'when you close yourself off emotionally. It's all well and good saying you avoid pain by avoiding relationships, but what about the wonderful things you're avoiding as well? What about the joy and the intimacy and the trust that come with finding someone you love?'

'I don't need to find someone I love to have that,' I remember saying. 'I have joy and intimacy and trust with my friends. What I don't have is heartache and insecurity and the loss of my *self*, and Lucy, trust me, I'm happy like this.'

'No pain, no gain,' Si sniffed, but then again he would, because no matter how many times we have this discussion, no matter how many times I try to explain how I feel about men, about relationships, Si just can't understand.

Which is why, I suppose, he's with Will now. Si has always settled for second best, for men who use and abuse him, because as far as he's concerned it's better than being on his own, although he doesn't use those exact words. Si always thinks he can change them. The worse they treat him, the more of a challenge it is, and I will say this for Will: he definitely poses the greatest challenge of Si's life.

I finish the rice cakes and head back into the kitchen, opening the fridge again just in case, but no, same old mouldy vegetables as there were half an hour ago. Aha! The freezer! I thank God, and thank Si, that nestling in among the frozen peas and spinach in the top drawer is the one thing that's guaranteed to make my night.

A Sara Lee frozen Cinnamon Danish that Si brought over one Sunday but that we never – for some extraordinary and inexplicable reason – got around to eating. Licking my lips, I set the microwave to defrost and linger in the kitchen, smelling the delicious cinnamony, almondy smells that waft from the left-hand corner of the kitchen.

I can't wait for the ping. I open the door ten seconds before it's ready and pull the Danish out, tearing off a large chunk even before I put it on a plate. Oh God, this is delicious, the soft dough and marzipan melting in my mouth, and I take the plate inside, vowing to eat only half and settle back into the sofa, plate balanced on my knees.

Ten minutes later I'm groaning with disgust, but even as I groan I'm licking my index finger and sweeping it around the plate to catch any crumbs I missed earlier. I've eaten the whole thing, and it was delicious, and I don't feel guilty. Well, not that guilty.

And let's face it. I'd never be able to do this if I had a boyfriend, would I? But James is a nice guy. James could be a good friend. I've always said I don't need any more friends, but that's mostly because Si has filled the role of boyfriend/brother/best friend better than anyone else I could have hoped for. But now that Will has come on the scene, maybe it is time I looked for someone else. Not to replace Si, because nobody could do that, but, even in the short time since he met Will, Si hasn't been around for last-minute cosy suppers at home. I haven't been able to pick up the phone to him at five thirty p.m. and tell him to meet me outside the cinema in an hour because we're going to the movies.

And maybe I have been feeling just the tiniest bit lonely since Si met Will. Then again, I muse, there is always Portia; yet, however close we were once upon a time, I can't help but feel that there's too much water under the bridge for us to be that close again.

I can still see the old Portia when I look at her, still have a vestige of the feelings I had all those years ago, but, although part of me steps back into the old role, the other part, the part that's spent ten years without her, knows that we've grown too far apart, that our lives are too different for us ever to be best friends in the way that we once were.

Yes, James would be the perfect friend. I resolve to phone him back, but right now, with bulging belly and lethargy inflicting every bone in my body, I can't be bothered. But I *will* ring him tomorrow.

The TV stays on for the rest of the evening. I mute it temporarily to phone Portia and Lucy, and I leave a message for Si, then carry on mindlessly watching, and find myself becoming really quite engrossed in one of those detective drama series, and I'm rooting for the good guy when the doorbell rings.

Shit. Now I know I said that James would be a perfect friend, but I've just reached a crucial bit where we find out whether the main suspect's alibi was in fact real, and this habit James has of turning up with no warning is beginning to seriously get on my nerves.

I stomp down the hallway and open the front door, ready to give James a mouthful but trying to swallow it before it comes out, because I don't want to frighten him off permanently, not when I've just decided he'll make the perfect friend.

I open the door, trying to smile, and on my doorstep is Si.

'Si! I was just thinking about you! What a gorgeous surprise,' I exclaim happily, giving him a hug, and when we pull apart Si gives me a wobbly smile and proceeds to burst into tears.

'Oh shit.' I usher him in and lead him to the sofa, sitting down next to him and rubbing his back until the first bout of tears has subsided a little. 'Cup of tea?' I say finally, knowing it will bring a smile to his face, as he always jokes that nobody in soap operas can ever deal with emotional outbursts, and all they do when someone's in a terrible state is offer to put the kettle on and make a nice cup of tea.

He smiles, rolls his eyes and starts crying all over

again. After a while I ask if it's Will, and he nods his head. I ask if it's over, and again he nods, and along comes a fresh spurt of tears.

Eventually he manages to calm down enough to tell me. I do make a cup of tea, and bizarrely it does seem to help, if only because he has to force himself to stop hiccuping in order to drink the tea. Once the hiccups have gone, he starts to take himself in hand and to take control.

Will had phoned Si at work today, and after a brief chat in which Si now says he could tell something was wrong, Si asked if they would be seeing one another later. Will said that Si could come over if he wanted, and that he'd be in around eight.

So Si duly went over, planning to have a talk with Will. Not *The Talk*, he said, just a talk about how important his friends were to him, and how important Will was becoming, and how life would be so much easier if he could try to get along. He was going to say that he understood his friends weren't Will's types, but sometimes, when you're trying to make a relationship with someone new, you have to think about somebody other than yourself.

But Si never got the chance to have any sort of conversation. Will opened the front door, then ignored Si as he walked back into the living room. And there, on the sofa, was Steve – a guy they'd met together in a pub a couple of weeks back.

Steve was exactly the sort of man that Si always runs miles from. Good-looking, arrogant, dismissive. Exactly, I thought to myself, like Will, except this Steve obviously didn't bother with the charm act at all.

Will went to sit back down on the sofa, pressed up next to Steve, and the pair of them sat there drinking their beers, giggling like teenagers at jokes that Si was clearly not in on.

So Si sat there for a while, watching them flirt, desperate to leave but hoping this was some horrible nightmare that would be over any second, when Will looked up with an expression of surprise and said, 'Are you still here?'

Shocked, Si stood up, as Steve snorted in amusement and Will buried his head in his shoulder to hide the laughter.

'Not interested,' Si heard Will say as he stumbled out of the flat. '*You're* boring as fuck, your *friends* are boring as fuck, and as for your *fucking* . . .' and he heard the laughter as he slammed the door.

It was a wonder, Si sniffs as he sits here on my sofa, that he didn't crash the car on the way back. It wasn't that Will was the love of his life, but the humiliation was awful. He'd never been so humiliated in his life, having to sit there and watch the two of them together, and then that sneering comment, the rejection.

'I can't cope,' Si says, his voice starting to break again. 'I can't cope with the rejection. Why does this always have to happen to me? Why? What have I done?'

And what can I say? What is there to say? Eventually I come out with a feeble, 'He wasn't good enough to even lick your bloody shoes,' which is the only thing I can think of.

'I know that,' Si says, which I suppose is something of a breakthrough. 'But that's not the point. He wasn't good enough for me, and he still managed to get the final word in and kick me once I was down.'

'You know what?' Anger is finally kicking in on Si's behalf. 'Alison Bailey said he was a *cunt*.' Si looks at me in shock because I spit the word out with relish and this is not a word *anyone* is accustomed to hearing from my lips, not least Si, who knows me better than most.

'She said he was a nasty evil shit who got a kick out of destroying people. He'd done it to some girl at work, and she said the best advice she could give would be to stay well away.'

Si starts to look interested, and because I can see this is helping I decide to add a few personal touches, a few flourishes of my own. 'She said that he plays mind-fuck, he gets off on playing psychological games with people and seeing what it will take to break them.' She may not have said that, but I know that's exactly the sort of person he is.

'I swear, Si. You may be hurting now, but Jesus, all I can think is that you got off incredibly lightly.'

'Did she really say all those things?'

I nod.

'He was a pig to Josh and Lucy, wasn't he?'

'God, yes. The worst.'

'So you don't think it's me?'

'Si, you're gorgeous. He's just an arse for not recognizing it.'

'Do you think that somebody, someday will recognize it?'

'Absolutely, one hundred per cent, definitely.'

'Thanks, sweets.' He gives me another smile that's a lot less wobbly than the last one I saw, and I give him a hug until he starts to sniffle again, warning that I mustn't be too nice or it will set him off again.

'You know what will definitely make me feel better?' he says suddenly with a faint twinkle in his eye, looking much like a naughty little boy. 'That Cinnamon Danish I brought a couple of weeks ago.'

'Ah.' I sit there as my brain works furiously trying to

think of an excuse, but I can't say that I had ten people over for tea last week, as Si would know I was lying, and, embarrassing as it is to have to admit I ate the whole thing by myself, he doesn't have to know the whole truth.

'It's in here,' I say, pointing at my swollen stomach.

'What? All of it?' Si's horrified as I shake my head and laugh.

'Don't be ridiculous. I've had it in the fridge for a week, and I've worked my way through it, ending with the last piece tonight.'

'So there's nothing left, not even one little piece?'

'I'm sorry. Nothing.'

'Well, there's only one thing for it, then,' he says, standing up and reaching for his coat. 'Come on, get your shoes on. We're going out for ice-cream.'

On any other night I'd tell Si to get stuffed because going out this late in the freezing cold is the very last thing I feel like doing, particularly after the entire cinnamon Danish, but tonight I have to show what friends are made of, so I pull some boots on and head out the door.

Half an hour later we're sitting in the window of Haagen-Dazs, rain splattering the glass, my wonderfully smooth locks having now, thanks to the rain, frizzed up to the usual Cath mess.

Si's spooning out the last of a tub of Strawberry Cheesecake ice-cream, and I'm watching him with my chin in my hand, nursing a large glass of water and doing my best not to be sick.

'Are you sure you don't want my last spoonful?' Si says, holding the spoon to my mouth.

'Absolutely not.' I shake my head as the Danish threatens to rise once more. 'But I'm glad you love me enough to ask.'

Chapter nineteen

'Cath, my love, do you think anyone would ever understand how much we appreciate a Sunday off? I don't know about you but I am absolutely exhausted.' Lucy kicks off her shoes and stretches her arms up to the ceiling, rolling her shoulders and sighing.

'And we thought running Bookends was going to be easy.'

'Not easy,' she says, smiling, 'but my God, I wish someone had told me quite how many hours we'd have to be working.'

'But think of all the benefits . . .' I make sympathetic noises just as the front door slams, and Ingrid and Max arrive back from the park.

'MUmmmmmmmyyyyyy!' Max comes hurtling down the hallway and flings himself into Lucy's arms, as she strokes his hair and covers him with kisses, and whatever animosity I may have felt towards Max in the past, I can see that he obviously does miss her right now, and my heart warms.

'What's that, my love?' Lucy says, gently detaching herself enough to take the piece of paper clutched in Max's hand.

'Darling, that's wonderful. Is that you with Mummy and Daddy? Why have I got blonde hair?'

'Because,' Max says, 'it's me, Daddy and Ingrid. I was going to draw you, but Ingrid plays with me more,' and with that he climbs down, too young to see how much he's hurt Lucy, but of course I can see the pain in her eyes.

She waits until he's run upstairs, and then rubs her temples with her hands.

'You see?' she says finally, looking at me. 'I can't blame him for that, he never sees me any more. God, Cath, I'm not suggesting it's any easier for you, but it's so heartbreaking when you know you're missing out on seeing your family.

'There I was, thinking I'd be home early evening to get Max ready for bed and make supper for Josh and I, and instead I find myself in the shop until at least eight or nine o'clock, and that's if we haven't got any events on.

'I hardly see my son, and Josh and I feel like ships passing in the night right now. In the mornings I pass him in the kitchen as I'm making a cup of coffee and he's grabbing his briefcase and running out the door, and if I'm lucky we have a chance to have a quick two-minute chat at night before I hit the sack.'

'Lucy, you're making it sound awful. I don't know what to say, because I haven't got anyone to worry about other than me, and quite honestly I love the fact that it keeps me so busy. It stops me worrying about not having a social life.' And it's true. I have never been happier in my life than this last month, since the bookshop opened.

I love getting to know my local community, because although I've lived here for years, I never really knew anyone outside my immediate social circle. I love getting to know the regulars, chatting about books with them, recommending things I think they might like, and then having them come back in a week later to tell me I'm right and they did love it. And I don't mind in the slightest the fact that I am working late almost every night, and that whatever social life I might have had has flown out the window without a backward glance.

Lucy looks at me with a smile. 'No social life? What are we, then?' and she laughs. 'The problem, my darling Cath,' she says eventually, 'is that I love it. I love Bookends and I love the fact that I'm a person again, not just Josh's wife, or Max's mother. I love the fact that I'm working with you and that I'm meeting people every day. I'm getting out there, achieving something, and Cath, I had forgotten, completely forgotten, what it was like to have a place in the world.'

'So how do you think you can resolve it?' I'm only slightly worried, because I know Lucy does love it, and, even though it's difficult right now, I know she'll stick at it and we'll find a way of making it work. It just might take some time, that's all.

'On the rare occasions I've managed to catch Josh he's said these are just teething problems. He says that hopefully we'll be able to take on more staff soon and just be in the shop for normal opening hours. I hope he's right, because I'm sure he's finding it incredibly difficult, me hardly being here.' Suddenly the light comes back on in her eyes and she flashes her megawatt smile at me. 'Anyway,' she continues, 'that's enough about my boring old life. I've been so wrapped up in myself I haven't even asked you anything. So what's all this about you and the lovely James going out next week?'

I called James back. I decided the best way of proceeding would be, rather than apologizing for slamming the door in his face and shoving the flowers back at him, to pretend that everything was fine and nothing out of the ordinary had happened. Obviously, as Lucy pointed out, I was running the risk of him thinking I was completely round the bend, but I'd prefer that to having him know I was furious because I thought he'd gone off with Ingrid.

He sounded guarded at the beginning of the conversation, but I can hardly blame him for that, and within the first two minutes I made him laugh by telling him about the dinner party he was supposed to have gone to, and then everything was fine.

He was astounded that Lucy had forgotten to ask him, which led to further tales of things Lucy has forgotten to do in the past, such as bring her passport to the airport with her on her honeymoon, buy Josh a birthday present for two consecutive years, and take a nightdress to the hospital when Max was born.

James tries to top my stories by telling me about his mother, who had a mental block with recipes and would always leave out a vital ingredient, so they'd sit down at night to Coq au Vin, without the chicken, Duck à l'Orange, without the orange, and Lancashire Hot Pot, without the potatoes.

We're both laughing on the phone, and I realize that half an hour has flown by without me even thinking about it, and suddenly James asks me out for dinner, and, well, I find myself saying yes, which I suppose means I'll be going out on a date.

A date! Why do I feel like such a teenager at the very mention of the word? But a date! I have to talk to someone about this, have to share it with someone.

Now, usually Si would have been my first port of call when asking advice, but right now he has done what he always does when he is dumped, which is immediately come round to me to have a good cry and get it all out, and then hibernate for a while to get his strength back. Once upon a time I used to feel shut out when he did that, but I'm used to it now, and I know that the only way to get the old Si back when he's been truly hurt is to leave him be, as he spends his evenings alone, in his flat, listening to old love songs and feeling sorry for himself, until suddenly he snaps out of it and demands we accompany him to some club, or bar, or cabaret.

He'll still take my calls occasionally, but in the hibernation period the answer phone goes on, and stays on, most of the time. If he is in the mood he will occasionally pick up, but more often than not we have to talk to the machine, knowing he's listening and saying that we know he's there and could he please pick up the phone, which of course he doesn't do.

But, being the good friend that I am, I went out and bought the videos of *Harold and Maude* and *Brief Encounter*, and sent them on a bike, together with a box of Milk Tray, which Si and I always giggle about, although secretly we adore them.

His hibernation periods can last for anything from one week to one month, but, given the shortness of the relationship with Will, and the fact that despite what he said I'm convinced that Si knew he wasn't The One, I'm expecting his cheery voice any day now on the phone.

But who am I supposed to share this with? This strange feeling in my stomach, which, unless I'm very much mistaken, feels peculiarly like butterflies, although it's been so long since I've been excited about anything I could be completely wrong.

But whatever the feeling is I'm dying to talk to *someone* about it. Si is incommunicado, Lucy is far too busy with the shop to really pay any attention, and Josh? Josh seems a bit distracted right now. Apparently – and Lucy says this is the only reason why she doesn't feel quite so guilty not getting home until late – he's got some huge deal going on at the office, and he's having to work all the hours God sends.

So I suppose the only person that really leaves, apart

from Bill and Rachel at the shop – although I like to keep my work very separate from my personal life – is Portia.

'Why don't we have a long girly lunch?' she says, when I phone her a couple of days later on the pretext of finding out how she is, but really to talk to her about James. I tried to keep it to myself, but two days was too much and now I have to talk to *someone.* 'My treat.'

Well, how could I resist?

I arrive at Kensington Place at exactly one p.m., and I'm shown to a table next to the window, where I sit looking at my watch, wondering when exactly Portia will turn up.

At ten past one I order a glass of white wine, and at quarter past I start studying the menu, deciding what I'm going to order.

At twenty past one, just when I've given up hope, I look up to see Portia grinning at me outside the window, and I grin back and relax my shoulders because she's finally here, although it appears it was a little early to count my chickens. Portia manages to take a good five minutes to actually walk through the restaurant, because it seems she knows *everyone* in here.

Every few steps she stops to kiss someone hello, or shake someone's hand, or have a brief chat, and my smile of greeting becomes more and more strained, but I sip my wine and try to look as if I really don't mind being kept waiting for half an hour.

Eventually she reaches the table and envelops me in a warm hug, apologizing profusely for being so late. 'I was in the middle of a script for the new series,' she laughs, 'and I was so carried away I had no idea what time it was.'

'Don't worry,' I say, not bothering to add that I only

had a limited lunchbreak and already I had pretty much used it up, travelling all the way to Kensington.

She orders a sparkling mineral water and pulls a packet of Silk Cut out of her bag, lighting her cigarette with a tiny platinum lighter that is so smart it could only belong to her. 'So,' she says. 'You look wonderful.'

'You liar,' I laugh, because my hair is back to the wild woman of Borneo, and I'm in my usual old black gear today, saving my pink sweater and grey trousers for the date.

'No, seriously,' she laughs. 'I mean, you looked completely fab the other night, at Josh and Lucy's, but you didn't really look like you.' My face falls. 'No, no,' she says quickly, 'don't be offended, but sitting here now, with your curly hair and no make-up, this is the Cath that we all know and love.'

'So what do you think I should do for my date with James?'

'Be yourself. Make-up and hairdressers are lovely for special occasions, but this is you, this is the Cath that he first fell for, so why change anything?'

I start to laugh. 'Portia! That's all well and good, but look at you, for Christ's sake! You're immaculate!'

'But that's different.' She rolls her eyes. 'Didn't I ever tell you that my mother says I emerged into the world wearing high heels and lipstick? The nurses at St Mary's couldn't, apparently, get over it.'

I laugh with her, but she can see there's something in my eyes and that all is not completely well, and to be honest, as excited and nervous as I am, I still can't get over the feeling that I'm standing on the edge of the precipice and I'm really not entirely sure I'm ready to jump.

'What's the matter?'

I sigh for a bit, then try to explain the way I feel. How I've managed to protect myself by surrounding myself with people I know and trust and love, and that anything outside of that group feels very dangerous, and very frightening, feelings I'm not used to.

'I do understand,' she says, smiling, when I've finished my halting explanation. 'Better than you might think. I know what it's like to want something very badly but to be too frightened of going after it because it feels dangerous. But Cath, I don't need to tell you of all the good things you could be missing out on by not going through with this. I'm sure Lucy's already told you.'

I smile, because of course Portia's right.

'But you know, if this helps at all, I've always thought that the one thing I would regret more than anything else in life is to reach the ripe old age of, say, eighty, look back on my life and think, "What if?" What if I'd done something differently, what if I'd followed my heart? What if I hadn't ended *this* love affair, or *that* love affair?

'And you know, even at thirty-one, I have regrets. There are things I wish I'd done in my twenties, things I wish I'd said to people, and things' – her eyes become increasingly wistful – 'I wish I hadn't said, hadn't done.'

'It's not too late, though? You're *only* thirty-one, Portia,' I laugh, trying to lighten things, aware that what she has just said is an almost exact echo of what James has already said to me.

'I don't know,' she sighs, then pushes a smile on to her face. 'I can't turn the clock back, but hopefully I can right some wrongs, and who knows, maybe even give myself some happier endings . . .'

There's a silence for a while, and eventually I pluck

up enough courage to say tentatively, 'Portia, when you talk about righting wrongs, we've never talked about those days.'

'Those days?'

'When we were all at university, and then, after that night, with Josh, how we all lost touch.'

She laughs. 'Oh that. That was nothing. I was just a silly little girl demanding some attention, and there's nothing to talk about.'

Relief seeps through me. 'Do you know, I've thought about that for years, I always felt guilty that we all drifted apart after that.'

'Cath, it was a long time ago and I can barely remember it. Really, it's not necessary to apologize. It's over. Forgotten.'

'But then we met that guy who knew you . . .' I trail off, aware that I'm getting nowhere, that Portia has always had an extraordinary ability to shut down when a subject is becoming uncomfortable, and this is what she's doing now.

She smiles and shrugs, and I know from days of old that it's the end of the subject: she won't talk about it any more, but God, I'd love to know what she meant about giving herself some happier endings, and right what wrongs? The only person *she* wronged back then was Matt, and he isn't around any more, at least not in our lives.

'How's the bookshop going?' Portia asks, expert in changing the subject.

'Fantastic. Truly unbelievable. I'm loving every minute of it, but poor Lucy's working like a demon in the café bit and she's absolutely exhausted. And then, to make matters worse, she got home the other night to find that evil little Max had drawn a picture of the family at nursery or somewhere, and instead of drawing Lucy he'd drawn Ingrid.'

Portia starts to laugh. 'Oh God, sorry,' she says, seeing that I'm not laughing. 'I mean, that must be awful for her, particularly because Ingrid's so gorgeous. I can never understand these women. Aren't they just asking for trouble by employing some stunning Swedish blonde as an au pair girl? Particularly when they're out working late every night.

'I just always think that the easiest thing in the world would be to turn to the au pair for a bit of comfort during those lonely evenings. Especially when she looks like Ingrid.'

'Well, no possibility of that,' I say. 'First of all, Ingrid's the prize bitch from hell.' Portia arches an eyebrow in surprise. 'Oh, come on, you saw her the other night, she's a nightmare, and as far as I can see her only saving grace is that Max loves her. Anyway, despite what you may think, Josh *adores* Lucy.'

'Does he?' Portia looks interested.

Now at this point it occurs to me to have a little gossip about Josh and Lucy passing like ships in the night, but, however tempting it might be, it really wouldn't be fair to Lucy, so I mentally zip the lip and decide that no matter what Portia says I will not be drawn.

'God, yes! Josh can't keep his hands off her. Really, it's quite ridiculous, I mean after all these years together you'd think some of the passion would die, but if anything it's the reverse.'

I'm not entirely sure what makes me go so over the top, but something in my gut tells me it's the right thing to be doing, so I go with it and add just a little more to be on the safe side.

'They didn't strike me as being particularly affectionate to one another,' Portia says, after considering what I've just said. 'They obviously have a good working relationship, but it struck me that perhaps the passion had gone. Oh well, I must have been wrong.'

'God, definitely. In fact Lucy was saying the other night that she's completely exhausted because she's working like a dog and then as soon as she gets home Josh wants to jump her.' I wasn't planning this last bit, but too late, it's already out there.

Portia looks surprised, and then she smiles. 'I like Lucy, you know. She's not at all what I expected, as you know, but I've surprised myself by how much I like her.'

'*Everyone* adores Lucy, she's wonderful.'

'Hmm,' Portia says, and sits back as our rocket and Parmesan salads arrive. 'She's certainly a wonderful cook. That food was amazing. Oh God, I haven't even asked about Si. You said on the phone they'd broken up. How is he?'

'He's probably about three quarters on the road to recovery,' I tell her. 'Hopefully about to come out of isolation and join the real world again.'

'Maybe when he does you'll all come to me for dinner. How does that sound?'

'Would *you* cook,' I say doubtfully, remembering her inability to even make a toasted cheese sandwich at university, 'or would it be catered?'

'Don't be silly, darling. Catered of course.'

'In that case it sounds fantastic,' I say, grinning, and she laughs, and I realize that although Portia will never be a proper replacement for Si, I'm having a good time here today, a much better time, in fact, than I thought I'd be having, and when Portia says, at the end, that we must do this again soon, I find myself agreeing.

*

'I'm back!'

'From where? Ibiza? Majorca? South Beach?'

'Oh ha bloody ha. From the land of lamenting and feeling sorry for myself. Oh, and by the way, I could kiss you for the videos. So clichéd, but absolutely perfect for squeezing out the last few tears.'

'Oh, Si, I've missed you.'

'I know, sweets, and I've missed you too. So, what's been going on since I've been gone? Has Portia run off with Josh yet?'

'Si! That's a terrible thing to say!'

'Joke, joke.' A pause. 'Well, *has* she?'

'God, Si, you are incorrigible. Of course she hasn't, although – '

'Although what?' he snaps, just in case I'm withholding some vital gossip from him.

'Although I did have lunch with her last week, and she was saying that she wouldn't be surprised if Josh ran off with, wait for it, Ingrid! Can you believe she said that? Ingrid!'

'I can actually.' Si's not laughing. 'She was probably just testing the waters to see if Josh has it in him to be unfaithful, checking to see whether he flirts with Ingrid or anything.'

'But Josh *so* isn't the type.'

'Not with Ingrid, no.'

'Meaning?'

'If Portia is after Josh, and I still think it's a distinct possibility, then it would make her job a hell of a lot easier if she found out that he'd already had an affair or two during their married life.'

'Well, I don't think that. When we had lunch she said that she had regrets, and she hoped she could right some wrongs and maybe give herself a happy ending, or something like that.'

'Uh oh. Doesn't sound too good to me. What does she mean by right some wrongs?'

'I know, that's what I've been trying to figure out. The only person I can figure out that she actually wronged back then was Josh, but it was so long ago, surely it's all water under the bridge now?'

'I just don't know. What about Matt? Now that *would* be weird,' Si laughs. 'Can you imagine if Matt turned up as well?'

'Maybe she's still in touch with him, it's the one thing I keep forgetting to ask.'

'Nah, I'm sure she would have mentioned it. So, sweets, how about a movie tonight?'

'Oh, Si, I would have loved to, but I can't.'

'You can't? You can't? Why on earth not? Don't tell me that in the three weeks since I've been away you've discovered a social life?'

'Charming. I see your hibernation period didn't sweeten your acerbic tongue. Actually, I've sort of got a date . . .'

'A *what*?'

'Well, Lucy's calling it a date, but it's probably not, it's just that James and I are going out for supper.'

'Oh my God! Oh my God!' I can hear Si doing a little victory dance at the end of the phone. 'How? When? Where?'

'Well, he called and then I called him back and then we chatted and then he said how about supper.'

'So where are you going? What time is he picking you up? He is picking you up, isn't he? What are you wearing? Oh my God! What are you wearing?'

I start laughing.

'Tell you what,' Si continues,'why don't I whizz over and help you get ready? I promise I won't embarrass you, and if I'm not gone by the time he comes over, I'll hide in the bathroom.'

'I know I should say no . . .'

'See you in ten minutes!' he whoops, and the phone is slammed down.

'Jesus Christ,' I say as I open the door to Si, laden down with bags.

'No, but I might be about to perform miracles,' he says, with a grin that tells me Will has been well and truly forgotten. He drops the bags and strokes his chin, studying me in the manner of a mad professor. 'I seem to recall your hair being gorgeously straight and glossy not so long ago,' he says, 'and I knew it wouldn't last so . . . tah dah!' and he pulls something out of one of the bags. 'I've brought the hair irons and the latest de-frizz serum.'

'Nope.' I shake my head. 'Si, I love you and I know you mean well, but I talked to Portia about this and she thinks that, rather than wear make-up and straighten my hair and everything, I should just go au naturel because that's how James knows me and he obviously likes me like that, so why pretend to be something I'm not.'

'Bollocks to that,' Si says, squeezing past me and whipping out the plug of my bedside lamp, replacing it with the hair irons. 'She's just jealous because she's not happy, and if she's not happy then she doesn't want anyone else to be happy either. She was always like that. You looked beautiful the other night, and we're going to make you beautiful again now.'

'Si,' I say uncertainly, 'are you sure?'

'Never been more sure of anything in my life. Now hand me that green bag, it's got the make-up in it.'

'Make-up? What the hell are you doing with make-up?'

'Remember Angel? The drag queen? I thought I'd keep the make-up as a little memento. I knew it would come in handy someday,' and with an evil grin he sends me off into the bathroom to wash my face.

Chapter twenty

'Oh, come on, James,' I laugh, 'I don't look that different.' He's standing on the doorstep and his mouth is hanging open as he stares at me.

'James?'

He shakes his head. 'Cath, I'm really sorry,' and he peers at me closely. 'It is Cath, isn't it?' And he grins.

'The new Cath,' I say. 'Improved, I hope.'

'You just don't look like *you*,' he says uncertainly, and my face falls as I realize that Portia was probably right and why the hell didn't I listen to her? I suppress the urge to run into the bathroom and scrub my face of all this gunk, and we stand awkwardly for a while on the doorstep.

'You know,' James says finally, 'I think you actually look very lovely, it just takes a couple of minutes to get used to.' I relax and ask him if he wants to come in, praying he'll say no because Si is, as promised, lurking in the bathroom.

'Just for a minute or two,' he says. 'We're only slightly early for the table.'

'Where are we going?'

'It's a surprise,' he says, and jumps at the sound of the toilet flushing. Shit. I knew Si wouldn't be able to lurk quietly until we'd gone. Sure enough, the bathroom door opens and Si strolls out, pretending to be surprised to see us both sitting there.

'Hello,' James says, with the good grace not to look the slightest bit shocked.

'Oh, I thought you'd both gone.' Si's wide-eyed and innocent look doesn't fool me for a second. 'Lovely to see you again, can I get you a drink?'

'Actually we were just leaving,' James says, as I gratefully smile and run off down to the bedroom to grab my coat.

'What are you doing?' I hiss at Si, who follows me in to tell me to behave myself. 'You said you'd lurk quietly. That's the last time I ever let you come over when someone's coming to pick me up.'

'Is that all the thanks I get for helping Cinderella go to the ball?' Si tries to look hurt.

'Come on, you're leaving too.'

I tell Si not to take his bags with because I don't want to have to think of an explanation for what's inside them, so he leaves them in the bedroom, ready to be collected the next day, and the three of us walk out together.

'Have a lovely time, children,' Si shouts as he climbs into his Beetle. 'Oh, and don't do anything I wouldn't do!' and with that he revs the engine and zooms off.

We drive through London, chatting quietly, although it's hard to hear over the sound of the windscreen wipers swishing through the October rain. I twist my body in the passenger seat so I can look at James's profile, and I marvel, despite not having done this for years, at how familiar this whole scenario is, how going on a date hasn't changed since I was a teenager.

I remember twisting my body exactly like this to talk to dates before. I remember the whole feeling of sitting in a darkened car, filled with nerves, apprehension, excitement, because neither of you yet knows what the rest of the night will hold.

We seem to be driving for ever, on the Westway, down

to Hammersmith, over to Putney, and eventually into Barnes, where James pulls over and parks the car, and we walk round the corner to a chic little French restaurant.

'I hope this is okay,' he says nervously. 'I thought of somewhere big and trendy, but the problem with those places is you can hardly hear yourself think, and I used to come here a lot when I lived in Hammersmith and I thought it would be perfect and the food's delicious.'

I realize that he's talking so much through nerves, and the realization that he's as nervous as I am makes me relax, and I smile my approval as we walk through the door.

We are shown to a corner table, secluded, discreet, and, although it is in Barnes, outside the trendy epicentre of London, the rest of the clientele look surprisingly smart, and I feel an overwhelming burst of gratitude to Si for doing a number on me, because I'm quite sure I would have been intimidated had I not had glossy locks and shining lips.

'Is this okay?'

I smile at James. 'Better than okay. It's perfect. To be honest I avoid the big, trendy restaurants you mentioned like the plague. Si drags me to them once in a blue moon, but this is much more my scene. I can hear what you're saying, for starters.'

'Good. I'd offer you champagne, but you don't strike me as a champagne type. What would you like to drink?'

'What do you mean, not a champagne type? What kind of type do I strike you as, then? A few pints of beer?' I start to laugh.

'Nah.' He looks horrified. 'Not beer. Lager, perhaps.' And from that point on, I start to relax.

*

Halfway through my second glass of wine I start to have a good time. Not that I wasn't having one before, but the alcohol loosens my inhibitions, and the more we talk, the more James smiles at me, the more attractive I start to feel.

Although attractive isn't quite enough. Actually, sitting here with the candlelight softly flickering on the table and James laughing at all my stupid jokes, I start to feel positively gorgeous.

And suddenly I realize what Lucy, and Portia, have been banging on about. I haven't felt like this in years. In fact, I don't think I've felt like this ever. I know I'm being funnier than I've been for ages, and that there is a real spark between us, something that I was perhaps vaguely aware of before, but tonight it seems to be growing into a flame after all.

And there seems to be so much to say. Neither of us can wipe the grins off our faces, and in our excitement our sentences are tumbling out, twisting and turning, overlapping, and it's all I can do not to leap on the tabletop and start tapping out a dance of joy.

This is what it's all about. *This* is what I've been missing out on. And Jesus Christ, no matter how much I love Si, Josh and Lucy, it's not a patch on *this*.

I'm in the middle of telling James why Geminis should never be trusted, and he's laughing even though he's already admitted that he thinks all this star sign stuff is a load of rubbish, when the door of the restaurant opens, and I can just about see through the smoked glass someone handing their coat in, and, as I carry on talking, the someone steps into the restaurant and it's Portia.

I stop in the middle of the story, and James turns round to see what I'm looking at. 'I don't believe it,' I say, about to push my chair back and call her over. 'It's my friend Portia.'

I start to stand up as the door opens again, and Portia's mystery date shakes the rain off his umbrella, and I smile to myself as I realize I'll get to know a bit more about Portia's private life, about which she seems to be so incredibly private.

The manager greets them effusively before leading them into the restaurant. Portia's companion has his arm around her to guide her to the table, and she makes a joke, and they look at one another tenderly and laugh.

And when he looks at her I sit back down with a bump because the mystery man with his arm around Portia, looking at her with an extraordinary amount of tenderness and – dare I say it – love, is Josh.

'Oh fuck,' I whisper, unable to tear my eyes off them, even as they disappear into the back room. 'He was bloody right.'

Extraordinary how magic can disappear in a split second. I, we, had been having such an incredible time, but the minute I see Josh and Portia together, my evening is ruined.

And poor James. It's not his fault. I start trying to explain, but it's too difficult and it hurts too much, and the only person I really want to talk to right now is Si, because he, after all, was the one who predicted this would happen right from the start.

So this is what she meant by giving herself a happier ending. This is why she kept asking the questions about Josh and Lucy. But Josh? I just can't believe Josh would do this. I can't believe he would treat Lucy like this. And if this can go wrong, this marriage, this partnership that seemed so perfect, then what in the hell hope is there for the rest of us?

'I understand, don't worry,' James keeps saying when I tell him that we have to leave, and even though I don't say why, he can see I've gone as white as a sheet.

He asks for the bill, and I'm so keen to get away from here, just in case they should come back through on the way to the loo or something, I forget all about the dilemma of should I offer, shouldn't I, and just let James pay the bill, my mind far too distracted by other things.

As we walk out, James turns, and I can see that he spots Josh and Portia, and that he really does understand, that it isn't just a meaningless platitude, and he looks at me sympathetically as I try to push away the feeling of dread that's now looming.

And God, how different is this car journey from the one a couple of hours earlier. James tries to keep the conversation going, but my heart just isn't in it, and after a while he gives up and switches the radio on.

We pull up outside my house and I know I ought to invite him in for coffee, to try to make amends, as the last part of the evening has disintegrated so badly, but the only thing I want to do right now is get on the phone and talk to Si, quickly, because he's the only one who will know what to do.

'Are you going to be okay?' James says, and I nod. 'You're not going to do anything rash, are you?' his voice slightly more nervous. 'Like call Lucy or anything?'

'God, no! I need to get this clear in my head first.'

'You know, you might be wrong. It might just be a friendly supper.'

'James, they were having dinner in Barnes when they both live in North London, and presumably they chose it because they didn't think they'd see anyone they know. Plus I saw the way they looked at one another, and it's just all so fucking obvious now.' My voice starts to rise with anger, and I stop and take a deep breath, forcing myself to calm down, even managing a smile for James's sake.

'I know this might sound like a lie, given the events of the latter part of the evening, but I really did have a lovely time.'

'I bet you say that to all the boys,' James says, a small grin on his face, 'next time it could be even better . . .' but my mind is back to Josh and Portia, and I'm climbing out of the car as James carries on saying something, but I'm not listening. I give him a distracted wave and let myself into the flat, heading straight for the phone.

'Si, it's me.'

'And what are you doing home at this early hour? Unless of course' – he drops his voice to a whisper, although God knows why because he's definitely on his own – 'unless the gorgeous James is in your bedroom, pulling off his boxers at this very moment.'

'We saw them. Josh and Portia. You were right.'

There's a gasp on the other end of the phone, then silence for what feels like a very long time.

'What?'

'I know. I feel sick. I can't believe it.'

'What do you mean, you saw them? Saw them where? What were they doing?'

'We were sitting in this little French restaurant in Barnes –'

'Why did you schlep over to Barnes?'

'I could ask the same of Josh and Portia, really, couldn't I? Except I doubt the answer would be the same.

I suspect that James chose it because it was lovely, rather than for its discretion. But anyway, there we were, when the door opened and Portia came in . . .' I proceed to tell Si the rest of the story, and when I've finished I realize from the silence that he's as shocked as I am.

'Jesus, Si. Say something. You were the one who said she was after Josh from the beginning.'

'I know, but I didn't think she'd actually succeed. I mean, Josh loves *Lucy*. What the hell is he thinking of?'

'I know. That's exactly what I thought. But more to the point, Si, what the fuck are we going to do?'

'Well, I know what we can't do and that's tell Lucy.'

'But we can't just sit back and watch the marriage of our best friends disintegrate. This is just horrific. I can't believe how horrific this is.'

'What about if we talk to Josh? Why don't we talk to Josh?'

'I just don't think I can, Si. Maybe you could.'

'Oh God, I don't think so. I hate these confrontations. Look, we're just going to have to sleep on it tonight. Maybe by the morning we'll have a plan of action.'

But of course we don't have a plan of action the next morning, and that's despite me having hardly slept a wink, tossing and turning, too busy thinking about Josh and Portia to get a decent night's sleep.

And do you know the worst thing about it? The worst thing about it, and I can't believe I'm actually saying this because it feels like such a betrayal, but the worst thing about it is that, seeing them together last night, they looked perfect. They looked far more *right* together than Josh and Lucy have ever done, and, as much as it pains me to even think it, they look as though they belong together.

I will never ever tell anyone I think this. Not even Si, not even during our numerous phone calls the next day, starting at eight in the morning and continuing until mid-afternoon, when I tell him to quit or someone will start suspecting something. This whole fiasco has brought out something incredibly protective in me towards Lucy; I feel that I ought to be close to her, to somehow try to shield her, and I follow her around for the rest of the afternoon, making sure she's okay, although the shop's so busy we hardly have time to speak, let alone have a proper conversation.

'Excuse me?' I look up from sorting out the new stock to see a middle-aged woman standing in front of me, looking imperious. I give her a smile and she, not smiling back, asks: 'Can you tell me where I'd find the new Dava Sobel?'

'Sure. It should be on that table at the fr . . .' I tail off as the woman starts walking away, no 'thank you', nothing, leaving me stranded in mid-sentence. Bill, who's manning the till, catches my eye and rolls his eyes. 'I hate it when that happens,' he says, as I sigh.

'Just tell me you'll be the one to help her when she comes back to ask again.' I grit my teeth, seeing that the woman has, as they always do, gone to the wrong table and is currently browsing through biographies. 'I don't think I've got enough patience to deal with that today.'

'No problem,' says Bill, stepping forward, as the woman marches back to the desk, saying in a loud, disgruntled voice: 'It's not there.'

'I'll find it for you,' he says with a smile, leading her away, and I huddle back behind the desk, wishing I were in a better mood, because normally these things just don't bother me, but today, obviously, isn't a normal day.

*

'Cath, darling!' Lucy's voice is breathless as she dashes back behind the bar, and for a second it almost makes me think that last night must have been a nightmare; it feels so unrealistic when Lucy's voice is still exactly the same. 'I can't believe we haven't had a chance to speak today. Give me a hand with these cups, and then you can tell me how last night went with the lovely James.'

'Lovely.' I try to make my voice sound as normal as possible. 'I'll tell you all about it later.'

'I've got a better idea,' she laughs. 'Josh has another meeting tonight, so I'm on my own again. I haven't got the energy to cook, but if you won't tell anyone we can order pizza and you can tell me all about it. How does that sound?'

Scary, is how it sounds, because I know that the memory of Portia and Josh together will loom all evening, but the desire to see Lucy properly, out of the work environment, to be somehow reassured by her, is far more overwhelming than the fear. 'Great.' I say. 'I'll supply the wine.'

'All right, my darling. We'll go home together. Whoops, Bill's calling you, must be about that order you put in yesterday.' Either that or another bloody customer.

In the event I end up going home first, because it's freezing and I didn't turn the heating on when I left, and the one thing I can't stand is going to bed in a freezing cold flat – it means I won't sleep for hours. So I dash home to put the heating on for later, and tell Lucy I'll be round in about half an hour.

It's ridiculous to feel even more nervous about seeing Lucy, seeing her socially, as opposed to in the shop, than I did last night when I saw James, but it's the truth. And I know I've spent the whole day in the shop with

her, but it isn't the same. I'm not altogether sure how
we've managed this, but during the day, at work, you'd
never know how close we are.

Despite that old myth that you should never get
involved in business with friends, we seem to have found
a way to make it work. It's not as though we don't talk
during the day, in the shop, we just try to keep it as
businesslike as possible, particularly given that Bill and
Rachel are around most of the time as well. And already,
in just over six weeks, we've developed a routine that
seems to work perfectly for us.

We tend to get in first, Lucy and I, usually around
nine, an hour before the shop opens, just to give ourselves
a bit of breathing space. Lucy sticks the coffee on, while
I check to see what was sold the day before, muttering
to myself in frustration as I try to decipher my own
handwriting, should I have been the one to have been
manning the till at the time.

And then Lucy brings the coffee over as I get on the
phone to the wholesalers to reorder the books that have
been sold, and to place orders for customers who are
looking for things we don't usually stock.

Yesterday a man came in and asked where he'd find
The Guide to Natural Plant Life in Outer Mongolia. I
checked the computer, because I knew he was the type
who wouldn't take no for an answer without actually
seeing me check the stock, and when I said I could order
it for him he flew into a deep rage and demanded to know
why, given that we are a bookshop, we didn't have it in
stock. I tried to explain that we cannot possibly stock
every book ever printed just on the offchance that
someone should want it, and that with more obscure
titles we do have to order them.

That really set him off. Obscure? he said. Obscure?

And then he proceeded to go into a detailed rant about how he had read this book twenty years ago and it had changed his life. Rachel got the giggles, which nearly set me off, and eventually, feeling evil, I sent him off to Books Etc., knowing full well that they wouldn't have it either, but figuring he could vent his fury on them instead, and I told him it was only a five-minute walk. Ha!

But, despite the occasions when people are just plain *peculiar*, I love it. We all do. And although we aren't actually in profit yet, it won't, according to Josh, be long now. It looks like I made the right choice after all.

I stand on the doorstep of Lucy's house, place a hand over my heart to calm it down, and ring the doorbell. I hear footsteps, and Ingrid comes to the door, followed closely by Max.

'Hello, Cath,' she says, with what looks like, unless I'm very much mistaken, a suspiciously warm smile. Has this woman gone completely crazy? I peer at her closely, refraining from asking her if she's feeling all right, and give her a faint smile in return.

'Lucy has popped out to get some vegetables. She said she would be back by half past. How are you?' she says over her shoulder as I follow her down the hallway, trying very hard not to step on Max, who is jumping from side to side in front of me.

'Fine,' I say slowly. 'Umm, and you?'

'Oh, fine,' she says breezily. 'Would you like a glass of wine? We are having one.'

'We?' I follow her into the kitchen, and I swear to God I'm not exaggerating this, but my heart threatens to leap into my mouth and I actually gasp because sitting at the kitchen table, as cool as a cucumber, is Portia.

I stand, frozen, in the doorway, and not sure whether to reverse immediately and run far away, or to walk in and pretend nothing's wrong, although considering I'm doing a very good goldfish impersonation right here, I think that it would be fairly difficult to pretend there's nothing wrong.

What the fuck is she doing here? Oh Christ, oh no. Please tell me she's not here to confront Lucy, to do something awful like tell Lucy that she and Josh are in love and Lucy should leave. Oh Christ. Get her out of here. Get me out of here.

And then I notice that Portia's expression is exactly the same as always, and she doesn't have any qualms at all about sitting at the kitchen table of her lover's house, and she probably isn't going to confront Lucy, she's probably here to see Josh before they go off to her flat for an evening of passion.

Christ. I could kill her.

I mean, does she have to be so obvious about it? Look at her, in her plunging shirt with her cleavage on view for all to see, what the hell does she think she's playing at?

'Hi, Cath,' she says warmly – bitch – standing up and coming over to give me a kiss as I stand there like a statue, hardly moving. 'I was just leaving.'

'Here to see Josh, were you?' The words are out before I have a chance to think about what I'm saying, and I can't hide the sarcastic, bitter tone in my voice. Portia gives me a strange look, and you know what? I don't care if she knows that I know. I want her to know because I will not play her game and I will not protect her.

'What?' she says carefully, looking at me strangely, and I know she doesn't think I know. For a second I think she looks flustered, but no, Portia's far too cool for that. 'I was just passing, so I thought I'd pop in and see if Lucy was home,' she says. 'I brought her this recipe book from Italy I'd told her about,' and she gestures to a cookery book lying on the kitchen table.

Ha. A likely bloody story. But what's really weird is that I've heard of unfaithful husbands buying their wives unexpected gifts when they're having an affair, but I've never heard of the mistress doing it. It's the classic sign, isn't it? The husband who never pays any attention to his wife, suddenly starts pitching up with roses and jewellery, saying that it's his way of apologizing for working so late all the time, when he's just trying to find a way to appease his guilt and live with himself.

I suppose the mistress isn't usually friends with the wife. Maybe if she were, she'd be doing exactly the same thing as Portia. Maybe she'd be turning up with cookery books too.

Or maybe she'd be turning up with any old lame excuse just to see more of the husband. At least Josh is out and she's had to put up with Ingrid, which is a punishment I wouldn't wish on my closest enemy, except at this point in time I feel it would take a lifetime with Ingrid to inflict the sort of pain I feel would be appropriate.

'Right,' I say slowly, nodding at Portia to let her know I know she's lying.

'Anyway,' she says, smiling brightly at Ingrid and slightly less brightly at me, 'got to go. Big night out tonight.'

'I'll just bet,' I say, and she stops and stares at me, then shakes her head as if I'm the one who's mad, and Ingrid shows her to the door. I can hear the two of them whispering in muffled voices, and Jesus Christ, I can't believe Portia is whispering about me to the bloody bitch of an au pair girl, but I don't care, at least I kept *my* dignity this evening.

'Are you certain you are feeling okay?' Ingrid says, walking back into the kitchen after the front door slams, and pouring an orange juice for Max.

'I'm not the one you should be asking,' I say pointedly, and Ingrid shrugs nonchalantly and goes out to call Max just as – thank God – I hear the key turn in the front door and Lucy walks in, only to be practically knocked over by Max jumping into her arms.

'That wasn't Portia I just saw driving off, was it?' she says, cuddling Max as she walks into the kitchen.

'Yup. She was dropping off a cookery book.' I point to the book as Lucy shrieks and immediately starts flicking the pages.

'Oh, she's such an angel! I can't believe she remembered this, how lovely. I must remember to phone her and thank her. Honestly, Cath,' and Lucy looks up at me, smiling, 'I cannot tell you how thrilled I am that Portia has come back into all of your lives, that she's now a part of mine. We're all very lucky, you know,' and she covers Max's face with kisses as he giggles and flings his arms round her neck, kissing her in return.

Oh bugger, I think, using Lucy's favourite expression. If only you knew.

Chapter twenty-one

A week later and I'm convinced Lucy thinks I'm completely mad. All day yesterday she kept catching me watching her with, as she put it, these big worried eyes, but every time she asked me what was wrong I just sighed, apparently, and said it was nothing.

Just before six o'clock I start telling people that we're closing, but, as usual, they all suddenly seem to have gone deaf, which I suppose can only be a good thing, really, given that there appear to be five deaf people currently in Bookends, which is infinitely preferable to no people at all.

'I'm sorry, but we are in fact closing now.'

'I'm sorry, but I'm going to have to ask you to leave.'

'I'm sorry, but we will still be here in the morning if you want to come and finish the book.'

And all this said with a polite smile. Eventually everybody leaves, and Bill, Rachel and I walk around the shop and put the books back where they belong, the shelves managing to get extraordinarily muddled up by the end of each day.

Bill and Rachel leave, and half an hour later I move over to the bar to see how Lucy is. She finishes wiping one of the tables, winks at me, then a few minutes later comes over to the table with two large milky coffees and a giant slab of juicy carrot cake with two forks.

Untying her apron she collapses into a chair and gives me a weary smile. 'How are you doing, my darling Cath?

And more importantly, what are you up to tonight?' she asks. 'Seeing James again or is it too soon?'

'Much too soon. I haven't even thanked him for last week. Damn. I meant to phone today.'

'Why not phone now?'

'No, it's okay. I'll wait until I get home.'

Lucy's smile disappears for a while and she stares into space, her mind obviously on other things. Poor Lucy. Oh God. Do you think she knows?

'Lucy? Are you okay?'

She looks at me with a smile and nods, but the expression in her eyes is one of sadness.

'Are you sure?'

'Well, no.' She says finally, and I mentally brace myself because if she actually asks me if I know anything, I just don't know what I'm going to say. Lie. You must lie. But I'm a hopeless liar. My face is, as Si always says, exactly like an open book.

I blush, I stammer, and I find it completely impossible to look the other person in the eye. Your classic textbook crap liar, so please God, don't let Lucy ask me, don't let her elicit my opinion on this.

'What's the matter?' As if I don't already know.

'It's us, I suppose. Josh and I,' and the smile has well and truly disappeared, which is when I realize that I never see Lucy's face in repose. She is always so bright, so animated, that seeing her like this makes it look as if all the stuffing has been knocked out of her. Which I suppose it has, if she's found anything out.

'Things just aren't right,' she continues after a long pause, looking up at me to see if I'm still listening.

'I know that things have changed, what with me working here, and Josh suddenly having this really big deal, and that we're not spending as much time together, but Josh seems to have taken it personally, and the less time he spends at home, the less time he seems to *want* to spend at home.'

'Have you tried talking to him?' I say, which is what I always say when I can't think of anything else. Plus, I learned it from Lucy.

'Ridiculous, isn't it? Here I am, having recently done that damn counselling course, and I'm married to a man who completely clams up at the first hint of a problem. The worst thing is that normally I can draw things out of him, but I feel so guilty at not being there, not being at home any more, I seem to have lost the ability to communicate as well.'

'Oh, Lucy,' I say sadly, rubbing her arm to comfort her.

'And I know this sounds ridiculous, but if I didn't know better I'd think he was up to something.'

I can't stop my sharp intake of breath, but luckily Lucy's looking at the table and she neither hears nor sees.

'Late nights practically every night, incommunicado because he's locked in meetings. God,' and she gives a rueful smile. 'They're supposed to be the classic signs of an affair, aren't they?'

'*Do* you think he's having an affair?' I ask, in what I hope is a nonchalant manner.

'Josh? Absolutely not,' and she starts laughing. 'But don't think I haven't thought about it. It's just absolutely not up his street, although God knows I wouldn't blame him, given the state of our sex life. I don't even remember the last time we had sex, and Cath, this is so awful, but I'm just too blasted tired.

'You know,' she says, looking up at me, 'often during the day I feel really rather sexy. I'll read something or

265

think about something, and I'll think, how lucky I am to be going home to a man that I still really fancy, and maybe tonight we'll make love and I spend the rest of the day looking forward to it.'

'And?'

'And then by the time I've got home and spent some time with Max, and had something to eat and jumped into a hot bath, I'm so exhausted I can hardly lift my feet, and it's all I can do to actually stand up and walk from the bathroom to the bedroom, fling back the duvet and climb into bed. That uses up any surplus energy I might have had, and then that's it. I'm fast asleep as soon as my head touches the pillow.'

'Lucy, if it's any consolation, it's exactly the same for me. It is exhausting, running our own business, and I could seriously do with a holiday, but don't the benefits outweigh the negatives?'

'In your case, my darling, yes, because, and Cath, don't take this the wrong way, but because you haven't got a family, but in my case, I just don't know any more.' She sighs deeply. 'I didn't mean that. Of course the benefits outweigh the negatives, I suppose it's just a question of finding the right balance.'

There's a silence for a while and I try to lighten the tone. 'Well, they always say that you stop having sex when you get married. You're just proving the rule.'

'But Josh and I always had the most marvellous sex life. Oh, Cath, I'm not embarrassing you, am I? Do you mind me talking to you like this? It's just that I have to talk to someone or I'm simply going to explode. Or implode,' she says sadly, 'which is infinitely worse,' and she smiles.

'It's fine. I don't mind at all. I just wish I knew what to say.'

'Josh and I always used to say how lucky we were that our sex life was still fantastic, but now . . .'

'Did you mean what you said about not blaming him if he were to have an affair, then?'

'No,' she sighs. 'Of course I didn't mean that. I'd be devastated if he were having an affair. It would be horrific. But trust me, Cath, I know I feel like I'm going crazy, but I honestly don't believe he would do that. I think, I hope, it's just a phase we're going through.'

'All marriages have their ups and downs,' I state sagely, praying that this is just a phase, that soon this will be over and Portia will have moved on.

'I know,' she says sadly. 'It's just that we've never hit a down like this before, and, although I know we'll come out of it, it's pretty bloody miserable when you're stuck in it.'

'What about pulling a big seduction number?' I say suddenly, as Lucy looks puzzled. 'You know, sexy underwear, stockings, the whole works. I always read those articles about women putting the sex back into their sex lives, so why shouldn't you try it?'

'You're not serious?' Lucy starts to laugh. 'I'd look like a trussed-up chicken in one of those outfits.'

'You wouldn't.' I start liking this idea more and more. 'You'd look gorgeous. How about if Si and I took you on a shopping expedition? If nothing else we'd have a laugh, and God knows we all need a laugh right now.'

'I'd feel ridiculous,' Lucy laughs, pretending to be embarrassed, but I can tell her resistance is wearing thin. 'Anyway, what on earth do you suppose I'd buy?'

'I don't know,' I chuckle, 'possibly a little French maid's outfit? Or how about a nurse's uniform, that always seems to do it.'

'God no!' Lucy starts to giggle. 'How impossibly naff.'

'But sexy,' I wink, and the pair of us snort our coffee out through our noses.

'Don't even think about it,' Si says, when I inform him of our plan.

'What? You don't think it's a good idea?' I'm staggered at his disapproval.

'Sweets, I think it's a wonderful idea. I think that, at the very least, it will be fun for Lucy and that's a bit of an accomplishment right now.'

'So don't even think about what?'

'Ann Summers. I wouldn't let you near the place. If we're going to do it, we're going to do it right, and the only place to go is Agent Provocateur.'

'Oooh,' I squeal, suddenly feeling like a little girl. 'Is that the place that sells those fluffy marabou mules? The slippers that no good housewife should be without?'

'Those plus a million other gorgeously sexy bits and pieces.'

'Let's go,' I say greedily. 'Today? Tomorrow? I want those slippers and I want them now.'

'Well, well . . . Who would have thought our Cath was a Brigitte Bardot in the making.'

'Not bloody likely,' I laugh. 'I've just dreamt of those slippers ever since I was about five years old. Can we go soon? Pleeeeeeeeeease? Pleeeeeeeease?'

'Only if you promise to buy me a leopard-skin thong.'

'It's a done deal.'

Si lets out a long sigh. 'On a more serious note, Cath, do you actually think this might work?'

'I don't know, but I'm not letting this marriage collapse without a fight.'

'I know,' he says softly. 'I feel the same way. Anyway, back to the real world, have you phoned the gorgeous

James yet to thank him and apologize for being so spacey at the end of the evening?'

'Oh God,' I groan. 'I feel so awful about that, shit . . . call waiting, can you hang on?'

'Don't worry, I'll talk to you later,' and he blows me a kiss and is gone. I press the appropriate buttons and say hello.

'Cath?'

Well, speak of the devil. It's James. 'I was worried about you, and I just wanted to phone to see if you were okay. Are you feeling better?'

'James, you're making me feel so guilty. All week I've meant to call you and thank you for a lovely evening, but I've been so busy I haven't had a chance.'

'It can't have been that lovely,' James says, 'not at the end, anyway.'

'Well, a bit traumatic, but the beginning was perfect, and had we not seen, well, you know. Had that not happened, the whole evening would have been perfect.'

'That's sweet of you to say so,' James says, and then we both sit there for a while as I wonder whether he's going to ask me out again, and actually hoping that he will, because I want to give this another chance, I want us to have an evening that really is perfect, from beginning to end.

But Cath the inexperienced idiot can't say that of course, so I just sit there in silence waiting, praying, for him to ask, and after a while he just says that he's glad I'm okay and that I should take care, and I put the phone down, suddenly feeling a deep emptiness.

Which is ridiculous, really. I mean, I hardly know him. It was one evening. There's nothing physical, no physical attraction, but I have to say I was looking forward to getting to know him better.

And even I'm amazed at how quickly I've managed to blow it this time. Oh well, there's only one thing for it. Eight slices of bread and half a packet of chocolate Hobnobs.

Chapter twenty-two

'Si really isn't that keen on Portia, is he?' A few days later it's a slow afternoon in Bookends, and Lucy's helping me tidy up the stock room. She tries to look nonchalant, but it doesn't work, and I know that this isn't the end of the question, that Si's reaction every time Portia's name is mentioned has only served to sow the seeds of doubt in Lucy's head.

'What do you mean?'

'Oh, come on, Cath! There's something going on, isn't there?'

All the colour drains out of my face, and, I swear, my heart actually misses a beat.

'What do you mean?' I speak slowly, trying to keep my voice calm and steady, and managing somehow, even though the voice sounds nothing like my own.

'For starters, you look like a ghost every time Portia's name is mentioned, and Si looks as if he's about to murder someone, probably Portia. What on earth is going on with her?'

Oh God, what do I do? Do I tell her? Should I confess? This is, after all, one of my closest friends in the world, and would I not be a better friend by telling her of Josh's betrayal?

What if the roles were reversed? Would I want to know? If I were with, say, James, and he was being unfaithful, and Si or Lucy found out about it, wouldn't I be more furious if I discovered that they knew and hadn't told me?

But then they say it's always the messenger who gets shot, and maybe it isn't any of my business. Or maybe I should just pray that it is, after all, a phase, and just cross my fingers and hope that it's all over soon.

I take a deep breath and look into Lucy's eyes, and I know immediately that I will not be the one to tell her, to hurt her in this way.

'What's going on with Portia?' I repeat, stalling for time.

'Yes, have the three of you had some kind of falling out or something?'

My relief is palpable.

'It's ridiculous that you and Si were so excited about seeing her again after all this time, and suddenly she's become *persona non grata*, and I can't understand why.'

I shrug. 'You know,' I say, after a while, 'it isn't anything tangible. I think that both Si and I have realized that ten years is a long time, and people change enormously in ten years, and I just don't think we have that much in common with her any more.'

Lucy's about to say something else when the door creaks open and Si staggers in, clutching his head and groaning in mock-agony.

'Fine, thank you,' I laugh. 'Nice to see you too.'

'Sssh,' he says. 'Hangover.'

'Let me guess . . . Turnmills *again*?'

He nods.

'So you've been out clubbing all night and you probably got home at, what, six this morning?'

Si nods.

'Which would explain why,' I look at my watch, 'at five minutes to four in the afternoon you're still feeling like shit. I hope it was worth it.'

Si looks up as a grin spreads all over his face.

'Uh oh,' Lucy laughs. 'I hope *he* was worth it.'

'Well, you know what they say,' Si sounds, and looks, brighter than he has done in ages. 'The best way of getting over someone is to find someone new.'

'No! Already?'

'Well, not permanently,' Si says. 'Definitely not relationship material, but gorgeous, gorgeous, gorgeous, and let's just say a good time was had by all. Meanwhile back at the ranch, how did the new sexy Lucy go down on Friday night?'

Lucy sighs. 'Going down was the last thing on my mind that night.'

'Now Lucy,' Si admonishes her, 'didn't I tell you it should have been the first.'

'I tried. Really, I did, but he didn't want to know . . .'

'Oh, Lucy,' I stroke her arm, and, fuelled by cappuccinos and carrot cake, the full story comes out.

Josh phoned early Friday afternoon and said he had a meeting but wouldn't be back later than eight thirty, so Lucy ran up the road to the beauty salon and had her legs waxed, even though they didn't really need it, just to be on the safe side. Then up to Waitrose, where she strode round the aisles smiling to herself, because here she was, playing the archetypal fifties housewife, shopping mid-afternoon for food for her husband's dinner, when tucked inside her cupboard at home were bags of gorgeously sexy lacy underwear with which to tempt him later that night.

She went home and slapped on a cucumber face mask while chopping and peeling, switching the radio on in the kitchen and dancing around in time with the music, feeling, for the first time in a long time, as if she were getting ready for something special.

At six o'clock, when the casserole was firmly in the

oven, the pastry had been carefully laid out over the tarte tatin, Lucy poured four capfuls ('Four capfuls!' exclaimed Si) of luxurious and horrendously expensive bubble bath into the hot running water, and lay back feeling excited, and sensuous, and completely relaxed.

Max, for once, seemed to be on his best behaviour, and after dinner and a story he climbed into bed, had a goodnight cuddle, and went straight off to sleep, leaving Lucy to finish her preparations.

She tipped her head upside down once her hair was dry and sprayed hairspray all over, so when she tipped her head back she looked wanton and sexy, in the way that Josh had always said he loved, although she could never be bothered to do it these days.

She stood in front of the bathroom mirror, a magazine laid out on the closed seat of the loo, its pages open to a beautiful blonde model advertising lipstick, and Lucy, not being an expert with make-up but being none the less exceptionally creative, tried hard to copy the make-up, brushstroke for brushstroke, line for line.

She shrugged off her huge old slightly grubby towelling robe and carefully pulled the new underwear out of the bag, folding the tissue paper and putting it back so as not to disturb the perfection.

And slipping her feet into her highest heels, she opened the wardrobe door back as far as it would go, and examined herself carefully in the full-length mirror hanging on the inside of the door.

'Well hello, big boy,' she said to herself, in an accent as close to Mae West's as she could manage, a slow kitten-like smile spreading on her face. 'Why don't you come up and see me some time?'

Si laughs briefly, breaking the spell, and even Lucy

has to join in. 'I bet you looked fantastic, though,' he says.

'You know what?' A genuine smile breaks through. 'I actually did, although I didn't look like me in the slightest. I looked in the mirror and there was this sexy, curvaceous glamour puss staring back.'

'What do you mean, it didn't look like you? You *are* a sexy, curvaceous glamour puss.'

'Oh, Si, I do love you. No, I'm not, nor would I normally want to be, but I didn't think I even had it in me any more to look like that.'

'Anyway, go on, what happened?' I'm getting impatient.

Lucy slipped a little black dress over the top and went downstairs to pour herself a glass of champagne, which always gets her in the mood for romance. The table looked beautiful. No kitchen, not tonight. The dining room was sparkling, candlelight glinting off crystal, and sleek silver candlesticks. Everything was perfect.

At twenty past eight Lucy took the casserole out of the oven and replaced it with the tarte tatin. She ran upstairs and blotted the shine off her nose, reapplied lipstick and a dash of lip gloss to give her a sexy pout, and took the ice bucket and champagne into the living room.

There she lit ylang ylang scented candles, put Nina Simone on low, and watched herself in the mirror as she waited for the front door to open.

After fifteen minutes she picked up a magazine lying on the coffee table and started idly flicking through, not really concentrating. Fifteen minutes is nothing, she told herself. Who could, after all, predict exactly when a business meeting was going to end?

She was telling herself the same thing forty-five minutes later. And again at ten o'clock.

But at a quarter past ten she stopped waiting. She kicked off her shoes and put the casserole – which had grown cold long before – into the fridge. The empty champagne bottle went in the bin, and the tarte tatin – Josh's favourite pudding – was tipped on top of the champagne.

And just as she finished clearing the dining room, disappointment, sadness and too much champagne making her movements slow and heavy, the front door opened.

'Sorry I'm so late,' Josh said, hardly glancing at Lucy. 'The bloody meeting went on for hours. I'm exhausted.' He was pulling his tie off as he put his briefcase down in the hallway, and finally looked at Lucy as she stood in the doorway in her little black dress and stockinged feet, lipstick chewed off, hair pulled back in a scrunchie, and for a minute her heart lifted.

'You don't mind if I go straight to bed?' Josh said, looking at her but most definitely not seeing her.

Lucy, deflated, shrugged, sighed, and took the champagne flutes into the kitchen, whereupon she threw them, slowly and deliberately, against the back door.

'Jesus!' Josh came thundering back down the stairs to survey the shards of crystal littering the kitchen floor. 'God, you must be more careful. Look, leave it for Ingrid to clear up in the morning. I'm off to bed. Night.' And he kissed her distractedly on the forehead, then went to bed.

'Do you know how I felt?' Lucy asks, sitting here with us now. 'I felt relieved that he hadn't even noticed, because if he had seen me, seen what I was wearing, seen the effort I had made, I would have been embarrassed, and that's the one thing I couldn't stand.

'And, as much as I hate to admit it, it does rather seem like dignity is about the only thing I've got left in this blasted marriage right now.'

'God, Lucy, it sounds horrific.' I take her hand and squeeze it, as Lucy rubs her eyes as if to rub out the memory.

'It's actually almost funny. It was like something out of a bad film. If we had ever actually got around to getting a dog, I probably *would* have told him his dinner was in the dog.'

'Given that it does actually sound like something out of a bad film,' Si says, 'I suppose we can assume that by the time you actually got to bed Josh was snoring like a baby, and lying on his side with his back towards you.'

'I know you're in the film business,' she says sadly, 'but do you always have to be so right about everything?'

And then none of us says anything, because although her last remark was punctuated with a brief smile, it isn't like Lucy to say something like that, and I know then that she is hurting far more than she is letting on.

'We could always go to plan B,' Si says, after a while.

'And plan B is?'

Si shrugs. 'God knows, but give me five minutes and I'm sure I'll be able to think of something.'

Lucy gets up and goes to the loo, and as soon as she's out of earshot I lean forward towards Si. 'I think maybe you should talk to him.'

'Me? Why me?' Si's voice is now back to its usual level, and he sits back in his chair, pointing at his chest indignantly before leaning forward again conspiratorially. 'Why not you? Josh has always listened to you.'

And it's true, Josh has. I'm not sure why, but perhaps because I've always had a proper job (as opposed to Si's sporadic bursts of creativity), because he knows I'm independent, he has somehow trusted me, and, although I do not want to do this, I think that Si may have a point. That if Josh will listen to anyone at all, he might listen to me, and at this point in time I can no longer sit back and watch his marriage disintegrate.

Since I saw him and Portia together, we haven't actually had a proper conversation. He used to call me in the office for long, cosy chats, but now that I'm in the bookshop, with Lucy, he only ever phones to speak to her, and even when I pick up the phone he usually sounds far too busy to talk. I don't even remember the last time Josh phoned me at home for a long chat, but then again I suppose I haven't exactly made much of an effort either.

But once upon a time what Si has just said would have been true, and perhaps it still is true. Si can see that his point has struck, and that I am thinking about it, so he carries on, telling me that Josh trusts me, and that we owe it to Lucy, and then finally that it's all my fault that Portia's back anyway, so I should take responsibility for getting rid of her again.

'Si! That's not bloody fair. You can't pin this one on me. There was no way I could have known what would happen with Josh, and anyway you used to talk about her all the time as well.'

'I know, I know. I'm sorry and I didn't mean that, it's just that I feel so bloody guilty. It is kind of our fault. I mean, if you and I hadn't dialled her number, this wouldn't have happened.'

'You know what? I don't believe that. Ultimately this

is Josh's decision, and neither of us is to blame. We shouldn't get involved at all, but I love Josh and Lucy too much to ignore this, so I'll do the only thing I can.'

'Which is?'

'Tell Josh that we know, and remind him of what he'd be losing if he and Lucy broke up.' But the very thought makes me feel sick to my stomach.

'And what if he says that Portia's the love of his life and she's the only thing he cares about?'

'First of all, Si, stop being so bloody negative, and second, I just don't believe Josh would do that, I just can't believe that.'

Lucy comes back to the table with a bottle of champagne that's part of our secret stash, well hidden in the stock room.

'Look at you two with your heads together, whispering furtively. If I didn't know better, I'd say you were planning a secret rendezvous.'

'You might say that,' Si sniffs, standing up and getting some glasses out, 'but I couldn't possibly comment,' and with that he pops the cork and the three of us start to drink.

Chapter twenty-three

Thank God my life seems to have found its equilibrium again. This whole Josh and Lucy thing has been so upsetting, that even when I tried to get on with things and forget about it, I still felt unsettled all the time, as if something terrible were about to happen, something I couldn't control, couldn't get away from.

I suppose it could just have been the fact that Portia had come back at all. Irrespective of her affair with Josh, I suppose it is bound to be unsettling when somebody new enters your world, changes the dynamic, disturbs the balance.

She's called me a few times, left messages, and I've managed to avoid the calls, telling Bill and Rachel to say I'm out (Lucy being the only one who never picks up the phone, as she's always run off her feet in the café) and screening my calls at home. Si, who's the only person who knows I'm avoiding her, thinks this is crazy, but it's so much easier to withdraw from the friendship than it would be to confront her.

And I know it's wimpy. I feel sometimes that I owe it to Lucy, that I should just pitch up on Portia's doorstep, screaming blue murder, but I was always in awe of Portia, all those years ago, and even though I'm an adult now and my life has moved on, when I'm around Portia I regress to those years, and I suppose if I'm really honest I'd have to say I'm ever so slightly frightened of her.

Which is why I don't say anything. Plus it isn't any of my business, although of course it is, because she is hurting one of the people I love most in the world, but, as Si keeps pointing out to me, she isn't the only bad guy in this scenario. I know it takes two to tango and all that, yet I can't help but feel that however clever and sharp Josh may be, he's also weak. I've always known that, and although I didn't think he'd be so weak as to give in to temptation quite this quickly, clearly I was wrong. But I still can't blame him as much as I blame Portia for tempting him in the first place.

I want to, but I can't.

Maybe it's my anger that's stopping me from confronting Portia. Maybe I'm so frightened of what I'll say to her, that it's easier to keep it contained, and to hope and pray that everything gets back to normal.

And the funny thing is that for the last week or so, Lucy seems much happier, and please let it not be premature of me to wish, to pray, that things might be cooling down.

I couldn't go as far as to say it's over with Portia and Josh, because he still arrives home late in the evening, claiming meetings or a heavy work schedule, which, as everyone knows, is always the classic excuse. And I still notice that Josh, who has always openly and lovingly declared his adoration for Lucy, now seems distracted much of the time, but Lucy has said that things have improved, and that, for now, seems to be enough.

She made me laugh this morning, telling me about Ingrid, who seems to be acting more and more strangely. Lucy told me how she got home last night and listened to the answer phone, the good news being that there was no message from Josh saying he had a meeting that night. And the bad news being that there was no message from Josh saying he'd be home for supper.

She poured herself a whisky, sat down at the kitchen table and kicked off her shoes, only for her mouth to drop open as Ingrid walked nonchalantly in and picked up her keys from off the kitchen table.

She had, Lucy giggled, outdone even herself. She was wearing a red PVC catsuit, which showed off her extraordinary figure extraordinarily, and her hair was scraped off her face in a slick ponytail.

'Off to an S & M club?' Lucy inquired politely, which is completely out of character, but, as Lucy admitted, she was too damned tired to keep up the good old British reserve.

'No,' Ingrid said, all sweet smiles that didn't, somehow, seem to go with her outfit. 'I have a hot date.' She then added, 'If I am not back tonight, you will not worry?'

'Well, uh, I suppose not, not if you tell me you won't be. Should I lock the front door, then?'

'I think so,' Ingrid said, waving goodbye and practically floating out of the room, as Lucy blinked a few times just to check she wasn't dreaming.

'God,' I laughed, listening to the story. 'She sounds like Denise Van Outen on Viagra. I hope he's worth it.'

'Oh shut up.' Lucy and I both giggled. 'You're just jealous. I bet you wish you looked that good in a red PVC catsuit. I know I certainly do.' And then her voice suddenly became serious and she looked down at the table before looking at me. 'I know this sounds ridiculous,' she said slowly, 'because I really don't think that Josh would have an affair, but you don't think . . . ?' She tailed off as I mentally willed my heart to slow down.

'I mean, it's just that Ingrid seems far happier suddenly, and she obviously is seeing someone, and you don't think that . . . well, you don't think Josh and Ingrid?'

'God, no!' I practically shouted. 'Not in a million years!'

Lucy looked relieved. 'Oh, okay, then, if you're sure.

Anyway, as it happens Josh was an absolute sweetie last night. He turned up with a huge bunch of flowers and whisked me off to Julie's for dinner.'

And apparently it was the first normal evening they'd had in ages. Josh had arranged for Laura to come and babysit, and once they were in the restaurant they sat and actually talked. Not about the bookshop, not about Max, not about Josh's work, but just talked.

They talked about themselves, reminisced about the first time they'd been to Julie's, and ended up actually laughing. It was, Lucy said, a beam breaking out on her face, wonderful. And wonderful because it was so *normal*. Not romantic, not earth-shattering, it didn't lead to passionate sex or anything like that, but she felt married again. And happy. And safe.

Si rang earlier and I told him about Lucy's evening, and he said it was a good sign. Not time to start breathing sighs of relief, he added hurriedly, but certainly promising that they seemed to be making time for one another again, although it doesn't mean it's over with Portia. Not by a long shot.

But I don't know any more. I think that maybe it was just a passing fling. That perhaps, like that one night all those years ago at university, it's over. But there's no doubt that something has happened, regardless of whether it may or may not be happening now.

And then Si asked me if I thought Portia knows that we know. I would imagine she'd have to be stupid not to, although the extraordinary thing is that she may have stopped phoning Si and I, having finally got the message, but she hasn't stopped phoning Lucy.

And that's what really pisses me off. She seems to have some sort of compulsion, but you would have thought she'd show a bit more subtlety. I mean, I've heard of mistresses secretly stalking the wives for a bit, just to find out what they're like, what they look like, what they do with their days. But not when they already *know* the wives. That's just sick. Or asking for trouble, but then maybe that's part of Portia's plan, part of her happy ending. To ensure that Lucy finds out, Portia will either have to tell Lucy or drop a hint, set up a situation in which there can be no doubt, and then Lucy will have to let Josh go.

Because right now I wouldn't like to place money on which way Josh would run if push came to shove, and if you ask me, which Si frequently does, he seems pretty damn happy having the best of both worlds: Lucy cooking for him and mothering him and keeping a wonderful home in which he barely has to lift a finger, and Portia taking care of sex, a few evenings a week.

But would he really leave Lucy? If push did finally come to shove, would he give all that up for Portia's life? Because I know it looks glamorous, and I know there have been times when I have been deeply envious of Portia, but would Josh really want to live that modern, trendy lifestyle?

Would he really be happy going out every single night, hanging out with media junkies at Soho House, nibbling Thai spiced fish cakes in restaurants, only ever going home to sleep, and even that is done between immaculate linen sheets that somehow don't seem to *do* creases.

Remember I have sat on Portia's sofa, and trust me, it is not a sofa that inspires you to kick off your shoes and curl up with the remote control while shovelling down a curry, which is Josh's favoured way of spending an evening.

And while I know there are some women who are prepared to compromise their entire *beings* for their man, Portia isn't one of them. Maybe once upon a time she would have willingly made a few sacrifices, but now, in her thirties, I realize that Portia has grown hard.

She is almost *too* independent, too self-sufficient, and if a man chose to enter her life – and I have to say I think most would be, after the initial glamour and excitement, scared off – but if a man did choose to enter it on a permanent basis, it would have to be on her terms or not at all.

And Josh might enjoy it for a while. For a while it might feel as if he had stepped into a film, but I can't see him enjoying it for ever, and I hope, I hope and I pray, that this is a passing fling and that Josh somehow has to exorcize Portia completely before moving on with his life. With Lucy.

A week later and I could almost have believed that it really was over with Portia, because ever since that night at Julie's, Josh and Lucy have been, well, they've been Josh and Lucy again. Even to the point where Lucy phoned this morning to say how about Sunday lunch, usual table, usual time? And without even thinking about it, without even checking to see if Si was coming too, I said yes.

As soon as I walk in the discomfort, the unsettled feeling I've been carrying with me, disappears, because there, in the corner, are the usual gang, and the scene is so familiar it is as comforting as travelling back to the womb.

A cafetière fights for space among the piles of papers, and I know exactly what papers will be there, and who brought what because the routine is the same every week, and even though we haven't done our Sunday lunch for a few weeks, I know the routine will never change. I know that Josh will have brought the *Sunday Times* that they have delivered every week, and the *Observer* that he will have picked up on the way, and that Si will have brought the gossipy tabloids to gasp over with Lucy and I as Josh pretends to be reading the serious papers, although he will be unable to resist the gossip and feign exasperation with us, but he will, eventually, join in.

A basket of croissants sits in the centre of the table, and Josh is buried in the Money section of the *Sunday Times*; Si is stuffing his face with croissant while simultaneously pointing out pictures in the *News of the World* magazine, and Lucy is sipping her coffee, laughing with Si at his outrageous comments.

I pull off my jacket and scarf, rubbing my hands together to warm them up as they're almost blue from the cold November air, and I drape everything over the back of the chair and sit down, helping myself to Si's fresh orange juice as Lucy calls the waitress over and orders more coffee and an extra cup, then telling her we're ready to order, although why they waited is beyond me because we always order the same thing.

Si has fruit salad because it makes him feel virtuous, and I think he thinks it counterbalances the fried eggs and toast he has afterwards. Josh has a full English breakfast, Lucy has scrambled eggs with bacon, and I have scrambled eggs, runny if that's okay, with bacon, sausages and copious amounts of toast.

It's not unusual to sit at this table, washing down all the food with gallons of fresh orange juice and coffee, for around three hours. Si's perfected the art of shooting filthy looks at the people queuing patiently by the door, waiting for someone to leave, and it's usually my guilt that eventually forces us up, magnanimously giving our table to the weary but grateful.

'So,' Si says when I've had some coffee. 'Heard the latest gossip.'

'Let me guess. Prime Minister run off with Meg Ryan? Queen pregnant again?'

Si raises an eyebrow. '*Real* gossip, sweets. Ingrid, it seems, has a ' – and he pauses to roll his *r*'s significantly – 'lurverrrr.'

'Oh, Si!' Lucy slaps him playfully. 'You are so beastly about poor Ingrid. I shouldn't have said anything.'

'So what else is new?' I shrug my shoulders. 'She did say she had a hot date the night of the red catsuit, and she said she probably wouldn't be coming home, so what's the big deal?'

'Okay, no big deal,' Si says nonchalantly, 'it's just that it's been confirmed now. She's going away with him next weekend.'

'Have you met him?' I ask Lucy. 'What's he like?'

'You know how private she is,' Lucy says. 'She hasn't said a word, other than to say her new lover is taking her to the George V in Paris for the weekend, and would we mind if she were gone for four days.'

'What did you say?'

'What *could* I say? Of course I said yes.'

'But weren't you positively dying to know?' Si's rubbing his hands together with glee. 'The George V is the best hotel in Paris, for God's sake! I bet it's some incredibly wealthy businessman with a fetish for rubber. He'll probably produce a bag of whips and chains once she gets there.'

'So does this new lurrve,' I pick up Si's inflection, 'mean that the dreaded Ingrid has become a nicer person?'

Lucy laughs. 'I'm not sure that nicer is the right word, but she's certainly more amenable. Cath, my darling, I'm still completely terrified of her, and the only reason I keep her is because of Max, but at least she seems a bit happier, which certainly makes life easier for the rest of us.'

'Oh well,' I say, shrugging. 'At least she's not stealing from you.'

'What?' Si's looking at me as if I've gone mad.

'I'm serious. One of the girls at work was telling me about a nanny they had, and every night when her husband got home he'd empty all the loose change out of his pockets and put it in one of those huge ketchup jars.'

'Yeuch,' Si spits. 'Sounds messy.'

'Don't be stupid, Si, it had been emptied and washed. Anway, they suddenly realized that all the pound coins and silver had gone, and the only thing left was a huge jar of coppers. She must have got hundreds.'

'Didn't they say anything?' Si's aghast.

'Apparently they tried to ask very nicely, but she got terribly upset, so they just left it and a week later she told them she couldn't work for them any more after being accused of something like that and she left.'

Si smiles. 'I suppose she took the kitchen sink with her?'

'Don't laugh.' Josh lays down the Money section and leans forward. 'Peter, one of the guys I work with, noticed that all his socks were disappearing. They couldn't figure it out and he kept buying more and more of these Italian silk socks that cost a bomb and can only be found in Harrods or somewhere.

'Then one day Peter's wife went into the au pair's room while she was out and her bottom drawer was slightly open and there were all the socks.'

'Bitch,' hisses Si, as Lucy and I start laughing, and Josh sits back petulantly.

'It's not the fact that it's only socks,' he justifies. 'It's the principle of the thing.'

'Yeah,' Si sneers. 'Bloody sock thieves. They should all be hanged. Anyway, serves him right for spending such a fortune on socks in the first place.'

'Christ, will you listen to us?' I'm suddenly horrified by our conversation. 'We sound so middle aged. Middle class. Talking about au pairs, for God's sake. What's happened to us?'

There's an awkward silence for a moment, and then the waitress arrives with our food. Lucy sits back and sighs with pleasure.

'God,' she says, sniffing, 'I can't tell you how lovely it is to be cooked for! Cath, I promise you I won't dwell on the subject because you're right, this conversation is just too awful, but I've just got one thing to add . . .

'We should actually count our blessings with Ingrid. She is a bit peculiar, but at least she's not dishonest, or a liar, or untrustworthy, and that's really the important thing. That, and the fact that Max, as we all know, adores her.'

'That boy really has no taste,' Si says acidly, with no shadow of a smile. 'Reminds me of his father.'

'Si!' Lucy and I exclaim at once, and Josh looks at Si in amazement, because there was more than a hint of viciousness in that remark, and although I know what he means, that he's talking about Portia, he has no right to be that obvious in front of Lucy.

'Si!' Lucy says again. 'Are you trying to say that Josh picked me in bad taste?'

Si recovers masterfully. 'My gorgeous Lucy,' he says, kissing her on the cheek, 'the one time in his life Josh has shown impeccable taste was in choosing you. No,' he says, catching, and holding, Josh's eye until Josh – almost imperceptibly – starts to squirm, 'I was talking about his clothes.'

I breathe a sigh of relief as Si reaches under the table and gives my leg a squeeze to reassure me.

'I mean, look at that shirt, for God's sake,' he says. 'Aren't you a bit old to be doing that whole student rugby thing?'

Lucy laughs and Josh looks down at his shirt. 'But I love this shirt,' he says. 'I've had this shirt for ever.'

'I know,' Si grunts. 'Looks like it,' and, as he picks up his fork and stabs a chunk of mango, I realize that Si is genuinely angry about this, and the only way he knows how to express it is to come out with these odd, vicious remarks.

Just as long as Lucy doesn't know.

We wander up to the O2 centre on Finchley Road for a lazy afternoon film, our breath visible in the cold air, and it feels lovely, it feels normal. I love this time of year. Early November, just as everyone starts to feel lovely and cosy, getting ready for the full force of winter, and the perfect time to disguise yourself with layers of snuggly warm clothes.

When Si walks me home I say goodbye knowing that this has been a perfect Sunday, and that it really doesn't get much better than this. Si is off to see a friend up the road, although he says if he's not there he'll pop back and we can have supper together.

Luckily for Si I have managed to go shopping this week. Unfortunately I went shopping at exactly the time they tell you never to go shopping, namely when you are completely starving. Starving in a supermarket completely obliterates reasonable thought, and instead of ending up with healthy, nourishing food that will last you a week, you end up with a basket of terrible fast food that is definitely bad for you and will probably be gone by the end of the night.

But even I couldn't have managed to polish off the contents of my fridge in one night, so Si can, if he comes back, look forward to a double cheese and pepperoni pizza, half a packet of onion bhajis, eight (I only ate two) pitta breads, the obligatory houmous and taramasalata, three quarters of a pack of pre-sliced Gouda cheese, a full and unopened packet of Chinese chicken wings, and a four-pack of white chocolate mousse.

Not a bad feast for a Sunday night, I think you'll agree.

I open up the Culture section, grab an old biro and circle my evening's viewing, and then, feeling absurdly decadent, start running a hot bath, even though it's only six o'clock in the evening. I think a glass of wine is called for, and I pour myself a glass of chilled Chardonnay and pad back into the bathroom, scraping my hair off my face with an elastic band that I pulled off a wad of post a few days ago.

And, soaking back into the hot water, I think how lovely today was. Even though we have spent our Sundays like this for years, it is only when you take a break, or when something threatens to disturb the routine, that you fully appreciate it when it is back to normal.

I pull off the elastic band and soak my head under water, loving the warmth, the feeling of being completely cut off from the world, and, reaching for the shampoo bottle, I come up for breath and lather up my head.

I dip under again and, as I emerge, shampoo still clinging to my hair, I keep very quiet because I'm sure I just heard the doorbell ring. A few seconds go by and there it is again. Definitely the doorbell.

Oh Christ. I grab a towel from the bath rail and, shivering, jump out of the bath, frantically rubbing the shampoo now dripping into my eyes, almost blinding myself in the process. I stumble to the front door, clutching the towel around me tightly, squinting out of the left eye because the right is now too clogged with shampoo and days-old mascara to open properly.

Now I know you should never open the door without asking who it is first, particularly not when you're female, single and living in London.

And even more particularly when you're half naked and wrapped in a towel, even if, as in my case, that's not a particularly appealing sight, given that the towel, for starters, is threadbare and not quite clean, and my face is streaked with mascara and my hair is still half covered in shampoo and is sticking up on the left side, but I was convinced it was going to be Si, so I didn't think twice.

Now I know you're not stupid, even though I, quite obviously am, but there on the doorstep, surprise surprise, is James.

Chapter twenty-four

'Ah,' I say, still squinting through the shampoo, slowly bringing James into focus.

'Ah,' he says, looking, it has to be said, slightly horrified by my appearance. 'I suppose I ought not to just drop in like this.'

'Actually I rather like people just dropping in. Except when I look like this of course. Do you want to come in and give me a few minutes?'

'No, no, don't worry.' He starts backing off. 'I'll ring you later.'

'James! Just come in, for God's sake.'

I practically pull him through the front door, push him on to the sofa and scurry along the corridor to the bedroom.

Shit. It's worse than I thought. No wonder he looked horrified, but, shoving the embarrassment aside, I run back into the bathroom, kneel by the bath and shove my head under water to quickly rinse my hair of the shampoo (I know it's more hygienic to use the shower but quite frankly I just didn't have the time).

I wash the mascara off my face, grab a hairbrush and run back into the bedroom, frantically pulling my hair back into the elastic band. And finally, letting the towel drop, I shove on some leggings and a baggy old sweatshirt, pausing before I walk out serenely to dash to the cupboard and pull on a bra because I do not need to hoist my boobs up from around my kneecaps in James's presence.

And eventually I walk sheepishly into the kitchen, as I shout at James over my shoulder, asking whether he wants a cup of tea. I hear him close a magazine and get up to join me in the kitchen, saying he would love one.

He comes in and sits down as I pick up the dirty plates that are covering almost every available inch of workspace and pile them in the sink, covering them with Fairy Liquid and hot water, then dig around for a bit until I find two mugs to wash up for us.

'It feels like ages since I've seen you,' I say brightly, as I open the fridge and tentatively smell the milk that, thank God, is still fine. 'What have you been up to?'

'Actually I've been incredibly busy painting,' he says, grinning, lifting an arm up from the table and examining the honey stain now spreading on his sleeve.

'Oh Christ! Sorry.' I run over with a cloth and clean the table, but James just laughs.

'Jesus, Cath. I remember that night you came over to the studio and it was a pigsty, you said you were worse than me, but I thought you were just joking to try to make me feel less embarrassed. But you really are more of a pig than I am, aren't you?'

'I can't help it,' I say, shrugging. 'I try so hard to be clean and tidy, but the pig inside just won't stay down. She's too strong. At least the mugs are now clean.' I grin, showing off the sparkling mugs, having scrubbed furiously to remove the week-old tea stains. 'So ... painting. What are you working on now?'

'You probably won't believe it. God, I can hardly believe it, but after you exhibited my stuff in the shop, *North West* magazine came over and did a feature on me, and suddenly I've got phone calls left, right and centre, asking where people can buy my work.'

'Oh, James! That's amazing!' I sit opposite him,

beaming, genuinely thrilled for him and completely filled with remorse, because I've been so wrapped up in Josh and Lucy that I haven't even given his exhibition a second thought.

'I mean, I'm not surprised,' I add quickly, because I'm really not. 'Your paintings are beautiful, but it's still incredible to have such a lucky break. Does this mean you'll be able to retire before forty?'

He grins. 'I don't think I've reached quite that level of success yet, but you never know . . .'

'Listen, today Bookends, tomorrow the Saatchi Gallery.'

'God, don't I bloody wish!'

'Stranger things have happened,' I laugh, 'to people who create things a hell of a lot more strange than you do.'

'Anyway, that's enough about me, what about you? How's everything with you?'

'The same.' I shrug, longing to be able to tell him exciting stories about my life, to make him laugh with witty tales of hanging out in glamorous places, but there's very little to tell.

'Had any more mad people in the bookshop lately?'

'Nah, and I'm slightly worried about it. I'm sure every bookshop should have its token eccentric.'

'I could always put an ad in the paper for you?' James grins. 'Wanted: true eccentric, sixty-plus, pink or blue hair, to add character and charm to local bookshop. No pay, but all the cappuccino you can drink. What d'you reckon?'

'I reckon you'd have to hire coaches to bring in all the lonely old dears who'd answer the ad,' I laugh.

'You could always borrow my nan,' he says. 'She's lonely.'

'But is she eccentric?'

'Not yet. But I'm sure she could learn. She could sit in the corner and screech at everyone in her thick Yorkshire accent.'

'And she wouldn't mind dyeing her hair pink?'

'It would make a change from misty mauve.'

'You are joking? Please tell me your grandmother doesn't really have misty mauve hair.'

'Okay, okay. She doesn't. But she was born in Yorkshire, does talk with a thick Yorkshire accent, and lists screeching as a hobby. God knows I should know, she's always telling me I don't ring her enough.'

I shake my head as I start to laugh. 'James, you do paint the most extraordinary mental pictures.'

'Thank you. That's the best compliment I've had all year. Now, there was something else I'd been meaning to talk to you about.'

'Yes?'

'My grandad.'

'You are joking?'

'Yes, actually. I know it's a bit of a pain in the arse, that I keep dropping in like this, but actually I hate the telephone . . .'

'James, love, you're an estate agent. You spend your life on the telephone, how can you hate it?'

'But that's work. That's exactly it. Once I leave work I hate the bloody thing, and it's much easier to talk to someone in person, particularly when you want to see them anyway, plus this is getting ridiculous now.

'The last time I tried to take you out for dinner it all ended up in a shambles, and I would really like to see you properly.'

'What do you mean, see me properly?' Although I

know what he means, and he knows that I know, because there's a huge grin on my face.

'I mean go out for dinner. Spend some proper time with you. Get to know you *properly*.'

'We could always start tonight,' I say coquettishly.

'Tonight?'

'We could have dinner tonight.'

'You're not busy?'

'Nope. The only thing is you'll have to wait around while I get dressed and stuff.'

James looks delighted. 'Tell you what,' he says, looking at his watch and standing up. 'If this is a proper date, and I bloody well hope it is, then I'll be back here at eight o'clock to pick you up. How does that sound?'

'Perfect.' I walk him to the door, and then a thought occurs to me. 'James, you know the last time we had dinner, when we saw Josh and . . . well, you know. Aren't you going to ask about Josh and Lucy?'

'Not my business, Cath.' He shrugs, at which point I'm incredibly tempted to kiss him. 'If you want to talk about it with someone, then I'm happy to listen, or try and help, but you should only tell me if you want to.'

'James,' I laugh. 'You're just too good to be true. I'll see you at eight.' And I close the front door behind him and squeal to myself for a bit, suddenly feeling things I thought I was incapable of feeling any more – excitement, exhilaration and more than a touch of anticipation.

I cannot believe that I have a proper date, and, more importantly, I cannot believe that I am actually excited about this date. It has been so long since anyone has made me feel these things, and even though I know I've avoided this for fear of getting hurt, there's something about James that makes me want to trust him.

And the more I get to know him, the more I like what I see. I thought he was so shy, so nervous at first, but I'm starting to see his sense of humour, and the fact that he's incredibly comfortable with who he is, and I like that about him. I could learn to like that a lot.

I dry my hair, change into something more appropriate, and when, at twenty to eight, the doorbell rings, I curse James silently for being so early, but thank God I am ready.

But it's not James, it's Si, and I have completely forgotten that he would be coming round for supper if his friend wasn't in, and I start to apologize, start to explain, when I notice that Si is as white as a sheet and looks suspiciously like he's about to throw up.

'Si? What is it? What's the matter?' I clutch him in alarm as he threatens to topple over, and then lead him inside, terrified of his shaking.

He sits down as if in a daze, and then turns to me. 'Will's not well.'

'Oh, Si.' My face crumples in sympathy, because, hate Will though I do, I can see that this is hurting Si, and that hurts me. 'I'm so sorry. Are you okay? Did you just find out?'

Si turns to me. 'Ian just told me.'

'Is it something serious?'

'Cath,' he whispers, turning to look at me, showing me the fear in his eyes. 'He's got AIDS.'

'What?' I never really knew what people meant when they talked about their blood running cold. Until now.

'He *said* he was fine. We talked about it because you know how completely paranoid I am, and he said he'd had a test last year and it was negative, and that if I was negative too, there was no reason to ... well ... you know, safe sex and everything.'

'Oh my God. Oh my God. Si.' My breath catches in my throat and I'm so angry, so frightened, I want to start shaking him. 'Please tell me you used condoms. Please tell me you didn't ...'

Si looks at me and then starts to cry, and I reach out and put my arms around him, rocking him to and fro as his body heaves with the sobs.

Four years ago Si lost one of his best friends. Jake was gorgeous. Funny, handsome, self-deprecating. They met at a cinema. Si, bored, took off for the afternoon and went by himself to catch a matinée. I remember he said he'd noticed Jake in the queue – and how, I laughed at the time, could he not.

Si caught Jake's eye, and Jake caught Si's, and although they weren't sitting together – Si was three rows behind Jake – there were only eight people in the cinema, and when the film was over Jake turned around and asked Si what he thought.

They went for coffee. Which turned into dinner. Which, at the time, quite probably could have turned into something more, but somehow the timing wasn't right, and instead of becoming lovers they became friends.

I remember feeling jealous of Jake. Jealous because despite the longer history that Si and I shared, there was an understanding between Jake and Si that I could never be a part of. Jealous because the two of them could go off and hit the clubs together, and even though I went, from time to time, I could never have as good a time as they could. And jealous because all of us could see that although they were only friends, Si had fallen hook, line and sinker, and if Jake's friendship was the only thing on offer, then that would have to be enough.

Jake was American, and very early on, before they even got to know one another that well – although of course Si was already secretly planning their cottage in the country, had already planted out the vegetable garden, named their two golden Labradors – Jake sat Si down and told him about his past. He told him about his youth, the years of anonymous sex with strangers, and he told him that, despite everything, he would not have lived those years differently.

Despite everything? Jake told him that when he first arrived in London he came down with a fever. One hundred and four degrees, vomiting and shivering, and he went to a doctor who tested him for HIV.

And because this was real life, and because real life doesn't always go the way we would like, Jake was positive. He was also devastated. He went through everything the counsellors told him he might experience: anger, fear, grief and, finally, acceptance.

His fever went away, the vomiting and shivering stopped, and he tried to pretend that everything was fine, that it had all been a nightmare, but of course it wasn't. Jake went to counselling, he met people living with AIDS, heard their stories, and somehow along the way he discovered that perhaps he was being shown a different way to live his life.

He learned that the challenge of having AIDS is not dying of AIDS, but living with AIDS. That it isn't an instant death sentence, that his life could be just as fulfilling, more even, than before: he could work with the community, give something back, make the absolute most of the rest of his life, however long, or short, it would turn out to be.

And Si listened to Jake, heard what he was saying, and when Jake finished, Si reached over and gave him a hug.

'I'm scared,' Si said. 'I have to be honest and if I'm honest then you have to know that it frightens me, terrifies me, because it, AIDS, has always been there, but it's never directly affected anyone who's been close to me. But I also know that you're one of my best friends, and whatever I can do for you, I will.'

They went to a bookshop that afternoon, and Jake pointed out the books he had read, some of which Si bought, to arm himself with information.

He learned to stop being frightened. He learned what was safe and what was not. And he learned that not every cough, every headache, every sneeze, was the onset of the downward spiral.

But Jake wasn't just HIV positive – Si always said he wished he'd met him years ago, wished he'd got to know him before the illness, even though Jake said he wouldn't have liked him as much, that he was a far nicer person since contracting HIV – Jake had AIDS, and although he had friends who had gone years without opportunistic infections, Jake was unlucky.

Soon after they met Jake developed PCP pneumonia. He'd already lost his appetite, had night sweats, but this was the moment he'd been dreading, the moment he hoped wouldn't come for years.

His CD4 count dropped to just under 100, he lost his appetite, his sleep, and his mood swings were frightening, but Si tried to fight for him, tried to find the strength to make him survive. Even during the times he shouted at Si, screamed at him to fuck off, Si sat silently, patiently, stroking his hair until Jake broke down in tears.

When the end finally came, all the people Jake had ever loved gathered together in the tiny terraced cottage he owned in Clapham. His mother and sister flew over from North Carolina. The friends came who had become closer to him than his family had ever been.

And then it was over. Jake was, finally, at peace, and Si, after cocooning himself away for months, gradually came out of his shell, and started to live in the real world again.

And since Jake, since reading the books, watching his friend die, Si has become the 'condom queen' of North London. (His expression, not mine.) AIDS, he has always subsequently said (an expression he picked up from someone else), is one hundred per cent fatal but one hundred per cent preventable.

And sure, he's had one-night-stands, brief encounters, but the one thing I was always absolutely certain of was that he had never, ever, practised unsafe sex. Not Si. So why is he sitting on my sofa crying, not answering my question?

I am about to ask again, when the doorbell goes. Oh Christ. James. Si looks at me questioningly and I whisper that I'll be back in a second. I go to the front door, feeling ridiculous for having to cancel again, but knowing that there's no way on earth I will leave Si like this.

And James can see immediately that there's something wrong.

'I don't bloody believe it,' he sighs, visibly annoyed. 'You're cancelling me again, aren't you?' he says flatly, and I can see that this time he really is pissed off.

'I'm so sorry, James, something has come up. I can't explain now. I'll have to explain later. Can I call you tomorrow?'

'You know what, Cath?' he says, and his voice is hard, and although I'd like to tell him why, I can't, and I know that he's upset, and this hardness is his way of covering it up, but if he gives me a second chance I will make certain he understands that it's not him, that I am not trying to avoid him. I start to speak but he turns to go.

'Just forget it. Let's just forget it.'

'James?' I plead softly as he looks at the floor. 'I am so, so sorry. I was so looking forward to this evening, and if there were any way I could go out with you, I would, but it's going to have to wait. I'm not cancelling, James, I'm just postponing.'

'How long,' he finally sighs, looking up at me and forcing a smile, 'do you suppose I will wait? Because I have to tell you, Cath, my patience has pretty much run out.'

'I promise I'll call you tomorrow,' I say, and this time he does turn to leave, and I shut the door and go back into the living room, to Si.

Chapter twenty-five

I know this isn't the time for recriminations, and I know that Si, above all else, needs support and understanding, but I'm in shock. I still can't understand how Si, the Condom Queen, could have risked everything for Will. Especially because we've always laughed in the past when Si's been told that people are fine – as Si has always said, 'He would say that, wouldn't he?', and it has never stopped Si from practising safe sex.

'I don't understand,' I keep saying. 'How? Why?' But having a test a year ago means that a year ago Will was negative, and evidently a lot can change in a year.

After a while Si calms down and starts to breathe normally, and soon he even makes a joke or two. I make tea, and I can see the warmth flow slowly back into his veins, and suddenly I think that we are being ridiculous. We are being overdramatic, we don't know anything for sure, and surely we should not be making these assumptions. Not yet. Not when this life feels so normal.

And I feel the maternal Cath kick in. The Cath that wants to make everything better, the Cath who will right wrongs and soothe the furrowed brow. And it might be inappropriate, what I'm trying to say, but I so want this to be some horrible nightmare. I just want to wake up and for everything to be fine.

'Si,' I start, 'I know this might sound crazy, but you couldn't possibly have it. You're as healthy as an ox, for starters, and so you slept with Will a handful of times without using anything, it doesn't mean you've got it.

' I remember reading an article about HIV,' I continue, my words tripping over themselves in their hurry to be heard, 'which said that it really isn't that easy to catch. In fact, there was some study taken about partners of people with HIV who hadn't known about it and were having unprotected sex, and all of them were fine.'

'Cath,' he says slowly, 'I have no idea whether you'll be able to understand this, but I've got it. I *know* I'm HIV positive.'

'Si, that's ridiculous. That's you being overdramatic. You can't possibly know that . . .' And I tail off because of course there is then only one question left for me to ask. 'What are you going to do?'

'I don't know.'

'Are you going to get tested?'

Si looks into his mug for a long time, and then looks back at me. 'Cath, this is something that I've thought about for years. All the time that Jake was ill I kept thinking about his courage and his bravery, and wondering what I would do if I were in the same position.

'What would I do if my glands swelled up for no apparent reason and then refused to go down. What would I do if a cold refused to go away, sticking around until it got worse and worse. And I always thought that unless I absolutely had to, unless I had absolutely no other choice, I would live in blissful ignorance because I never thought I'd be able to handle the results.'

'And now? How do you feel now?' My voice is gentle, but I'm still trying to take this in.

'Jake must have changed my attitudes far more than I had thought.' He looks up at me and shrugs. 'How could I *not* know? If I *am* positive, then the best thing I can do is to know now, to deal with it now, to take whatever drugs I might need. But you know what the worst thing is?'

I shake my head.

'I've got to have the test, but there's an incubation period of three months, and the last time we slept together was the beginning of October, only a month ago, so it might not even show. Then again, I suppose we did meet in July, so who knows, I might get lucky.'

'Oh God, Si.' I can feel my own tears welling up. 'You can't have it. Please say you haven't got it.'

'Cath,' and he tries to smile. 'It's only a virus, for God's sake. I'm going to go tomorrow.'

'Can I come with you?'

'That's what I was going to ask. The only thing I'm pretty certain of right now is that I couldn't handle getting the results on my own. I want you to come.'

'Where will you go?'

He mentions the name of a GUM clinic at a local hospital. A clinic that specializes in testing for sexually transmitted diseases. A clinic that gives you the results within an hour, where you can remain anonymous, where even your GP doesn't have to be told.

'And you're sure you can handle the results?' I'm amazed that, once Si had got over the initial shakes and tears at the prospect of a positive result, he is now so calm. I keep waiting for something to happen, for the histrionics to start, because this is not the Si I know and love, this is an altogether calmer version, and I'm not entirely sure how to play him.

'You know,' Si says, looking up at me with a smile, a genuine smile, 'I can't believe how well I'm handling this.'

'Jesus. Neither can I.'

'You know, Cath, it doesn't mean AIDS. Not necessarily. Not yet. People can go for years and years being absolutely fine. Now, with all these new drugs, these cocktails and combination therapies, they're talking about twenty years, no problem, and who knows, by then they'll probably have found a cure.'

'Si.' I shiver. 'You're spooking me. Stop talking as if you already have it.'

All of a sudden he looks lost again, like a little boy, and I put my arm around his shoulders and give him a squeeze.

'I'm scared, Cath,' he says. 'I'm really, really scared, but if I have it, then we'll just have to deal with it.'

We sit in silence for a while, and eventually I ask, 'Have you made an appointment?'

'I have to phone first thing in the morning. I'm just praying they'll see me first thing, because the one thing I don't think I can cope with is the wait. Once I know, then I can just get on with my life, but I have to know.'

'Do you want to stay here tonight?'

'I don't know,' he sighs. 'I'm not sure whether I can handle being on my own, but on the other hand part of me wants to go back home, to climb into bed with the duvet over my head. I just don't know.'

In the event Si doesn't stay the night. He stays until midnight and we talk softly about the implications of being HIV positive, about what he might do, how he might tell people, how it will affect his life. And of course we talk about Jake, which is something we haven't really talked about before now.

When Jake died, Si, as always, shut down, and even when he came out of hibernation he still found it difficult to talk about him. We'd all learned to leave the subject alone unless Si brought it up, which he rarely did.

But tonight it's as if the floodgates have opened. Si talks about how much he loved Jake, and then, later, sheds more tears as he remembers his illness, his pain, and sobs in my arms as he cries that he does not want to go through this.

There is nothing I can say. I am still numbed by the horror of it all, because, out of all of us, Si is, or I should say, was, the most careful. He was the one who would shout at me on the rare occasions I got carried away by the moment, forgetting the condom in the heat of passion.

When Si eventually leaves, I sit for a very long time on my sofa, and I do something I have not done for years. I pray. I, who have not believed in God since I was a little girl, who do not believe in religion, sit there with my eyes clenched tightly shut, and I pray that if there is someone out there, then he must make Si be negative.

I pray and I pray, and I offer a few disjointed lines from the Lord's Prayer, half remembered from school assembly all those years ago, in the hope that this will appease any God that may be up there. I even offer myself up for sacrifice.

'I will do anything,' I pray, 'anything you want, as long as you make Si well.'

After a while there is nothing more to be said, and I climb under the covers in bed, closing my eyes and praying for a quick and dreamless sleep, but nobody hears that particular prayer, and I lie wide awake for hours, thinking about Si and wondering how I'm going to cope.

The phone rings at eight o'clock the next morning. Si tells me to get my skates on, as he'll be picking me up in fifteen minutes to go to the clinic. I ring the bookshop and leave a message on the answer phone, telling Lucy I'm going to be in late as I'm not feeling well and am off to the doctors, but that I'll call her later. I figure that after the test, when the results come back negative, I can always explain my late start away with a stomach bug.

Si sounded suspiciously cheerful when he phoned, and when he eventually arrives I look at him with concern, my head slightly cocked to one side, and I ask gently, 'How *are* you?'

'Oh God,' he moans, raising his eyes to the heavens. 'Don't you start already.'

'What? What have I done?'

'That sympathetic look. The cocked head. "How *are* you?"' He imitates cruelly, accurately, and I apologize and laugh.

And all the way to the clinic Si seems in great spirits. If I didn't know better, I would think we were going out for breakfast, or for a walk in the park, and we talk about everything but the main event until we actually arrive.

Even then, looking for a meter, driving around until Si spots someone leaving and nips in to steal their space, even then we both avoid talking about it. It's only as we reach the building, as we climb slowly up the steps to the entrance and ring on the doorbell, because it's so early, only then does my breath catch in my throat, does the colour drain from Si's face.

We are shown into a front-facing waiting room. Slightly shabby, rather gloomy. I note that piled on a coffee table are old, faded copies of *Hello!*, *OK!*, various glossy magazines, and I wonder whether it helps people take their mind off the results, to read these magazines, or whether they are far too frightened to pick them up in the first place.

A nurse comes in. Australian. She is bustling, matter-of-fact, smiling, and I think that whoever employed her is a wise person indeed, for she is exactly the sort to make you feel comfortable. Despite her youth she clucks like a mother hen, even while handing Si a form on a clipboard to fill in.

He picks up the pen to complete the form and I see that he is shaking. Normally, knowing how much Si loves forms, I would giggle with him over the questions. Many's the time Si has saved junk mail, only because it contains a questionnaire, and for years he would make me save the surveys in the glossy magazines, because he just loves answering those questions.

But this form is different. And now is not the time to comment, to make a joke, to say anything at all. He ticks the boxes silently, chewing on his lower lip slightly, which surprises me, as I have never seen him do this before. When he is done, he stands up and hands it to the nurse just outside the door.

'The doctor won't be a moment, love,' she says. 'He'll come out and get you in a second.'

And less than a minute later a door at the other end of the waiting room opens, and a young, dark-haired man in a white coat comes out, clutching the clipboard and looking at Si with a smile. The doctor.

'Please come in.' Si stands up and just as he turns to go he holds my gaze and I nod because there is still nothing to say, and he walks to the door, which shuts behind him.

Now I understand why they have copies of the magazines. I flick through *Hello!*, glancing at the photographs but barely taking them in, tapping my right foot quickly on the floor, a nervous habit that hasn't plagued me for ten years.

The door of the clinic opens again, and a girl comes in, young, pretty, trendy, and the nurse hands her the clipboard and she sits opposite me, head down, deep in concentration, and she looks so calm, so together, I wonder what circumstances might have brought someone like her here.

But of course, I mentally kick myself. AIDS, HIV, does not necessarily choose its victims because of their sex or their sexuality. I am reminded of a story I heard a long time ago, when we had just left university, when everyone laughed at the government campaign, the warnings of a worldwide epidemic. Not us, we thought. Never us.

A student from our university who had had two lovers. One, a long-term relationship of two years, and then, just after they broke up, a summer fling with a boy a couple of years older.

And then, a year or so later, she started to feel ill. Nothing serious, just tiredness, a few headaches, swollen glands. The doctor offered her an HIV test, just so they could rule out the possibility, he said with a smile, just so they could firmly discount it, and she laughed, because how on earth could she possibly have HIV?

The test came back positive. It seems the summer fling had unknowingly contracted it from someone who had slept with someone who had caught it from who knows where.

I don't remember the girl's name. I remember she was a friend of a friend, not someone I actually knew, but someone I could well have known. Someone who would have been at the same balls, the same parties, walked down the corridors of the same halls of residence.

Someone, in fact, much like me. And mostly I remember being shocked that someone like me could contract HIV, because of course that wasn't supposed to happen.

But we now know it does happen. I sneak furtive peeks at this girl, this girl scribbling on the clipboard, and I know that she is just as susceptible as Si. And then I check my watch.

Twenty minutes. Why is this taking so long? And, just as I think that, the door opens and Si walks back into the waiting room.

'Well?' I try to gauge the result from his expression, but there is no result, not for another hour or so.

Si shrugs, and we huddle together for privacy, as the door has now opened again and the waiting room no longer feels quite so safe. 'He was lovely,' he says, almost in a whisper. 'Not at all what I expected. He's worked with people with HIV and AIDS for five years, and was very calm, very matter-of-fact. I almost feel normal.'

'What did he tell you?'

Si glances at the girl still filling in her form, then back at me. 'Look, shall we go for a walk? He said at least forty minutes, and I can't talk in here, I need some air.'

'Good idea.' I grab my coat and we walk out into the cold crisp air.

'So?' I say, taking Si's arm and falling into step.

'So nothing I didn't know already. We established the risk factor, that I'm high risk, having been exposed to the virus, and then we talked about the impact if I'm positive. How I would deal with it, what I would do in terms of counselling, what's available to me, plus all the practical stuff like how it affects things like insurance and foreign travel.'

'Was that it?'

'No. He also said all the stuff that they say now. That HIV is a virus, not an instant death sentence, and that people can live completely normal lives, and there are drugs that blah blah blah.'

I stop and look at him. 'Blah blah blah? Now there's an interesting medical definition.'

'I'm sorry.' A big sigh. 'It's just that I've heard it all before, and I know it's true, but it still means that I am probably not going to see old age, and that when I die it will be horrible and painful and degrading, and even though I know that being positive doesn't mean instant death, all I keep thinking about is Jake. At the end.'

'Oh, Si,' I groan, stroking his arm, because I cannot think of anything else to say. And eventually I look at him with worried eyes. 'And what if you *are* positive?'

'If I'm positive, then I'll go to counselling and I'll take whatever drugs I have to take and I'll deal with it. Come on. Let's go back.'

We go back, and again, as we ascend those steps, that feeling of gloom overtakes me, but my heart doesn't jump into my mouth this time. That doesn't happen for a little while longer. We sit in the waiting room, and I manage to entice Si back to a semblance of his normal self by showing him a picture of Courtney Cox in a particularly disgusting dress, and in the middle of our laughter the surgery door opens and the same doctor appears.

He comes over to us and again says, 'Please come in.' And although the words themselves are completely innocuous, although they have no power to harm, there is something about his expression, his lack of smile, the sympathy lurking just behind his eyes, that makes my heart start to pound, and my breathing tight and sharp.

'Back in a sec, my darling,' Si says, winking at me,

putting on his old self in a bid to cover the fear, then, just as he goes, he leans down and kisses my cheek, and that is when I feel the tears burning, but I will not let them out. I will be strong for Si.

And anyway, I have never been the best judge of emotions. Perhaps I imagined this. Perhaps the doctor has the same expression whatever the verdict. I look up, and the girl, the trendy, pretty girl who is presumably now waiting for her results, smiles at me.

'Awful, isn't it?' she says softly, and I nod, not daring myself to speak, because her sympathy will ensure the tears come thick and fast if I so much as open my mouth.

She smiles at me in sympathy, and I think: she knows. She looked up when the doctor came out, she saw his expression, and she is thinking the same thing as me. I flick the pages of the magazine, furiously, blinking back the tears, not seeing anything at all, and when I reach the end, I flick back to the beginning again, my foot tapping all the while.

Twenty minutes go by, and then the door opens and Si reappears, smiling brightly, and, if I didn't know him as well as I do, I would think that the smile means everything is fine, but I know that smile. That is his false smile. His forced smile. He is stuffing leaflets into his pocket, and I stand up and follow him down the stairs and into the cold sunshine, and all the while he keeps smiling.

'Si?' I stand in front of him on the pavement, and only then does his smile start to fade.

'Positive,' he whispers, and I put my arms around him and feel his stiffness, his resistance, but whether he needs this or not, I need to do it.

'Regent's Park?' I whisper, because it's not far, and because I know he loves the rose garden, and because I sense that he needs to be reminded of things that he loves, and that it is far better for him to be out amidst beauty than at home alone.

We get in the car, not saying anything, and drive to Regent's Park, then walk through the gate, around the small boating lake and into the park. All the while Si does not speak.

My arm is linked through his, and I squeeze him tightly, reassuring myself that he is still there, the same old Si, and although the temptation is to keep looking at him, to check if he's okay, I know this would infuriate the hell out of him and so I resist.

And finally, when we reach the rose garden, Si gestures towards a bench and we sit down, and he starts to speak.

'I have to make an appointment with a counsellor,' he says, drawing the leaflets out from his pocket and looking at them blankly. 'And I have to go for regular check-ups, my CD4 count and Viral Load Tests. I have to go back in a week for the first round of tests. And my diet probably needs looking at, although he said there were courses I could do to learn about all of this stuff, to get support, and . . .' He stops, sighing.

I say nothing, just stroke his arm.

'Oh, Cath,' he says, and his voice sounds incredibly sad. 'How can my life have changed so drastically in one day? How can everything have been fine yesterday morning, and everything be so awful today? How can we even be sitting here talking about T-cells, and check-ups, and drugs, I mean, why me? Why did this have to happen to me?'

'Nothing has changed,' I say, putting my arms around him. 'You are exactly the same person sitting here today as you were yesterday. And you'll be exactly the same person tomorrow, and the day after that, and the day after that. The only thing that's changed is that you've caught a virus, and you have to be more careful with your health.

'But Si,' I continue, 'you have friends who love you and, touch wood' – I slip off a glove to stroke the bench – 'your health. It's a virus, Si, it's not the end of the world.'

And then we both sit there, holding hands, looking out over the park, and we stay there for a very long time.

Chapter twenty-six

I call Lucy in the shop, and luckily I do sound terrible, and she thinks I'm ill before I even have a chance to deliver a made-up excuse. She tells me to tuck up in bed and not to worry about anything, which is what I wanted to hear, as I need to spend the rest of the day with Si, but it nevertheless strikes me as slightly ironic, given that I'm the one who is absolutely fine. In shock, certainly, but fine.

But Si is fine too. Or should that be too fine. After we leave the rose garden he tells me he really feels okay about this; he says that, bizarre as it may seem, it somehow already feels a part of him, feels like his destiny, and it's not the worst thing in the world that can happen, and he really can deal with it.

I don't know what to do with Si today. He is too calm, too quiet, and I suggest lunch, even offering to treat him at the Ivy, which would normally be his idea of heaven (although God knows how we'd ever get in at such short notice), and he just says no, he's fine.

I drag him down to Marylebone High Street and we find a small café and tuck ourselves away in the corner, ordering cappuccinos and baguettes, but as soon as the food arrives I know that I have no appetite, that I couldn't eat this if you forced me, and of course Si pushes it away as soon as it arrives.

So we sit and drink our coffee, and I pull out the lettuce from the baguette and shred it slowly on to the tabletop, and then Si draws out the leaflets again and this time we really look at them, read them, read about courses for the recently diagnosed, the importance of regular check-ups, the life expectancy growing longer and longer.

And when we have finished the leaflets I pull my diary from my bag and rip out a clean page, and we write down the places Si is going to contact this afternoon when he leaves me, the support centres he will visit, the places he will turn to for help.

'Doubtless the doctor at the clinic will go through all of this with me next week,' he sighs at one point, but I ignore him because I can see that this is helping, to actually do something practical, to make a list, and even if it is not helping Si, it is helping me.

Eventually we leave and Si drops me off. I practically beg him to let me come over in the evening, but he says he will be fine.

'You won't do ... well ... you know ...' I can't help but ask the question.

'Anything stupid?' he says, grinning. 'No, Cath. I'm fine. Well, I'm not, but I'm certainly not unfine enough to down a bottle of paracetamol, if that's what you're thinking.'

'Will you ring me later?'

He nods. 'And sweets? I don't know how to tell Josh and Lucy. I know I have to, but I need to do it in my own time, in my own way. Is that okay?'

'God, yes!' I'm mortified that he thinks I would take it upon myself to tell them, almost as if this were mere gossip.

'I'm sorry,' he says. 'I didn't mean to offend you, my love. Listen, I'm going to go home and run a nice hot bath, and I promise I'll ring you afterwards.'

*

He does ring, and he says that after he dropped me off he took the long route home, via a bookshop – not, obviously Bookends, as he couldn't face seeing Lucy – and picked up some books about HIV and AIDS, and is planning to curl up for the rest of the afternoon and read them.

I do the same thing in my flat. I curl up on the sofa and open a novel I've been meaning to read for weeks. I scan the first page, desperate for some form of escapism, desperate for something to take me out of myself, but every time I reach the bottom of page four I realize I haven't got a clue what I've just read, and I have to start all over again.

Eventually I put the book down and run a bath myself, wondering how I'm going to kill the hours before bedtime, wishing today had never happened, wishing I could have a *Groundhog Day* experience, relive today, make everything normal again.

I do manage to kill some of the hours before bedtime. Some, but not all. I speak to Si a couple more times and he sounds fine, says he's going to have an early night, a quiet night, give himself time to digest everything.

But I can't sleep, and when, at twenty past one in the morning, the phone rings, it doesn't surprise me in the slightest, and I pick up the phone to hear jagged sobs at the other end.

'Ssh, ssh.' I try to soothe, feeling Si's pain as if it were my own.

'I don't want this to be happening,' he sobs, his voice blurred with alcohol. 'Why is this happening to me? What have I ever done? Why me?'

'I'm coming over,' I say, and, without giving him the time to say no, I pull a coat over my pyjamas, shove my feet into boots, grab my car keys, and I'm out the door.

Six minutes later I'm on his doorstep, and he opens the door, his T-shirt wet with tears, his face puffy and blotchy, hiccuping as he tries to stop crying, and I put my arms around him and start crying too.

I stay the night, although we don't really sleep. We sit up, still talking, still trying to make sense of it all, and eventually, at around seven, we both fall asleep on the sofa.

Obviously I can't go into work the next day. Lucy offers to come round in the evening with home-made tomato soup and Lemsips, but I tell her that whatever this flu-thing is, it's probably contagious and I'll be fine.

I spend the morning with Si, and he phones the hospital and makes an appointment with a counsellor for that afternoon. This time, he says, he wants to go alone.

I manage to make some headway with my novel, but by early afternoon I feel so guilty about leaving Lucy in the lurch, that I consider walking up to Bookends.

Then again, how on earth would I have made a miraculous recovery in so short a time? I decide to phone instead, and when Lucy comes to the phone I'm astonished by the exuberance in her voice.

'Darling Cath! We are worried about you. Rachel says take lots of echinacea. Tell me you're feeling better? Have you dosed yourself up with lots of ghastly lotions and potions?'

'Yes, and I'm feeling much better, even though I hardly slept last night. How is everything in the shop today? You sound positively ecstatic.'

And Lucy, bless her, drops her voice and I can almost see her bringing the phone up to her mouth as she checks that no one's listening. 'Actually, I didn't sleep much myself last night,' and her voice is positively purring.

'Lucy! You didn't! You and Josh? SEX?', at which Lucy giggles.

'God, Lucy! That's amazing! No wonder you sound ecstatic. How was it, or need I ask?'

Lucy sighs with pleasure at the memory. 'Oh, Cath, it was so *lovely*. So unexpected and so, so lovely.'

She tells me that Josh had been just like his old self all day yesterday. That getting together as a gang to have our regular Sunday lunch seemed to have somehow brought them back together again, reminded them of how things used to be before she opened the shop.

They went home last night and Ingrid went out, as she always does these days, and Max went to bed, as he rarely ever does, and, instead of burying himself in a pile of paperwork in his study, Josh opened a bottle of wine and sat down at the kitchen table to talk.

And they found themselves laughing together over some silly story Lucy was telling, and Josh put the dishes in the dishwasher after supper and then stood behind Lucy as she finished clearing the table, put his arms around her and gently kissed the nape of her neck, 'Which,' she said guiltily, 'always turns me to jelly.'

And that, as they say, was that, but God, what a pleasure it is to hear Lucy laughing again. It is a welcome and uplifting distraction, and what a relief to know that whatever was going on between Josh and Portia must surely now be over.

'Oh, Cath,' Lucy sighs. 'I feel that everything's back to normal. It's all been so upside down for so long, but now I've got this lovely feeling that life is back on track. Now, sweet Cath, to change the subject entirely, or rather to get back to the original subject, what is happening with the lovely James?'

I don't know where to start. 'You know how some things are just meant to be?'

'Yes?' She is eager, expectant.

'This, unfortunately, isn't one of them.'

'But that can't be true. What on earth makes you say that?'

'Every time we try and get it together, something happens to pull us apart, and I can't help but feel that this just isn't meant to be. And God knows I'm happy enough on my own, so maybe this is how I'm supposed to carry on.'

'Nope.' She is determined. 'I refuse to accept that as a reasonable answer. If things keep going horribly wrong when James invites you for dinner, why don't you try to reverse your luck by inviting him?'

'What?'

'Make dinner for him. Every man adores a home-cooked meal.'

'Even when it's burnt scrambled eggs?' The thought of cooking fills me with horror.

Lucy laughs. 'No, my sweet, I shall cook for you both and he'll never have to know. I'll make a delicious meal and drop it off at your house. You can pass it off as your own. And who knows, if you get lucky I won't even have to worry about *afters*.' This last word said with a chuckle and probably a leer.

'Dinner? At my place?' God, now there's something I haven't done for at least five years.

'Yes. It's perfect. If I were you, I'd drop in and ask him just as soon as you're back on your feet. He'll be over the moon.'

By Friday I figure Si is doing just about okay, or at least okay enough not to need me on permanent standby, but

I still feel incredibly fragile. I know I should be going back to the shop, but if Lucy starts being all warm and maternal towards me, I'll probably just lose it.

But by Friday afternoon the guilt takes over, and I do go in to Bookends, and everything's fine. Lucy's fine. Bill and Rachel have been working like demons, and Lucy's so busy chatting up the regulars she doesn't really have time to fuss over me as she normally would, which is truly something of a relief.

But then the shop suddenly empties, and Lucy puts down a teapot and flings her arms around me, and I bite my lip to stop the full flood of emotion. 'What are you *doing* here? I told you not to come in until Monday.' She peers at me closely. 'Cath, my love, you look terrible, you ought to be in bed. You're all pale and slight.'

Pale and slight. Why is Lucy the only person who could get away with calling me pale and slight? It brings a smile to my face and Lucy says, 'That's better. Why don't you sit down, I'll make a fresh pot of tea, and then I think it's back to bed for you, young lady.'

Half an hour later, I push open the door of the estate agent's and, much like a Wild West saloon, the room goes quiet as five pairs of eyes eye me up and down, presumably assessing how much I would be willing to spend.

The silence lasts a second. A second that is evidently enough for them to realize I won't be buying that eight-bedroom house in Aberdare. Nor even the three-bedroom conversion in Greencroft. Nope. I am not a buyer to get excited about.

I have never seen the office this busy before. Five men seated behind five large, trendy beech desks, all talking into their phones, some of them managing to conduct conversations into their mobiles at the same time. And these men all look identical. All short, young and dark, neatly packaged in slick dark suits, their eyes constantly roaming, their voices filled with a confidence their age would not suggest.

And then I see James, right at the back, looking completely out of place, with his laid-back manner, lazy smile and tousled light brown hair.

'Can I help you?' the bimbo-esque receptionist inquires. I smile and shake my head. James wipes the smile from his face and looks at me sternly as I walk towards the back of the office to talk to him, trying to ignore the eyes that appear to be watching my every move.

'Hello.' His voice is guarded. 'What can I do for you, Cath?' Oh God. Have I blown it? Have I been so completely stupid and blown it? I look at his arm where the sleeve is rolled up, exposing strong muscles and light brown hair, and my stomach lurches as I realize that I do, in fact, desire this man.

That I have not felt desire for anyone for a very long time. And that I cannot blow it again. I bite my lip as I start to speak.

'Well . . .' I'm nervous, and I don't want to blurt out a dinner invitation in front of the receptionist, who has left her desk at the front and is hovering near by, pretending to look for something.

Thankfully James picks up on my discomfort, and he ushers me into a room at the back of the office, where there's a large sofa, and I sit down as he stands in front of me and raises an eyebrow, still as cold as before.

'James,' I say. 'I have to apologize. I don't know why things come up every time we try to get together, but I feel terrible about it and I was just passing and . . .' I am

about to ask him for dinner, but I can't quite manage it.
'. . . and I just wanted to come in and say how sorry I
am.'

'Yes?' James looks up sternly as the receptionist
hovers by the sofa, all pretence having gone out the
window.

'Just wondering if you wanted coffee?' she says
brightly, and I say no, because there is something very
disconcerting about the way she just appeared when
something interesting was being said. Reluctantly she
walks back to the front of the office, and James waits
until she's safely ensconced behind her desk and out of
earshot before continuing.

'God, Cath,' he sighs. 'This is just so exhausting. All
I'm trying to do is take you out for dinner and you're
just making it so bloody difficult for me.'

'I . . . er . . .' I'm floored. I don't know what to say,
and the emotion that I've been suppressing is suddenly
threatening to spill out all over this lovely white sofa. I
try to blink back the tears that well up out of nowhere,
but they don't go away.

'Cath?' James looks concerned, and sits down next to
me, trying to look into my eyes, which are busy failing
to stop the tears trickling down my cheek. 'Jesus, Cath.
You're not okay, are you?' And his voice is so gentle, so
caring, that I find myself doing an enormous hiccup and
then the hiccup turns into sobbing, and I'm reduced to
a wailing heap on the sofa.

I'm aware that this is the most exciting thing everyone
in the office has ever seen at work, but he stands up and
pulls the door closed, and when he comes back he sits
next to me and rubs my back, just as I did with Si.

And it works. It is soothing and calming, and after a
while, when the sobbing has gone back to being merely

hiccuping, I take a deep breath and James says, 'Can you talk about it?'

I start to shake my head, but then the tears start rolling down my cheeks, and I know that I can't keep this to myself any more. And I know it's selfish, I know it isn't about me, but there is nobody I can confide in, and I need someone to support me.

I wouldn't tell Lucy. Nor Josh. They are our closest friends, and it is up to Si to tell them, but I trust James, I don't know why. Perhaps because that night we saw Josh and Portia together he never asked about it, was so obviously not interested in the potential for gossip. I'm sure that whatever I say to him will go no further, and that I just cannot keep this to myself any longer.

And slowly the story comes out. I don't refer to Si by name. *A friend* is what I say, because it makes me feel as if I am still protecting Si, although it is clear from what I say, from the closeness of our friendship, that it could only ever be Si.

I talk about the helplessness I feel; about the fact that this is not supposed to happen to someone like him, not supposed to happen to one of my best friends. I tell him what I told Si, about it being a virus, about people living with it for years and years, but then I tell him that I've also seen the films, seen the photographs, and that however far we have come, is AIDS not the inevitable outcome?

And as I talk about it, I picture Si, frail, skinny, hollowed-out cheeks, and I start to cry all over again.

'Can I make a suggestion?' James says gently, quietly, still rubbing my back until I am calm again. 'I think that first of all you should also go to see someone. I don't know what exists for friends and family of people with HIV, but there are bound to be groups, counsellors, people who can talk to you, help you, because your friend isn't the only one who's suffering, and you need to learn to deal with it as well.'

I nod mutely.

'But you're the only one who knows right now, is that right?' I nod. 'Do you think your friend is planning to tell more people? Because it's a hell of a burden to shoulder on your own.'

'I don't know. I don't think he's thought that far ahead.'

'Where is he now?'

'Oh shit.' I check my watch and stand up, grabbing my bag. 'He must be home from the hospital. I've got to go.'

'You're sure you're okay?'

I nod, heading for the door.

'Cath?' I turn just as I'm stepping out. 'You know that if you ever need to talk, you can just pick up the phone or come over.'

'You know, James, you're amazing. I don't know what to say, thank you just doesn't seem enough.'

He smiles. 'Don't be silly, that's what friends are for,' and he leans forward and kisses my cheek, squeezing my arm at the same time. I walk into the street and go home to phone Si, having completely forgotten that I was supposed to have proposed dinner.

Chapter twenty-seven

The nights are not good. Si seems to get far more frightened at night, and among the many books he's bought are first-person stories of people living with AIDS, or people who have lost loved ones to AIDS.

He reads, nightly, about watching people you love die a horrible, painful death. He reads about people who go blind, contract tuberculosis, Kaposi's sarcoma. And when he reads these stories, although he says it helps him to feel not quite so alone, he cannot help the terror striking.

During the daytime I'm there, on the end of the phone, to keep him sane, to remind him of what the doctor told him at the clinic: that at last there are effective treatments, that the average prognosis, before people became ill, used to be ten to twelve years, but that now, with these new treatments, that has been significantly extended.

You, I say repeatedly to Si, will be around for *years*. Twenty or thirty *at least*. And I don't just say this to make him feel better, I say it because I genuinely believe it. I say it because if Si refuses to be positive about this, then someone else will have to do it for him and that someone will be me.

So, as I say, the daytimes are not quite so bad. During the day we even manage to have occasional conversations in which the words HIV or AIDS don't even figure. But it's during the night that he gets the fear.

During the night when he phones me up, either crying softly, or the weight of the fear pressing down on him so much he can hardly speak, just needing to know that someone is there for him.

Lucy asked me yesterday if everything was okay with Si, because he hasn't returned her calls. What could I say? I told her that he was fine, very busy, and that I hadn't spoken to him much either, and then I busied myself with ringing a wholesaler to stop her asking any more questions.

And I ring Si when I get home and ask him whether he's thought any more about telling Josh and Lucy. This, apparently, is one of the issues the doctor brought up in his first counselling session. Whom he should tell, and how.

Si has decided, he tells me, that he does want Josh and Lucy to know because we, after all (and at this point he puts on a cheesy American accent), are his *family of choice*. He hasn't, on the other hand, decided quite how to tell them, but is thinking of throwing some kind of dinner party, a miniature version of the film *Peter's Friends*, to break the news. Except, he says, right now he can't think of anything more terrifying.

His real family, he says, do not need to know. They live far away, they wouldn't understand, and it took them years to come to terms with the fact that he's gay, never mind being diagnosed as having HIV to boot. 'What would be the point?' he says. 'If I'm not ill, what's to tell?' And I believe him when he says he is doing the right thing.

He has not taken drastic steps to change his life, not yet. He has not done any of the courses, or started regular counselling, but he has been to the clinic, had his CD4 count checked to measure the strength of his immune system, and had his first Viral Load Test to measure the amount of virus in the blood.

At the moment his Viral Load is huge, but apparently that is to be expected, given that he has contracted the virus so recently, or at least any time between July and October. It will take a while for his immune system to settle down. But, all in all, so far, so good. He is fine.

After the tests at the clinic, walking up the street, he told me he saw Portia. Another time he would have spoken to her, another time when he had not been leaving the HIV clinic, had forgiven her the affair with Josh.

That day, he said, he couldn't face her. He didn't have the patience or the will to pretend to be nice, to be normal, and he didn't want her asking what he was doing there.

Was it definitely her, I asked? Yes, he laughed. There's no mistaking Portia, so he ducked into a doorway at the hospital and turned his back until she had passed, praying he didn't feel a tap on his shoulder; praying he hadn't been spotted.

'I suppose, at some point,' he says wearily, 'everyone will have to know. How do you explain sudden rigorous hygiene, washing your hands every time you touch an animal, or washing fruit and vegetables scrupulously?'

'You could always try telling them you're pregnant,' I offer, grateful for the laughter that ensues.

It is a Thursday night and Si has come over to watch Portia's series. We have ordered a Chinese takeaway, as we have always done, and Si is bemoaning the fact that we've slipped these last few weeks and have, you might say, somewhat lost the plot.

'How much do you want to bet,' Si smirks, just as the

titles start, 'there's a new character called John, or Joe, or Jason, something like that, and he's a local estate agent with a crush on Katy? Oh, and he's a fabulously talented artist on the side.'

'Oh fuck off.' I throw a cushion at him and he ducks, chuckling, but it's true, the thought has occurred to me, particularly because I have managed successfully to avoid Portia for quite a few weeks now, not returning her calls, pretending to be out when I listen to her voice on my answer machine. She may well take her revenge via the television programme.

And then we both settle down to watch. Jacob and Lisa are having marriage problems, but, astoundingly, Jacob hasn't turned to Mercedes's arms for comfort.

'Well, he couldn't in the TV series, could he?' Si sniffs. 'Mercedes is an angel who could never do anything as evil as split up a marriage.'

No, in the series Mercedes is there to offer support to Jacob, a shoulder to lean on, although naturally everyone gets the wrong impression.

'Oh shit.' I turn to Si in the commercial break. 'Have we got it horribly wrong? Do you think we've completely misinterpreted everything?'

'Jesus,' Si says, turning to me. 'I don't know. I mean, Portia would never portray herself as the marriage wrecker on TV, but . . .' he says, tailing off.

'Then again,' he says, 'what was she doing at Josh and Lucy's all the time? Remember all those times you pitched up to see Lucy, and Portia was sitting at the kitchen table, being all smug?'

'Yeah. Good point.'

Si makes a worried face at me. 'God, I hope we weren't wrong. I'd feel awful if we were. I mean, I was *so* rude to her when she phoned up that night we were babysitting.'

'Oh, I shouldn't worry,' I say breezily. 'I'm sure she'll get her revenge on the show. Sssh, sssh, here it comes.'

For the next fifteen minutes we sit there transfixed as Jacob makes a pass at Lena, the gorgeous Danish au pair, after they both find themselves in the kitchen in the middle of the night, both unable to sleep.

'Jeeee-sus,' Si whistles, as we watch them tumble to the floor in a fit of passion.

'No way,' I whisper. 'Josh and Ingrid? It *can't* be.'

And Si raises an eyebrow.

'Well, it could be,' I mutter reluctantly.

'Bugger,' Si says, getting up to go to the loo during the next commercial break. 'You know what this means, don't you?'

'What?'

'First of all that we're going to have to start hating Josh again, and secondly' –at this point he lets out a long sigh – 'secondly I'm going to have to apologize to Portia. Oh God. What a total nightmare. Thank God there are only fifteen minutes left. I mean, what else could happen?' And he disappears into the bathroom.

When he comes back he sits down with a sigh. 'Cath, I've had enough.'

'What?'

'This is ridiculous now. You and I sit here speculating about the state of Josh's love life, and the only person who seems to know what's going on, other than Josh of course, who would never tell us, is Portia. You've got to confront her.'

'Me? Why the hell must I do it?'

'Because I'm not feeling well, and anyway you were always closer to Portia. I think you need to call her.'

'Si, I'm sorry you're not feeling well. Even though I don't believe you, but there's no way I'm doing this on my own. I'll only confront her if you come too. The three of us could meet and talk about it. We could ask her straight out, because the one thing about Portia is she's a crap liar, and your bullshit detector's far better than mine.'

'Oh shit,' he suddenly whispers. 'Do you think Josh and Lucy are watching? Because Lucy might be thinking what we're thinking . . .'

'Oh shit. I'll call them.'

I pick up the phone, praying they're out, that they haven't seen the programme, and Lucy picks up the phone, out of breath.

'Lucy? It's me.'

'Cath, my sweet! Everything all right?'

'Fine, fine. Did you see the show?'

'The show?'

'Portia's show. Si's here and we thought perhaps you'd be watching it.'

'Oh bugger, damn and blast,' Lucy says. 'I completely forgot. Josh is out again tonight and put the strawberry jam down, there's a darling. Sorry, Cath, I've been busy helping Max make jam tarts. Did I miss anything?'

Thank God.

'Nope. Just the usual. I'd better not keep you. It sounds messy.'

'Oh God,' Lucy groans. 'My darling Cath, if you only knew.'

I put down the phone and smile at Si. 'Do you want the good news or the bad news?'

'Good news.'

'She didn't see it.'

'Bad news?'

'Josh is out again.'

'Oh shit. Where's Ingrid?'

'I don't know. I didn't ask.'

'Oh God. Cath? Do you really think that Josh and Ingrid have been having an affair?'

'Well, hopefully Portia will be able to shed some light on the matter once and for all.'

I ring Portia mid-afternoon, when Lucy's furiously busy serving the rush of customers that always seems to appear from nowhere on a Friday afternoon. We arrange to get together for a drink on Monday evening, and I manage to make my voice sound as normal as possible. Even though I'm convinced she knows why I'm phoning, she doesn't give anything away.

We don't mention the show. In fact, she doesn't mention the fact that I've obviously been avoiding her, just sounds genuinely thrilled to hear from me, and as soon as I mention getting together she suggests Monday, which is rather keen, even for Portia.

'Cath, can you come here a sec?' I say goodbye to Portia and wander over to Rachel, who's looking upset. On the counter in front of her is a dog-eared copy of a novel that's currently number four in the bestseller charts.

'What seems to be the problem?'

A young woman in a black puffa jacket with a sour expression on her face gives a deep sigh. 'As I was just explaining to your colleague here, I was given this book for my birthday and I already have it, so I'd like to exchange it.'

'Oh, I see.' I pick up the book and examine the bent spine, the creased pages, the coffee mark on the cover. 'Normally that wouldn't be a problem, but it does appear to have been read, so I don't think there's anything we can do.'

She looks up disdainfully. 'Actually, it was like that when I got it.'

I almost start to laugh. 'What? Had a bent spine and coffee stains?' My voice is as disbelieving as my face.

'Yes,' she says, her voice dripping with sarcasm. 'I imagine that's what happens when you open a bookshop that has a café in it.'

'Right.' I can see I'm getting nowhere, and quite frankly, although it's quite clear she's trying it on, I have to remember that the customer is always right, and that it's far better to keep her happy than to refuse an exchange and have her tell all her friends.

'No problem,' I say, smiling. 'Why don't you have a look for something else?'

'I'd rather have the money,' she says, evidently amazed that it's this simple, to which I nod, pull £5.99 out of the till and hand it to her.

'Have a nice day,' I say, as she turns on her heel and walks off.

'Cath, did you see this?' Rachel, who's been standing next to me the whole time, opens the flyleaf of the book to reveal the following:

2 November 1999
Dear Caroline,
Happy Birthday!
Lots of Love,
Emily xxx

'I can't believe that!' Rachel gasps. 'I can't believe she brought it back when it's not only been read, but also inscribed! Jesus Christ! What a nerve!'

'Rachel.' I turn to her with a shrug, knowing that

it's yet another book we'll just have to write off. 'The customer, unfortunately, is always right.'

At the end of the day Lucy brings me over a pile of books that have been left in the café. 'Cath, my love, are you going to be around the weekend of the twenty-seventh? You and Si, actually. It's just that's the weekend Ingrid's off to Paris with the grand passion, and bloody Josh has just announced that he's got to go to Manchester for a meeting, and normally I wouldn't mind but you know how I can't bear being on my own, and I thought the three of us could have a lovely cosy evening on the Saturday and maybe you'd stay?' She pauses to take a breath, and my blood runs cold.

I think back to last night. To Jacob and Lena grappling on the kitchen floor in the TV series. Ingrid and Josh. It can't just be a coincidence, that they're both away at the same time. Oh God. Oh no.

But how would Portia know? How does she know all this *stuff* about our lives? And then I remember the time I came in and found Portia sitting in the kitchen with Ingrid. They'd obviously been chatting, had evidently become friends, and Ingrid must have confided in her, must have told her what was going on.

'Cath? Are you listening to me?' Lucy's voice filters through as I try to collect my thoughts, and I manage to tell her that the twenty-seventh sounds fine, and I'd have to check with Si, but even if he couldn't make it I'd definitely be there.

And she walks off back to the café as I stand there feeling sick. I don't understand. How could we not have seen this? How could we have thought that Josh's affair was over just because he and Lucy are having conversations again?

I can't understand what's going on. I sit there feeling confused – first Portia, now Ingrid – confused and hurt, so I do what I always do when life throws these obstacles in my path – I go home and ring Si.

He picks up the phone sounding morose, and I start by telling him about Portia, that we're meeting her at the Groucho on Monday at seven, and then I tell him about Josh being away on the twenty-seventh, when he interrupts.

'I couldn't actually give a fuck about Josh being away,' he starts, the coldness in his voice almost making me jump. 'I've got AIDS, Cath.'

I am about to interrupt and tell him that he hasn't got AIDS, that he is HIV positive, which is a very different story, when I realize that he has been drinking, and that now would perhaps not be the time to say anything at all.

'And before you say the usual shit about me not having AIDS, you know and I know that it is just a matter of time. All I ever wanted from life was to be happy, and what bloody chance do I have of meeting Mr Right now? No bloody chance, that's what, and there's no point in you saying anything because you don't know the first bloody thing about it.

'You have no idea how it feels to be me right now. You don't know what it's like to have this death sentence hanging over you. God,' he snorts with drunken laughter, as I wonder whether I should just put down the phone, because Si in vindictive drinking mood is not a good thing.

But no, I am a friend, I will be here for him and I will listen so he knows that he is not alone in this.

'At least you, Cath,' he continues, laughing out loud, 'don't have to worry about AIDS. Jesus, it's the least of your concerns. Your legs are stuck so tightly together it would take a man a lot stronger than that bloody James to prise them apart.

'And relationship? You don't know the meaning of the word. You're so fucking frightened of getting hurt you attach yourself to me, Josh and Lucy, like a fucking limpet, just so you don't actually have to put yourself out there in the big bad world and risk finding love.

'You're like a bloody robot. You don't have a clue, and then you tell me I'm not going to die and I'm expected to believe that? Coming from you?'

I have had enough. The tears have already started to drip down my face, but Si doesn't need to know that. He just needs to know that I won't take this abuse. Not from my best friend. Not even when I know he's going through hell.

'I'm not going to listen to you any more, Si,' I say gently.

'Why? Because the truth hurts?'

'I'm putting the phone down now,' I say, and, as I gently place the phone back in the cradle, I can hear Si shouting, 'Cath? Cath?' but I then unplug the phone, together with the answering machine, from the wall.

And I curl up on the sofa, hugging my knees to my chest, and I let the tears stream down my face, because I know that Si would never have said those things if he wasn't drunk, and frightened, and filled with rage at the injustices of the world, but I also know that everything he said he believed.

He's just never told me before because he didn't want to hurt me, and the only way he would ever dare tell me was when he had the false courage that alcohol had given him.

And the worst part is that I know he's right. He's right

about me closing off from the world. Running away from anything that isn't safe and familiar. Running away from James.

After a while I get up, splash cold water on my face and pick up the phone to ring James. I listen to his answer phone, and then, after the bleep goes, I still haven't formulated anything to say, so I gently put the phone down.

Si was right. The truth does hurt. But sometimes hearing the truth can inspire you to do things differently. I am going to get hold of James, invite him over for dinner and seduce him.

And just because I put it off until tomorrow because I suddenly realize that the emotions of the day have severely taken their toll, doesn't mean that I'm not going to do it.

Trust me.

Chapter twenty-eight

At half past four on Monday a woman walks into the shop with a large bunch of flowers and asks for me by name before handing me the flowers. This is vaguely cheering because today has been the day from hell.

I just feel that everything is going wrong in my life. Too much is changing too quickly. I can't blame Portia for that, but her return has damaged the equilibrium far more than I could ever have anticipated.

Which I suppose is ridiculous, because whether Portia had come back or not, Si would still have met Will and would still have contracted the virus, but nothing feels safe any more, and I seem to spend most of my time waiting for the next bomb to fall.

And can it really be simply coincidence that everything seems to have changed since she first turned up at the party at Bookends? If it were only one thing, I could handle it. If, say, Si had been diagnosed, and everything else was fine, I could cope. But Si's diagnosis, and Josh's affair, and then to have Si turn on me, is just too much.

Just for a change I didn't sleep well over the weekend. I spent the entire two days on my own, unable to face anyone, and at night everything that Si had said kept going through my mind, and I kept telling myself that I would feel better about it in the morning, but each morning, as soon as I awoke, I knew that the black cloud was still there.

And I haven't called him. Perhaps I should have done, because he, after all, is the one who is truly going through hell, whereas I am just experiencing it second hand, but I need some time and space to forgive him, and I'm hoping that a few days will be enough.

He won't be coming tonight. Won't turn up after the conversation the other night, if, that is, he remembers anything at all, because God knows how much alcohol he had, in fact, consumed.

And now I have to deal with Portia myself, which is fine, especially given that she was clearly not the object of Josh's affections. I am only slightly astonished at how quickly I have managed to forgive her that alleged infidelity, although quite how quickly I will forgive her for disrupting my life, our lives, beyond all measure is another story indeed.

I drop the flowers off at home, waiting until I'm in a cab on the way to Soho before opening the card, although I already know they'll be from Si. Sure enough: 'For Cath. I'm so, so sorry and I'm too frightened to call. You're a far better friend than I could ever hope for, and I need you. Please forgive me. Will explain when you call. Will you? Soon? Love you, sweets. S.'

It doesn't even bring a smile to my face, not yet, not when the hurt is so raw, but I tuck the card safely in my diary, knowing that it will be something I will keep.

I am shown into the bar at the Groucho, and I see Portia instantly, because at this hour the bar is not yet crowded. She is sitting in a corner, sipping a gin and tonic, looking stunning.

I walk over and she stands to greet me, her face lighting up when she first sees me, the smile fading as she realizes I am not smiling in return, or not, at least, with quite the same brilliance.

'Cath.' She opts for the double kiss on the cheek, her

voice warm but businesslike. 'You're looking great. It feels like ages. What can I get you?'

A gin and tonic arrives and I sip it slowly, thinking how easy it would be to fall into the arms of alcohol when under stress, how I may not be able to forgive Si for what he said, but I can certainly understand how he came to say it.

We make small talk for a while. I talk about the shop and how busy we've been, and she tells me she has also been travelling for work. Last weekend to New York, this weekend Europe.

We talk about New York. About where she stays, what she does. I say that it is somewhere I have always wanted to go, but I am quite sure that if I went, I would never return, because my love for the city would be so strong.

'How do you know that?' she laughs.

'Because of Woody Allen and *NYPD Blue*,' I reply, in all seriousness, and even as she's laughing I wonder whether she is mentally filing this away, only for the phrase to pop up in a future episode of the series.

The series. How can I sit here and pretend that I am here merely on a social call, a catch-up, an innocent girls' night out? How can we talk about New York, and Woody Allen films, and work, when she is exposing all our secrets in her series, when we don't even know what some of those secrets are?

'Portia,' I interrupt her gently, mid-flow. 'There's something I need to talk to you about.'

'Ah,' she sits back. 'I thought there was something,' and she shrugs. 'I thought, when you phoned, that perhaps I had been going mad, that perhaps you hadn't been avoiding me all these weeks.

'I wasn't going mad was I?'

I shake my head. 'No, but that's not what I want to

talk to you about, that was Si and I thinking that you and Josh were having an affair, because I saw you in Barnes one night, in a restaurant, and I was so furious with you, but now, obviously, we know that's not true, and anyway, that's irrelevant, that's not what I wanted to talk to you about.'

'Hang on, hang on. You saw us in that restaurant?'

'Yes, but it doesn't matter now,' and I'm about to continue but I see that I have truly thrown Portia, and I stop, astonished, and curious to hear what she is about to say.

'Oh, Cath, I didn't know. No wonder you and Si had been so awful to me. I can't blame you. But you know we didn't have an affair, Josh and I, although not for want of trying, on my part, anyway.'

I stop, astonished at Portia giving away so much information. 'What do you mean?'

She sighs. 'I mean that for years I had always thought that Josh was the one to get away. You know how they say there's always one? A lost love? I convinced myself it was Josh, and that if Josh and I were together, then I would live happily ever after.'

Aha. Her happy ending. Despite myself I'm amazed that Si was right, that there was an ulterior motive behind it all.

'I managed to persuade him to come to that restaurant that night, and I only managed it because he was tired, and lonely, and things, as you probably know, weren't going that well with Lucy, and I thought it would be the perfect window of opportunity.

'He needed someone to talk to, and I made sure he knew I'd be listening, and then I planned on bringing him back to my place and seducing him.'

Jesus. What a bitch.

'I know what you're thinking,' she says. 'And I agree. It was disgusting behaviour, but I hardly knew Lucy then, and I'd spent ten years thinking about Josh. Ten years thinking that he was the only man who could ever make me happy, and here he was, telling me he was unhappy. God, Cath. I'm only human.'

I don't say anything, just wait for her to continue.

'And you know, he was so grateful for my being there. He was so sweet to me, so tender towards me, I really thought it was going to happen.'

'So what happened?' I prompt as she lapses into silence, evidently thinking back to that night.

'It didn't take long to see that Josh saw me as an old friend who was concerned, who would be there to listen, and that was it. He sat there and talked about his marriage all night. He talked about Lucy, about how much he loved her, how special their relationship was, and how he couldn't understand why they seemed to be drifting apart since Bookends.'

'So you didn't try to seduce him?'

'Even at the beginning of the evening I still thought I would. I thought it would be the perfect time, but the more he talked the more I realized that he really loved Lucy, and that I'd be wrecking a marriage that had been perfectly happy apart from this one glitch that would soon sort itself out.'

'But Josh was always in love with you. You know that.'

'Of course I knew that, which is why I was so convinced I could get him. And you know what, Cath? Maybe I could have done. But I knew it wouldn't have been fair, and I also knew that he and Lucy were meant to be together. Not him and me. I'd been building this fantasy for ten years, and I understood that night that reality would never match the fantasy.'

I sit there in silence for a while, stunned. Stunned at her honesty, and the courage it must have taken to walk away. And stunned at my behaviour, mine and Si's, for jumping to conclusions and behaving so appallingly towards her.

'But you know,' she says, after a while, 'life works in very mysterious ways.'

'What do you mean?'

'I needed to be here now, to meet up with all of you again. Just because Josh wasn't The One, doesn't mean that things won't work out, just not in the way that I'd actually planned ... well ...' She is about to say something more but evidently changes her mind, and picks up her drink with a smile and a small shrug.

We sit and talk softly, and another hour goes by, and there is such an air of intimacy, of trust, that when Portia asks about Si, asks how he is, where he is, I almost find myself telling her. But I don't. Not quite.

We carry on talking, and the conversation moves on to sex, and we start laughing as we remember exploits of old, and then sex becomes safe sex, which becomes AIDS, because that was always Portia's greatest fear.

And I tell her I have a friend who has just been diagnosed HIV positive. I don't mention names. I don't say it is a particularly close friend. I just say a friend. And Portia becomes very quiet. Too quiet. And I suspect she knows, but she won't say anything.

'How is your friend taking it?' she says quietly.

'Nobody knows yet, except me. And you now, obviously. How is he taking it? Not great. At times I think he's fine, he's accepted it, realized that it doesn't mean, as you said, death. And then he phones me in the middle of the night, drunk, frightened, furious, and I know that he feels it's the end of the world.'

'Has he started counselling?'

'Not really. He's been to the HIV clinic, and he's got all the leaflets, but he hasn't joined a group, although God knows he needs to.'

Portia appears to be deep in thought, and eventually she asks, 'Cath, do you think he'd talk to a friend of mine?'

'What for?'

'I have this friend, Eva. She's a bit older than us, mid-thirties, but she's been diagnosed as HIV positive for thirteen years, picked up during her early twenties in New York when she got into a drug scene, and she's the most amazing woman I know.'

I sit forward in my chair, interested.

'I think that your friend should meet her, because she's incredibly inspirational. She turned her life around when she was diagnosed, and she has this extraordinary outlook on having HIV.'

'How did she turn her life around?'

Portia smiles. 'It's a long story, but I think she's someone he should definitely meet. We should put them in touch with one another, and she could tell him her story herself. I don't know your friend, obviously, but Eva is a great healer, and it might help to see things from another perspective, turn him around, if you like.'

'Portia, I don't know what to say. That would be wonderful.'

'Don't be silly,' she says, giving me a sad smile. 'It's the least I can do.'

And it's only the next day that I realize I didn't even mention Josh and Ingrid, the very reason for meeting her in the first place. Somehow our rediscovered friendship got in the way of the accusations, and I never got around to it. Si said that he would ask, but then said that if Portia was that friendly with Ingrid, which apparently she is, she would hardly tell us the truth, given how close we are to Lucy. So we're still in the dark, but quite frankly there are far more important things to deal with right now.

And I'm not sure what I expected from Portia, but I'm pretty sure I didn't expect *this* from her. Not in a million years did I ever think she would be the one to dive in and rescue Si, but by introducing him to Eva, by offering us help and then immediately coming up with a day and time, this is precisely what she has done.

I told Si what Portia had said, and Si said I could tell her, as long as I swore her to secrecy. Of course she said she already knew it was Si, and that she wouldn't dream of telling a soul, other than Eva, of course.

And I can't help but feel that Si and I have been far too unfair on her – have misjudged her enormously, because every time we think she has betrayed us, we end up being wrong. And although Si was right when he kept saying she had come back for a reason and it wouldn't be a good one, I think she has now redeemed herself.

Si phoned me on the Wednesday afternoon, the day of Portia's dinner, and said that he couldn't be bothered and was about to ring to cancel, but somehow – God knows how – I managed to talk him into going, and then sat on tenterhooks, waiting to hear what happened.

When Si got home, he was buzzing. He phoned me immediately, told me that already, after spending an evening with this woman Eva, this woman who was HIV positive, he felt entirely different.

She was tiny, he said. Tiny, dark, very pretty, and

the picture of health. She sat there drinking sparkling mineral water, listening to Si, before quietly telling her story.

In 1980, when she was fifteen, she fell in with the dope-smoking crowd at school. No big deal. She did it because everyone else was doing it, and because it made her feel, for the first time, like she belonged. Most people grow out of it, but Eva didn't, she did the reverse, and within a couple of years she had progressed to speed, and soon, because other people did, and because she fancied one of the boys in her crowd who did, she was using heroin. The remainder of her school days were blurred by the heroin, as were her emotions, and at twenty she took herself off to New York, hoping for a drug-free stay and a fresh start.

Within two days of arriving at JFK she was living with a coke dealer, and *using* again. This time she started hanging out in 'shooting galleries'. Grotty rooms in old brownstones in the wrong part of town, havens for the junkies who would score from the dealer on the corner, then go to these rooms as safe places to shoot up. And Eva, the youngest of them all, would be given their leftovers, together with the dirty needles that had been passed around the entire room. And of course she didn't know. No one did.

Back home, two years later, Eva went to university. Middle class, bright, she was studying Philosophy, Politics and Economics, and trying, unsuccessfully, to give up heroin, turning to alcohol on the rare occasions she managed to go without.

And then the 'tombstone' adverts appeared. Adverts warning about AIDS and HIV, warning of the dangers of unprotected sex, of not knowing your partners' sexual history. Of shared needles and drug use.

It couldn't be me, she thought. Things like that don't happen to middle-class girls like me. To rule it out, she went to her doctor and requested a test. Two weeks later she went back in for her results. The doctor said, distractedly, you're positive. Go to the STD clinic at the local hospital.

Twenty-one years old, HIV positive, perhaps she should have felt that her life was over, but Eva didn't feel that. She didn't feel anything, her emotions still cushioned by the drugs, the drinking, and it was only a year later, when she lay in bed, thinking about her lifestyle, about how she was treating herself – smoking, drinking, not eating – that she realized she had to make a choice.

She realized that by giving in to HIV, by expecting it to take her life, she was removing all choice, and that, for her, was untenable. She didn't choose to die, she suddenly realized. She chose to live, and she refused to give in to the fear, because fear, she still says, is the most toxic thing of all.

A year after being diagnosed, Eva set up an illness and recovery group. She threw herself into working with AIDS awareness groups, for various charities, teaching, helping, advising. Then one day she woke up, and, in spite of everything she'd done, everyone she'd taught, she still felt that one day this *thing*, AIDS, was going to get her.

And that was when she decided it wasn't. She turned to Buddhism, to believing in one day at a time. She stopped believing there was no point in training in anything worth while because her life was about to end, and started to train in Cranio-Sacral Therapy, finding a spirituality there that had been missing in her life.

And she found a therapist who refused to allow her to

become a victim. If she had a cough, her therapist would turn to her and say: 'So you've got a cough? So what?' He didn't say it would be the onset of PCP pneumonia. He didn't say it was a symptom of full-blown AIDS. He said it was just a cough, and you know what? He was right, and she learned that even when you have been diagnosed, not everything is HIV related.

Now, thirteen years on, she is the picture of health. It may not work for everyone, she told Si, as she was coming to the end of her story, but what works for her is to believe she's fine.

'And she really is,' Si told me, in wonder, in awe, and then he said goodbye and put down the phone, because he had the rest of the night to think about what she'd said.

Chapter twenty-nine

'Cath, my love?' Si and I are walking Mouse on Primrose Hill, and Si is almost, almost, back to his usual self. Of course he's not the same, he says that something inside him has shifted, but the clouds have passed and his outlook is sunny again.

He and Eva swapped phone numbers. She said if he ever needed to talk, all he had to do was to pick up the phone, and I know they've got together a few times since then.

She took him to Body Positive in Greek Street, where she seemed to know everyone. She introduced him, made him feel welcome, and persuaded him to sign up on the Recently Diagnosed Course.

His first session was last Saturday. He phoned me from Soho Square, just around the corner and said, 'Cath, wish me luck. I'm going in.' I laughed and told him I'd keep my fingers crossed, and told him to call as soon as the course was finished.

He called the next morning, because a couple of people also on the course had invited him out for a drink afterwards, and instead of hitting a busy, buzzy bar in Soho, they went to a quiet little pub on the other side of Regent Street, and spent the evening sharing their experiences.

'Cath,' he said, sounding brighter than he had for ages, 'I feel like I can finally see the light at the end of the tunnel. Christ, I can't even begin to tell you how much better I feel. How *normal* I feel, now that I know I have this support.'

And he told me about the course: about having to wear a name tag, which everyone groaned about, but which seemed to break the ice; about sitting in a circle and introducing your neighbour to the rest of the group, having to find out when they were diagnosed, plus a couple of other, silly things that made everyone laugh.

They were told about Body Positive as an organization; about HIV, the immune system, the tests that they would come to expect. And towards the end of the day they gradually shared their stories, their feelings, and for the first time Si saw that he was absolutely not alone.

They were told what would happen on the rest of the course: about meeting dentists, dieticians, complementary therapists; about dealing with transmission, reinfection and the practicalities of living with HIV.

He decided today that he will start treating himself to a weekly massage, and has already booked his first one at the Brick Lane Natural Health Centre, which only surprises me because, in the past, he's always taken the piss out of people who actually believe in that stuff. Yet another thing that has changed.

For a Saturday, Primrose Hill isn't too crowded, the darkness of the sky with the impending threat of rain evidently putting people off, and Mouse is happy to run around looking for fellow four-legged playmates.

We huff and puff our way up the hill (well, me, because Si's a damn sight fitter), and when we reach the top I collapse, as usual, on one of the benches and beg for mercy as Si agrees to give me five minutes' rest.

'Has Portia told you about Marcus?' he says, after we've been sitting for a while.

'Portia, your new best friend?' This is somewhat sarcastic, I know, but ever since Portia introduced Si to Eva, she's been promoted from evil wicked witch of North London to Saint Portia the Heavenly Angel. I'm not jealous, it just pisses me off slightly.

'Now, now. She'll never take your place, Cath. But she has this friend, Marcus, and he's got an apartment in Tenerife, and apparently he lets his friends use it when he's not there.

'He's offered it to Portia in a couple of weeks, but she can't go, too much work, so she thought I might like to go.'

'It sounds amazing! Who would you go with?'

'Actually, I thought I might go on my own . . .'

I shoot him a worried look, but he starts laughing. 'No, no, don't worry, I'm not going to sink into a deep depression and throw myself off a cliff or anything. Actually I'd just love some peace and quiet, and I think the sea would be incredibly healing for me.'

'Si, come on, you'd be lonely as hell.'

'You know, six months ago I would have agreed with you, but everything's changed now, and, bizarre as this sounds, given all that's happened, I feel incredibly serene at the moment.

'I just want to go by myself, read my self-help books, sunbathe and sit on the terrace at night, breathing in the smell of the pine forest and listening to the sea.'

I snort with laughter. 'Pine forest? As if! God, Si. Ever the Romantic.'

'Only this time there's no man involved. Nor is there likely to be.'

'Si, being HIV positive doesn't preclude relationships, you know. It just means you have to practise safe sex.'

'Do I know it doesn't preclude relationships? Darling, you're talking to the expert. I've been through the whole safe sex issue with the counsellor, and it's not the practicalities, it's just that it's the very last thing on my agenda right now. I need to heal myself, and until I'm whole I won't be ready for anything else.'

I press my palm on to his forehead. 'Simon Nelson, are you sure you're feeling all right?'

'Oh ha bloody ha. Meanwhile, how about moving that big bum of yours and getting some exercise?'

'Yeah, yeah,' I mutter, 'I see that some things, like insults, never change.'

We carry on walking round the field, Si picking up sticks and branches that are just beginning to fall off the trees, and throwing them for an ecstatic Mouse.

'There's something else I've been meaning to tell you,' he says. 'About telling the others. I think it's time I told them, now that I'm doing the course and I'm coming to terms with it. What do you think?'

'I think that if you're ready, and you're sure, it would be the right thing to do. How are you planning to do it?' I don't tell him that Lucy and Josh know that something is up, even though they haven't got a clue what it is. They know because when Si was in 'the darkness', as he put it, he cut himself off from everyone except me.

And even now, since Eva and the course, he's still been reluctant to see them. He's changed, he says, and he doesn't want them to see the change until he's ready for it.

'I've decided to hold a dinner party,' he announces grandly. 'Well, actually I thought it would just be us, you, me, Josh and Lucy. I thought when I'm back from

Tenerife, but definitely before Christmas. Give me a chance to dust off Queen Delia, because God knows she hasn't seen the light of day for a while.' Si stops and looks at me, anxiety clouding his expression. 'Cath, do you think it's a good idea?'

'That you tell them? God, yes! Definitely.'

He sighs. 'The thing is that I'm sure Lucy will be fine with it, but what about Josh? You know how straight he is, I think this might completely freak him out, and I couldn't bear it if he did one of those numbers where suddenly he'd start dragging Max away or something because he thinks I'm infectious.'

'Sounds like heaven to me,' I mutter, but then I compose myself because Si is genuinely worried. 'First of all I'm sure Josh wouldn't react like that, and secondly, even if he did, do you really care what that unfaithful sod thinks?'

'I suppose not. Anyway, I may as well get it over and done with before I go away. Do you really think I'm doing the right thing?'

'I really think you're doing the right thing.'

We wander round Primrose Hill, then sit outside one of the cafés for a quick coffee, where Mouse misbehaves himself horrendously by trying to mount every dog – male and female – that has the misfortune to pass. After we've dropped Mouse back, I tell Si to let me off at Bookends, because, even though it's my day off, I can't resist seeing how busy it is every Saturday.

And at the end of the day, I get home and am about to listen to my messages, when the phone rings. It's James.

'And what are you up to now?' he asks, when I have

finished burbling my news down the phone, trying hard to push the picture of his forearms out of my mind. 'I hope you're doing something extra special.'

'Actually I'm staying in,' I laugh. 'Everyone's busy, and I'm treating myself to a lovely lazy night in.'

'Cath, you can't possibly stay in tonight. It's not allowed. You are, on the other hand, allowed to have a lovely lazy night in, but I'm afraid it will have to be at my place, because I'm bored too and I want some company. Say, eight-ish?'

How could I possibly refuse?

Just before I leave the house I record a message on Si's machine telling him he's a pain in the arse, but that I've finally done something I think he'd be proud of. And it isn't a shopping spree in Designer Heaven.

I check myself in the mirror and grin at my reflection, which, thanks to the stress of the last few weeks with Si, is looking just the tiniest bit smaller, and are those . . . could they possibly be . . . cheekbones?

Ten minutes later I'm standing outside James's door, and when he opens it he gives me a big hug and immediately hands me a glass of champagne.

'Hmm,' I say, as soon as I walk through the studio and into the living area. I inhale deeply, sniffing what smells suspiciously like lavender furniture polish, and today, unlike the last time I visited, James really has put me to shame. Today the piles of papers have all disappeared and the furniture is gleaming, helped somewhat by the flickering candlelight emanating from the huge gothic torches on either side of the fireplace.

'This smells far too clean for you, James,' I say, running my finger along the coffee table and feigning surprise at finding no dust.

'Oh, please, you've only been here once. And correct me if I'm wrong, but aren't you the woman who wouldn't know clean if it came up to her on the street and spat in her eye?'

'Charming! As it happens, James, I vaguely remember you saying that housework wasn't your thing either. In fact, no, no, I remember you saying you were horribly messy and couldn't get your act together.'

'Let's just say I wanted to prove to you that I had another side,' he laughs, sitting down next to me on the sofa.

'I can see,' I say, raising the champagne glass together with an eyebrow. 'Are we celebrating something?'

'The fact that you haven't cancelled me, perhaps?' he says, grinning.

'Now, now. The night is still young. Give me half an hour and I'll be doing another runner.'

'You had so better not do that,' he says sternly. I apologize and tell him that really is the last thing on earth I will be doing tonight.

'So.' He reaches for his glass on the table.

'So.' I smile, as we toast one another.

'To health, happiness and your future as a bookshop mogul or, failing that, a cleaning woman.'

'A bookshop mogul or a cleaning woman?' I laugh. 'What a choice!'

'Look at it this way,' he says, taking a sip. 'You'll be the Mr Waterstone of your generation, or the Mrs Mop, even if it kills me,' and I laugh.

'How's your friend,' he says, putting the glass down. 'Is he dealing with it better now?'

'He's really okay, actually.' I flush slightly at the memory of the state I was in the last time I saw James, but he doesn't mention it, and I push the thought out of my mind and carry on. 'He's started doing a course for people who have been recently diagnosed, and he's met this amazing woman. She's had it for thirteen years, and it's just completely changed her life, for the better. So he seems to have started coming to terms with it now, which is extraordinary, given the state he was in.'

James shivers. 'Horrible thought. Here we all are, thinking it couldn't happen to us, and boom, suddenly someone you know gets it and it completely changes your opinion.'

'God, I know. Tell me about it,' and I lapse into silence, desperate to talk about something else before I start getting morose, but luckily James seems to realize and he changes the subject.

'Just keep still!' he says suddenly, and I freeze, expecting him to brush off an insect of some kind, but he reaches down and pulls a sketchbook out from under the sofa. 'Keep still!' he says, grabbing a pencil and starting to sketch.

'Wonderful, wonderful,' he murmurs in a crap French accent that makes me laugh, even as he stares at me intently, glancing at the paper as he scribbles away, then back to me, as I start to feel increasingly uncomfortable. 'Beautiful, beautiful.'

I sip the champagne awkwardly, trying to keep my face as still as possible, just opening my lips a tiny bit to sip the champagne every now and then, and eventually James puts the pencil down, closes the sketchbook and picks up his glass again.

'So how's everything at Bookends?'

'What!' I practically shriek as I dive for the sketchbook, and he leaps out of my way as I open up the page to reveal a beautiful little sketch that looks exactly like me, only far, far prettier.

'This is beautiful!' I gasp, 'even if it is the most flattering thing I've ever seen.'

'Rubbish,' James says. 'That's exactly what you look like. Trust me. I'm an artist,' and I start to laugh.

Soon we have relaxed into the sofa, talking softly, about relationships, marriage, and then, after a while, about Josh and Lucy.

I tell him how hurt I am by Josh's behaviour, that it's putting me in an impossible situation, and that I wouldn't wish this upon anyone, to know about an affair and not to be able to tell. The weekend that Josh is going away with Ingrid, I tell him, Si and I are spending Saturday night with Lucy, and I don't know how good either of us will be at pretending that everything is normal.

And James surprises me yet again. He surprises me because on the one hand I think of him as this estate agent who has a huge talent for painting, and who doesn't seem to take life very seriously, and then on the other he can be incredibly wise and sensitive, weighing up a situation and offering exactly the right advice.

He thinks that, however much we love Lucy, and love Lucy and Josh as a couple, it is not our place to interfere. He says that he knows it must hurt, but that whatever will be, will be, and that nothing we say or do will resolve things. It may in fact make things worse.

He says that sometimes an affair, while not, obviously, the ideal, can make a marriage stronger. That there are usually reasons why one of the partners is straying in the first place, and often when they stray a step too far, they realize what it is they actually have at home, and come bouncing back with all the vigour of a newly-wed.

But of course who can say if the trust will ever be there again?

He asks whether, if push came to shove, I would have to make a choice, and I have to stop for a while, amazed that my immediate and unconscious answer would be Lucy. Amazed because had he asked me this question six months ago, I would undoubtedly have said Josh, because Josh, after all, has been my friend for far longer.

Josh and I have a shared history, a common past, have known everything about one another since we were eighteen, but all that has now changed, and his infidelity has placed a wall between us, just as Bookends has permanently cemented my friendship with his wife.

I realize that Josh and I haven't really spoken for months, that I have done my utmost to avoid him, and that the overwhelming emotion I have when Josh is around is anger.

But I know that James is right, that there is nothing I can say, or do, to change things. He goes to the kitchen, pulls another bottle of champagne out of the fridge (which is slightly worrying only because I haven't eaten anything and I'm beginning to get seriously light-headed), then sits down again, a few centimetres closer.

Now this, I have to admit, would normally startle me, but the champagne is definitely starting to have an effect, and I note the closing distance between us with nothing other than amusement.

But then he really startles me.

'What about you and relationships?' he says, out of the blue. 'How come you're still single?'

I start to laugh. 'That's like asking how come the sun is yellow. Or a tree is green. It just is. It's a fact of life. Didn't you know that even the name Cath is synonymous with singledom?'

James smiles. 'You're happy being single, though,

aren't you? You're so independent, you never seem to need anybody. Christ, it's taken me weeks to even get to see you by myself.'

'I don't know about that. I've just always been incredibly happy with my friends, and I suppose I never have really needed anybody.'

'It's funny.' He shakes his head. 'When I first met you I thought you were incredibly tough, but you're really soft inside, vulnerable. Oh God, I've gone too far. That sounded so naff, I'm sorry.'

I start to blush, he starts to blush, and we both start speaking at the same time. I stop to let him carry on, and he does, looking at his glass rather than at me, and I know that he's uncomfortable saying this, but he obviously feels he needs to make a point. 'Look, without wanting this to sound like a line, I just think that you ought to let that softness show more often. You're far more attractive when you do.'

I laugh nervously, because no one's called me *attractive* in a very, very long time, and even then I'm not entirely sure they meant it, and then, without even realizing it's happening, he's kissing me.

Or I'm kissing him. Either way, we're kissing, and once I've got over the shock, because I cannot even remember the last time I had a proper, passionate kiss (although this is far more gentle than passionate), we pull apart and I cannot wipe the smile off my face.

'Is this okay?' James whispers, and I nod, wondering whether it's the champagne or the kiss that's keeping this dopey grin on my face, but then not wondering for too much longer as he kisses me again.

'Shit!' I jump away as champagne pours on to my trousers, my having become so carried away the glass just flopped from my hand, and James laughs.

'Let me get a cloth,' I say, but he shakes his head, takes me by the hand and leads me up the stairs.

I follow him mutely, feeling as if I'm in a dream, because this surely can't be happening, not to me. I just don't *do* this any more. I don't have sex. Aaargh! *Sex*! Oh God. He's leading me to the bedroom.

Fortunately the grin is still plastered to my face, hiding this inner turmoil, but anyway, my body doesn't seem to be listening, as it follows him up the stairs and into his bedroom as if on auto-pilot.

The grin disappears pronto as he starts undressing me. Oh God, I pray, as he unbuttons my cardigan. Please let my bra not be too old, please let it not be too grey, and I have to admit I do lose the passion of the moment as I furiously try to remember which bra I put on this morning, and when was the last time it had been washed.

Two minutes later I breathe a sigh of relief as James switches off the main lights, a soft glow coming from the small lamp on what is obviously his – right – side of the bed, and I make a mental note to stick to the shadows on the left.

And then I don't have to think any more, because what has felt like a film, suddenly starts to feel very real indeed, and I close my eyes, wrap myself around James and . . .

. . . beautiful, tender, loving, warm, comfortable . . . shall I go on? How could I have forgotten? How could I have lived without this? How could I have run away from this for so many years, when it isn't scary at all, it's absolutely right, and lovely.

It's so lovely that just after James has entered me (condom-encased, of *course*), just after he's whispered, 'Is this okay?', just as he's starting to move inside me, I start to cry. Not like that time in James's office. Crying this time with pleasure. With forgotten memories. With sheer and utter bliss, and despite the tears I'm smiling, and although James is concerned, I reassure him and soon there's nothing left to say.

. . . And, let's just say that Si was right, it is *exactly* like riding a bicycle, and everything I thought I'd forgotten comes back in a flash, and it feels wonderful.

Better than wonderful. Perfect.

I have to get up three times in the night to pee, which is hardly surprising considering the amount of champagne I had to drink, but every time I come back into the bedroom to see James lying there, the duvet thrown back from his naked body, I can't help but grin to myself again.

And every time I climb back into bed, rolling over to my side, away from him so he isn't hit with the full force of morning mouth, he reaches over for my hand and gives it a squeeze, falling asleep again, holding my hand.

James sleeps like a log. I listen to his breathing and roll over to watch him when I am quite sure he is asleep, because sleep is evidently not on the agenda for me tonight, not after this.

But eventually I seem to drop off for a short while, and I swear, if it is at all possible to fall asleep smiling, then that is what I do, and as I give in to sleep I think that it's not that I had forgotten how lovely sex could be, it's that it never *was* this lovely before.

I wake up before James the next morning. I creep out of bed and pull on my clothes, making my way to the bathroom to brush my teeth as best I can using my finger, and leave before he wakes up.

And it doesn't feel quite the same in the morning. In the cold light of day I'm frightened. No. Make that terrified. I'm terrified because I have now put myself in the position of potentially being hurt, and that is something I have managed to successfully avoid for years.

And James could really hurt me, I think, coming back out of the bathroom and sneaking a final gaze at him before he wakes up, before I leave, avoiding the inevitable awkwardness of the morning after. Look at him lying there, his hair even more tousled than usual, his lips puffy with sleep, so vulnerable and soft and *gorgeous*, I could almost squeeze the life out of him.

He opens his eyes. I jump slightly, and he smiles sleepily, holding out his hand, and I wasn't expecting this. I walk over and perch on the edge of the bed, and he pulls me down for a kiss, while I thank God I had the presence of mind to get up and swallow toothpaste.

'Where are you going?' he says.

'Home.' I start to get up. 'So much to do.'

He hoists himself up on the pillows and rubs his eyes, looking so much like a little boy I want to just take him in my arms, but of course I can't do that. I have to leave.

'Cath,' he says, holding my hand and looking deeply into my eyes. 'Don't leave. Don't put the barriers up again, you don't need to, not with me, and not after last night.'

I falter, not knowing what to say, and he can see there's a chink of hope.

'Tell you what. I'll get up and we can go out, get the papers and have breakfast together. And before you say no I bet you didn't have any plans today anyway.'

'Oh, okay,' I finally grumble, standing up and walking out of the room to avoid having to see him naked in the cold light of day, because I'm sure I would just shrivel with embarrassment, and more to avoid him seeing the huge grin that has just lit up my face. 'I'll wait downstairs.'

Chapter thirty

Si and I stop at the corner shop en route to Lucy's to pick up some wine, even though it's hardly necessary, with their well-stocked wine cupboard, and a couple of giant bars of Cadbury's Dairy Milk, because there's no better sustenance for a Saturday night in than chocolate, and then we roll up at Lucy's.

I haven't said anything about James. Ridiculous as this may sound, this is my secret right now, and I want to keep it precious and safe, at least until I know it's not just a quick fling.

'Who is it?' Max's voice wafts through the door, loud and clear. I look at Si, but he just grins and keeps quiet, so I give it a whirl.

'Hello, Max. It's Auntie Cath and Uncle Si. Are you going to be a good boy and open the door?'

There's silence from the other side, and I can tell that Si is loving every second of this. I make a face at him and eventually he leans down and says, 'Max?'

A pause, then, 'Yes?'

'It's Uncle Si. Do you want to see what I've got for you?'

Another pause. 'Yes.'

'You can't see it if you won't open the door, can you?'

Brilliant. Si and I stand on the doorstep listening to Max's thought process, and then, when Max decides that in fact Si's plan is not flawed after all, the door slowly opens, and we look down into Max's expectant face.

'Okay, Max.' Si crouches down and looks him in the eye. 'Which would you prefer? A fire engine or ... a piece of chocolate?'

Max stops to think. 'A fire engine,' he says eventually, as I start to laugh.

'Oh well. Chocolate will just have to do.' Si shrugs and hands him a small Dairy Milk, which doesn't seem to go down at all badly, and makes a change from Si's most recent presents for Max, which include a sailor, a policeman and an Indian warrior. Although Si would not dream of saying anything to Josh for fear of compromising his son's impending masculinity, Si is aiming to keep going until Max has the entire set of the Village People.

'Cath! Si! I'm in the kitchen!'

'There's a surprise,' Si laughs, and we walk down the corridor, taking off our coats as Lucy appears in the doorway.

'Quick, quick, big gossip! Huge!' She hurries us into the kitchen, where bowls of guacamole are already sitting on the table, with nachos waiting to be dipped in and a bottle of wine.

'You've got to sit down because you're never going to *believe* this!' Lucy is bursting, bursting to tell us something, and I'm assuming it's good news, because if she'd found out about Josh there's no way she'd have this mischievous look on her face.

'Pour some wine, quick. Okay. Listen. I can't believe this myself. This weekend is the weekend that, as you know, Ingrid's away with the mystery lover.'

'Yes?' Si and I both say simultaneously.

'Do you want the short version or the long version?'

'Short,' I say, as Si says, 'Long.'

'Oh God. Well, the middle version is that Ingrid had

366

said the mystery lover was picking her up this evening and I was supposed to be at work and we'd got Laura to babysit, but I got home earlier than I'd planned, and you're never going to believe what I walked in on . . .'

Si and I shoot each other worried glances, but no, it couldn't possibly be Josh.

Lucy sits back and grins like the cat that got the cream. 'I walked in on Ingrid and the mystery lover locked in a passionate embrace in the kitchen.'

'And?' Si's now starting to look bored. 'Some swarthy Italian? Playboy type? Medallion and hairy chest?'

Lucy shakes her head, her smile growing wider. 'Nope,' and she pauses dramatically until even Si starts to look interested. 'It's *Portia*!'

'WHAT?' Si knocks his wine glass over, my mouth falls open and my chin hits the floor.

'You *are* joking?' I leave it to Si to speak, as I am, for possibly the first time in my life, completely speechless.

'Nope.' Lucy shakes her head. 'I know! *Portia*! Isn't it *extraordinary*!'

'Extraordinary. Are you sure?' Si's now looking doubtful.

'Sure? Si, they pulled apart looking terribly embarrassed, and then Portia shrugged and said we had to find out sometime, and they both grinned and left the house holding hands.'

'Noooooooooo,' I manage to breathe out eventually, my eyes as wide as saucers, because this is the very last thing I ever expected. I mean, Portia? Ingrid? How? When? Oh Christ. This is just too much for me. I sit down, mouth still agape.

'I know. Portia and Ingrid! In *lurrve*!' Lucy's loving every second of this.

'Actually,' Si says, 'I always thought Portia had a leaning towards her Sapphic sisters.'

'Did you bollocks!' I respond, because it's the first I've heard of it.

'What?' He looks at me, innocence personified. 'Just because I may not have mentioned it to you doesn't mean I didn't think it.'

'Yeah, right,' I say, grinning, because I know, and he knows I know, that this is absolutely rubbish. 'But Christ, how did this happen?'

Lucy shrugs. 'Ingrid's hardly likely to tell me the whole story, is she?'

'Didn't Portia drop any hint at all when you were over there the other night?' I turn to Si.

'No. We didn't even mention Ingrid. And anyway, what's she going to say, oh by the way, Si, I know we've known one another for thirteen years, but I'm now a lesbian and I'm in love with Ingrid?'

'Si, wouldn't she be bisexual rather than a lesbian?' Lucy, ever politically correct, interrupts.

Si shrugs.

'But Portia!' It hits me again. 'It's just unbelievable.'

'You should have seen Josh's face!' Lucy starts to laugh.

'Josh?' Si and I together, and I suddenly think, God, were we wrong again? And a deep shame engulfs me as I realize that yet again Si and I have jumped to conclusions and punished Josh for something he evidently hasn't done, and I shoot Si a worried glance, only to see him shooting exactly the same back to me.

'I thought Josh was away?' Si manages to sound breezily nonchalant as Lucy's busy concentrating on unwrapping the Dairy Milk.

'He was supposed to be, but it got cancelled at the last minute.'

'So where is he now?'

'Still trying to pull off this big deal. He's upstairs in his study, working, and I know I should have told you he'd be around but quite honestly he'll probably be stuck up there all night and I haven't seen the two of you like this for ages, and I didn't want you not to come because you thought Josh would be around.'

I for one, am completely speechless, and I can see that Si is also lost for words, but thankfully Max chooses that moment to disrupt the shamed atmosphere in the kitchen by zooming around the kitchen table with Pokémon in hand, screeching into chairs and making a huge amount of noise, until Si scoops him up and asks whether he'd like a story.

Lucy looks at him gratefully, and as Si carries Max out of the room he turns to me and says, 'Come on, Cath, it'll be good practice. Come and help me.'

Lucy starts to laugh. 'Good practice? Good practice? My darling Cath, you cannot mean to tell me you're already talking sproglets, are you? Although heaven knows it's about time.'

'Don't even go there,' I whisper furiously, because, okay, okay, I confess. Lucy does know about James – I had to tell *someone* – and I don't want her saying anything, but luckily Si is standing at the foot of the stairs, just out of earshot, making big eyes at me and frantically waving me over.

'Okay, I'm coming.' I get up and as soon as we're safely upstairs Si sends Max off to find last year's Furby, telling him that the Pokémon wants to destroy it, and then whispers, 'Christ, we've got to apologize to Josh. I feel awful.'

'I know. But what are we supposed to say?'

'Oh, God knows, but I think we just have to do it.' He shoots a glance at Max, who's on his hands and knees rifling through the toy chest and muttering to himself as he pulls the toys out.

'Will he be all right?'

'He'll be hours,' Si says, pulling his sweater up to reveal a small brown and white Furby nestling in his waistband. 'I had to pull the bloody batteries out to stop it speaking Furbish.' He rolls his eyes as I start to laugh. 'Come on, let's go and find Josh.'

As we walk up to the study door we can hear the sounds of typing, and Si makes the sign of the cross, pretends to pray, then knocks on the door. The typing stops.

'Yup?'

'Josh? It's Si. And Cath. Can we come in?' Si is already opening the door as he asks this, making it a purely rhetorical question, and Josh swivels round from his desk.

'Hi, guys,' he says nonchalantly, which, if you didn't know any better, you might think was a sign that there was nothing wrong, but there is a warmth missing in his voice, and I suddenly realize how awful this must have been for Josh. We are, after all, two of his best friends, and for weeks now we've been giving him the cold shoulder without letting him know the reason why, and poor, poor Josh, with all his insecurities, must have felt terrible. Why did I not think of this before?

'Josh, we need to talk to you,' I start, then stop, because how on earth do you explain, or justify, or apologize for what we've done?

'The thing is,' Si says, moving across the room to the futon pushed against the wall and sitting down. 'We feel ridiculous and we feel ashamed because we thought you were having an affair with Portia – '

'Well, actually that was my fault, because I saw you in Barnes one night with Portia and I immediately jumped to the wrong conclusion, but then we discovered you weren't,' I interrupt.

Si continues, 'But only because we then thought you were having an affair with Ingrid.'

Josh just sits there and looks at us, not saying a word, his face giving nothing away.

'And now we know that you didn't, you hadn't, and we feel terrible because we've been so awful to you, but we were only trying to protect Lucy,' I say lamely.

There's a long silence.

'What made you think I would be unfaithful to Lucy?' Josh says after a while.

'Well, you were hardly ever here, and you kept having these late meetings and then, when you were here, you weren't interested in sex . . .' Whoops. I think I've just gone too far, and I see Josh clench his teeth, which means he is seriously pissed off, but, repressed as he is, he won't be letting it out, which is something of a relief.

I shrug apologetically. 'I'm sorry, Josh. We both are. We were just so angry and upset at the thought of you hurting Lucy.' Si and I hang our heads in shame.

And Josh shakes his head, looks at the floor, then up at the ceiling, then at the floor again. 'I didn't know what it was,' he says eventually. 'I couldn't figure out why the pair of you had just switched off. At least now I know.'

'Oh, Josh, *please* forgive us?' I can feel my eyes welling up, and I feel terrible, and I know I won't feel good again until I have his forgiveness.

'What can I say?' Josh looks first at me, then at Si. 'You're my oldest friends, and I suppose, at least, you've been honest with me. But why didn't you say something before? I mean, if you thought I was having an affair, why didn't you confront me with it instead of just cutting me dead? Christ, we're not children any more.'

'But we've never had to deal with this kind of situation before,' Si says. 'And I agree, with hindsight we were absolutely wrong in what we did, and we would never do that again, and if we ever have a problem in the future I swear to you we'll sit down and talk about it.'

'You mean, if you ever think I'm having an affair again?' but Josh's voice is soft and I can see he's forgiven us.

But before Si has a chance to answer, the study door is pushed open and Max stands there, eyes bright and alert, the war between Pokémon and Furby completely forgotten.

'Daddy?' he says, climbing on to Josh's lap. 'Can I go to affair too? And can I have a toffee apple and a candy floss?' The three of us start to laugh, and it is the first time I have ever wanted to kiss Max.

Chapter thirty-one

'Not . . . *SEX*!' Si squeals, when I finally admit every-thing, having successfully managed to keep it from him, and now realizing that I have to give him something to look forward to when he gets back from Tenerife, and what would be better than gossip?

'Yes,' I admit reluctantly, after much sighing. 'I did it. We actually had sex.'

Si screams down the phone, and we both start laughing. 'And what's more,' I say gleefully, 'you were absolutely right about it being like a bicycle, and it was lovely.'

'You witch! You complete witch! I can't believe you waited a week to tell me. I *knew* it. I knew you looked different! So how do you feel?'

'Amazing.'

'And you spent the rest of the weekend with him?'

'Yup.'

'And you've seen him how many times since?'

'Almost every night,' I admit sheepishly.

'OH MY GOD!' and this time he shouts so loudly my eardrums practically pop, but then he recovers and says very seriously, 'Now, Cath. Don't do what I've always done. Don't jump in feet first looking for a big relation-ship. You must take it slowly, play it cool.'

'Oh fuck off,' I snort, and he laughs, because this is, of course, what I have always said to Si.

'Details, details,' Si says, 'I want details. Oh no. Oh bugger. I've got to go.'

'I know,' I chuckle maniacally. 'That's why I left it until now to call. Oh well,' I say, letting out a dramatic sigh. 'You'll just have to wait for the details until you get back from Tenerife. Have a lovely time. Bye.'

'CATH!' he shrieks. 'Don't you dare. Oh God, oh God, I can't bear this. I have to wait a whole week. Just tell me one thing, when are you seeing him again?'

'Wednesday night,' I say. 'He's taking me to the theatre.'

I can hear the awe in Si's voice. 'The theatre, indeed? Now that sounds serious.'

'Look, you. You're going to miss your flight. And I'm going to miss you. Will you take really good care?'

'Yes, yes. Fuss, fuss.'

'No, I'm serious. Look after yourself, and I'll see you the weekend after next and I love you.'

'I know, sweets.' He blows me a kiss down the phone. 'I love you too.'

For someone who has spent years erecting barriers around her love life, I'm doing a remarkably good job of letting them down.

But perhaps the strangest thing of all is that it simply doesn't feel scary. If I didn't know better, I'd say it felt *right*, but of course I do know better, so instead I'll say it feels *easy*.

So, so easy. Although it's been years, I well remember the men who didn't call, who'd phone to cancel ten minutes before I was due to see them, who'd say they would phone and then never would.

And maybe it's different because I've known James for a while now, or maybe it's because he has more integrity than anyone I've ever met (and that's saying something for an estate agent), but he does exactly what he says he's going to do.

When he says he's going to phone, he phones. If he says he'll pick me up at seven thirty, he's on the doorstep at seven twenty-nine. There is no messing about with James, and I always, *always* know exactly where I stand.

God. I could get used to this.

For the first time in my life I can see what successful partnerships are made of. Not that I was completely blind to them before, but I'd never actually experienced it for myself, and now, since James, I can absolutely see what it is that makes it work.

Because we just get on so well. I feel totally, completely, one hundred per cent relaxed in his company. There are no games, no insecurities, and I have never felt quite so comfortable being myself with anyone other than Si, Josh and Lucy.

Yes, yes, I know it hasn't been long, but when you're seeing someone all night, almost every night, it's remarkable how quickly a relationship can progress.

And as for my fear of relationships, of exposing myself, even that seems to have disappeared pretty damn quickly. In fact, since the morning after the first night we spent together, I haven't even felt a flicker of fear, but then again I suppose I haven't had to.

James calls me in the shop every day, at least twice a day, and we've been, as I already said, together every night. I know it's slightly early to say this, but it does seem that already we're settling into a pattern. Lucy, of course, is over the moon; she was almost bursting with excitement when I first told her, and now I can't wait for Si to get back so I can fill him in.

I wouldn't normally drive to Heathrow to pick anyone

up, not even Si, but he happened accidentally-on-purpose to leave a copy of his itinerary at my house before he left, and at the time I'd planned to ignore it, although that was before my big adventure with James.

So here I am, and the bloody flight's delayed, and there are hundreds of people milling around, and it's far too early in the morning for me to be doing this.

I grab a coffee from a stand and buy a paper, and when I've finished ploughing through I realize that the flight has now landed, and I rush to Arrivals to surprise Si.

He is almost the first one through, which doesn't surprise me, as he's such an incredibly neat and orderly packer that he usually manages to get away with hand luggage only. I push my way to the front so he can see me.

He's sharing his trolley with another man, around the same age, and they're both laughing and talking animatedly as they walk through, so animatedly they don't see me until I'm practically on top of the trolley.

'CATH!' Si throws his arms around me and lifts me up, which is no mean feat, I can tell you, and when he puts me down again, a split second later, his grin is ear to ear. 'I can't believe you're here!' He turns to the man with him, 'And there we were, about to jump on the train to Paddington. Thank heavens for large mercies.'

'Not that large.' I smack him, and he winces in mock pain.

'Cath, this is Paul,' he says, standing aside for me to have a good look at his companion, who grins at me, showing rather gorgeous dimples in his cheeks, and warmly shakes my hand. 'I suppose you won't believe me if I tell you I've heard all about you and all of it's good?' he says, smiling.

'You were doing so well until the last bit,' I say, grinning back, thinking how attractive this man is, and wondering how on earth they met.

'Paul was staying in the apartment next to mine,' Si explains, reading my mind. 'We met on the first day . . .'

'And haven't been apart since.' Paul squeezes Si's arm as he looks at him affectionately, and I feel a jolt of excitement.

Si catches my eye, gives me a half shrug, a big grin and an unsubtle wink, and it's all I can do not to grab him and twirl him around the Arrivals lounge, so thrilled and proud am I.

And Si looks fantastic. Not that I was expecting anything less, but he looks tanned, healthy, positively *glowing*, and I know that sun, sea and sand alone haven't given him this glow, even if the sun was amazingly hot for December.

I grab the trolley and the three of us walk to the car park, leaving Paul in charge of the bags because Si insists on accompanying me to the car park pay machine.

'Well?' he hisses, just as soon as we're out of earshot. 'Isn't he *gorgeous*?'

'Gorgeous,' I echo, laughing. 'I can't believe you. I mean, I expected you to come back looking all lovely and tanned, but I certainly didn't expect you to have some beefcake on your arm.'

'Well, sweets. Neither did I!' I look at him slyly as I feed the coins into the machine. 'I *swear*! I really wasn't, and wouldn't you know it, just when I've reached the point where a relationship is absolutely, one hundred per cent not what I want or need, I go and meet someone lovely.'

I turn to him slowly. 'Did I just hear you use the word relationship? Is it time for the onion rings yet?'

'No,' Si laughs. 'It's not a relationship, but we've had

an incredible time, and he's sweet, and bright, and funny, and for the first time in years I haven't fallen head over heels.'

'Yeah, right.'

'No, I'm serious, Cath. If anything he's been the one doing all the chasing. Meanwhile, speaking of chasing. You're still having sex, aren't you? It's written all over your face.'

'Never mind me, did I just hear you right? You? Playing hard to get? Come on, Si, I know you too well.' But his face, surprisingly, is serious.

'I promise you, Cath. I kept telling him I wasn't interested, but he didn't want to hear it.'

'Does he . . . ?' My sentence tails off, because I'm not sure whether I should be asking this question.

Si shrugs and nods. 'That's the thing. I kept saying no, and he kept saying why not, and in the end I just told him, which was bloody scary because even though I kept saying no, I fancied him like you can't believe, and I knew he wouldn't want to know after I told him.'

'And?'

He grins. 'And I was wrong. He's fine about it. Says he'd already sort of figured it out.'

'And?'

Si shoves me playfully. 'And he'd brought condoms. Thank God.'

I hold up a hand, putting on my best schoolmistress voice. 'Too much information, Mr Nelson.' And he laughs. 'Christ, come on, he'll think we've done a runner,' and we both rush back to see Paul smiling as we approach.

'Done the post-mortem,' Si pants, as we move off towards the car. 'And you, Paul, will be glad to hear you pass with flying colours.'

'I don't remember saying that,' I say, mock-indignant.

'You didn't have to,' he says triumphantly, and Paul looks at me and shakes his head, as if to say, what can we do.

'So how's the great romance coming along?' It's Saturday and Si's just picked me up, on our way to see Lucy.

'Hmm? Fine,' Si says, most uncharacteristically.

'Fine? Fine? What the hell's fine supposed to mean?'

'It means it's fine.'

'Okay,' I sigh, wondering why this suddenly feels like trying to get blood out of a stone. 'Let's find the simple way of doing this. Are you still seeing him?'

'Yes.'

'Do you still like him?'

'Yes.'

'Does he still like you?'

'Yes.'

I hold my breath, then quickly ask (although I already know the answer), 'Does this mean this is The One?'

'Don't be ridiculous, Cath,' he says. 'I hardly know him.'

And it floors me. I mean, what is there to say? This is Si, who always, *always* falls in love within about five minutes. This is Si, who's planning a life together after ten.

'Si? Are you *sure* you're feeling all right?'

'Cath, I have never felt better in my whole life.'

Chapter thirty-two

I haven't spoken to Portia since that night, but not because I haven't wanted to. I so valued that night at the Groucho, that night when she reminded me of why we were friends, why I loved her so much, but I didn't want her to think I was prying, and I didn't know what to say about Ingrid, so I've just avoided the situation altogether.

I've thought about her, of course, and thought how strange it is that life should turn out like this, and how Portia is the last person I would have expected to have a relationship with a woman.

I'm sure an amateur psychologist might say that she had been hurt too much, too often by men, but I'm not sure that I agree. Looking back, over the years, I can see that, although everyone fell in love with Portia, it was the women with whom she really bonded.

God, I remember how inseparable *we* were, how much I worshipped her, and I wonder what I would have done had there ever been a time when our friendship might have progressed to more.

It's not something I've ever thought about before now. Not that it repulses me or offends me, it just never occurred to me, but now, and I know this sounds ridiculous, but now I almost feel rejected, and I keep thinking, how come she never made a pass at me?

And I've really tried to think, to remember whether she had, but maybe she hadn't admitted anything to herself then, maybe they were merely feelings, or fears, that she pushed down until she thought she'd pushed them away.

Lucy says that maybe Ingrid is her first, that it's not unusual for people to fall in love with someone of the same sex and for that person to be their first and last, but somehow I don't think that's the case with Portia.

Would I ask her? I'm not sure. I will always treasure the Portia I knew when I was eighteen, and the friendship we had. And I will always be indebted to her for introducing Si to Eva, for showing him that not only is there a light at the end of the tunnel, but that it burns strong and bright.

But however much I loved her then, however close I felt to her that one night when she explained her affair-that-never-was with Josh, she simply doesn't have a place in my life any more. She talked of happy endings, and before she came back I always subconsciously thought that I wouldn't be able to have a happy ending unless Portia was around, but now I think I was wrong.

I think that all those years of thinking about her, talking about her, building her up into something she couldn't possibly have lived up to, weren't so much about missing her as about needing to have some kind of ending. In fact, I couldn't have put it better than Portia put it herself, although she was referring to Josh at the time. Reality could never match the fantasy. That was always the problem, and it was just a question of stopping the fantasy.

Not an ending in the sense that I'm wiping her out of my life again, but an ending in which we both acknowledge the past, forgive one another, and then move on. I realized, that night at the Groucho, that she had forgiven me, but I still needed to forgive her, for walking away from us with barely a backwards glance.

Lucy has called it closure, and that feels exactly right. It feels that finally, at the ripe old age of thirty-one, I am able to close the chapter on Portia, to sever the ties that have bound me to her all these years, and to let her go.

Which is not to say I won't see her. She and Si are growing closer, and I'm sure she'll be there, at his dinner party, tonight, although I'm not sure how often Josh and Lucy will want to see her, Ingrid now spending almost every night at Portia's, which is, as Lucy keeps saying, not what they're paying her for.

And, as Josh has already pointed out, however much he may like Portia, the last thing he wants to do is socialize with Ingrid on a regular basis. They do seem to be very much a couple, which is making it rather awkward for Josh and Lucy, given that Ingrid is still their au pair.

Perhaps I am over-analysing all of this. Perhaps it is merely as simple as my life moving on: I have the career of my dreams now that I have Bookends; I have a relationship with James, and I am happy. No, more than happy. Content. Deeply content, and perhaps it is this that is allowing me to let go of the old life and welcome the new.

Because God knows a lot has changed. Not that I was unhappy before, but I can see now that Si is right when he says that I was in a rut, that we all were. Bizarre as it seems, Si thinks that there is a reason for him being diagnosed positive. He has started to involve himself far more in the world of alternative therapies, and has been talking about training in acupressure massage himself.

As for Paul, it actually does seem to be materializing into something important, and Si does have a point when he says he would never have met Paul had he not been diagnosed.

Si tries to give the impression that he takes Paul for granted, but nothing could be further from the truth, and I adore watching them together. Because Paul does something I have never seen anyone do to Si before, ever. He mothers him. I popped in there the other night and Paul was clucking round Si like a mother hen, which Si was pretending to find irritating, but of course he was loving every second of it.

Even Josh and Lucy have changed, grown far closer, since the 'affair that never was'. It may not have actually happened, but there's no denying that the pair of them drifted apart, too caught up in their separate lives to give one another time, and the actual physical act of having sex with someone outside the marriage was just a formality.

They make time for one another now. They talk to one another, and at least twice a week they ensure they have dinner alone, just the two of them, to keep the romance alive (incidentally, the Agent Provocateur gear hasn't been wasted after all).

I had always thought of myself as the observer in this group, the one who watches silently as the action happens to everyone else, but I can now see that this isn't the case. Si has become just as much of an observer, only he chooses not to keep his observations to himself. He speaks 'his truth' frequently now, along with many other truths that I don't necessarily want to hear.

This, by the way, is all part of his new philosophy of taking each day at a time, living in the present, and realizing that life is too short not to say the things you mean, which was fine in the beginning, but I swear he's starting to take advantage of it now, and some things I just *don't* need to hear.

Other things, however, I do. He finally told me that I just could not go around looking like Michael Jackson circa 1978 any longer, and if I didn't go and get my afro seen to, he would refuse to speak to me for evermore.

I did it for Si, not for me, because some things will never change, and although I would like to make Si happy by waking up one morning with a huge interest in clothes, and hair, and make-up, it just isn't me, and you can only force these things for so long.

But I agreed to make concessions with the hair, and I'm glad I did. I had it professionally straightened, with some sort of reverse perm solution. It hasn't gone quite as straight as Si would have wanted, but it does now slip down my back in large, loose curls, and is about six inches longer, and secretly makes me feel far more feminine.

James adores it, as he's now able to run his fingers through it without the fear of coming across a stray bird's nest or two, but the loveliest thing about him is that he thinks I'm perfect. He lies in bed at night, stroking my thighs, not even flinching at the orange peel effect of cellulite under his hands, and he thinks I'm beautiful.

And having him think I'm beautiful has started to make me feel beautiful, and this is perhaps the biggest change of all, because apart from one day, in the hairdressers with Portia all those years ago, I've never felt beautiful before.

'Crisis, crisis.' Si's on the phone, sounding desperate. 'I need lemons. Oh God, I can't believe I forgot the lemons. Cath, can you bring me lemons?'

'Now?' I'm standing in the living room, water dripping into a big puddle on the carpet, as I still haven't got round to getting a walkabout phone and I still have this ridiculous thing about taking a phone call, even when you're in the bath and have an answer phone that functions perfectly normally.

Si grumbles to himself for a few seconds. 'Oh, okay,' he mutters eventually. 'I suppose you can bring them with, but you *must* be first. Seven thirty sharp. Can you do that?'

'Okay. Where's Paul? Can't he get lemons?'

'Nope. He's gone out to get some more crackers and his mobile's not on.'

I already know that tonight will be the dinner party to end all dinner parties, and not because Si intends to reveal his *coup de grâce* in what will doubtless be the most dramatic way possible. I know because Si has been planning this for days. He has planned the menu, the flowers, even the place settings, because this will not be eaten off our laps while sitting on the sofa, oh no. Paul has borrowed a trestle table from a friend, to be covered with a crisp damask tablecloth and tiny tea lights in glasses ('Candles, my darling Cath,' said Si, the other day, 'are just so *done*.'), all to be placed in the centre of the living room, which will be lit by the light of the fire and the tea lights alone. The champagne will be on ice, and Si's beloved opera will be playing softly in the background as we take our seats.

Portia was going to come tonight, although there was a question about Ingrid, Josh still being extremely uncomfortable, both with the fact that Ingrid is Portia's lover, and also, more importantly, with the fact that she's his au pair. Luckily for all of us, Portia had already accepted an invitation to some media do with Ingrid, and although part of me is fascinated to see them together, the other part is relieved they won't be coming, because, let's face it, Ingrid is not exactly my favourite person.

Paul, naturally, will be there, having been Johnny to Si's Fanny Craddock all week, and James has been invited as well. James knows about Si, he would have had to be stupid not to guess, and he knows that tonight is the night he is planning to tell everyone, although, as James has pointed out, everyone knows, apart from Josh and Lucy.

'Is there not something slightly ghoulish about calling everybody together to announce it in this way?' he asked, the other morning, and I was surprised to find myself saying that it is, in fact, quite the reverse. I know, beyond a shadow of a doubt, that it will be, is meant to be, a celebration of life. Of friendships, both new and old.

'Cath! Look at you! You look all gorgeous and sparkly, like a film star!' Lucy is as exuberant as ever as we approach them, shivering on the doorstep in the cold December air.

'Look at me? Look at you!' I laugh, admiring her slinky red dress and tiny glittering beads threaded through her hair.

Josh leans down and gives me a kiss, and I am relieved to see that he has truly forgiven me, and the twinkle in his eye tells me everything is back to normal. He shakes James's hand as Lucy links her arms through James's and smiles up at him with a wink.

'Could it be you, young James, making our Cath look so sparkly?'

'I'm certainly trying,' he laughs, as the buzzer finally lets us in, and we all fall into the hallway and up the stairs, chattering as we rub our arms to warm up.

Paul answers the door, and I introduce him to James,

Josh and Lucy, all of whom have heard about him constantly since Si's arrival home, although mostly from me, it has to be said, and I watch them closely to see if he wins them over.

More fool me. With that large, open smile and trusting eyes, how could he do anything other than win them over? Si runs out of the kitchen to greet us, then runs back in to stir the soup, and Paul opens a bottle of champagne and pours it, shouting for Si to come in and join us for a toast.

'To old friends,' Si says, as we all raise our glasses and echo his words, and as I take a sip I catch sight of Lucy, who has a huge smile on her face, and she stands up.

'And to new arrivals,' she says, as we all say 'new arrivals', and Si puts an arm round Paul as I squeeze James's leg.

'*Tiny* new arrivals,' Lucy says, stressing the word 'tiny' and looking around the room at each of us, as Si squeals and runs over to her.

'Are you trying to tell us there's a tiny bun in there?' he says, patting her stomach. She nods and he throws his arms around her, and I go to give Josh a kiss.

'We were planning to wait until twelve weeks,' Josh says ruefully, 'but my gorgeous wife evidently couldn't keep it to herself.'

'And when are we all going to be together in such beautiful surroundings again?' she says, and Josh leans down and kisses the top of her head as she leans into his arms.

'Lucy, I'm thrilled,' I say, although quite frankly, given how I feel about Max, I'm hardly relishing the prospect of yet another devilspawn-child-from-hell, although if I'm honest Max does seem to be getting slightly better, and I *am* thrilled that they're thrilled, because that's all that really matters.

'Oh bugger. The canapés.' Si stands up and puts down his champagne glass, but Paul jumps up. 'Don't worry,' Paul says. 'I'll get it. You stay and chat.'

I catch Lucy's eye and she raises an eyebrow, and I know we are thinking exactly the same thing: that all these years we thought that Si was waiting to be someone's wife, but not only does he now appear to have found a wife of his own, he's obviously thrilled to pieces with the arrangement.

Lucy has followed Paul into the kitchen, ostensibly to offer help with the canapés, but actually to find out whether Paul is really as perfect as he seems (and by this time I'm pretty sure that he is), while James and Josh are deep in conversation about children.

I squeeze in next to James and pretend to look interested, as Josh explains how children have changed his life.

'But Cath's not ready, are you, Cath?' And Josh and James both look at me as I stammer slightly, because up until now of course I haven't been ready, but then I've never wanted to say never, and a part of me had always hoped that my lack of maternal instincts had been down to not finding the right man.

But of course I can't say that here, so I simply shrug my shoulders and give what I hope is an enigmatic smile. 'I'm only thirty-one. I've got plenty of time to worry about children.'

Si raises an eyebrow and I scowl at him as he starts to laugh, and Lucy, typically, chooses just that moment to walk back into the living room bearing a tray of pâté and crackers.

She sets the tray down on the coffee table, then hurries

over to the sofa and sits on Josh's knee. 'Children? Cath? Are you thinking of children? Gosh, that would be lovely! Imagine, we could all go off to Tumble Tots together.' She couldn't even hope to hide the excitement in her voice.

Si takes one look at my stricken face and starts to laugh, as I go pale because this is all sounding horribly like I've been talking about James to everyone and telling them that I'm planning marriage, children, the whole works, when I haven't done that at all.

I don't dare look at James, because I'm sure he's getting the wrong impression. I clear my throat and say, 'No, Lucy. I'm not thinking of children, certainly not in the foreseeable future.'

'I've got an idea,' Si pipes up. 'You know how in America they give twelve-year-olds realistic dummies of babies that scream all night to put them off having children? Why don't you give Max to Cath for a week or so to see how she likes being a mum?'

My mouth opens and closes in a remarkable imperson-ation of a goldfish, and Lucy and Josh start to laugh, not altogether unaware of my feelings for Max.

'Oh ha bloody ha,' I manage eventually, sneaking a look at James to see his reaction to all of this, and very relieved to see he's laughing with the others, breaking off only to gaze affectionately at me and plant a kiss on my lips, as Lucy catches her breath and tips her head on one side with a ridiculously soppy smile.

A bell goes off in the kitchen, and Si stands up and calls everyone to the table, where we stand for a while, oohing and aahing over the crystal rose bowl in the middle, the beautiful calligraphy on the name cards, the candlelight flickering off the silver.

'I must say, I do feel special,' Lucy says, pulling out

her chair. 'This feels like we ought to be in some rather grand castle somewhere – '

'Instead of in a poky one-bedroomed flat in Kilburn?' I say.

'Poky? Did I hear you describe my palace as poky?' Si looks at me in mock anger.

'Moi? I wouldn't dream of it. Mmm, something smells completely gorgeous.'

Si dashes into the kitchen and emerges moments later with a tureen of soup.

'I wish I could take credit for this – ' he says, placing it on the table.

'But Queen Delia got there first?' I say, unable to resist.

'Actually, Paul got there first,' and we all turn to look at Paul, who pretends to look humble and then laughs.

'Before you call me Queen Paul, I have to say I'd be happier as Prince Charming.'

'Prince Charming it is.' Si looks at him affectionately, and, given that the champagne has already had its desired effect, we all loudly raise our glasses and toast Prince Charming, who duly bows his way back into the kitchen to fetch the croutons.

James starts off quietly, getting used to the whole crowd in all their boisterous glory, but the alcohol keeps flowing, the conversation starts rising, and soon he is as loud as the rest of us.

I watch him, watch him banter with Lucy, with Si, and I smile to myself as I sip from my glass of red wine, delighted at how he fits in, how James could never be the sort of person I'd ever have to worry about.

We are so busy having a good time that I completely forget that there is a reason for tonight, and it is only when all the food (broccoli and stilton soup, roasted rack of lamb with apricot stuffing, hot chocolate soufflé with vanilla sauce) has been served, when we are all groaning and complaining about the amount of food, that I wonder whether Si is still planning to make his announcement tonight.

For he looks so calm. So content. And the Si I know, the Si I *knew*, would be having a huge anxiety attack right now, palms sweating at the prospect of revealing his innermost secret.

I am about to follow him into the kitchen to ask, because I am quite sure he has changed his mind, when he comes back into the living room bearing a cafetière, and calls for silence.

'Speech, speech!' Josh calls drunkenly, as Si shushes him with a benevolent smile.

'Believe it or not,' he says, as Paul runs back in with a tea-towel, 'there is a reason for this little dinner.'

'To drink fine wine and get pissed?' Josh has, as he always does when drunk, regressed back to his student days, and Lucy puts a hand on his arm to silence him, because the atmosphere is now changed, and it is no longer appropriate for Josh to shout out anything.

'I have an announcement to make, but first I want to say I'm absolutely thrilled that Max will have a little brother or sister, and the fact that such a lovely and unexpected announcement was made earlier this evening, makes what I'm about to tell you much easier.'

My heart starts pounding, and I can't even imagine how difficult this must be for Si. James reaches for my hand under the table, and I squeeze it hard, staring intently at Si's face.

'But I want you to know that it really isn't a big deal. I mean, I thought it was, at first, obviously, but being diagnosed as HIV positive only means I have a virus, not that I'm going to die. Well, hopefully not yet, however much you might want to kill me at times.'

If you weren't concentrating, you'd almost miss it, so casually does Si weave this into his sentence, but then I look at Josh, who, even in the candlelight, suddenly looks completely pale, and at Lucy, whose eyes are already brimming over as she stands up, knocking her chair over as she runs over to Si to give him a hug.

'It's okay, Lucy,' Si murmurs into her hair, rubbing her back, then carefully letting her go.

'The thing is, you're basically my family, sorry, James, I know you're the latest addition and you probably weren't expecting to be drawn into a drama quite so soon.' James smiles at Si and shrugs as if to say it doesn't matter, and I love him for that. 'But I need you all to know, and I need your support.

'Lucy, Josh, you probably have things you want to ask me, and I've started going to a course for, well, for people like me, and one of the things I've learned is that it's incredibly important to be absolutely honest with one another, so if there's anything you want to ask me, well, now would be a good time . . .'

The questions come thick and fast. Mostly from Lucy, once she has recovered from her tears. How long did he have, had he been ill, how had he caught it, what did it mean, were there new treatments . . .

Si answers them quietly and patiently, and even I am impressed with the depth of knowledge he has acquired in so short a time, and it is only when he has said all that he has to say, that I realize Josh still hasn't said a word.

'Josh?' Si speaks gently, as Josh raises his eyes, looking completely shell-shocked. Josh starts to say something, but then leaps to his feet, walks to the door and slams it behind him, without a word.

Lucy, stricken, apologizes for him, then runs after him, the door slamming behind her. The four of us who remain speak in hushed voices, concern for Si mingling with outrage at Josh, and fury.

It might be half an hour later. Or maybe an hour. But the doorbell rings and I open the door to find Josh standing there with Lucy. Both of them have swollen faces, and eyes puffy with crying, and they walk in wordlessly, Lucy coming to sit down with us, and Josh walking over to Si.

And I see something I never thought I'd see Josh do. He puts his arms around Si and starts to cry, and Si comforts him, patting his back and telling him it's okay, as the rest of us suddenly decide to start the washing-up, walking quickly into the kitchen.

'Is Josh okay?' I whisper to Lucy, as James and Paul busy themselves putting more coffee on.

'Shocked,' Lucy says. 'You know what Josh is like. He thinks HIV means AIDS, which he thinks, means death, and he just went into shock. I've been sitting out there for an hour trying to explain what it really means.'

'Lucy, did you know?' I don't know what makes me ask this question.

She shrugs. 'I guessed. Si hadn't been his usual self, and I woke up one morning and just knew. Although I kept hoping I was wrong. But I knew something was wrong with you as well, and you stopped talking about Si for a while, but . . .' She stops and sighs. 'Not that it really matters now.' She turns to me, her face filled with concern. 'Is it going to be okay?'

And I stand in the kitchen, listening to James and Paul clattering about with coffee cups, looking at Lucy's puffy face, turning so I can just see, through the doorway, Si and Josh sitting together on the sofa, talking softly, and I feel an incredible peace come over me. In the heart of – as Si would put it – my family of choice.

'Do you know,' I say, smiling, seeing Lucy's face relax as she looks into my eyes, as I suddenly know what the answer is. 'I really think it is.'